A BAC

b

In a recent unpublished survey

Merle Seton and Jem Masters, it [has been revealed that] [illegible] soldiers will use their weapons against an oncoming enemy. The majority will either fire in the air or not fire at all until they literally see “the whites of the eyes” in the foe conducting its onslaught. The “reluctant 76” will hope that the firepower of the majority will be enough to suppress the hostiles who in fact have their own “reluctant 76” who are hoping for the exact but opposite effect.

The reluctant 76 also includes the .076 who will fire at each other, at their officers or at themselves. 76% of those will miss their targets mostly because their guns jammed.

Next, they surveyed second and third clarinets in high school bands and discovered that only 24% of that woodwind section actually played the notes of the music in front of them and the “reluctant 76” only played 24% of those notes and only the ones that they were sure of reaching and only at those rare moments when the orchestra leader was paying attention to them.

Seton and Johnson were unable to demonstrate the high relationship between those second clarinetists who would play the notes and those who would fire the guns. Most of the students who played the notes were also in the honors sections of their classes and were among the least likely to end up in the infantry although those who entered the military and became officers were the most likely to be fired upon not only by the enemy but by their own men.

Armed with this improvised information, I leapfrogged to the conclusion that only 24% of readers read the forward to a book with the 76% majority, “Just trying to get through the goddamned assignment," went right to the first page of chapter one, where the skirmish began.

As this is a forward to a book that supposedly will be written by my friend Ice Rivers, probably next century, I can pretty much assume that very few readers will read this preamble ; three times fewer than the minuscule amount that will read Ice’s book in the first place if it ever comes out which provides me with great artistic license and assures my continued obscurity. Even I myself haven't read Ice's future book "Early Boomer" which as all English teachers know, doesn't prevent me from teaching it, criticizing it, grading it or forwarding it.

So let's go forward shall we which of course means going backwards to Aristotle. Aristotle was the first famous student of Socrates which means he was the first to misunderstand Socrates. Plato was the great student of Aristotle. Plato took notes and through his misunderstanding of his own notes based on the misunderstanding of Socrates by Aristotle, he somehow arrived at a philosophy that yielded a semblance of the philosophy of Socrates which Plato did not understand. So to insure further progress, Plato wrote very little about his understanding of Socrates because there was very little of Socrates that Plato understood.

Plato had the solution. He would depend and insist upon his students taking notes when he was teaching. Those notes constituted the misunderstandings that Plato' students had of Plato which were meager understandings of Aristotle's original misconceptions of Socrates.

Thus Plato and his students stumbled upon the misconception known as metaphysics. Centuries later when I studied the accumulated ruins of metaphysics, I came to the conclusion that it was 'close but no cigar'.

One day I was smoking a cigar when I met Ice Rivers. We got to talking about all this stuff because I was putting together a seminar on "Metaphysiction" which I considered an evolution of metaphysics. "Metaphysiction" is the culmination of written communication which means that in one and the same time it is singular and plural, it is biography, autobiography, fiction, faction and non-fiction all delivered from different points of view all at the same time because past, present and future are all present at all times with only the present being "visible" or "real" or "sane". Metaphysiction embraces misunderstanding and includes misunderstanding as a milestone in the mastery of itself.

When I first presented this concept to Ice he said, " I got it" which means that I must have presented it incorrectly which again was "good but no cigar". I lit another cigar. I threw in a few contradictions, a couple of faulty syllogisms, overgeneralized non sequiturs, sincere ironies, a dash of gentle sarcasm, upside down sonnets along with the all important factoids who add questionable backstory and are not quite human enough to be considered humanoids. I was pretty sure I nailed it when I asked Ice if he understood what I was professing and he said. "You lost me at alpha, whatever you said next was Greek to me."

That made me feel confident enough in my thinking that I wrote up a fake course description and submitted it to a local community college where they were running short of adjunct professors willing to work at minimum wage to instruct what had been identified as high risk students.

I did just that. I hoped that at least one of my students would take notes and pass his misconceptions back to Ice who said he would use them in his book if I would write a forward to the book which is still under construction as I complete this forwarding task which very few will ever read and if you are amongst those few who are reading this as we come to the conclusion of the forward that means the book was finished. I sincerely hope that you misunderstand and from what I know of Ice, I'm confident that you will.

Doot Doo.

- Thornton Krell

- February 1992

ABOUT THE AUTHOR

Ice Rivers is the pen name of a retired English teacher from Rochester, New York whose identity is known to only his friends and students. "Ice" is an international blogger at ABCtales.com, he is a published poet as well as an accomplished photographer. He has been on the front page of the New York Times and featured on Entertainment Tonight.

He is a five time winner of the Democrat and Chronicle Golden Pen Award.
His photography has been displayed at the George Eastman House as well as Kevin Shaugnessey's pizza shop in Newport. His canvasses currently hang in the home office of Wahlburgers, the clubhouse of Champion Hills and the living room of Kathy McMorrow.

He is a graduate of Geneseo State which means he is a friend of Buzzo, Thrall, Marion, DeCamp, Mead, Majors, Gerling and Woods.
He is A Rochester Red Wing Stockholder

He has a Masters Degree in Career Development from RIT.

He currently resides in Huntersville, North Carolina.

He is a cancer survivor so far.

INTRODUCTION

An essay is a recounting of thought processes. All essays begin with, include or accentuate an idea. An idea is a collection of thoughts that relate to each other. A sentence is a group of words that expresses a complete thought. An essay is a collection of related sentences. The essay represents the mental meandering that a specific idea or problem ignites in the mind of the essayist. The essay itself is the words that stay in the wake of reflective, ideaphoric meandering.

The idea at work in THIS essay is the difference between an essay and a story and how the addition of story adds metaphoric resonance to an essay. As I write THIS essay, I'm thinking about that idea/problem. If I can add a story to my thought process, it elevates the essay out of abstraction into the physical world, which is to say, into metaphor.

One morning, while struggling to help my students write more engaging essays, I coined this phrase "adding action to abstraction guarantees metaphor". Even as those words came tumbling out of my mouth. I had to stifle a laugh because, to me at least, they sounded unexpectedly intelligent.

My students, observing me stifling myself, began to laugh which caused me to bag the stifle and laugh right along. I turned the unexpected phrase into a song. I started slapping my thigh, snapping my fingers and singing "add action to abstraction oh yeah." This impromptu song and dance number got me laughing even harder which in turn made the students laugh harder which caused me to slap, snap and sing even more.

In the midst of this cacophony, as well as within this essay, a point is/was being made: namely that when we add action to abstraction, a metaphor emerges.

See what I mean.

In the midst of THIS essay, I told an action story about my class.

A story is a recounting of the chronological order of physical and mental action, with an emphasis on the physical. The order can be altered through flashback or flash forward, and swerves can be signaled by foreshadowing. The story within THIS essay chronologies like this: First I came up with the phrase. Second, I started to laugh. Third, the students started to laugh. Fourth, I sang and danced. Fifth, the students started to laugh harder. End of story.

A story may or may not need abstraction. Often, abstraction added to a story becomes tangential, thus superfluous. As a personal rule, action added to the abstraction of an essay is a safer bet than abstraction added to the action of a story.

An essay is more likely to end with a conclusion based upon logical and intuitional persuasion than is a story which ends with the recounting of the last episode of chronological action.

All things considered. I'm an essayist.
Expect baseball, boxing and blues
Expect dreams, distance and destiny.
Expect pee, poems and poison.
Expect radiation, reflection and romance.
Don't expect chronology or linearity.
Don't expect precise pagination.
Don't expect a novel
That's another story altogether.

Here's THIS story.

PLURAL IS THE NEW SINGULAR

Roses are red. Violets are blue. I'm a schizophrenic and so am I. So what the hell is a couple of weird guys like us doing in a nice place like this.

As usual, we are trying to make something out of nothing and then make a big deal out of that something while preserving its basic obscurity so it won't escape and wreak the havoc it usually does when the recluse becomes a wreck on the loose.

We offer proof that plural is singular as we try to discover what we've never possessed and try to rediscover what we possessed and lost while hoping this is the last place that we will have to look.

We come to this place for what fills the space rather than for the blank space that is this place before we begin to fill it.

Somebody built it so we come like pilgrims minus our Mayflowers.

We come to this place to forgive as the hyacinth leaves its gift of fragrance on the heel that crushes it. Even if that heel is Mark Twain or Sam Clemens who was himself another plural singular.

We're here because we're on vacation between infinities and yesterday we came out of sedation.

We're here for the aardvarks, the alligators, the beer, the ballgames, the celebrities, the movies, the dinosaurs, the essays, the hats, the dreams, the radiation, the fiction, the faction, the fields, the family, the fairways, the fuzzy science, the metaphysicition, the magic, the poetry, the realism, the magic realism, the students, the teachers, the parents, the children, the auto-biographical blarney and for everything except a gazillion dollars because we're here for the heart.

I and Me and Thornton too if the time is right.

We're here because faith has revealed to us that we still have a job to do and this place is part of that job, a legacy according to my doctor. We're here to warn about fear of doctors which I've had even before my first movie.

One last chance.

Stop in and watch us work. You'll laugh. You'll cry. Warning; there is plenty of death, a dearth of sex, a sense of impending doom, a presence of yearning and way too much urine.

You'll learn and as you learn, you teach and all teaching is about forgiveness.

Just remember, all generalizations are false including the last two which causes a contradiction which means one of them may be true in spite of itself or this whole place is one beautiful paradox or two.

In other words

I'm listening to my muse sighing lies

A voice so sweet could never tell the truth

So if my typing takes you by surprise

Or illuminates the notions of youth

Be patient with the liberty I take

Interpreting these shortwaves to my heart.

Her song momentarily stops the ache

Thrusts it headfirst into obscure art

Not yes or no but ancient and true

Verse ricochets through my solar system

Until it finally gets home to you

Passing off with point guard precision

Through that danger zone of grinning willows

To the safe harbor, your dreams and pillows.

INDIANA SPIN

We thought we had located heaven but we had to pass through Indiana first. I was wondering why the hell somebody decided to name this state "Indiana" when we cruised into a blind spot.

The first moment that I realized we were in a blind spot was when I saw the front fender of the semi smashing through our driver's side window. We were going 70 minimum, I don't know how fast the semi was going but it was passing our van. Somehow the driver never saw us when he attempted to change lanes.

I remember flying up in my seat and hitting my head against the roof of our vehicle. Then the swerves began as the semi hit the brake while it pushed us down the road. For a moment we were perpendicular with the eighteen wheeler and taking up both lanes. I remember thinking…we can't die here. I've got to teach next week. Nobody will know who the hell we are…our friends back home will never understand how we came to crash and burn in this weird place.This can't be the end but it must be. Nobody ever lives to tell this story.

We disengaged from the semi and the high speed spin began.The laws of physics must be obeyed. The swerve into spin continued forever. I lost consciousness. When I came to a second or a minute, an hour or a lifetime later, our totaled van was in the median between the lanes of a four lane highway. I figured that I had just learned how to die. It was simple really. You hit your head and the video tape called life goes dark for an undetermined time and when you wake up, you're in a median in Indiana.

Slowly, I got the impression that I might be alive but what about Lynn? She was driving. She must be dead. I saw the fender smash through her window. I saw the flying glass Her head was against the steering wheel.

There was blood.

She had to be dead.

The whole goddamned thing was my fault.

I was the one who thought we could find heaven.

Whatever this was; it didn't look like heaven.

I had a lot to learn about heaven.

I had a video camera. Soon I would use it. In my dreams, the camera never works. I hit the "on" button and the light flashed. Whatever this was, it wasn't a dream.

To my mortal amazement, Lynn was as alive as I.

To my immortal wonder, perhaps she was as dead as I.

I saw the truck coming through her window. No way that she could have survived that collision as long as there were laws of physics that governed force, mass, speed and velocity. If she was alive…these natural laws had been circumvented which put us in the realm of the supernatural where we have remained ever since.

And the blood? We both had slashes above our right elbow from the shattered glass….nothing serious. We were able to exit the vehicle without much trouble. I went to my video camera. It seemed to be working.

I turned on the camera and started recording. The semi had come to a stop about 150 yards in front of us. The driver was still in the cab. I pointed the camera in the other direction and noticed a person coming towards us.

I kept the camera aimed at his face so I got a closer up look than I would have without the camera. I focused on his eyes. For all I knew, this might have been St. Peter. His eyes told me that he thought he was looking at a couple of ghosts. When he got within speaking distance, I put down the camera.

"I saw the whole thing," said St. Peter, "I thought you guys were goners? Are you okay?"

I wasn't sure.

We walked around to the side of the van. Lynn was leaning up against it. I kept the video running. The tape would later be seen at least three times on national teevee.

FORWARD FIFTEEN TO DREAMLAND

We have blizzard conditions in upstate New York.

On polar vortex days like this, we hibernate and daydream of Summers past and Springs to come We thank God that it's February and not November as the end is now in sight.

I remembered back to the sunny afternoon when Lynn and I celebrated our fifteenth wedding anniversary. We thought it would be loverly to re-visit some of the places where our relationship began and our love blossomed. After stopping at a few such places, we decided to drive to Sea Breeze, good old Dreamland Park on the shore of Lake Ontario. Dreamland Park is an old fashioned amusement park featuring the famous Jack Rabbit one of the first of the wooden roller coasters.

Dreamland Park was the site of our very first date which occurred the afternoon after the dance where she saw me standing there and astonished me by asking if I wanted to dance.

I don't think I would have had the nerve to ask her, so radiant was she as she continues to be.

I did have the nerve to kiss her during our second slow dance which was our third dance in a row. I'll never forget those first three songs. "Hurt so Good" by John Mellencamp. "Loving You" by Elvis and "It's All in the Game" by Tommy Edwards. When in "All in the Game", Tommy sang "and he'll kiss your lips" I kissed her lips.

Our lives were changing by the second. She was at the dance with a gal pal of hers and had to take the friend home. She gave me her number and wondered if I would call. We kissed goodnight. I raced home and called her immediately.

We talked on the phone until sunset and decided to rendezvous the next day.

She asked me where we should meet and I picked Dreamland Park, which was closer to her house than to mine. I suggested we should meet at three on the merry go round.

She agreed.

I got there twenty minutes early so had my choice of what horse to ride. I chose the white one that went up and down. Even then, I sensed that this was going to be an afternoon we would never forget. I rode the carousel a few times before she showed up. Her first sighting of me would be aboard the white horse. She made me feel brave. I wanted to be a hero. Prince Charming Valliant.

She appeared like a dream, exactly on time. I signaled her to climb on the carousel. She did and we began to go round and round as the ancient calliope added more melody to our moments and memories. I was cool and in control. I knew I was making a good impression.

Fifteen minutes later, we took a whirl on the Tilt-A-Whirl one of those rides in which the cars are traveling in one direction while spinning in another. This is when I discovered vertigo. It is impossible to be cool with vertigo. Suddenly I was sweating profusely and whispering to myself 'stop the machine' as I closed my eyes and tried not to hurl.

My heroic facade was permanently as blurred as my temporarily whirled vertiginous vision. She took it all in stride. We staggered over to a bench next to the Jack Rabbit. I had to lie down. My equilibrium was gone. Even prone, the world was barely tolerable. The mighty had fallen. She could deal with it. We made our way to the Arcade where we skeed a few balls then hit the photo booth to memorialize the very beginning.

Twenty-six months later we got married. We've been on the merry go round ever since with more than an occasional side trip to the Tilt a Whirl.

So fifteen years later, we returned to Dreamland Park for the first time in all those years. Things had changed in the park.The original merry go round had burned to the ground and had been replaced. The only way you could get in Dreamland was to pay for an all-day ticket.

We only wanted to take one ride on the carousel.

As we approached the gates, a burly security guard was comforting a little girl who had become separated from her parents. We waited for the guard to finish before we asked his advice on how we might celebrate our anniversary with one ride on the carousel.

He directed us to the Park office where someone would be glad to take care of us. We made our way to the office and related an abbreviated version of our love story to the person behind the window who said, "What a great story. I'm sure it will be no problem. Let me check with my boss."

A few minutes later a very friendly young woman who looked disconcertingly like Annie from Field of Dreams emerged and said,"I just heard your story. Let's go take a ride on the carousel or two or three if you'd like. Right through these doors"

Beautiful.

The three of us walked through those doors. We headed over to the carousel. I climbed aboard the white horse and she got on the chestnut horse next to mine. The night was warm. The Polar Vortex was unimaginable. Romance lives in memories of Dreamland even in the midst of February hibernation.

Whenever she loves me, I am brave.

BEATLEJUICE

I had zero symptoms and was feeling fine. I just wanted to get the hell out of the office. I had no intention of taking the finger ride. I hate and fear doctors.

In his ongoing attempt to convince me that my situation was serious when I refused biopsy because "I didn't want to know," the urologist asked the old question in a new way. "what's the difference between ignorance and apathy?"

We answered the new question in our old way. "we don't know and we don't care"

This time the doctors said; "wrong answer" and made a decision.

A month and a half later, we were sitting in the pre-op room telling the nurse, who had recently graduated from groin holding, our life story and our love story and how hard it was at times to know the difference between Iowa and heaven but after all these years, if it were anything Iowa would have been purgatory at best.

We started to wake up when the IV needle went into our hand. Apparently what we were doing was real yet nobody seemed particularly worried not even us. We were in a place like this. When the doctors came in, we tried to apologize to them for our past hostile, ignorant and apathetic behavior which they couldn't possibly have forgotten although they seemed to be pretending that they had.

Next came in the doctor who was going to knock us out. We had been told that he looked like a kid but he was very good at what he did. We told him all we wanted was some Beatle juice. He sorta smiled and said, "I can do that". The nurse said we can play some Beatle music in the operating room if that's what you would like.

They wheeled us into the OR. Sure enough we heard the Beatles singing "Love is all you need".

A couple of hours later, we woke up. We had confronted our first fear, The biopsy was over. We went home and resolved to forget that this was probably not the ending, this was more like the beginning. Soon we would know and now we cared, not in the old way but in a new way.

Yes, we have cancer.

Who are we? We are I, in all my different hats and moods. We are all those who love me and all those whom I love and all those who love them. We are everybody who knows me and everybody who knows them. We are everybody who reads about us.

You are we.

Our cancer will affect you as it affects all of the we's of all the folks who have or had this cross to bear. You know us, some of you know us better than others. We are public people who seek a private place; a place like this. We've been in a lot of places from the front page of the New York times to the middle of Entertainment Tonight ahead of Bob Hope. We stay awhile, make a difference and head out for some place else.

Now, we are here in a place like this.

Some of you, even in a private place like this recognize us from our work and from our past shared experiences and now know my great secret.

We don't want to be the "about" in the "holy shit did you hear about them?"

We have cancer and we don't want the whole world to know until we want the world to know and we'll let you know when that day comes. We promise.

We intend to describe this journey with accuracy and honesty soo, you can tell others what we say but please don't tell them whom we are unless you are speaking for yourself because you are we and we are you and we are altogether

Goo Goo ga joo.

So what do you think when we say the word “cancer”.

Everybody thinks something different and everybody is probably right to some degree. We’ve changed our understanding of the C word as well as the meaning that we give to the C word since we now have to apply it to ourselves and thus to you. The word that best conveys our current interpretation of the C word is this: TREATABLE.

Please stay tuned; for we’re very sure that this is part of the job we were put here for, especially in a place like this.

You are welcome here as welcome as we are.

DOIN' DA DEAN

You've had a tough day. Nothing traumatic but deadly in its own way. Repetitive. Uninspiring. Marginalizing. Alienating. Too listless to even qualify for frustrating. One of thousands of days like this that will be forgotten by everyone everywhere including you except in your subconscious where it will feed into your recurring nightmare of helpless, hapless abandonment.

Ya know what I mean?

Of course you do.

Well, I have come up with a remedy.

Actually, James Dean started it in *Rebel Without a Cause*. Here's how it works.

Position your hands so that your left thumb is under your left ear with the pointer finger above the ear....your little finger should extend almost to what is/was your hair line. Now do the same with your right hand.That's right...thumb under ear... pointer finger....little finger....yeah..yeah...you got it.

Now pull backwards with both hands as if you're trying to remove the wrinkles from your forehead and widen your eyelids....really pull Goddam it...pull.

Now, look in the mirror and scream at the top of your lungs...."YOU'RE TEARING ME APART!" Hold the pose for three-seconds...keep pulling....now open your eyes as wide as you can just before you stop pulling.

There you did it. Are you starting to feel a little better?

Does your day seem a little different from all the other days that were exactly like all the other countless days/daze until you did the Dean and tore yourself apart?

If not do it again or even better yet, if you live with someone ask them if they have a moment and repeat the exercise right in front of them.

Having a forgettable argument with the spouse? Dean me up, Scotty.

Just found out ya got cancer? Do Da Dean

If you want to have a truly memorable, good or bad, day...go downtown and start doing the Dean in front of people that you don't even know

In the movie *Disaster Artist,* James Franco who once played James Dean in a biopic did a tremendous imitation of Tommy Wiseau doing a crappy imitation of James Dean doing the Dean.

Look at all the attention Franco has gathered. Yikes.

If you can get somebody to take your picture while you're doing the Dean and you paste it on facebook without any further comment, you will get some likes which will brighten up your day.

Caution, when you're doing the Dean and the photographer is getting ready to snap the image....don't anticipate the click. It's hard to do especially if the photographer is one of those "okay one, two, three" types. At the count of two, you're liable to pose a little bit which cuts down on the vulnerability which gives the exercise its authenticity resulting in an homogenized look referred to as a Clean Dean.

A great place to do the Dean is at a sporting event where you can exercise at will and yet give the illusion of containment.

Once a year, the State of the Union speech is a great motivator. I did the Dean at least a hundred times during the last one...slightly more than one a minute. When I went to sleep that night I dreamt that Elvis Presley was president.

Finally, a wonderful time to do the Dean is immediately after reading an instructional essay on the cathartic effects of the exercise.

Like right now. Try it. Your dreams will improve.

STILL IN THE GAME

I'd miss Mr. Baseball more if I didn't dream about him so often.

I dreamt about him again last night. He was laughing and healthy. I remember telling him in the dream "Hey Dude, I thought you were dead". To which he responded "Do I look dead to you". In my dream/s he looks as far from dead as imaginable. He's radiant with vibrant light. He even looks like he dropped twenty pounds. We're laughing like we always were. Laughing and talking wonderful trash.

I call him Mr. Baseball because he won a bet with me and the stakes were whoever won the bet had to be called Mr. Baseball by the loser for the rest of their lives.

I didn't mind calling Mr Baseball Mr. Baseball because it ended another argument we had going. His first name was Gerry and my given first name is Jerry. We both claimed that one of us was an imposter with the wrong letter starting his name. I'm Jeremiah, he's Gerard.

Mr. Baseball taught Spanish. One day I walked past his classroom and we exchanged winks. He held up five fingers which I knew meant that he had five weeks left until retirement.

He was a world traveler and had big plans.

His wife Rosie had her retirement dinner that very night.

Rosie and Baseball attended Rosie's dinner and midway through the meal, according to Rosie, Baseball turned to her and said, "I feel like I've just had a shot of Novocain."

With that, he collapsed on the floor.

They rushed him to the hospital. He had suffered a massive stroke. The doctor's said he wasn't going go regain consciousness. Rosie was faced with the decision....should they keep him on life support or let him go.

Rosie chose support.

Mr. Baseball was still in the game, at bat but it was the bottom of the ninth with 2 outs, two strikes on the batter and the home team down by 10.

Much earlier in Mr. Baseball's game but only a couple of years in the past. We were walking in the hallway together when the secretary from the main office breezed by us. As she passed Joanne observed "you two guys are the slowest walkers I've ever seen."

Then in a flash she was down the hall at full giddyap with what we called her purposeful stride.

I've always been a slow walker unless I was late for a class or headed for the men's room. In retrospect, I'm not sure if Mr. Baseball was a naturally slow walker. The extra weight that he had gained over the years had resulted in a bad back and bad knees. Both the back and the knees would become factors as the innings of our lives passed at differing velocity.

Of course we were talking baseball. The prospects of the Chicago Cubs was the subject when Baseball, as he liked to do, swerved into another ursine subject from a Christmas party past.

"Remember that fiberoptic bear," Mr Baseball asked.

I did and he knew damned well that I did.

That's why he asked the question in the first place. To piss me off.

As I was remembering, Joanne still in giddyap passed us going in the other direction."Whatever you two guys are talking about it must be interesting" Jo observed.

"It sure is" said Mr. Baseball.

Mr. Baseball and I had been talking about a Christmas Party and the gist of a Christmas Past.

I hadn't attended a Christmas Party for 30 years. At the last one I attended everybody got smashed which presented a vibrational, intuitional overload resulting in way too much information and a couple decade long grudges

I was working in the building where Mr. Baseball was teaching Spanish.

A few weeks earlier, my wife Lynn and I had gone to the movies with Mr. Baseball and his wife Rosie. We had dinner at Bugaboo Creek after the movie and somehow the conversation turned to an oncoming Christmas party. Although I was now retired, I had been filling in for a woman who was on maternity leave. I wasn't crazy about the assignment. I had been a twelfth grade teacher and all of a sudden I was teaching ninth grade.

God bless anybody who teaches ninth grade.

I had started my career there. It was kinda cool that I was finishing it in the same building, the same room in fact that I had begun thirty-five years prior. I liked the people, teachers and staff, who worked in the building. They treated me with respect and kindness. They liked to say that I was their idol because I was retired.

When I shared my hang up about Christmas parties, Rosie , Lynn and Baseball gave me a collective 'get over it' response. To my surprise, Lynn seemed interested in attending the party. She told Mr. Baseball to " pick up two tickets for us" and we'd pay him at the party.

Since I hadn't been to a faculty party in decades, I wondered how the attendees passed the time before and after the buffet. Baseball told me that a "white elephant" activity was on the agenda. I didn't know what a white elephant activity entailed so I asked Baseball to sum it up for me.

"You bring in some piece of junk you've got hanging around the house that you don't want, you don't know what to do with and yet you don't want to throw out. You wrap the junk up as nice as you can or in your case have Lynn wrap the junk. You give your precision wrapped junk to somebody else. They give the piece of junk that they don't want to you and everybody's happy, sort of"

The whole exercise sounded like a microcosm of most of the relationships that I'd observed in my lifetime and thus possessed a certain minimal degree of validity along with existential possibility....

A week later, on a snowy December night, Lynn and I arrived at the scene of the party. I had forgotten about the "white elephant". I asked Lynn if she remembered and of course she had it "covered".

We entered a little early so we had our choice of seats. We saved two places for Rosie and Mr. Baseball. As it turned out Chris, the principal and his wife along with the vice principal Ken and his wife chose to sit with us.

Once the crowd had gathered, Chris went around with a manilla envelope which contained a bunch of numbers. I found out that I had to draw a number from the envelope. The number that I drew would have something to do with the order in which I would select from the well wrapped white elephants on the "elephant" table.

Mr. Baseball picked first and pulled out the number 4 which he immediately described as "Lou Gehrig" the famous first baseman of the Yankees....the Iron Horse....the luckiest man....wore number 4. Lou Gehrig was Mr. Baseball's father's favorite player. Lou had died with the disease that now carries his name.

I picked next and pulled out the number 32 (Jim Brown)

I shrugged as once again, I was at the bottom of the barrel. I glanced at Mr. Baseball and tried to make the best out of yet another calamitous draw. I expected to see a big shit eating grin; instead I saw a shadow of worry cross Mr. Baseball's face. The cause of the umbrage was not yet discernible to me.A few minutes later I understood why the moon shadow had danced across the face of Mr. Baseball.

Sadie, the school psychiatrist, explained the rules of the White Elephant game. "Each person draws a number. The person who draws number 1 goes first, picks any gift/elephant....opens it and sits down. Number 2 person has a choice, he/she can pick a gift from the unopened/mystery elephant prize table OR if he/she likes the gift that number 1 opened, he/she can ignore the mystery pile and STEAL what number 1 had just pulled from the pile which would send Number 1 back to the pile to pull another prize and on and on until all the elephants are gone and everybody has what they have. The higher the number you drew, the more elephants you have to choose from. Stealing is encouraged but no elephant can be stolen more than three times and no elephant can be stolen back to back"

I had the highest number which meant I would have the choice of any elephant that hadn't been stolen three times OR the last wrapped prize in the pile.

The person who drew Number 1, a math teacher named Betsy, stepped up to the table and picked out a nicely wrapped medium sized prize. She opened the prize package and inside was a little teapot, short but not particularly stout. Person 2 stepped forward, inspected the teapot, shook his head and opened a package that contained three frosted martini glasses. Person 3 a business teacher unwrapped an elephant that contained a dozen cassette tapes from the 70s/80's.

The next person to choose was Mr. Baseball. Baseball slauntered up to the prize table. In case you haven't heard the word 'slaunter,' it's an uncomplimentary verb that Lynn used to describe the slow walk employed both by me and by Mr. Baseball. Slaunter means a slow, sloppy saunter.

When Mr. Baseball got to the table, he turned his head to look over his left shoulder then turned it to look over his right shoulder then shook his head and shrugged. His body language indicating that he didn't want anything that had been chosen so far so WTF, he might as well choose from the pile where he picked the very package that Lynn had wrapped and which contained an empty wooden box containing A to Z dividers in which coupons could be kept and organized.

Lynn was delighted, Mr. Baseball not so much. His thrall diminished even further when he returned to our table and I loud whispered to Lynn in a volume meant to be overheard "we've been trying to get rid of that piece of junk for years".

Once again it dawned on me that we had a decent deal. I didn't know if Lynn understood our good fortune so I mansplained to her that we had the last number and that meant we could steal ANYTHING that had been chosen. To illustrate my superfluous explanation, I asked her if she wanted the martini glasses. She said,"we have more martini glasses than we need already."

Next, a very pregnant woman picked a huge package from the table which was obviously a stuffed animal of some sort. The package turned out to be a gigantic teddy bear which Laura said would be perfect for her baby to play with in a couple of years and for the rest of her life. Everybody, almost everybody oohed and aahed at the appropriate cuteness of the story. Laura was the first person to be pleased with her selection.

Almost everybody was shocked when two picks later, Rose a recent grandmother said, "I'll take Teddy, thank you". Rose went over to Laura and took the teddy bear that Laura's child would seemingly never cuddle.

Laura, clearly disappointed, picked again. This time the elephant turned out to be a series of interlocking picture frames for three by five photographs which Ivan a photography teacher commented, "Oh that is so stolen." and took the frames from Laura who immediately took the teddy back from Rose.

The game was heating up.

Lynn nodded, willing now to steal.

And Mr. Baseball still had our junk.

Two picks later, Ava stole the teddy bear from Laura. According to the rules, Ava owned the bear.

Next came a random stampede of elephants including but not limited to an attache case, a toaster, a fiber optic bear, a plastic chess set, a glass sculpture, a glow in the dark snowman, box of golf tees, a wallet, a pair of gloves and another ten items whose non-descript existence escapes my recall.

As the game went on, patterns seemed to emerge, Laura kept opening the best packages and those packages would be stolen from her. This happened at least three times. The later it grew, the more enthusiastically folks waved their newly acquired pieces of junk hoping that whoever's number was up would steal the junk from them and give them another shot at the elephant.

Remember, the junk that each of them was trying to get rid of was the very junk that somebody else had already successfully gotten rid of by getting rid of it to the very people who were trying to get rid of it again in the hopes of getting yet another piece of junk that they would be less willing to get rid of…

The usual.

"This box contains all twenty-six letters of the alphabet; great for coupon clippers and debt collectors."

"Everybody loves to play chess. Chess sharpens the mind. Here's a beautiful little chess set."

"Don't you dare come over here and take my fiber optic bear."

"This whatever it is would make a great whatchamacallit."

When only a few items remained on the table, we had to get serious about our decision making. Like most husbands, my happiest moments come when I'm able to put a smile on the face of my wife. Like most husbands, I always want to know what it is that my wife wants Like most husbands I ask her what she wants too much which irritates her because at a certain point I'm supposed to know what she wants without asking her and if I ask her what she wants at the point when I'm supposed to KNOW what she wants without asking well, she "doesn't want anything, thank you" and that's not good.

I was approaching that sensitive point when Lynn astonished me by looking directly into my eyes with an expression that was very close to "kiss me" and saying with purrfect clarity. " I love that fiber optic bear. Get it for me."

All of a sudden I was elevated to the next level…Knight errant…man on a mission. I had an opportunity to earn a smile.I was in perfect position.

The fiber optic bear had drawn zero attention through the entire game and this was the end of the game. Brad the librarian had drawn the bear early and throughout the game he had used reverse psychology "Don't you take my fiber optic bear. I love this bear. etc" all of which proved ineffective as he was still stuck with an unwanted bear which would be in Brad's garbage can within 24 hours.

When my turn came, the bear was right there.I went to the table. I listened to the various offers. "I know this is gonna break your heart, Brad, but give me that bear."

Brad didn't even fake heartbreak, when he handed me the bear.

I took my trophy back to Lynn. She looked at the bear with tenderness and then turned her loving eyes for towards me. She gave me a sweet kiss on the lips as almost everybody cheered. Momentarily I was young and brave.

In the meantime, Brad had decided to keep the game going by stealing once again from Laura. I wasn't paying much attention. I was focused on my refountained youth and courage. The reverie was rudely interrupted when Laura, the oft-wronged Laura, burst into my space. "I'll take the bear,Jer."

"Don't take the bear, Laura," I pleaded as my courage began to dissolve.

"Hey, you're retired and you make more money than anybody here so say goodbye to the bear, Jer"

Laura and the bear trundled back to the other side of the room.

It was my turn to choose again. If I took the last elephant, the game would be over. On the way to the table, I forgave Laura. She had a bambino on the way plus she had been stolen from at least four times and was still being tortured by Ava and the teddy bear. Mr. Baseball was still saddled with my piece of junk.

I decided to keep the game going, maybe I'd get another shot at the bear.

Once again I heard the cacophony of pleas.

One plea stood out. "Jerry, take this whatever it is and assign your students to write a composition to figure out what the hell it is."

I stole the whatever it is/was from a weird guy named Chuck, a science teacher well known for incomplete passes at female colleagues.

The stolen object was a glass "sculpture" about a foot long and ten inches high. The "sculpture" looked vaguely like some sort of drug delivery system or a synthesis of Sideshow Bob and a snake crawling out of a saxophone resting on lava. Trying to be good natured and retain composure. I said that I would indeed use this as a composition subject. I brought the questionable "sculpture" back to my seat where Lynn looked too flabbergasted to speak.

Chuck followed me over to my table and stole from Mr. Baseball our cardboard classification system.

I heard Chris, the principal mutter under his breath...."what's Chuck gonna do with THAT? Keep record of his strike outs?"

Mr. Baseball jumped to his feet and slauntered over to Laura. "I'll take the fiber optic bear." Baseball came back to our table, and set the fiber optic bear next to Lynn within her reach but far beyond her grasp.

Laura took the attache case from Ken.

Ken ended the game by choosing the last elephant which turned out to be a candy jar full of Hershey kisses.

For a moment, I thought that Baseball had redeemed the bear in order to gift it to Lynn.

"Hey Baseball, I'll give you this beautiful glass sculpture for the bear."

Baseball turned to me with the previously absent shit eating grin and said, "Why should I take that ugly thing back, I've been trying to get rid of that piece of shit for the last five years."

The party was over.

A few minutes later Lynn and I were silently driving home in frigid, black ice weather that could be described as an Arctic assault appropriate only for polar bears.

MAN HAT ON

Sixty-eight years ago, Doc Zilla bought a Stetson. Doc died thirty-five years ago. He passed the Stetson on to my father who immediately passed it on to me. Vin thought that I would think that the hat was retro. I did.

I thought the lid was retro which meant I thought it was gimmicky in a cool way and would separate me from everybody else. I was too young for the hat.It separated itself from me.

I proved that conclusively a couple years later at a disastrous cabin party. It's always nice to have Jack Daniels in the room but not a good idea to give him the mike. Consequently, I told everybody off in a tragic effort to save the world before peeling out bareheaded at 90 miles per hour. Not only had I left behind a few acquaintances but more importantly I left behind the Stetson. I never saw the hat again. I hope it found the head of someone more worthy.

I vowed that someday, somehow, when I was ready, I would get that hat back again. I had faith that a path to the Stetson would be revealed to me. I started wearing baseball hats as a penance. They separated me from nobody except Yankee haters and Red Sox fans. I can't say that I missed them.

I am a patient man except for doctor's for whom I refuse to be either patient or a patient…thank you John Barrymore.

I also believe that vocabulary shapes destiny. I didn't have an articulate enough hat vocabulary to describe the Zilla Stetson that I was seeking and until I did, the lid would linger somewhere out there beyond my destiny.

All this happened during my first marriage. The marriage outlasted the hat but not by much even though Jack Daniels had permanently left the building.

Lynn came into my life after both my hat and my first wife were long gone. Lynn never saw my hat and I had trouble explaining it to her. Lynn had seen my first wife a few times and had no trouble explaining her. Because we are human, it is easier for us to explain than to understand.

Lynn also had no trouble explaining baseball hats and how juvenile she thought they were especially for a guy like me who still had "good hair".

I began this story as a thirty year old kid trying to ironically wear a man's hat and then I devolved into a man wearing a kid's hat. One day, Lynn and I decided it would be better if I tried being a man wearing a man's hat. With this agreement, revelation ignited somewhere in the near future, we simply had to make our way into that future and the mystery would appear to us in the form of realization. That's the way the world works. When you say something in the present and you really mean it, that something starts to happen in the future. As we approach that future, the gimmick is to hold onto the vision we had and keep it in place until we reach that future and POW there it is.

Of course, you've got to really mean what you say and since most of us most of the time don't really mean what we say the future is catastrophically non-linear brightened by the good fortune randomly generated by occasional, almost accidental outbursts of optimistic sincerity from a nearly forgotten past.

About a month later a visual clarity trumped my vocabularic inadequacy and a path to the hat suddenly appeared. Then, out of nowhere, Lynn suggested that we go see *The Aviator* which was screening in the discount house a couple of miles away. The discount house known as Movies 10 is the last stop for feature movies before the brief hiatus when they disappear and are prepared for Netflix etc.

In other words this is their last stand at the box office. The popcorn costs as much as the viewing of the movie which is a straight up perk to the discount chain dispensaries.

I'm not a fan of bio-pics especially if they are built around people and events that I can remember. I always remember the people and the events depicted as so much more complex and dramatic than the condensed imitations that constitute the majority of biopics. I already had a full dose of the real Kate Hepburn and wasn't thrilled about watching Blanchett channel Hepburn in a battle of dueling Kates.The deciding vote as usual belonged to Lynn.

We went.

During the showing itself, I fidgeted in my seat. I put my elbows on the back of the seat in front of mine and rested my chin on my palms. Typical sulking jerk exercising a little pent up passive aggression.

We were the only people in the theater.

All of a sudden on the screen, DiCaprio gets out of a plane or a car or something. I'm shocked to see that he's wearing my hat.I leaned back in my seat.

"That's my hat. DiCaprio's got my hat," I whispered too loudly.

Lynn shushed me.

A little later DiCaprio and the hat appeared again on screen. This time, Lynn whispered to me in a far more appropriate volume, even though we were the only two nuts in the dark. A light had gone on in her head. "Oh THAT's your hat. I like it."

I said, "That is exactly my hat."

I didn't have the words but I had the image, the visual. Usually when I write, I have the visual and the vocabulary comes to me. In the case of the hat, I had the image and now, if you've seen the movie, so do you but I still can't give you the words. We're making progress though, ain't we?

With visual vocabulary firmly in place and with destiny drawing closer to revelation, I made an appointment to meet the Master Hatter.

Lynn and I went to lunch before the appointment and our conversation dangled a few minutes past the appointed time to meet the Hatter. We arrived late and were informed in no uncertain terms that we would have to wait because the Hatter "is a busy man". Or we could just leave. Whatever.

We waited an hour in his tiny vestibule while people came and went, collecting their laundry. Eventually, the Hatter made his way to the counter of the dry cleaning establishment that serves as a front for his creativity. He makes his hats in the back. The dry cleaning joint is the cottage for his industry.

It became very evident that when you talk to a clear eyed man like the Hatter about hats, you better know what the hell you're talking about and if you don't have the coin or the courage to purchase the hat that you better know what you're talking about well then, he knows that you know that he knows that you're just wasting his time as well as your own, only his time is more valuable than yours because he knows what he's doing and you don't know what the hell you're doing. Etc.

I told him I was in the market for a hat. I told him about the Doc Zilla hat; how I had come to own it and lose it. He seemed interested or at least interested enough to ask the essential question. "So, what kind of hat are you looking for?"

I knew the answer, sort of. I told him I had just seen *The Aviator* and the hat in that movie was exactly the hat that I had lost and wanted to regain. I asked him if he had ever seen *The Aviator*.

As soon as I asked him that question, something in his demeanor changed. Up to the Aviator question he had been more business like than friendly, more challenging than engaging. He was sizing me up. As a hat maker, size definitely mattered.

At that point, he invited us to step out of the vestibule, past the counter, past the racks and racks and racks of other people's clothing. The Hatter invited us into the backroom where he interviewed serious hat seekers. We had passed the entrance exam.

As we made our way to the inner sanctum, we passed a stool upon which was a beauty of a hat.

"Now, that's a hat," I said in passing.

"That's MY Hat" replied the Master Hatter.

I still lack the chapeau vocab to describe that hat on the stool but suffice it to say that a hat made by a master hat maker for his own dome is indeed a joy to behold. The Hatter picked up on my joy regarding his hat which made the dozen steps into his back room much less threatening.

I knew the Hat maker's name but he didn't know mine. Many more people seek the Hat Master than are sought by him. I had told him my name when I called to make the appointment. I told him my name again when we met at the counter. When we got to the backroom, he told me something I already knew and asked me something that I had already told him.

"My name is Brown" said the Hat Maker, "what's yours?"

After he said Brown, I resisted the urge to say, "If you tell me again, I'm gonna knock ya down".

"They call me Ice" I said.

Brown resisted the urge to say, "That's cool".

We shook hands.

"Now, tell me again. What kind of hat do you have in mind?"

"Did you see *The Aviator*?", I replied again.

"Oh yeah" said Brown.

Once again, I felt more at ease, more connected. Movies are readily available cultural metaphors. Whenever we share metaphor we share a bit of truth."Leonardo DiCaprio was wearing my hat in that movie. Do you remember that hat? That hat is my hat or should I say that hat was Doc Zilla's. THAT is Exactly the hat I'm looking for."

"Exactly THAT hat?" Brown asked

"Exactly," I asserted.

Brown said, " Look at the top of that hat rack. Do you see that hat? That is exactly the hat in the *Aviator.* Reach up and get it. Take a look for yourself".

I followed his directions. I pulled the hat down and took a close look.

"It looks like the Aviator hat" I estimated.

"I've got news for you Ice. Not only does it look a lot like the hat DiCaprio wore in the movie. It IS the hat he wore. I made that hat for the movie and you've got that hat right in your hands."

"THIS is the hat that Leo wore in the movie? What's it doing here?"

"Often when I make hats for movies, they send the hats back to me. I hold on to the hats and keep them safe in case the film makers have to reshoot a scene and they don't want to screw up the continuity. That's the actual hat I made for Martin Scorsese to use in *The Aviator* to go on the head of Howard Hughes as played by Leonardo DiCaprio."

"Leo wore this hat," I asked incredulously.

"That EXACT hat" said Brown.

I tried on the hat.

Size matters. The hat was too big.

“Whoa, Leo’s got a big head” I observed.

“Why don’t you try Richard Gere’s hat from Chicago? That one’s on the back behind Leo’s hat”

I pulled down the Chicago hat and tried it on for size. Gere’s hat was too small.

“ I think you’re closer to Leo than to Richard, Ice. Gere wears a seven and a quarter. Leo wears a seven and five-eighths. Figure you’re about the size of George Clooney. I’m working on his hat right now”

When Lynn and I were waiting in his vestibule, Brown had been making a hat for George Clooney. "George is a seven and a half” said the Hatter. “It’s better to have a fit that’s a little loose rather than a little tight. We call that ‘headroom'."

Brown took out his measuring tape and wrapped it around my dome. “Seven and a half, Ice. Same size as George.”

I had my size. I had my style. Not bad for a guy coming in with zero hat vocabulary. Still, as I looked at the Aviator hat, something was wrong. It was the hat band. The Doc Zilla brand was a darker brown. Hatter grabbed a darker brown band, a 'chocolate’ brown and wrapped it around the Aviator hat that I had on my head.

Thanks to Jack Daniels, I couldn’t remember the last time I saw the Doc Zilla hat. I could remember a picture someone had taken of me the last time I wore the hat when I was trying to save the ozone and preserve the integrity of art with profanity while insulting everyone around me in a dazzling triple play of boorishness.

Not a pretty picture, except for the hat.

The picture was in black and white. I recalled a differentiation in the tone of black between the hat and the hatband. The hatband was definitely darker as was the one that Brownie wrapped around the exact Aviator hat. Still uncertain, I asked for a second and third opinion.

Both Lynn and Brown agreed that the combination looked great but the final decision was mine. I decided I would go for MY hat which was Doc Zilla's hat which because of the darker hat band wasn't EXACTLY Leonardo's hat which wasn't actually Leonardo's hat anyway but Howard Hughes's hat as played by Leo as envisioned by Martin Scorsese and his wardrobe director. I am my own wardrobe director and I sure as hell am not Leonardo DiCaprio nor Howard Hughes nor Martin Scorsese.

As if reading my mind, Brown said "Leo's surprisingly tall"

"Do you know Leo?" I asked

"I fitted him for that hat you got on your head. I'll tell you something else, Leo's weird."

"Whaddya mean Leo's weird," I wanted an answer because I didn't want to believe that Leo was weird. Considering Brown was running his hat business out of a dry cleaning store, I thought maybe it was the Hatter who was mad. That's been known to happen.

"Let me tell you about his fitting," Brown began.

"First of all, Alec Baldwin didn't like the hat that I made for him. I had to calm Baldwin down by explaining that the hat was authentic to the year and to his character as well as the fact that the hat had been made to the exact specifications sent by the wardrobe director and approved by Marty himself."

"Baldwin finally calmed down and headed back to his trailer, hat in hand. Without Baldwin around, the atmosphere grew less tense and more expectant. Everybody knew that Leo was next on the schedule which was a big deal all the way around. Right on schedule, the door opens and in walks Leo. A silent, barely visible swoon filled the room. Leo's a lanky guy, surprisingly tall as I said before and very thin. He introduced himself as Leo. I introduced myself as Dave. We shook hands. I pulled the hat out of the box. This is when Leo got weird. I stepped forward to put the hat on his head. Leo stepped backwards, spooked, and he disturbed the air between us with a double open palm, ten finger pushback. The signal was clear. 'don't touch me, man and get that hat away from me'. Feeling like I had caught the plague after stepping in a pile of dogshit, I took a few steps back," Dave recalled.

"With that, Leo turned his back on me and walked across the room to the full length mirror. He stood in front of the mirror, studying his reflection for what seemed like an hour but was probably five minutes. The room was completely quiet. After about forty-five minutes or maybe four, I whispered to the wardrobe assistant on my left. 'What the hell is he doing?"'

"She whispered back, 'I think he's getting into character'."

"A minute or fifteen later, Leo turned away from the mirror and headed over in my direction. The guy coming over to me, however, was no longer the guy who had turned his back on me 300 or 3000 seconds earlier. The guy coming towards me was young Howard Hughes. Leo was gone and Howard Hughes was ready to be reunited with his hat."

"I put the hat on 'Howard's ' head. The fit was perfect as I knew it would be. The studio had sent me the exact measurement of Leo's head as a reference. With his hat on his head, the reincarnated ghost of Howard Hughes walked back to the mirror. He tilted his head from the left to the right. He pulled the back of the hat down, which made the front of the hat tip up slightly. He nodded in approval."

"Howard Hughes turned away from the mirror and paused for just a moment. In that moment, Leo took Howard's hat off his head. He walked towards me, hat in hand. He was a different man from the man on whose head I had placed the hat a minute ago. In the space of about ten minutes, this guy had become two entirely different people."

Leo/Howard looked at me and said, "that's exactly the hat, Dave"'

Dave continued "We shook hands again. I'm pretty sure I was shaking with Leo and not Howard because the handshake was strong and Howard Hughes wasn't known for the strength of his handshake. I thanked him for the compliment. Apparently I had the right guy as I called him 'Leo'. He after all had called me 'Dave'. I guess it was right because he went on his way and as he left, the swoon in the fitting room became more visible as did the relief. That's what I mean when I say, 'weird'. I've met a lot of actors but I'd never seen anybody do that or have that effect. Baldwin, the actor, didn't think his hat looked good on him. DiCaprio had no concern how the hat would look on him because it wasn't his hat anyway. The hat belonged to the character of Howard Hughes. Before Leo could evaluate the hat, he had to see the hat through the eyes of the character. Like I said, concluded the Hatter. Leo's weird."

By the time the Master Hatter had finished his Hollywood tale and the weirdness of Leo, I had already decided that I wanted the hat.

But there were complications.

I didn't want Leo's hat or Howard's hat. I didn't even want Doc Zilla's hat anymore. I wanted MY hat and the hat that the Hatter put on my head with the darker band was exactly that hat. The deal was almost done.

The price tag was next and it was hefty.

We entered the area between stimulus and response.

That time of final objection which comes before the moment of acceptance or rejection.

Lynn, who is all about maintenance, found her voice. "Well, it's a nice hat but a very expensive hat. I'm concerned about the care of the hat. How will it stand up to water? What if the hat loses its shape? If he gets caught in the rain, can he bring the hat back to you for reshaping. Will rain ruin this hat? Can he wear it in a rainstorm?"

The whole deal was up in the air with the machine gun of those questions.

I was worried.

I should have had more confidence in Brown.

He looked Lynn straight in the eye and said, "Mrs. Rivers, the hat is made of beaver and beavers are pretty good with water."

Bam the first volley returned

"And remember," the Hatter continued, "when it begins to rain, that's not the time a man takes OFF his hat. That's the time he puts it ON. He'll be wearing this hat for the rest of his life so if you divide cost by years, this hat is a bargain."

Game, set, match.

We ordered my hat.

I've worn it ever since.

I don't wear it everywhere. I only wear it on those occasions when I want to look exactly like myself.

One of those times occurred a couple of months ago when I was invited to a beer tasting event put on by the alumni foundation of one of my colleges. By this time I was full of radiation and barely able to control my urges and there was only one small water closet at this event so we stayed very close to it and I rushed it a couple of times in the hour that we spent.

At this event, I noticed someone at the bar. I couldn't take my eyes off this guy. Every time I looked at him, he was looking somewhere else. When I find myself in that situation, I'm pretty sure that the person looks back at those moments when I'm not looking.

Finally, I went to Lynn.

"See that guy sitting at the bar? Is that Beau?"

Beau is my son from my first marriage. I hadn't seen him nor spoke to hime in almost twenty years.

Lynn said she thought it was Beau.

I tried to figure out what I would say to him of if I should even say anything after so much pain. I decided I would say something. I didn't know what. I figured the words would come when I got there. I headed over in his direction.

He was gone.

I don't know if he saw me or not but if he did, he saw me looking like myself.

DEER LAKE AND BEYOND

I read his auto-biography, *The Greatest.*

Towards the ending of his book, Muhammad Ali invited anyone who had read the book that far to come and visit him at his training camp where they would be welcome. He even gave simple directions. Go to Deer Lake. Go to the gas station in the middle of town. Turn left at the gas station. Come up the mountain road. Watch for the boulders along the side of the road. The boulders have names of past champions painted on them. If you see them, you're in the right place. Drive to the top of the road. Park your car.

I had a few days off with no particular place to go. I had a truck. I had a wife and a three year old son. We got in the truck. We trucked to Pennsylvania. We drove to Deer Lake. We found the gas station.

(Oh my God there's the gas station)

We turned left on the mountain road.

Oh My God, there's the boulders.

We were unmistakably on the turf of Muhammad Ali... We kept going. We parked the truck.

I couldn't believe how simple it was. Exactly how Ali described it in his book. We were on the property of perhaps the most famous man on earth. No one had stopped us. Searching for parallels. I tried to picture myself pulling into Ronald Reagan's ranch. I imagined security guards with sunglasses and rifles. I imagined a few years in federal prison.

Here there was no security, only a collection of cabins and 7 A.M. Pennsylvania morning silence and fog. I was happy just to be there enjoying the electrified serenity. I didn't dare wish for anything more. For all I knew, I was breaking a law.

What was I going to tell the cop? “I read the book. I turned at the gas station. I thought I was welcome, etc.” I didn’t think that sounded too good.

My son climbed out of the truck and headed over to a boulder. We looked at a few of the boulders. I told him a little story about each of the names on the boulders.

Then I heard my wife say, “Ice!” I walked back to the car, just a few steps away.

“Does Muhammad Ali have a mustache," she asked.

“Not that I know of. Why do you ask”

“Because some guy with a mustache just walked into one of those cabins”

She pointed.

Almost immediately, I saw a back emerging from that cabin. Only one person on earth had a back like that. Muhammad Ali

“It’s him," I whispered in alarmed awe. In fright, the usual choice of fight or flight arrived. Fight? Well, this was the heavyweight champion of the world I was looking at and I was an interloper on his property. Fight wasn’t going to work for damn sure. Flight? I could back up, grab my son and take off, if not like a robber in the night certainly like a stalker in the sunrise.

By this time, Ali was a few feet from my truck.

I stepped out of the truck and walked towards him. "Good morning Champ” felt about right so I dropped it on him.

He looked at me, through me and somehow spotted my son.

“Be careful your boy over there on the rock”

I glanced over and there was my boy precariously perched on the Jake LaMotta boulder. When I came back to the truck, Ali was waiting for me.

"Ya wannna see a magic show" said the Greatest to my boy and me.

I said "Sure,I'll get my wife"

He nodded. He waited.

A few moments later, my wife, my son and I were following Muhammad Ali into his empty mountain gymnasium. He opened the door, we four went inside. Ali locked in on me. He asked me what I did.

I told him I was a teacher.

He replied in a voice so soft barely audible, the whisper of an old man. If"you so smart? What did Lincoln say when he woke up with a hangover?"

"I don't know Champ" I responded.

"I freed the who?", Ali answered.

And there it was, one of the most heavily identified and analyzed racial figures of all time was making my acquaintance with a complex little ethnic joke.

I didn't know what the hell to do.

I laughed.

We all did.

It was the right thing. I was still the most important man on earth in the eyes of the most famous man on earth.

For the next half hour he made scarves come out of my ears and made cards disappear all the while making the three of us, feel as if we were the absolute center of his universe. A couple of times I almost felt sorry for him, he was trying so hard to please. Then I would remind myself where I was and whom I was attempting to feel sorry for.

Muhammad Ali

Somewhere during the half hour, other people began to show up.

Soon the number was up to fifty and Ali was still locked on us.

He had other people to lock on. Another day in training camp was beginning as our time together was ending. Ali knew hows to close.

His last few words to me were these

"You a teacher...be good to those kids. Tell 'em this story"

Then he feinted that left jab at me.

That was goodbye.

We would meet again.

FLASHBACK

I got blizzarded and sold out of the first Ali-Frazier fight.

Yes, a March 8 blizzard made driving nearly impossible and I lived a long way from the Auditorium. The Auditorium was the theater that screened the HBO production of Ali-Frazier. Back in those days, a pay per view event did not appear on teevee. We had to travel if we expected to participate. By the time glascaded to the Auditorium, the unthinkable had happened. The venue was completely sold out and occupied. Absolutely zero tickets were available.

We cross-countried home and listened to a heavily edited version of the fight on the radio in my living room along with brother Deke and the great Johnny Crown. I'll tell the story of that evening some other time, for now it's merely prologue. Let's just say we lit our victory cigars too early and with fake confidence.

Ali lost.

I vowed I would NOT miss the rematch.

As usual, I overcompensated.

When the inevitable rematch was scheduled for Madison Square Garden, I contacted my buddy Kevin in New York City and asked him to pick me up two ringside seats for the fight; one for me and one for Deke.

The ringside tickets cost an unheard of 100 bucks apiece.

The day of the fight arrived. We put on our rented tuxedos and flew to New York. All of our buddies were going to watch the fight on closed circuit again at the Auditorium. This time everybody bought their tickets in advance. My pals gave us a big send off at the airport as part of their pre-fight celebration.

We arrived in The Apple and made our way over to Crazy Joe's apartment. We had a few beers at Joe's and headed to the Garden. The gigantic poster in Times Square at the time was of Al Pacino as Serpico.

We made our way to the Garden.

We paused outside for gyros and souvlaki.

We went inside.

Our "ringside" seats proved to be pretty far from ringside because even though we wore tuxedos our name wasn't Sinatra or anything close to that although the actor who played the Son from Sanford and Son had the seat next to mine.

Big time, baby.

I had a nice new 35 millimeter Canon DSL. I was proud of that camera and thought I was Ice Sports Illustrated Photographer Pacino. This was the first time that I was ever in the same room as Ali and Frazier. It would not be the last.

CHAN SHAKE HANDSHAKE

There's a line in the Grateful Dead's "United States Blues". "Shake the hand that shook the hand of PT Barnum and Charley Chan." Now if you shook that hand, then anytime anybody shook your hand they would also be shaking the hand of Charley Chan.

That's a Chan shake.

We're all in one big fraternity without the gender restriction and the secret handshake. The unifying, not so secret handshake is our humanity. When we literally do shake hands, we emphasize the familial nature of our humanity and we pass it on. We drop our weapons.We've all got powerful Chan shakes to pass on to one another. Here's a very brief snapshot of what you get when you shake my hand.

I shook hands with Jim Irwin, a man who walked on the moon.

I shook hands with Norman Baker who navigated the papyrus raft the Ra across the Atlantic from Africa to South America.

I took part in Hands Across America. I was standing at the very beginning of the East Coast line in Battery Park looking directly at the Twin Towers.

On my way home, a couple of days later, I happened to run into a woman who had been at the end of the line in California. Naturally, we shook hands which linked the line in the East with the line in the West; a cross country handshake.

So that covers the United States from shore to shore and extends to South America to Africa and then flies us all to the moon.

Not a bad distance.

To fill in some other blanks, I shook hands with Muhammad Ali. Imagine all the hands that have shaken Ali's hand and all of the hands that have shaken the hands that Ali's hand. Lot's of people starting with uh, pick two, Malcom X and the Beatles.

Let's call our individual articulated collective handshakes our Chan Shakes. Chan shake with me and you get all of the above.

Before leaving the Chan Shake, lets momentarily go in another direction. Let's call it Face in the Crowd.

Thousands of people saw Buddy Holland and Bobby Darin perform live.

Thousands of people saw Elvis perform live twice.

Thousands of people saw George Harrison perfom live.

Thousands of people saw Dylan and the Band on their Planet Waves tour.

Thousand saw the Dead on their Wake of the Flood tour.

Thousands saw Secretariat win the Triple Crown at Belmont.

Thousands saw the Mets clinch the National League Pennant at Wrigley Field in 73.

Thousands saw Affirmed win the Triple Crown at Belmont.

Thousands saw Seattle Slew win the Triple Crown at Belmont.

Thousands saw Foolish Pleasure win the Run for the Roses under the Twin Spires.

Thousands saw the match race between Foolish Pleasure and the mighty Ruffian which ended in tragedy at Belmont Park.

Thousands have seen World Series games between the Yankees and the Dodgers at the old Yankee Stadium.

Thousands of people saw Joe Frazier fight Muhammad Ali at Madison Square Garden,

Thousands have visited the Field of Dreams in Iowa.

Thousands have been on the front page of the New York Times.

Thousands have been on Entertainment tonight.

Thousands of folks have given commencement addresses at a high school graduation.

We're probably getting close to three or four million here.

That's a lot of people.

How many people have done all of the above.

I'm guessing one. That would be me.

Whereas the Chan Shake is an exercise in universality, this one is an exercise in uniqueness. We're all unique and we're all faces in the crowd.

Let's shake on it, while we still have time.

FRONT PAGE TIMES

Thousands of people have had their picture on the front page of the New York Times. Aside from possibly Muhammad Ali, I haven't met any of them. Except for myself. Yup, my picture made the front page of the Times. Here's the scoop. I was sitting around my house one day when the phone rang. The caller was a researcher from the Times who was gathering information for a writer who was planning an article about feminism in America.

I hit it off with the researcher. I had her laughing hysterically as she asked me yes or no questions about feminism that I turned into short answer/essay replies. Most of my answers were coming from the perspective of a guy whose marriage was on the brink of ending and who was realizing how little he knew about women, marriages, feminism, and life in general.

I was skinny as a rail from the worry of impending marital catastrophe. I had even shaved off my beard for the first time in many years so I had a weird mustache working on the grill of a guy who still was learning how to wear the expressions on his face without the benefit of the beard to camouflage a startling degree of vulnerability.

I was suffering from sobriety as well.

So, I was bitterly honest in my conversation with the researcher which she found hilarious. Nothing is as funny as sad truth, Nothing as sad as funny truth.

She said that she would pass on my opinions to the lead reporter and recommend that the reporter get back in touch with me because, according to the researcher, my answers were not only honest and hilarious but as near accurate and sensible as any she had received during the entire process of the researching that she had done on the subject.

Sure enough, the writer doing the story called me back a couple hours later. Same thing all over again. Different questions....similar wounded, truthful, ironic replies. The writer had the same reaction as the researcher. Laugh, larf, laugh.

After about ten minutes into this routine she asked if she could use my quotes in the paper. I said sure.

The interview continued......the larfing, the wisecracking, the comedic pain, the receptive audience.

After 10 more minutes she asked "Can we use your picture?"

Again I said sure. She thanked me for the various permissions.I thanked her for the patient, active listening. A couple hours later, I got a call from the local AP photographer. Would I be available for a picture in the next hour or so? I told him that I was ready now and wouldn't be any less ready in an hour... so come on over. The guy showed up. Big guy. Big beard. He wanted to know for what subject the picture was being taken. I told him it was for my opinions on feminism. The guy took a spit take and asked me "well what are your opinions on feminism".

I told him that I was glad he asked. I'll rant them to you and instead of posing, you can just shoot all you want during the rant and then pick out something you like. I only remember the beginning of the rant. It started like this: "Women? I'll tell you about women!", slapping the back of my right hand against the palm of my left. This was followed by a ten minute imitation of Ralph Kramden going off on "goddamned bitches, kings and castles and flights to the moon" etc with forehead slapping, hand clapping, finger snapping, eye rolling gestures as Gleason-like as I could make them.

All made tongue through cheek.

The photographer was laughing so hard that he could barely snap the pictures. He took at least a roll of film during that ten minutes.

Remember rolls of film?

36 exposures.

Now all of this was pre-internet. I didn't have a subscription to the Times.

For the next couple of weeks, I went to the drug store near my house that sold the Times. I'd pick up the current issue, scan through it and put it back.

I was beginning to think that I had imagined the whole thing.

Then, one Sunday, I went to the drugstore. I didn't have to leaf through the pages. There it was. My picture, front page under the headline "Americans Assess Fifteen Years of Feminism".

And there I was.....mid rant.......palms up....shoulders ashrug....body language screaming "I don't know what the hell to make of it because I don't know what I'm talking about.

They included only one of my quotes in the article itself as apparently they figured they could let my picture do my talking and in retrospect....it kinda did.

After fifteen years, Americans didn't know what the hell to make of feminism.

SHOWDOWN ON MAIN STREET

Every so often, I'll find a volume in my office library that takes me by surprise. I don't remember acquiring the book so I don't remember the moment that it arrived in the 'brary nor the duration of its shelving.

Such a volume was "Main Street" by Sinclair Lewis . The volume is paperback and the publishing date is 1980 so it couldn't have been hiding for more than thirty-seven years before it leaped into my hands.

Although I don't remember when or how I got it, I can understand the reason why. Sinclair Lewis was a favorite author of my father who kept in HIS library both "Babbit" and "Arrowsmith". When I first became aware of his library shortly after becoming aware of reading and books, I asked him about the books: "Babbit" which I hoped was gonna be about baby rabbits and "Arrowsmith" about Robin Hood. I was probably five years old at the time.

After he told me that they weren't about rabbits nor archers, I asked the inevitable followup question "What are they about?".

He explained that they were big person's book and I probably wouldn't like them until I got big but when I did, I would.

I opened the book anyway hoping to find some pictures like I had found in his history book and his book by a guy named Collodi named "Pinocchio".

No pictures in Babbit or Arrowsmith.

I stashed the disappointment/anticipation away in my memory with the vague concept that someday or other, someway or other I would be big and would read "Babbit".

Many years passed and somehow someway Donald Trump became president of the United States. In the furious backlash that followed I became aware of a book by Sinclair Lewis called “It Can’t Happen Here” which was regaining relevancy at the conclusion of 2016.

I went to the public library to get a copy but they didn’t have one.

I ignited a search on Kindle fire and found a copy. I bought it, read it, loved it, was amazed how prophetic and hip it was. Sinclair Lewis was in the pipeline.

Fired up another look in the pipeline and there it was; “Babbit”.

99 cents.

I’m big now. Much older than my father was when he read it. I figured I could read it now. I did. Loved it. Found it totally relevant. Started talking to my reading pals about Sinclair Lewis most of whom thought I meant Upton Sinclair.

“I haven’t read him since high school. His book made me sick that’s about all I can remember” as they remembered “The Jungle” by the wrong Sinclair.

So I took a detour and read “The Jungle”. It was as depressing as I knew it would be but the price was right on Kindle.

99 cents.

I read and appreciated the novel for its historic and reformative value but Upton Sinclair was no Sinclair Lewis.The next day, I was browsing through my private library and there it was......"Main Street" by Sinclair Lewis.

Now comes the showdown. I had the paperback in one hand, my Kindle in the other. I searched for “Main Street” on Kindle.

Found it.

99cents.

I hit the button to buy.

Now the two formats of "Main Street" walked down a dusty Main Street at high noon in my mind. Kindle drew first. I opened up that format. I went the distance. I never opened the paperback.

Given the choice between new school and old school reading. I chose new school. Once a child learns to walk, he rarely crawls.

The showdown and the result of the showdown shocked the hell out of the dusty little town called my intellect.

Here are some of the reasons why Kindle won.

I can read the Kindle in the dark. I prefer darkness when I read. It reminds me of my childhood when my parents demanded that I turn the lights off at night and I wished I had a little tiny night light that I could read by without turning on the bedroom light and getting busted. Now I have one. I can even read without waking up my wife.

I can change the font size on the Kindle. I have learned that during some sessions I prefer larger print which is of course less a strain on the eyes. Other days I shrink the size so that I can read faster. I find a co-relation between the two.

Kindle comes with the dictionary and wikipedia link up. Prior to Kindle, I never bothered to look up a word that I didn't know. I wasn't gonna go from paperback book to paperback dictionary and slow down my reading time. I read everything in context so it didn't matter at all if I didn't recognize a word. I still got the picture. Now with Kindle, I can get that definition almost instantaneously. My vocabulary is growing which is illuminating my past life as well as enriching my present life even as it influences my destiny.

In other words, I'm learning to read all over again.

As I learn how to read, I will learn to take firmer possession of the intellectual property that my reading has gained for me. As you can see from these words that stay, I am becoming more interested in writing ABOUT what I have read which locks down that comprehension and retention in my mind.

When I read, I make mental notes about concepts that come up in the source material that remind of an idea that I am approaching. With the Kindle I am learning how to highlight that particular material and lend my notes permanency. An infinite set of inspiration points that tend to piggy back one another, when I compose.

Yup, when I got "big" enough, Sinclair Lewis leaped into my hands and changed my life. When the student is ready, the reacher will appear.

Now to wrap this up, let me compare and contrast Sinclair Lewis with Upton Sinclair or vice versa.

Let's look at their awards.

Upton Sinclair won a Pulitzer which makes him a literary All Star.

Sinclair Lewis won a Nobel which makes him a literary Hall of Famer.

In other words, Upton is no Sinclair and Sinclair is no Lewis.

DOCTOR IN THE DARK

I was still afraid of the dark when my father took me to my first movie. I didn't think that the dark itself could hurt me but maybe something in the dark that I couldn't see would. In the light, there were quite a few things that I could see that would hurt me. The doctor was foremost amongst them. He seemed like a nice guy at first until he stuck a needle in me after saying that it wouldn't hurt. It hurt and from that point on, I hated and feared doctors. They seemed to be two people; a smiley guy and a monster who punctured you. My fear of doctors was about to metastasize and nearly cost me my life. The scene of that first flick was the Dryden Theater in the George Eastman House. I had already freaked out at the Elephant head "trophy" on the wall which we passed by on the way to the theater. The whole place struck me as scary.

We took our seats. The curtains were drawn and the lights went out. This was bad. I had no idea what was about to happen next so I covered my eyes. I opened them when the music came on, I wasn't afraid of music but this music didn't sound like any music that I had ever heard before or wanted to hear again.

I can't recall all of the processes and wonders and horrors that I experienced over the next ninety minutes other than wanting to get the hell out of the place. The movie was *Dr. Jekyll and Mr. Hyde* starring John Barrymore.

The film was silent but words were far from necessary. I realized that every time one guy drank a potion he turned into another guy and even though both guys were scary, the guy who appeared after the potion drink was so upsetting that I closed my eyes and prayed that he would go away before he hurt me. Of course when that guy finally disappeared, I was confronted with my foremost fear figure...a goddamned doctor who might somehow come off the screen and attempt to stick a needle in my arm.

I figure I was maybe four years old at the time which means this happened in 1950/51. The movie was free as were all the movies at the Dryden back then, that's why we were there in the first place. Barrymore's Dr Jekyll and Mr.Hyde was made in 1920. In 2020 that would be like a movie that was made in 1990. Barrymore's face and famous profile provided the horrifying special effects.

When we got home, I was very upset and so was my mother when she found out what movie we had gone to see that afternoon. She yelled at my Dad and that argument was almost as scary as the movie itself as if both of them had sipped a potion. Not only was this the day of my first movie but also the first time I saw my parents mad at one another.

It was a long time before we went back to the Dryden. The place still scared me but both my mother and my father assured me that I would have a better time. We all three went together. I didn't freak out at the elephant head and I knew the place was gonna get dark. Dark was never as dark when my Mom was around. This time what came on was a Tom Mix movie with Tom defeating the bad guys and riding away on his horse Tarzan.

I lost most of my fear not only of the movies but also of the dark. For every Mr. Hyde or Dr. Jekyll that threatened me, I could always count on a Tom Mix to save me.

Mix and Mom and Dad.

WISCONSIN MILK

The eighteenth ward on the East Side of Rochester was full of grocery stores, what we now would call Mom and Pop shops.

It wasn't unusual for the shops to have different prices for similar items. On Wisconsin Street, all my relatives and friends were up to date on the economic differentiations.

One afternoon, I was spending time with my grandmother when my Uncle Tommy who lived across the street entered the scene. Like most of my relatives on the street, he enjoyed sending me to get "yourself some candy". Usually, he'd send me to Mary's Sweet Shop on East Main. Mary knew all my Wisconsin kin. She had known them since *they* were kids walking up to the shop to get themselves some candy. This time Tom needed a quart of milk and he was aware of a milk war going on between the shops. He gave me a nickel for candy and sent me on my way, telling me to make sure that I went to the Dago's store and not the Jew's store.

I wasn't really listening when he gave me the task because I was thinking of the candy that my nickel would buy. I headed down Wisconsin to Atlantic Avenue rather than up Wisconsin towards East Main. I wasn't thinking about milk, I was thinking about Mary Janes and Tootsie Rolls.

When I got to the store, I had forgotten which store that Tommy had sent me and I wasn't too sure which store was which anyway. I bought my candy first. While eating the candy, I remembered that I was supposed to go to the Dago. I didn't want to get the wrong milk so I innocently asked the person at the counter if this store belonged to the Dago or the Jew.

The owner asked "Who sent you?"

"My Uncle Tom."

" I thought so," he said with a smile. "Where did he tell you to go?"

" He told me the Dago had cheaper milk today so I should go there."

Of course I had no idea what "Dago" or "Jew" meant other than what I supposed was the name of two competing grocery stores, one of which was the right one because it had cheaper milk today.

The proprietor said, "You got it right son. I'm Luigi and this is the Dago store. The Jew is on the corner of Main and Wisconsin across from Engine 12. Tell your uncle that Luigi says hello"

I bought the milk and brought it back to Tom who was still chatting with Grandma only some beer had been added to the chat. My Grandma called beer her "medicine" which I thought at the time and now realize that's exactly what it was.

I gave Tom the milk and the change. He took a look at the change and asked me where I had gone. I told him that I had gone to the Dago store. He asked who waited on me and I told him Luigi and that Luigi said "hello"

"Luigi huh? There's no Luigi at the Dago store! Was 'Luigi' bald."

"Yeah Tom, Luigi was bald."

" You got your stores mixed up. You went to the Jew. The Jew is bald and his name is Norm." Tommy started laughing just as I'm sure "Luigi" had laughed a few minutes earlier. He had put one over on the Mick. Luigi knew that his milk was more expensive that day and that Tom knew that he knew.

"Next time I send you to the Dago, head for Mary's Sweet Shop and you'll meet Tony. Tony's the Dago"

I always kept them straight after that.

It was that kind of neighborhood, everybody playing tricks on everybody else... nobody taking offense. In retrospect, I have often wondered why I headed towards Atlantic that day instead of heading to Main and Mary's. It's clear to me now, so many years later. The store on Atlantic, be it Dago or Jew, was less of a walk than the store on Main.

The store on Atlantic was more convenient.

HENRY THE BARBER

Just as dogs were once wolves, barbers were once doctors.

I remember going to the doctor before I remember going to the barber. Perhaps this is why I was afraid to go to the barber as a child. My father took me for my first hair cut.

He took me to Henry……the neighborhood barber. Henry cut everybody's hair in the East Side of the eighteenth ward. He had been cutting my father's hair since my Dad had come back home after his time in the Philippines during WW 2.

When I saw Henry in his white smock, I didn't want to enter his shop. I was afraid that it would hurt. My father reassured me that it wouldn't hurt but he had told me the same thing the last time we went to the doctor's office.

It had hurt.

I was comparing smock to smock while standing between the barber poles. Henry, in his momentarily empty shop must have seen the terror outside on the sidewalk. Pretty sure my father had been telling Henry about me every two weeks when he sat in Henry's chair to get his trim.

Henry stepped outside his door. "Vinnie is this big boy your son?"

"Yeah, Henry he is"

" Nice to meet you, son. Your Dad is so proud of you."

Henry shook my hand and before I knew it, I was sitting in his chair.

Now that I think about it, I'm pretty sure that Henry was authentically moved as he must have recalled my father as a boy sitting in the same chair that I was sitting. Pretty sure he had been concerned about my father during the war and happy when

"Vinnie" had returned. Pretty sure a lot of neighborhood guys who went to war never returned to Henry's chair. Pretty sure he had known about my Mom's pregnancy. Pretty sure my father had sat in this chair the day that I was born. Pretty sure Henry had smoked one of the celebratory cigars. Pretty sure, they had discussed well in advance. What kind of haircut I would get this first sitting and what my mood would be.

Henry was more ready than I. He gave me the same kind of haircut my father had been getting for years. It was called a GI.

Henry had cut many a GI. He was good at them. He didn't hurt me one tiny bit. I liked that.

I would return to Henry's shop for many years always getting the GI.

Always feeling relieved and connected.

Pretty much up until the Beatles hit, when I stopped getting haircuts for a long time.

Every once in a while I would walk past Henry's shop but I didn't want to visit. I was kinda guilty that I wasn't seeing him regularly anymore. He hadn't done anything wrong.

I don't think many people were seeing him regularly anymore.

I went to college.

Whenever I came home, I cruised past Henry's shop until Thanksgiving. The shop was gone. Salons were destroying barber shops. Henry had sold his shop and according to rumor had moved to Florida.

The neighborhood had changed as well and was on its way to dangerville. Neighborhood kids were getting GI's courtesy of Uncle Sam and heading to Nam.

People were getting hurt.

The barber poles were fading memories.

I still hated doctor's which almost killed me 40 years later.

I never forgot the day that my Dad told me the truth.

He told me that it wouldn't hurt.

Barbers were no longer doctors.

HUMILIATING CATHY

During my Parsells Avenue days, my playmates regarded me as the smartest kid on the block which I knew was far from true. That erroneous regard was based upon reading and spelling skills. I had only one challenger and that was my next door neighbor Cathy. In second grade, my classmates would always request that I did the reading in the class. They preferred my reading even to the teacher 's because I read with so much "expression". I got used to being the main reader in our class until one day Sister Agnita called on Cathy to read. Cathy stepped up and read with expression, pronunciation and accuracy. I enjoyed her reading as well. Over the next few weeks Cathy and I were equally called upon to read. We were the bluebirds.

Then one day, Sister Agnita brought a children's magazine to school. Up to that point, our reading had all been done from the infamous Dick and Jame reading primers and we read them in the order that they were presented in the book. Sister called on Cathy to read new material from the children's book.

Cathy was silent as if she didn't hear the teacher's request.

The teacher repeated her invitation. Cathy repeated her silence but added a discernible blush. Sister repeated her request. Cathy repeated her silence but this time added tears. The teacher called on me. I read the story no problem.

Cathy was never called on again and eventually left the bluebird nest. One day in her backyard, she explained her silence to me. Cathy couldn't read. Her mother, competitive with my mother, had heard about my reading success and became determined that Cathy would shut me down. Cathy was forced to memorize the reading assignments that we had each night for homework.

Cathy's reading was rote memory and recitation.

I couldn't imagine how difficult it must have been for Cathy to memorize all that stuff every night and be ready to recite and lie the next day in such a way as to reveal that she couldn't read a lick.

I liked Cathy. She was a friend of mine and a playmate. I hated to see her get humiliated and lose all of her self-confidence. Cathy's was the first humiliation that I remember seeing in school. I would see many others as a school boy and hear of many others when I became a teacher. I hated them. I felt sorry for the humiliatee. Moments like this were the beginnings of my teacher education. I learned the basic must to avoids in teaching. Humiliating a student being close to the top of the list. I vowed to become a teacher and NEVER humiliate a student. This came in handy when I ran into Laird, my first dyslexic student. As soon as I realized his discomfort, I made a point of talking to him. He explained the problem to me tearfully and I tearfully began to understand. Laird taught me for the rest of the year and forever.

Cathy moved from Parsells Avenue a few years after the incident. Maybe she became an actress. She would have been good at that if she had the confidence. I never saw or heard from her again.

My reputation as a "smart" kid in the neighborhood hood grew at Cathy's expense,

I knew better.

GREEN TREE PHARMACY

Green Tree Pharmacy was next door to Henry's Barbershop. I got my hair cut at Henry's every two weeks. Every two weeks, I would stop at Green Tree Pharmacy. Green Tree had unusual comic books.

I had read many comic books but comics were getting blamed for "juvenile delinquency". They were becoming harder and harder to find. We weren't delinquents. We just liked comic books even if and probably because they were horrifying and violent… but no the government had to step in and start censoring them leaving us with Donald Duck, Mighty Mouse, Little Lulu etc. To put it mildly, the edge was off but at least we got Be Bop A Lula out of the deal.

And eventually Mad magazine,

Green Tree sold Classic comic books. They were a little more costly than other comics. Classic comics cost 15 cents.15 cents was equivalent to 3 packs of baseball cards. Baseball trading cards were the coin of our realm on Parsells Avenue.

I got 15 cents a week allowance. 15 cents was an entire week.

One November afternoon after a cut at Henry's, I stopped into Green Tree and noticed their Classic display. I had to judge the books by their cover because the word was out how much juvenile delinquents liked to read a comic book on the shelf and not buy it. As soon as I got near the display, the white coated pharmacist was hovering over me to make sure that I didn't grab a free look. I didn't care for the pharmacist who looked like some kinda doctor.

One of the covers had caught my eye. It showed a Civil War scene with Yankees charging forward, cannons blasting and bombs exploding overhead. The comic was called *Red Badge of Courage*. I plucked it from the display.The pharmacist walked me over to this counter. I gave him my allowance. Baseball cards wouldn't be out for six months so I had money to burn.

When I got the book home, I read the Red Badge over and over again. Lots of blood, lots of explosions, lots of corpses, lots of history as well as a message about war and bravery and cowardice. I kept expecting the hero to be awarded a badge and it took me a couple of readings to realize that his blood was his badge of courage. It was easy to recognize a new dimension of comic story telling.

On the back cover, they listed the names and numbers of all the Classic Comic books. I noticed one called *The Hunchback of Notre Dame*. I figured that was a football story. I wanted it.

Two weeks later, I was back at Green Tree with my fresh GI haircut. Once again, the pharmacist intercepted me as I walked in the door. Together we walked over to the Classic display where I cast my eyes on *Hunchback of Notre Dame*. The cover took me by surprise as I was expecting a half back rather than a Hunchback.

We walked back to the counter. I gave him my allowance.

When I got home, I met Quasimodo and Esmerelda. I learned that Notre Dame was not only a football team but also a cathedral in Paris. I learned about impossible love and sacrifice. I learned about romance and humiliation.

My collection had begun.

So had my literary education.

Over the next months I added *Oliver Twist*, *Dr Jekyll and Mr. Hyde*, *Fang and Claw*, *Bring Em back Alive*, *Tale of Two Cities*, *Don Quixote*, *Huckleberry Finn*, The *Deerslayer* , *Call of the Wild* and *Cyranno De Bergerac*. I read all of them over and over.

The pharmacist began to take an interest in me and my reading.

One day in January when I walked in he said, “Hey, guess what just came in.”

He answered his own question a moment later when I was too shocked by his friendly attention to respond.

He said, "I figured it was time for some Shakespeare so I ordered Hamlet and it arrived this morning."

As he took me over to the section I was facing a decision. I had intended to buy *Around the World in 80 Days*. I had heard about Hamlet but thought it was Omelet and I didn't like omelets so I couldn't figure out why this Shakespeare guy would be writing about eggs. Of course the yolk was on me.

I asked the Pharmacist what it was about. He hesitated for a bit. In retrospect I realize that he was trying to figure out a way to explain Hamlet to a kid that he knew only because he saw the kid for about two minutes every two weeks but the kid obviously had a literary interest.

God bless him. He gave me the best answer. He wasn't a grouch after all.

"It's about a ghost."

I bought it. I read it. Over and over.

Now 60 plus years later, having introduced Hamlet to dozens of classes of high school students, hundreds and hundreds of developing intellects; I realize how right he was. Hamlet is about a ghost and that's what I would tell my students in the very beginning. I would also add how,"when people ask me about a play or a ghost story or for that matter any drama, I usually say 'well it's not exactly Hamlet'. What we are about to study is EXACTLY Hamlet." and we would begin and for many of us never end.

DADDIO

When I was a pre-school child I played with miniature plastic cowboys and Indians. My parents referred to them as "characters". I liked 'em all, the cowboys and the Indians. Sometimes they got along, sometimes they fought. They always had personality, thus individuality.

They were part of an ongoing story that I was continuously creating. When they fought, someone would get wounded usually in the shoulder. At some point, I became aware of the concept of deaths well as the concept of loss and burial.

One day there was a big war in the story and four characters died. Two of my favorites died in that war, an Indian swinging a tomahawk and a yellow, plastic cowboy who was charging forward with a rifle. For some reason I called the yellow soldier Daddio and the Indian with the tomahawk was Tommy. Tommy was made out of some kind of weird rubber.

After the war, I couldn't just bring them back…they were dead. They needed to be buried. I buried them one day. Literally. I dug four little holes. Four shallow graves.I put rocks/sticks over the spots where they were buried; two in the front yard and two in the back. The back yard had a cherry tree; a hill, a garage and barbed wire keeping our yard separate from the yard next door. It was big enough that later we would learn to play baseball back there.

Daddio was in the front yard. Tommy was in the back. Another character was buried near each of them I didn't want to lose them forever. I just needed them to be dead for a while…a week or two. I was interested to see what the other characters would do when Tommy and Daddio were gone. I wondered if the survivors had learned any lessons about love and war and death and loss while I was learning about their learning.

The surviving characters were alarmed when they heard about the four burials. They indicated that the loss of life was not as frightening as the undertaking. I learned that they realized that they were not actually alive so the loss of life was no deterrent to their belligerence. Burial was a different story as they were afraid that I would not be able to locate the burial sites and therefore Daddio and Tommy et al would be lost. As I learned then and we all know now, toys fear being lost.

They immediately went back to war and said they would continue the carnage until I buried them all or I brought Tommy and Daddio back to the surface.Furthermore, they wanted me to start using red nail polish to indicate their war wounds. I thought that was a good idea so I did.

A couple of weeks passed

After a lot of bloodshed, I decided enough was enough so I went out to retrieve the buried leaders to stop all the suffering.

I found Tommy and his companion in the front yard. No problem. I found Daddio's companion in the backyard but I couldn't find Daddio. I must have forgotten to put a marker over his location.

Daddio was gone. I dug a dozen holes and I got the kid from across the street to dig a few holes with me.

Suddenly the backyard was a real big place.

My parents were getting worried.

We never found Daddio.

I returned Tommy and his companions to the wounded.

The polished characters decided they didn't want to play anymore and neither did I.

Lost and loss and learning.

That same week, I saw my first baseball card.

Roy Face

Everything changed.

I've just seen a face. I remember the time and place.

The face that I've just seen is the face of Roy Face. What a face on Roy's Face.

He looks like a juvenile delinquent skeleton skull with a Pittsburgh Pirate lid on its dome and a forkball on its mind.

I see him in my memory as I remember the buried Daddio.

Roy Face's face was on the first baseball card I remember which was the moment I stepped away from wounded plastic characters.

I haven't thought of Roy Face's face nor of Daddio for a long time.

The last time I thought of Daddio before yesterday was when I remembered a poem that I had written 40 years ago called One of My Childhood Burials.

That poem disappeared as well.

I gave it to a fake Elton John who was going to use it as the lyrics to a song he was supposedly writing. According to his plan, I was gonna be the fake Bernie Taupin within that collaboration and we were gonna get rich.

Right around that time another person wanted to collaborate with me on writing porno. She was the wife of the man who once was the kid across the street who helped me dig some holes when we were looking for Daddio. Her name was Christine Sullivan but she called herself Michelle Le Carte.

This was Michelle's proposal to me: "I've got a filthy mind and you know how to spell."

She disappeared almost immediately as did the poem, the fake Elton John, the imaginary song and the anticipated riches of each goofy dream.

The Roy Face card had disappeared long before that, 3 or 4 years after the burial of Daddio.

But here's the kicker. Here's what I know now that I didn't know then.

Nothing ever disappears.

Things get buried.

Things get lost.

We forget.

Matter is indestructible.

If I went back to my old backyard and dug it up,

I would find Daddio.

Daddio is plastic so Daddio didn't decompose.

He's still in that backyard,

two miracles and a life short of sainthood.

Buried.

The backyard is more real than real estate

The backyard is also the subconscious.

Everyone has a backyard.

Daddio is one of millions

of memories,

that lurk in my backyard.

Everyone, everything and every thought

ever is in all backyards.

Daddio is everywhere.

In the backyard of everyone

reading these words.

Always been there

Everything in the backyard

is trying to come to the surface,

to get back into memory,

to be unearthed,

discovered,

remembered,

analyzed,

misunderstood,

turned into an idea

an elaboration

a formulation

a realization

an inspiration……

Roy Face

Fake Elton John

One of My Childhood Burials

Michelle LeCarte

Linda Lipstick

They all made it to the surface yesterday,

because Daddio came to the surface and elevated them with him.

They connected.

They ascended.

Happens everyday to all of us all the time.

Occasionally we write it down

or play it on a trombone

or dance in the moonlight all alone

OH SUSANNAH

When I was a child, I believed everything I heard on radio or teevee. I believed that the United States was fighting against gorillas in Korea. I believed there were ghost riders in the sky. I believed that somehow it could get so hot that you could freeze to death and that sometimes when it rained all night, the weather could still be dry. I believed that some guy from Alabama with a banjo on his knee was goin' to looziana his true love for to see.

Oh Susannah really blew my mind and still does to this day.

When I got a few years older, shortly after I believed that a flying dinosaur named Rodan was terrorizing Japan, I began to smarten up some. Around this time, I was encouraged to pick out an instrument and take music lessons. Elvis hadn't arrived yet so I didn't even think of guitar and the school didn't teach it anyway because the school was recruiting kids to play in the school orchestra.

I chose the clarinet. I had no idea what a clarinet even looked like but it sounded cool, a lot cooler than violin and different from trumpet which most of the guys chose as their instrument. Only two or three other kids chose clarinet.

My parents bought me a good one and made it clear that I should take it seriously because it was a serious instrument. I started taking lessons and I guess I was pretty good because I got a lot of encouragement from my teachers and assurance that when I got a little older, I would be in the orchestra especially if I practiced maybe even first clarinet (whatever that was)...so I practiced even though I didn't enjoy playing. Practice became a drudgery and I took no joy in it.

Meanwhile rock and roll was starting up and I loved that. I noticed there was never a clarinet in a rock and roll band which only added to my disinterest and disdain for the instrument but I kept practicing and by the time I was in fifth grade, I was ready for the recital which was the last step before joining the orchestra.

My music teacher picked out my solo. She chose, Oh Susanah.

The recital was just something that I had to do so I got ready but my heart wasn't in it. My best friend Frankie was also in the recital. He played the piano but he hated that as much as I hated the clarinet. He never practiced and was scared shitless of the inevitable recital performance.

On the night of the recital, I was scheduled to be the fifth performer and Frankie was gonna go third. The place was packed with parents and friends and catching vibes from Frank, I too became petrified. Frank preceded me and froze. He screwed up his "Hunting Song" and had to start over three times. He finished the fiasco and sat down next to me, nearly in tears. I figured the same thing was gonna happen to me. I was gonna freeze and maybe even squeak. While the fourth kid was playing her solo, I wanted to get the hell outta there but realized that I was trapped.

I got my introduction. I walked up on the stage and played the song perfectly. My practice had paid off. I never played better. My parents were very proud. They remarked about how calm and composed I was during the performance and that I had played the song "perfectly" which in fact I had.

I got a nice round of applause. I returned to my seat as relieved as I had ever been in my life, at the perfection of my performance but rather because the pressure was off and to my amazement, I had come through in the clutch.

To this day, I have never had anything turn out as well as Oh Susanna did that night.

I had cinched my place in the orchestra which was kinda cool but nothing I was thrilled about.

I wanted to play baseball. I wanted to play football. I wanted to have hair like Elvis. I wanted to play the guitar.

Frankie quit the piano that night. The reason he chose to play the piano in the first place was because he had one in his house. I kept playing the clarinet for the next three years. I spent a lot of time over at Frankies house where he would occasionally play "The Hunting Song" on his piano. He would play it perfectly and always end by saying, " I screwed that up" During that time, we joined the Boy Scouts. We were trustworthy, brave reverent and prepared. We joined Little League. I travelled to Ireland, couldn't wait to get home and play ball. I went to the Eastman school of Music. I practiced. I went on my first date. My parents made me play the clarinet on our porch for my date. Her name was Terry and she was my childhood friend who had moved away but came back when I asked het to go with me to be on Dance party which was our local equivalent to American Bandstand. We were on teevee and I was with the prettiest girl.

Oh Susannah had been very good to me.

It was the end of something and the beginning of something else.

A few weeks later, I saw Buddy Holly live. I heard my first electric guitar courtesy of Duane Eddy.

I stopped practicing. I settled for second clarinet.

And rock and roll and baseball and cigarettes and girls.

No more gorillas in Korea.

Don't you cry for me.

YES WE ARE AFRAID

We are afraid.

We've been cat scanned and bone scanned. Our secrets photographed. Even the secrets of our secrets are now up for inspection; an invasion of privacy in search for a truth that is out there and in here at the same time.

Today is Saturday.

Our day of reckoning is Monday.

Monday is the "consultation" with Dr. Somebody who performed the biopsy and is the office mate of Dr. Somebody else who made the bad news call and described the secret secret by a number; Gleason score 7.

I'm pretty sure that Dr, Somebody Else made all the bad news calls for the office. He had a perfect voice for it. His voice was a baritone that sounded as somber as the fateful message that he delivered which began with "I'm sorry to inform you that you do have cancer."

The various scans would reveal the level of spread that the cancer had achieved in its attempt to take over our world. All we know so far is that it's a Gleason 7 and has been around "for years". I picked up his hint…if I had come in sooner, they would have caught it earlier.

Trying to imagine the first words of the consult……the first dozen words.

Gleason score 7 might be amongst those dozen words.

Like many guys my age, 7 is my favorite number because it was on the uniform of Mickey Mantle and of course we all love Ralph Kramden aka Jackie Gleason. Both men, however, are long deceased which is a condition more in my mind than ever as we go forward with the pessimism of intelligence, the optimism of will and the courage of caution.

We are afraid but we are not worried.

Fear is the natural reaction to mortal threat and the place where courage can be found. Fear is the department of defense. The only thing we have to fear is fearlessness itself. We embrace our fear. We confront it with a minimum of worry and awareness of faith.Yet there is regret as we prepare to confront the scans of my secrets. It's as if I'm expecting to see all of the cigars, the cigarettes, the potato chips, the red meat, the diet cokes, the pasta, the reefer, the Budweisers, the lack of sunscreen during all that golf and swimming, all of the things that over the years have been revealed as carcinogenic killers all of which we have enjoyed. We are about to see the damages and dread the "I told you so" as much as the damages themselves.

We don't dread the reckoning as much as we are afraid of it. We can handle it, whatever it is. Worry or dread is not going to change the results of the cat or bone scan. We can even write a little bit. Ice has taken over that delight in the last week or so and managed to keep the cancer on the low, which we very much appreciate.

Stay tuned and focus on the word TREATABLE. One way or the other, we'll be back soon. See ya on the other side in a place like this.

WHY DO WE FEAR FEAR

The only thing we have to fear is to fear fear itself. Why do we fear fear? Fear is an involuntary response to the possibility of pain or death. Fear is intuitive and will do the best it can to help us survive and/or endure.

Fear is different from worry. Worry is voluntary.

We can choose to pick that worry phone up or we can choose to put that phone down or never answer it at all. If the worry is connected to pain or death, don't worry, fear will take over and do it's best to see us through.

For those of us who worry a lot under the mechanism that most of what we worry about won't come true which makes worry sort of a protective amulet, we need to be careful to make sure that worrisome weather doesn't turn into a climate of anxiety.

So here's the deal…if you're worrying about say the results of a bone scan that you took last week…worrying won't change the results of that test and you will be dealing with those results soon enough anyway so why let them get in the way of enjoying the days before the result is revealed?

I know this sounds simple and truly it is, we just love to make things more complicated for various, very human reasons. Perhaps we should all return to the mid-20th century to our once and future idol Alfred E. Neumann and "what, me worry?"

Some of my teachers said reading Mad magazine would ruin my life. By that time, of course, I was already a faithful reader of Mad magazine so I began to worry that I was already in trouble or my teachers were not as infallible as I thought they were.

It's almost impossible today to recognize how popular, subversive and influential Mad magazine was in the middle to late fifties and early sixties. The price was 25 cents (cheap) and Alfred E. Neumann appeared on every cover.

Alfred E was the “what me worry kid” and free as he was of worry, his dim grin suggested a wacky degree of self-satisfaction over confidence mixed with despair not recognizing the validity of anything or anyone including himself and the very magazine he was representing.The epitome of authentic absurdity resonant with the times and reflective of the times ahead. The fifties ended and not everybody was worried, although we should have been.

But I was and still am. I worry a lot, always have. Trump just landed in Saudi surrounded by Arabs with swords. Yeah, I’m worried but I’m not afraid of fear. Maybe my teachers were right.

THE BARON'S ROBE

It was the second professional wrestling card at the brand new War Memorial. My father had two ringside seats. In hindsight, he might have got them for nuthin' because he was a fireman and he was wearing' his formal uniform. I think he was on duty.

He took me with him.

He had taken me to the first card as well. Vern Gagne beat Yukon Eric with the use of a steel chair hitting Eric on the head above Yukon's half ear which had been famously sheared by Killer Kowalski a few years prior.

I was so proud of Vin that he had done such a cool thing as getting ringside seats. Only a few of my friends had even been to the sparkling new building. None had been to a wrestling match, much less ringside. It was 1957. Since it was my second appearance at ringside, I thought I knew what I was doing.

The first match of the card pitted babyface Tony Sillipinni against heel Baron Gatoni. Tony was a huge crowd favorite because he was a local guy, a former great athlete at Jefferson High School. Tony was a young, clean cut high flyer who would years later change his name to Tony Marino and become a Madison Square Garden midcard mainstay.

His opponent, Baron Gatoni was known as "The Barrel Chested Baron". Baron had long black hair that grew way past his shoulders which in the days of flattops, crewcuts and duck asses made him look like an insane Italian Rasputin who represented everything that was despicable about unrepentant, non-English speaking immigrants as he cursed the crowd in an unidentifiable language and prepared to beat the beejezuz out of the local kid.

Needless to say, the Baron generated a lot of heat.

Back in those days, kids were encouraged to rush to the ring and get the autographs of the good guys. The wrestlers were encouraged to give them which was an important part in the identification/differentiation ritual. Good guys gave autographs. Bad guys....Nobody even tried.

I got Tony's autograph, still have it somewhere.

I returned to my seat. The house lights in the Memorial dimmed and the ring lights flamed on as the two grapplers approached each other. With Baron's attention focused on Tony, he failed to see a "fan" approach the ring. The fan grabbed Gatoni's robe from the entry stairs and with jingoistic courage threw it under the ring to the applause of the assembled crowd. Gatoni didn't see the pilferage but I did.

The match continued for the allotted nine minutes. To the delight of the crowd, Tony pinned Gatoni after the Baron had broken all of the standard rules, had thrown stiff arms at the crowd and had begged for mercy in a disgraceful display of cowardice.

Most of the crowd turned its attention to the entrance of the next pair of wrestlers, one of whom was another local kid name Bob Marella who went on to become Gorilla Monsoon and a WWE Hall Of Famer.

Some in the crowd were still threatening Gatoni. He didn't have much time to get outta there. He couldn't find his robe. He didn't have a clue where it was but I did. I crawled under the ring, retrieved the robe and handed it to him. He looked at me with an expression of kindness, understanding and even wisdom; emotions that he had clearly avoided during his performance in the ring. Under his breath, the Baron said, "Thank you. You got guts". The expression took only a split second. I was the only one who saw it.

Then he changed his face into a bullying scowl.

He grabbed the robe out of my hands like he was stealing it and ran back to the locker room while the crowd booed like crazy. I went back to my seat and the booing continued, except now some of the boos were headed in my direction... aimed right at me. I was getting some of the left over heat.

I made my way back to my seat where Dad, distinguished in his formal blues, had my back so nobody insulted me upon my return and the boos became redirected at the next 'furrier' to enter the ring, Frank Valois "The Mad Lover of Paris".

My father was proud of what I had done. He asked me what The Baron had said. I told him what the Baron said and what I had thought. I had thought and still think that it doesn't take "guts" to do the right thing, the obvious thing, the polite thing.

A few minutes later an attendant came to my seat with an envelope from the dressing room. He said, "Joe told me to give you this." Inside the envelope, was a crisp dollar bill along with a Baron Gatoni autograph.

The Baron was really a guy named Joe.

Back in those days, a dollar was a lot of money. I was flabbergasted and tried to give the money back to my Dad. He said, "You keep it. Get some cards with it."

Up until that time, the most I had ever spent on baseball cards, even though they were the coin of the realm on Parsells Avenue, was a half a buck. My wild Irish Aunt Rose had given me a half-dollar piece and when I told her that I had intended to spend it on cards she said, "Don't tell your mother." I said I wouldn't and I didn't. The idea of buying ten packs of cards from Dee's delicatessen at a nickel a pack had seemed so extravagant as to border on sinful. Now here was my father green lighting me to buy twice that amount with the money that I got from "Joe".

I bought the cards the next day. One of the cards that I got was a Willie Mays card. The Willie card would make a double for me and I was the only kid on the Avenue to hav even one Willie. The bully on the street, Big Duke Clod had been making my life miserable for the proceeding couple of weeks for not trading the Willy Card for him in exchange for two or three of his worthless doubles that I already had. I didn't let the jerk know that I had a double and traded him the old Willie card and got a better deal than he had offered me a couple of days earlier. Plus he laid off me for a while.

I learned an awful lot from that episode. Sixty years later, I'm still trying to figure out all of the ramifications that adventure had on my personal and professional life. As I type this, I suspect they were immense.

LEARNING TO MISUNDERSTAND SEX

When I look back at my childhood, I'm staggered by the innocence.

I grew up deep in a city in the time that it was inevitably turning into a war zone.My next door neighbor was named Mrs. Good. Her yard was separated from our yard by barbed wire.I always called her Mrs Good. I called her husband Bill.

Bill was easy going. I found out decades later that one of the reasons Bill was so calm was that every day he drank whiskey on his walk down the Avenue from the bus loop on the corner of Parsells and Culver so that by the time Bill got home to Mrs. Good, Bill had a good buzz on.

Next to Mrs. Good lived the bad influence of our neighborhood...a kid a few years older than me and my friends. His name was Kenny but he called himself Duke. We were all afraid of Kenny/Duke and that's the way he liked it.

When he wasn't listening, we called him Big Duke Clod. Of course, he never knew that.

Needless to say, there was bad blood between Duke and Bill and Mrs Good especially if a ball got knocked into her yard. Clod's house was also separated from the Good House by barbed wire. We learned how to climb barbed wire early on the Avenue. When we got into Good's backyard, we were amazed at how well taken care of it was. Fountains, flowers a cherry tree etc.

Duke's backyard was all concrete.

My backyard was almost as nice as Good's.

We had a cherry tree back there and a summer house and a shrine to St. Theresa which of course had been blessed by Father Murphy one proud day.

We learned to play baseball in my backyard.

Every once in a while, a pop foul would land in the Good yard.

The Goods' didn't mind if we went in their backyard as long as we asked them.

Duke wasn't gonna ask anybody about anything, especially when he could pound one of us until we climbed the barbed wire.

Mrs Good loved my parents who called her Connie.

Every once in a while, she'd catch us in her yard without asking permission. When she did so, she immediately told my parents. My parents would get kinda mad at me but they also thought that Connie was overreacting.

Before reaching baseball age, I used to run around in my beautiful backyard and didn't always have clothes. No problem. I hadn't yet learned about shame or secrets

That would take awhile.

Duke helped with that.

He also helped me to misunderstand sex.

One of the first sexual misrepresentations that Duke hit me with was this:

"How'd you like to go to bed with THAT?" Duke would ask this as a reaction to seeing a pretty girl walking down the Avenue. He would say this when looking at an actress in a movie magazine. He would say this all the time.

I didn't know what the heck he was talking about but I kind of figured out that what he meant was the girl or woman or picture of a girl or woman that he was questioning me about was someone he thought was attractive.

I learned to say, " Yeah, I'd love to go to bed with THAT".

I can't be more than seven years old at the time.

Later he would ask if I'd like to JUMP in bed with that BROAD

Of course I would LOVE to JUMP in bed with that BROAD.

I figured Broad mean't woman and jump in bed meant that the woman was good looking.

Other little neighborhood kids my age didn't quite know how to answer Duke's question. He called those kids Fairies. He made them eat grass

The only fairy I knew about was Tinkerbell who I kinda liked. I couldn't figure out what was wrong with being a fairy but I didn't want to be called one. I could avoid this by giving Duke the right answer when he asked that question.

"Of course, I'd LOVE to JUMP in Bed with that BROAD" I'm no fairy. I don't need to eat grass.

In the twenty-first century, I knew that there is a relationship between distance and time. Back in the mid-twentieth, at the age of eight, thirty miles was a world away from Parsells Avenue. Crystal Beach was thirty miles away.In the summertime, which in itself was a loooonnng time, I spent most of my weekends far, far away from the city at place called Canandaigua Lake at a beach called Crystal.

Duke Clod was nowhere in sight but his influence tended to linger.

I was blessed to be relatively middle class so guess who WAS in sight…that's right my relatives especially those on my father's side. Many of them had collaborated on the actual construction of 'the ranch house' which was the name of the second cottage that my grandfather built in 1952.

I caught a lot of that sound and fury which later proved to have great significance By 1954, the arguing, cursing and drinking that went on during the building of the "Ranch House" had dissipated. The place was inhabitable and open to all my kin.

Not all my kin appreciated the muddy road to the ranch house nor the 'honey bucket' that passed as the toilet nor the fact that the only water available other than the lake required a trip to the well and a return trip bucket lugging fifteen pound of water,

None of this bothered me too much so we were the most regular visitors to the Ranch House.

One time, we were down at the Ranch and my Uncle Bill showed up. Uncle Bill was an elegant old guy. Always well dressed and in great posture, Uncle Bill was an engaging figure whom I saw rarely enough to render mystical. The main thing about Uncle Bill is that he was ancient. My grandfather, even though everybody called him Danny Boy was old but his brothers Mike and Bill were older still. Bill was the oldest of them all. He was known, naturally, as Old Uncle Bill.

Me, I was the first son, the grandson, the first nephew and the youngest kid at the Ranch House. I was held in a position of esteem.

Everybody knew my grades were excellent, that I read with uncommon comprehension as well as speed. I had a commensurate vocabulary and consequently admirable spelling ability. Most important of all for life at the Lake, I could swim. All my relatives knew this.

What they didn't know was the influence and existence of Big Duke Clod.

Sooooo, one July weekend, I found myself alone in the company of Uncle Bill. I found a movie magazine lying around. I was looking through the magazine when I came across a picture of Anita Ekberg.

I had never seen anyone who looked quite like Anita Ekberg. If you have never seen Anita Ekberg, take a minute to google her and maybe you'll see what I mean.

I figured I'd ask Uncle Bill if he had an opinion about Anita Ekberg.I called him over. I showed him the picture and asked 'Hey Uncle Bill, how would you like to jump in bed with that BROAD'

It's hard to describe the look that crossed Uncle Bill's face at that moment. It was a look that reflected him grabbing a visual of his 200 year old self jumping in bed with Anita Ekberg which he must have been spontaneously cross-referencing with the dueling visual of his 60 pound, 8 year old grand nephew jumping in bed with Anita Ekberg.

The expression transmogrified and concluded when he must have visualized all three of us ...he, me and Anita Ekberg all jumping into bed together.

To this day, I've never seen an expression like it. Basically it was a look of astonishment with shades of consternation, curiosity, fear, hopelessness, surprise and suspense all colliding in a complicated, asymmetrical smile.

A smile was his answer to my question.

So I took it to the next level.

I'd LOVE to JUMP in bed with that BROAD.

Silence again.

Then after a moment an even more complicated smile accompanied by a couple blinks that might have been intended to be winks. Somehow, I stopped myself from asking Uncle Bill if he was a fairy.I knew Goddamn well thatI wasn't.

I definitely wanted to go to bed with that Anita Ekberg broad.

EXACT ROCK BUBBLES

Every time I make the effort to look at the past, positive experiences look the same only better; the Kodachrome effect.

One hot July afternoon in my boyhood, my father and I were splashing around and cooling off in the shallow waters of Crystal Beach, Canandaigua Lake. Crystal Beach is very rocky bottomed in the shallows.My father picked a rock from the bottom, examined it closely and showed it to me and said, "Take a close look". After I looked at the rock closely or at least what I considered closely at the time, he took the rock from my grasp and threw it in the water, maybe ten feet away.

"Bring that rock back to me, Son."

I walked 10 feet to the approximate spot where I thought the rock had entered the water. When I looked into the crystal clear water, I saw what sorta looked like the rock, The only problem was that the rock next to the rock looked like the original rock as did the rock next to that rock as did the one next to that one as did all the rocks in the area as in fact, I realized, did all the rocks in the lake. I became aware that the lake was full of thousands if not millions of rocks. I chose one and brought it back to my father.

"Is this the rock that I threw?", he asked.

"Yes," I answered.

"How do you know for sure?"

"It looks like the one you threw, doesn't it?" I answered his question with a hopeful question of my own.

"Did you notice that they all look like the one I threw?"

"Uh huh."

"Only one rock in this entire lake looks EXACTLY like the rock I threw, precisely like itself in every way. The rock that you brought back, is not the one that I threw."

I could have been discouraged, could have pouted, could have left the water but knowing what a good teacher my Dad was, I realized I was about to learn something so I was curious rather than afraid. I asked the question that he clearly wanted me to answer, a question that would change my life.

"How do I find the exact rock?"

"The exact rock is the one with bubbles coming from it. Look for the bubbles and you'll find the exact rock."

I picked another rock from the bottom. I examined it more closely and noticed a couple of unique features.I gave it to my father to scrutinize. Before throwing the rock, he gave me another bit of advice. "Don't walk to the rock. Don't run to the rock. Running riles up the water and makes the bubbles harder to see. Swim to the rock like a fish, underwater with no splashing and eyes wide open. Shallow dive for the rock as soon as I throw it. The faster, the calmer you get to the rock, the more bubbles you will see."

He threw the rock into the water again about ten feet away. I hit the water as soon as the rock did. The moment that I opened my eyes under the surface, I could see the bubbles.I swam to the bubbles rather than to the rock. The exact rock was right where it was supposed to be, under the bubbles.

My father was telling the truth. I grabbed the exact rock and brought it back to him.

He kept throwing that rock, I kept finding it. The throws kept going further and further. The further the throw, the fainter the bubble trail by the time I got to the rock. When I focused on the bubbles, I didn't have time to complain about the distance. When focused on the bubbles, I didn't have time to worry about the depth even though I was now in over my head. The depth made the bubbles fainter, yes, but the bubble trail grew longer and even more beautiful in its fragility.

Eventually, I reached my childish limit for distance and depth and breathless time under water.I lost the exact rock.

I came back to Dad empty handed. I had transformed that rock into a kind of treasure and now it was gone forever.

My father could read the loss and disappointment in my eyes.

"Don't worry Ice, there's a million rocks in this lake and most of them haven't moved for decades. By moving your rock so many times, you changed the lake a little and for the better. Let it go. It's safe and it's where it belongs. Let it go and let's get something to eat."

We climbed out of the water. We walked up the steps to the road leading to our cottage. When I got to the top step, before I hit the road, I looked down at the water.

Another treasure had been added. An every day rock had been paid attention to, thus enriched. My Dad had taught me a lesson. The lake looked the same only better. And that as they say, was just the top of it.

FULL

At first, I was a "when are we gonna get there" type kid, like every kid on early journeys.

The monotony of every journey was interrupted by stops at service stations. Whenever we stopped into a station, my father would ask for "a dollar's worth". My first memory of that request goes back to a time when gas was probably about a dime a gallon. My Dads' dollar's worth of gas bought us ten gallons.

I didn't understand what " a dollar's worth" meant until I was about 10. By the time I was 10, I had a brother to share the ride with so the trip wasn't so boring. He took over the "when are we gonna get there" duties while I was punching him in the shoulder... He had no idea about the cost of gas.

Gas stations were on every corner. Occasionally, they would drop the price on one corner only for the purpose of luring the customers to that corner and away from the other three corners. Eventually, they all drove each other out of business but that's another story.

I was 12 when we took a trip and got caught in a gas war.

My Dad noticed the economic combat. He drove and drove looking for a station that was selling gas at 16 cents a gallon. He passed many a station selling at eighteen and a couple selling at 17 cents. Finally, on the verge of empty, with my 5 month pregnant mother making her condition and discomfort VERY clear, my father spotted a sign that read "gas sixteen cents a gallon a mile ahead". Vin said, "That's as low as it's gonna get."

We made the mile on fumes. We pulled into the station. Sure enough, the price was right. Dad said something that I'd never heard him say before. He said, "Fill er up!" and he did so with pride and a wink at Mom. We caught the wink in the backseat. Mom was looking out the window. She missed it. Intentionally. The attendant filled the tank, wiped the windows, checked the oil and wished us all a good day. We felt like we were rich.

We pulled out of that station. We went down the road, not even half a mile when another sign appeared “absolute lowest price on gas…. 15 cents a gallon”. We all noticed the sign but out of respect for my father we didn’t say anything (although my mother turned and winked at us and we winked back).

When we reached the 15 cents a gallon station, my Dad immediately pulled off the road and up to the pump. For the second (and maybe last time) and the second time within five minutes, he said, “Fill er up”.

The attendant agreed to do just that and he had a grin on his face as he realized that for this car, for this family, on this trip, his price had won the gas war with the morons down the road.

He stuck the nozzle in the tank and began pumping. The price on the pump read 2 cents when the overflow began. The attendant stopped pumping, rubbed his eyes in astonishment and said two words…two words that live today in cherished memory as we think of journeys, times and lives passed.

The attendant said, “It’s full.”

My dad handed the kid a dime and told him to not bother with the windshield “keep the change”.

For the rest of our lives, as we tried to figure out our father, at those moments when his wisdom, common sense, cheapness and courage was beyond our reckoning, my brother and I would look at each other and simply say, “It's full.”

When his life journey ended. When I held his urn before passing it to my Mom who would put it into the ground, I whispered to my brother “it’s full”.

SKINNING THE CAT

The swing set was on a hill overlooking the crystal water of Canandaigua Lake. Nothing fancy at all. Two swings suspended by thin chains. We had learned how to swing in the city, in the playground, fifty feet from the jungle gym. We had left being pushed behind.

We knew how to walk backwards as far as our legs would take us and then jump on the swing. Thus we gained momentum.When we swung back to the start position, we would cross our legs as the momentum reversed. When we reached the limit of backward momentum we would stretch our legs straight out. This initiated and accelerated the forward motion taking us higher faster.We called this "pumping".

When we really got going, we'd stretch that chain out to its maximum and our height was nearly as high as the balancing bar on the set.Twelve feet high.The swing set on Crystal Beach was the same swing set that my father had used when he was a boy.He knew all about it.He told us about the leap of death.

When the swing had gone forward as far as the swinger dared to take it, the leap began.With legs outstretched, the swinger released from the swing and flew into the air with all the momentum that physics would allow. Regaining balance in the air, the swinger would drop to the ground and land on both feet.The further the drop, the more deathly the leap.

The first leaps were tentative but as confidence grew so did the risk and the thrill.We learned to launch ourselves into motion on that hill above the lake.At first release on that hill above the lake, it looked as if we would fly all the way into the lake.We knew what we were doing and we were fearless.We were kids having fun.

Then my father told us about the ultimate.

Skinning the Cat.

To Skin the Cat meant to gain so much momentum from your pumping that the swing went all the way over the top of the swing set. After skinning the cat, a leap of death was the coup de grace.

My father claimed he had done it.

Thinking of the possibilities, we tried all summer. Although there were many leaps of death nobody ever skinned the cat. Finally on the last day of summer, we persuaded our father to get on the swing.

He got on the swing and took off. He took it higher than we had ever seen.So much power...so much grace..so much skill...so childish. When he had gone higher than any of us had gone...he took the leap.He landed perfectly.Like a father should.

"What happened to skinning the cat" we asked.

"Wait until next summer" He replied.

We thought that there would always be another summer.

TERRI AND BILL AND KEN

My wife was telling me about the intoxicating smell that came from the packaging of Barbie dolls and Barbie accessories back in the day. I related that smell to the smell of a pack of baseball cards back in my day.

My father was a smoke eater. Neither the Barbie smell nor the card smell opened his olfactory doors to any extent.He knew as much about dolls and cards as we knew about hooks and ladders.

Sixty years ago, I was losing the urge for cards. My sister, however, was in the 'She Loves You' stage of her Barbie mania.

She wanted/needed a companion for her Barbie. She needed a Ken and Christmas was approaching. My father was all over it. Pretty sure he told my Mom "I got this".

Christmas arrived.

The gifts were under the tree.

One of the packages was a man wrapped rectangle.

Everybody knew what that rectangle contained under the ribbons and bows.

My parents distributed the gifts. Sweaters and shirts and socks came first while anticipation for the 'good stuff' built to a crescendo as the packages dwindled. The good stuff was always at the end and the best thing was the last thing. Finally, the only package left was the rectangle.

My sister was getting warmed up for that fake cry of surprise that we gave when we got what we wanted although we knew that it was coming. My Dad, full of confidence and good cheer handed her the rectangle.

Terri opened the package slowly, savoring the moment. All eyes were upon her. "Oh my God…thank you sooo much…it's a…" She hesitated to make sure…the plastic didn't smell right.

"A *Bill*!?"

"You got her a *Bill*, Vinnie" asked my mother in subdued shock.

"Yeah," answered my Dad. The guy at the store told me Bill was better than Ken."

He knew he was in hot water. Even though he was used to heat, This heat grew to stifling in a matter of seconds. There were no hoses available.

My sister, to her credit, refrained from dousing the fire with tears.

I'll never forget the way she said, "It's a Bill."

The celebration continued although smoke was filling the room.

As I recall the moment today, I can imagine what was going through my father's mind when he bought the Bill. To him, a doll was a doll and the fact that one doll looked exactly like the other doll and yet cost half as much made the Bill a much better doll than the Ken.

Hands down.

No doubt.

My sister guessed the inevitable solution so she wisely underplayed her reaction. She took the Bill upstairs to meet Barbie. The meeting was awkward, I found out later. Neither Bill nor Barbie knew quite what to say.

Of course, my mother knew what to do. The next day, Bill disappeared and Ken had a great first date with Barbie.

Everybody was happy, including my Dad.

Over the next year he would ask Terri about Bill. One day, he walked into her room to watch his beautiful daughter play with her Barbie and her Bill.

My father looking at Ken and mistaking him for Bill said, “Bill and Barbie look happy.” My sister agreed. So did Ken and Barbie.

FICTION IS THE NEW TRUTH

I'm pretending to be a writer. I'm also pretending to be the narrator in an ongoing story in which I am pretending to be one of the main characters created by the writer that I am pretending to be.

And most of it is true except, of course, for the lies which I tell to the characters that I pretend to create as a fictional writer and whom I pretend are my confidantes.

In return, I realize that the characters that pretend to confide in the character that I pretend to be are also telling the truth most of the time except when they lie to me which sort of defeats the purpose of them pretending to confide in me which is quite an amusing technique for the writer who is pretending to be me and as such is pretending to write about pretending to be amused by a technique that reeks of despair and mistrust.

It all goes back a few years ago to that moment when Jeff Bridges came to town and I pretended to be sitting next to a character who was pretending to be Stingray. Stingray was pretending to agonize over the integrity of taking a picture of Jeff Bridges after he had learned from a character pretending to be a blue haired old bitch that photography of any kind was prohibited.

Very near to that moment, Stingray realized that he was in fact The Dude that Bridges had tried to portray in The Big Lebowski and therefore he was a fictional character looking at the actor who had pretended to play him.

Of course, even that fictional character was me pretending to be him.

When it all became too much for Stingray, he spotted me pretending to be Thornton Krell sitting next to him. I pretended that Sting was perceptive enough to realize that the guy who was pretending to sit next to him was also the guy who was pretending to be the writer that had got Sting into this situation in the first place and who therefore probably knew how to get him the hell out of there.

And that's where fiction started to become the new truth. Some call it the beginning of metaphysiction but they misunderstand.

And that's the "truth."

CALL ME STINGRAY

Clearly, I'm not as stupid as I appear to be or pretend to be, that wouldn't be possible although it might be preferable to the marginal state of bliss that I occupy now as I try life with double elephant ears for pockets, while I wander from the concrete concession stand that I call home.

No, I'm not stupid. Ya see, it's a combination of the oversight committees of my internal legislation combined with poor intelligence gathering that is responsible for the current comedy of errors that I laughingly call my existence. It's not Trump's fault nor Pelosi's fault that keeps me from dreaming the American dream.

I'm all about the Dream.

Dude is the American dream for me.

Dude is Jeff Bridges.

Big Lebowski.

Dude is my idol.

I love the Dude, man. When I found out the Dude was coming to town, I rubbed a couple of nickels together and headed to the Dryden Theater at the George Eastman house where Mr. Kodak himself screened movies for his guests until he decided that his work was done and he shot himself in the heart at this very house. Somehow, I had another double sawbuck so I took the tour of the house, checked out the elephant head in the lobby overlooking the giant organ and an array of flowers and gingerbread houses. I strolled into the exhibition hall and looked at the photos on display taken by Jeff Bridges. Next, I bought my ticket for the flick that Dude was going to introduce in the theater.

I'm an hour early. I walk down to the front. Figure for the money I'm paying, I might as well get as much indoor times as I can. Rochester is one cold, dark, dangerous town. So, there I am sitting safely, minding my own business when out of nowhere, a white hair walks up to me and spying my unhidden camera says in a real snotty voice..“You can't take pictures in here.”

Wait a minute, I think to myself. I'm in the home of the guy who popularized photography, the guy who made the art available to the masses as well as the messes and here's some drainer telling me I can't take pictures even though I'm using a Kodak camera loaded with Kodak film and I'm wanting to take a picture of a guy because HIS photographs are on display in the exhibition section of the museum. In other words, I'm a photographer in the birthplace of photography trying to take a picture of a photographer and somebody tells me “no”.

I should be more specific about the drainer. She looked a lot like Barbara Bush in Bar Bar's days as first lady with the shocking white hair. The imitation was breathtaking. Part of the breathtaking aspect was the “perfume” she was wearing. Imagine the smell of lilacs inside a trash bin, well that was the stench that was taking my breath away. I whiffed her before I saw her and by the time I saw her, she was in my face telling me what not to do.

God I hate that.

I had paid six bucks to get in and six bucks is a whole different ballgame to me than it is to the fake Barbara Bush. Six bucks has bought me four days and four nights of winter warmth at Movies10 which costs a buck to get into the theatre and once you're in, if you play your cards right, you can hide out for twelve hours. Six bucks is what I paid to get a picture of Jeff Bridges. Six bucks should entitle me to that.

BarBar stalked away leaving a trail of fetid flower stank residue. The guy sitting next to me, another early arrival, looked astonished or alarmed or whatever you call an expression that is a combination of thunderstuck bemusement and outrage. I'm no stranger to that expression. I get and give that kinda look quite often

I had been talking to this guy a few minutes earlier and I can tell you what kind of guy he was. He was the kind of fiftyish guy who looks like he's pretending to be someone else and the person he's pretending to be is a shorter version of a fake Donald Sutherland.

He told me his name was Ice but he was pretending to be Thornton Krell.

I don't need notes to remember stuff like this so I never take 'em. You're gonna have to go with my shaky recall.

I would hesitate to call Ice a dude although he was too old to be a nerd, too tall to be a dweeb, too small to be a doofus, too friendly to be a dork and too well informed to be a nimrod. I guess he was just a normal guy . Still, even he didn't know what to make of the fake BarBar.

I said to Ice, "There ain't no signs around here that say you can't take a picture."

Ice reached into his pocket and pulled out one of those fancy phones.

"I didn't see any signs either," he said with a 'we're all in this together but you're the one who got busted by a fake Barbara Bush as if you were Al Franken on a plane' kind of wink.

I wondered if the photographic prohibition was posted on my ticket. I looked at the ticket which didn't look much like a ticket ,just a crumpled piece of green paper featuring a large ADMIT ONE. Nowhere on this ticket did I see anything about not taking pictures.

I showed Ice my ticket and he pulled out HIS ticket and goes right to the fine print.His ticket cost thirty-five bucks and since we were sitting right next to one another the main thing his fancy ass ticket bought him was more writing because his ticket said that photography was prohibited at the request of the artist.

Let's see…no prohibition on my later cheaper ticket …clear prohibition on Ice's reserved more expensive ticket. This pretty much sums up my life. Forget about being reserved. Show up early and the cheaper you live, the more freedom you have.

So me and Ice sat there like twin particles ready to collide at the edge of a black hole. Something was about to happen but nobody knew exactly what. I wondered if perhaps Ice's last name was Jones.

We both got out our cameras and our contradictory tickets. I'm trying to feature the Dude prohibiting photos in a situation like this and I can't see it. One thing we know about the Dude…he **abides**.

I'm tawkin' bout the Dude who always adhered to a pretty strict drug regimen to keep his mind, ya know, limber. What kind of limber minded photographer like Jeff Bridges would bar other photographers from taking pictures of El Duderino himself. Also, I hoped to ask Jeff a few questions. Did he do his own bowling scenes and because of the whole brevity thing did the Dude prefer being called El Duderino, Duder, His Dudeness or simply the Dude or Dude?

Decisions were soon to be made.

Making decisions without accurate intelligence is like applying mathematical theories to non-mathematical facts. It's like grabbing a pool rack and putting the rack into sink full of swamp water in the hopes of creating a liquid triangle or a fertile delta. It don't work. I've tried versions of that experiment many times if not most of my life.

And once again, at the Dryden, I found myself trying to rack up innocent water although this time I was closer to Ice than to actual water. I've also learned that when you subtract mathematical theory from contradiction, you eventually wind up with paradox. Ice, although heavier than water floats upon it. Paradox means you face a crossroads of two clear ,equally balanced, oppositional ideas options that are uncompromisingly win/win or lose/lose in their execution.

Sink or swim

Contradiction also abides

Then, the curtain rustled and out comes the Dude himself in the person of Jeff Bridges. Dude looks exactly like he does on screen except a whole helluvalot smaller. As I decided whether or not to take his picture, at least ten guys ran down the aisle like stealth bombers in hoodies and beards, snapped off several rounds of flashes and then ran back down the aisle, out the door, into the parking lot, into their POS cars and down East Avenue towards Wegman's before BarBar could even get her panty hose unwadded.

Dude didn't look like he minded the snapping. I suppose it helped that the stealth crew snapped him before he even had a chance to give two shits.

Dude, as Jeff ,started to speak about how misunderstood his father Lloyd's career had been as the teevee series "Sea Hunt" became a mixed blessing for the Bridges' family. The money was the good part. The bad part was that the viewing audience thought that Dude Dad Lloyd actually *was* a skin diver, actually *was* Mike Nelson the role his Dad had played on the teevee show. Dude said most of his life somebody has been coming up to him all teary eyed and saying, "Thanks to your father, Mike Nelson, I've become a skin diver and all my children want to become marine biologists or harbor masters."

Imagine, confusing an actor with a role that he played

One of my childhood friends had the same confusion, sort of. I guess that's why he started calling himself "Mike" and strapping a waste basket on his back, sticking a garden hose in his mouth, putting a pair of underpants over his face and a huge pair of rubber galoshes on his feet, he would "skin dive" by crawling around on his belly in his backyard in the rain until he reached the end of his hose and crawled back before his air ran out remembering all the while to keep the crawl slow as to avoid the bends.

Good thing my friend didn't see "High Noon" when he was a kid, otherwise he might have grown up either a craven coward or a "boy not a man" as Katy Jurado had called Dude's Dad when Dude Dad bailed out upon the return of Frank Miller as the clock ticked real time towards noon.

In real time at the Dryden, Dude was five feet away and looking straight at me, I was coming to a conclusion of my own. It was the flash in his face not the photo itself that the Dude objected to and wanted to minimize with the small print on the fancy ticket. Since my disposable didn't have a flash, all I had to do was wait until Dude looked away for a second and I could snap his picture as I felt that I had the right to do. In all likelihood, the flashless picture wouldn't come out anyway. Dude wouldn't know that I had taken a picture that didn't come out and everybody would have a win. Paradox confronted and overcome. Slick as snot on a doorknob.

While I waited Dude kept rappin' and looking right at me while he spoke.

The way he was looking at me, reminded me of the phenomena of paired neurons. You see, when we watch somebody do something that we've done, paired neurons fire off in our brain similar to the neurons firing off in the brain of the person who is doing something that we've already done. If you play the guitar and then go and watch somebody else play the guitar, you are having a whole different neurological experience than a person who doesn't play the guitar. And the guy playing the guitar can usually recognize you in the audience because he can feel your neurons firing in synch with his which makes him play the guitar better which makes you get more into his performance and fire more neurons which makes his guitar play even better and refire etc ad infinitum.

Anyway, this is the way that Dude was looking at me.

Certainly, I was firing 'you are the Dude' neuronic vibes to the Dude but to my amazement he was firing back 'no YOU are the Dude' neuros back at me. I wondered if anybody else noticed. I took a quick look over at Ice who was trying to pair up with the vibe and cop off it but he was unable to because he was taking notes, just as I suspected.

I turned my attention from Ice back to the Dude who took my glance at Ice as a vibe breaker rather than an icebreaker. Dude looked away. My opportunity arrived. I snapped my camera. The camera didn't flash. Dude never noticed.The whole transaction didn't count. Like an at bat that takes six pitches; two fouls and four balls.

And just like that, except for reflection and analysis minus thought and regret, it was pretty much over. Dude never looked back. He finished his spiel and took a seat in the middle of the theatre to watch the screening of his Dad's old flick. He didn't take any questions from the audience. Pretty sure he snuck out early.

My job was done as well. I didn't see any sense in keeping my seat way over to the right of the screen in front of the vacated rostrum. I went up to the balcony and found some degree of calm along with an opportunity to reflect; using my feelings rather than my thoughts to process what my intuition had gathered. Certainly, paired neurons were firing between the Dude and me. What was he doing that I do? What was he doing that I was going to do in the future? What had I done that he had done? What did he know that I knew that only we two knew? What did I know that he NEEDED to know and was surprised to find out, was that I knew it and knew that he knew that he needed to know. Or vice versa.

First, I felt that it was" The Big Lebowski" film that had brought us together but my intuition told me that the neuron firing was too intense for that shallow of a conclusion. There is a big difference between a guy in a movie and a guy who's a fan of that movie, not that Jeff wasn't a fan of the Dude. Even I know that. I recognize the difference between illusion and delusion. Movies themselves are an illusion created by light and dark. Believing that movies are real and not reel is a delusion.

Dude had been in movies, I considered my whole life to be a movie or if not a movie, at least a book and if not a book at least a story in that book and if not my WHOLE life than at least the last three hours of it or maybe my short term life was three hours within which a story could be noted, imagined, located, decided and written by somebody else and that was the purpose of my life and after that I would disappear and exist only in words that stay or in the memories of everyone who read those words.

If this was true, then I was a fictional character.

Now, one thing a movie star knows a lot about is fictional characterization. Stars earn their money playing them. When Jeff looked at me, his realization neurons fired off this message: "the guy in front of me with the crappy camera is LIVING what I do for a living. He's a fictional character in a story and he doesn't understand that, A) He's fictional B) He's in a story C) As a fictional character he's got a lot more in common with the Dude than I do and D) This whole realization/connection/neuron firing thing (myself included) is part of the story that this guy is the only fictional character within but also the unreliable narrator of."

That's exactly the moment that Jeff ricocheted my "you are the Dude" vibes to him with an even more powerful, "no dude, YOU are the Dude" dude vibe back at me just before I turned away and looked at Ice and snapped my flashless photo.

With that, I realized the truth of my situation. I was the fictional part of a factual story.

I was part of a faction. I was and am a factoid like Thornton Krell and Jem Masters

That's my story folks although I didn't write it. Ice Rivers wrote it based on his notes which means its inaccurate in the first place as is all metaphysiction.

He gets the credit or the blame.

GOLF

Golf took a gigantic leap forward with the invention of the hole.

Up to that point, golf was simply a lot of people with sticks and balls walking around some very lovely terrain doing all sorts of things with their sticks and balls.

Most of the people with balls were men who were trying to get the hell outta the house/cave because the “woman’s driving me bonkers , etc.” I’m sure it was all very spontaneous, creative, individualistic, time consuming, non-judgmental; usually comic in its pointlessness but occasionally tragic in its masculine temperamentalism.

Then somebody dug a hole in the middle of the environmental splendor. The idea was to try and use a stick to put the ball into the hole. Since putting the ball in the hole was the final act of each hole, the stick used to ‘put’ the ball in the hole came to be known as the ‘putter’ which originally rhymed with footer because sometimes a golfer in frustration would just kick the ball into the hole. Eventually the stick for putting the ball in the hole took on a new rhyme. Putter began to rhyme with both nutter and mutter. A lot of nutters muttered about their putters until they just kicked the ball in with the foot which was counted as a put not a putt.

In another example of the beauty and simplicity of our language amidst the wonder of rhyme, the word hole rhymes with the word goal. At first there was only one hole in the whole three mile walk and players counted the number of swings it took to finally put the ball into the hole. Putting was not as essential a skill as it is now.

The goal of the hole, although it increased judgmentalism and decreased individuality, proved to be a such a great idea that another goal was eventually dug into the ground and then another and another and another until somebody said, “Damn, how many holes we need for this game?”

With our human tendency toward excess, 175 holes were dug before the guy who was digging the holes realized that he had enough of this and decided he would just as soon go home and listen to the troubles of the wife than dig any more of these goddamned holes which were a lot bigger than the tidy holes that we have today.

The first holes were big enough to bury an eagle in case one of them got killed during the invasion of their air space by the men with sticks. It became a short-lived superfluous tradition because no one ever killed an eagle although many smaller birds were dispatched. Dispatching a small bird was considered a good thing and came to be known as a birdie.

Eventually the size of the hole was reduced to the height and width of three golf balls which because they were made of wood and were almost impossible to hit into the air was a lot bigger than the golf balls of today.

After playing a couple rounds of 175 hole golf, it was determined that too many goals produced a "game" strikingly similar to no goals at all because everybody quit at different time and in various degrees of rage having long lost the number of swings needed to reach the breaking point.

It was at this juncture that Lord Ferguson Calloway, came up with his revolutionary idea. " A half dozen isn't enough," thought the good Lord "and neither is a dozen. I got it. Of course, a dozen and a half is ideal."

And thus we arrived at the first course of eighteen holes.

Par is the standard for each hole.

Par is an exemplar representing skillful reaction to the specific problems presented by each well defined goal/hole.

As each hole developed a standard level of difficulty measured by the number of swings required to put the ball into the hole, someone else came up with the idea of adding all the standards together and coming up with a standard for the entire course.

Shortly after coming up with the standards for each hole and then the entire course, some other wizard...perhaps Lord Bellamy Foxtrot decided to record all of those standards so that each golfer at the beginning of his walk had a clear idea not only of the goals of the "game" but also of the standards of each individual goal and each individual course. Individual holes from different courses could be compared as well as courses themselves.

The longest most difficult holes required five swings of the stick to put the ball into the hole.

Shorter holes required four swings.

The shortest holes required three swings.

Since most courses contain four holes that allow five swings to meet the standard, four holes that allow three swings to meet the standard and 10 holes that require a standard number of swings to be four. Add that all up and most courses have a par of 72 swings to put the ball into eighteen holes.

A score of less than 72 on most courses is considered under par.

Under par is good because it means it took less swings to complete the course than the standard requires.

A score of 72 means, a round of golf played exactly to the standards of the course.

A score of 73 or above means over par which indicates a playing of the eighteen holes with a number of swings more than needed by better players to complete the course. Each hole is its own measure of standards. If the goal is achieved on each hole by taking one less swing than the standard, that effort is called a "birdie". If it takes 4 swing to put the ball into the hole of goal that has been established as needing 4 swings to complete that effort is known as a "par".

If it takes one swing more than the standard for putting the ball into an individual hole, that effort is known as a "bogey". Two strokes over is a "double bogey" Three strokes over is a "triple bogey" Four strokes over par on a par four is known as a "snowman"

Five strokes above par has no general name but there is a name for anyone who regularly needs more than five extra shots and there is a term. That name is "duffer" and that term is "pick up the goddamned ball and either get off the course or go on to the next hole."

Most of us are duffers in this world. It takes us a lot more time to finish a task than it takes other folks to finish that same task. We keep reinventing the square wheel.Not only does it take us more time but the task we completed is a shittier version of the task completed by people who possess what I have come to know as "talent".This lack of talent however usually doesn't stop us from trying to achieve the impossible while ignoring the possible.

Not too long after the invention of "the hole," another great moment in golf arrived; the invention of the green. The green is the closely mowed area immediately surrounding the hole. If the hole stands for the essential goal then the green stands for the important goal, a more general place to aim. To reach the green predicts looming realization of essential pursuit.

A century or two after the invention of the green, another great moment occurred; the invention of miniature golf. Let's skip the whole driving and fairway thing. We're not as interested in the journey as we are in the destination. We read the last chapter of a mystery novel first so we know who did it all along and who cares about anything else?

Miniature golf is a concentration of essential goal with a diminishing interest in important goals. As it turned out, many people became activated by the single minded pursuit of the essential and thus the world discovered a new use for miniature windmills, aquariums filled with enamel fish and plaster dinosaurs holding fake candy canes.

Shortly after the concept of truncated activation peaked with miniature golf, some true star invented yet another form of abbreviation namely the "driving range". This one deals with the other end of the spectrum and once again gets rid of the "hole" as history once again rhymes with itself in a colossal retreat. Here the golfer can exercise a specific strategy, while sacrificing other important activities including the essential goal.

Both of those innovations diminished the concept of "walking" which at one time (before the invention of the hole) was in fact the primary goal of the game. Unless you count the husband's goal of getting the hell out of the house and the wife's goal of getting him the hell out of the house yet keeping him away from the harlots. Everybody used to win.

Miniature golf requires some walking while the driving range requires only getting out of the car and waking to the tee, usually grabbing a beer on the way. This means that the guy gets home before either he or his wife wanted him too or he stretches it out by stopping off somewhere and sometimes with a "golf instructor"

Shortly after the appearance of driving ranges and miniature golf courses, another synthesis reared its head. This manifestation included some walking, some iron driving, an important goal (The green) and an essential goal (the hole). This innovation became known as par three golf as the fairways were shorter and narrower and the expectation is to be able to reach the essential goal with two swings and a putt..

Even with this myriad of manifestations, golf has remained a non-essential activity. Therefore, people discover or ignore the game based on their own interest and time table. Some folks activate through miniature golf. Others activate through the driving range. Still others activate because of the par threes. It's impossible to choose between the game of golf and these three activators other than for purely personal reasons including the need to go "shopping" by the wife and the need to get the hell out of here by the husband who fully realizes how much his wife cherishes her private time.

I'm going to step away from the history of golf, like a pro who hears a fart in the gallery.

I'm gonna talk about My game.

TAWKIN' BOUT MY GAME

I'll tell you about MY game. Since it's my game, it's my rules. My game is all about forgiveness. This is why I prefer to play alone. When I do play with someone else, the game is best ball. My partner and I are playing against the course by co-operating with one another.

Here's how it goes; my partner drives.His drive is straight and true and right down the middle.I hit my drive straight into the woods. Together we go look for my ball.We find it and we head to HIS ball, the Best ball...hence the name of the game.

We take our second shots. His shot lands in the trap. My shot lands on the green.We retrieve his ball from the sand. We putt from my ball on the green.

My approach putt is short. He knocks his putt in. We have a birdie...The hole was a par four and we took three strokes to get it in. We're pulling for each other on every shot.

Best ball.

When I play alone, I start out with a mulligan. That means sometime during the round, I won't count a shot that I hit. That non-shot is called a mulligan. I only allow two putts of the first green.I'm not warmed up yet so...two's the limit.

When I hit the ball into a trap, I just pick the ball up and underhand it out of the trap onto the green.

If I hit the ball into the water, I go to the place where my ball hit BEFORE it went into the water and I hit it from there. Every horrible shot I hit, I find solace in the reality that no matter how bizarre the shot...I've definitely hit worse.

If the ball gets lost in the woods, I play as if it went into the water. I never forget that I'm here to relax and now here to recover.

I usually have my camera with me and I take pictures. I keep score in my head. If I score five on each hole that's 45 as I only play nine holes at a time.45 is pretty good.

That night as I go to sleep, I replay all of the forty-five shots in my head which usually puts me to sleep.Sometimes, I'm out on the course all by myself with no one else in sight.

At those moments, baby I'm a rich man.

Today, I'm a richer man. I won't be alone. I'm playing a best ball threesome. Because we have three guys hitting every shot, we'll have a lower score than any of us would have had if we had played alone.My partners are Deke and Crown.

Deke, Crown and I have done a lot together. We did the great American road trip in my truck from the Atlantic to the Pacific. We camped out almost every night under the stars down by the river. We visited the Ponderosa Ranch in Nevada and got drunk in the saloon where the Cartwright's drank. We played blackjack every day and learned to count cards only to lose everything one endless night in Lake Tahoe. We got kicked out of Candlestick Park.

We've been to the Kentucky Derby, the Preakness and the Belmont.

We've been through births, deaths, wedding, divorces, sickness, health and every stop in between.

We've climbed mountains and worked on Horse farms.

When Crown was an MP, he arrested Jane Fonda.

Deke got married at Graceland

Deke and Crown were there the night that Pete Rose broke the record for all time hits.

Crown and I saw Secretariat win at Belmont.

Deke helped my dying father into the ambulance in which he died.

Crown had a heart attack at the Kentucky Derby and since then has had colon cancer and open heart surgery.

Nobody can plank like Deke.

One thing we had never done before is play golf. Two years ago, it looked like Crown wasn't going to survive his illnesses. Last year, I had my moments of doubt. Deke is the youngest of us and still is in great shape. He doesn't owe anybody anything. Everything is paid up. His house. His car. His college loans. His credit cards. Everything. So we've lived this great life together but until yesterday we had never played golf together.

Deke hadn't lifted a club in 10 years.

Crown, like me, played only 27 holes last year.

I can't lift the ball out of the hole anymore which explains why I NEVER miss a five foot putt. If it's within a club length, it's in the hole. It's a gimme.

Crown can't get the ball out of the hole either. At least he thought he couldn't. Yesterday on the third hole, he reached down and plucked it out.

Way to go, Johnny

Now, because Deke is still flexible enough to pick the ball up out of the hole, we had no excuse to take gimmes on any putt. That killed us as we missed one five footer after another over and over and over and over ad museum. We played amazingly from tee to green and from a distance might have passed as younger men but when we got on the green……fuggedaboudid.

Of course we used carts as this is the reason that God invented them.

And brothers And friends

The sky was blue, the clouds beautiful. We talked about life. We laughed. We rejoiced. We remembered. We were present with our eyes on the ball. It was worth the wait.

Golf they say is a sample of sorrow

A walk in the park scarred by frustration

Then we hit THAT shot...come back tomorrow

For more sorrow amidst celebration.

We retain our most ironclad of grips

We visualize keeping elbow tight

We take dead aim and we let er' rip

When we lift our eyes we see ball in flight.

When we lift our head a little too soon

Too anxious to see the ball in the air,

We won't see the sky, the sun or the moon

We'll see our ball on the tee sitting there.

We promise to always keep our head low

Then we strike a beauty and on we go.

SALAMANCA FUNDAMENTALS

My former brother-in-law Tim and I were great friends before both our marriages crashed. Tim was a lumberjack, a master with ax and chain saw.

One afternoon, Tim and I were working on a case behind the cabin that he had literally carved out of the forest for himself and my first wife's sister deep in the hills of Salamanca. Somehow or other after about ten beers apiece, the conversation stumbled towards golf, specifically the origin of the game, more specifically the origin of golf clubs and finally the origin of the clubs called woods/woods called clubs.

I speculated that in its most primitive incarnation, cavemen just used the all purpose clubs they had for survival, courtship and domestic tranquility. These clubs were made of wood. From the first moments of civilization, clubs have been a factor.

Tim liked that idea. Next thing I knew Tim had his chain saw fired up and was cutting into a log. Wood chips flew everywhere as Tim transformed the log into an L shaped object, handed it to me and said, "Here's a wood."

I held the club in my hand. The "wood" weighed about seven pounds. I told Tim the club was a little too cumbersome. Tim fired up the chainsaw again and trimmed about two pounds off the club while shaping a bit of a handle on top and leaving most of the weight on the bottom.

He handed me the reshafted club and I took a few swings between a few swigs. The club felt great but what I wondered was what did the first golfers hit with the first club. As we worked a little deeper into the case, we began to speculate on that problem.

Once again, Tim fired up his chain saw this time transforming another piece of wood into a solid kinda round object about the size of a baseball. Tim handed me the object and said "here's your ball."

As I looked at the "ball" I was amazed to observe that an object with so many flat sides could resemble something round. The invention of the ball caused more casework and label laughter.

Here's where I made my only contribution. I went over to the nearby woodpile, found a sturdy splinter, handed it to Tim and said, "Here's our tee". Tim took out his jack knife and whittled a roundish, flattish hollow at the top of the splinter. We put the "ball" on the "tee" and returned to the case.

At this point our wives, annoyed by our prolonged absence from the cabin, burst upon the scene and were immediately irritated by what they saw. In the midst of her aggravation, Tim's wife grabbed the "club" that was leaning against a tree, walked over to the "teed" up "ball" and furiously and unknowingly hit the greatest golf shot I had ever seen with the first and only swing of her life. The "ball" flew twenty yards, bounced off a couple of rocks, rolled a few feet and disappeared from sight.

Fueled by the combination of apology, concern and amusement that most men use to confront irritated spouses, Tim and I went to look for the "ball" as the sisters stormed back into the cabin muttering something about "five more minuted" and "wastes of time".

The ball had found its way into a "hole" dug at some time long ago by some person or something. The "hole" was almost the exact size of the "ball". Up till that point, this was the first hole in one that I had ever seen.

FACTION IS THE NEW FICTION

As our president demonstrates each and every day, alternate truths are just a click away. Trump has already presented more than a thousand versions of the truth and since our country is based and was founded on the concept of a fantasy land, we get to choose how many of these alternatives we will swallow to determine whether or not we are red or blue with white still being a wild card.

Currently, we are trying to interpret the alternate truths that have led to the “invasion” of immigrants. Red is more convinced of invasion than blue. Red folks are even more convinced of invasion by whites and they have the history to prove it which everybody kinda ignores and for which ignorance many a casino has been built and many tobacco products sold.

We don’t really know who shot either Kennedy. Even *Helter Skelter* begins to wobble as yet another alternate reality by Vincent Bugliosi to avert attention from Hollywood. Oh and OJ was not guilty until he was.

As usual, Tarantino got ahead of the game with his altered visions of the past including the death of Hitler (*Inglorious Basterds*) and the once upon a time on Cielo Drive cancellation of Helter Skelter by Leo and Brad.

All of this alteration of history can be summed up in the word “faction," Faction is both more and less than fiction and non-fiction. Faction is the intentional fictionalization of non-fiction in order to tell a better story. One of the ways to achieve faction is to have the story itself written by a fictional character If the author isn’t real neither is the story no matter how closely it sticks to the facts. If the author is “real” person, she/he can grab the faction mantle by the utilization of an unreliable narrator.

Holden Caulfield admits to being a liar, right off the bat.

The Girl On The Train was drunk.

The Woman in the Window is a man

So faction is reality filled with interesting, conspiratorial lies.

Faction is the new fiction as well as the new non-fiction.

All it takes is a fraction of fiction to turn non-fiction into faction

And a fraction of non-fiction to turn fiction into faction.

Then all you need is some characters and action

And ya know what else helps a lot

Some rudimentary semblance of plot.

And for a dash of innovation

Add some internal motivation.

Who cares about "truth?" Truth is 'soo' two years ago and it was shaky then.

We don't need it.

Fuggedaboudid. We got faction and I know you love it so I'm gonna give you some more. Because I'm neither real nor reliable although, unfortunately, I'm sober.

And speaking of faction.....

GLOVE STORY

A guy named Arthur Gregor walked out of the classroom, apparently on his way to the john. The boy on the way to the john, Arthur Gregor Junior, almost always suspected that he had a sex problem.

The reason Arthur Gregor suspected he had a sex problem was because his father, Arthur Gregor, suspected that he, the father, had a sex problem. Arthur Gregor Junior's mother Sara knew that her husband had a sex problem but she didn't know exactly what it was nor how to describe it which led Arthur Gregor Senior to have even greater suspicion about the sex problems of his son etc.

So one day when Junior was eight, his parents took him to a psychiatrist named Dr. Schinetzki. Schinetzki suspected that he himself might have an undefined sex problem, that is why he specialized in detecting sex problems in others.

When Junior walked into Schinetzki's office, he had no suspicion that he might have a problem with sex. He was eight years old. He didn't have any idea what sex was. So Schinetski started showing Junior some pictures and asked him to identify the pictures. The pictures were very concrete; an apple, a desk, a lamp, a shirt, a dog and then a bra.

Junior nailed the first five and then the trouble began.

Junior hesitated when he saw the bra. He knew what the name of the item was but he didn't want Dr. Schinetski to know that he knew what it was for fear that Schnitetski would tell his parents that their child knew what a bra was which of course he would have and that would have been considered normal and that might have eased the suspicion that Senior had about Junior which might have eased the suspicion that Senior had about himself which may or may not have dented the wall of certainty that Sara had constructed about her husband and hence her son.

Tragically, Junior chose to overthink the situation. He figured that no "normal" kid his age should know what a bra is or where it goes or what it does.

Junior decided that he either had to continue in silence as he contemplated the picture which he figured would be suspicious or he could mis-identify the picture. Junior chose option two.

"Well, Arthur, can you name this picture?" asked the good Doctor with an edge of impatience in his voice while pointing to the bra.

" Oh yes, Doctor. That's a glove"

"Very good young man" said the doctor and moved on to a picture of a goat, and then a telephone and then a piggy bank all of which Arthur identified.

From that day on, the suspicion of Arthur Senior about Arthur Junior began to grow and then one day that suspicion appeared within Arthur Junior and it started to grow.

That day was a Sunday in January

The next day, the day after sexual suspicion started within his son, Senior uncomfortably explained the birds and the bees to his boy and Arthur began to believe that bees were having sex with birds and if he got stung by a bee, he could get pregnant.

When Senior got the report from Schinetzki, which indeed cast suspicion upon the sexual inclinations of his son, he did what any other father who is suspected of unusual sexual inclinations by his wife would do. He over-reacted. Senior figured that if he could ease his suspicion about his son which would enable him to ease his suspicion about himself which would lessen the infuriating certainty of his wife which somehow had become the deciding vote in every domestic disagreement.

Senior bought Junior a pair of gloves. When he gave Junior the gloves, he said "these are gloves, son . Do you understand me? These are gloves. They keep your hands warm. They protect your hands".

This was the beginning of Arthur Junior's compulsive, lifelong search for definition and overstanding.

And gloves.

It was May. Junior's hands were already warm. Still, his father insisted that Junior put on the gloves immediately. When Junior put on the gloves he remembered his session with Schinetzki. The gloves made him feel guilty. Eventually that guilt would transform into suspicion of sexual abnormality. Every time Junior put on a glove of any variety, for the rest of his life, the whirlwind of self-doubt reared its furious head and reaped its own devastating harvest. The wearing of the glove would both cause and ease the internal whirlwind.

Senior insisted that Junior always have a supply of new gloves. Senior insisted that Junior concentrate on three sports, baseball, hockey and golf. All three sports required a glove.

The incidents with the baseball glove were particularly painful.

Senior bought Junior the most expensive ball glove that he could find which amounted to three hundred plus dollars in today's money. Junior wasn't any good at baseball but he had the best glove so he made the major leagues in his local Little League. When the manager asked him what position he played Junior said "shortstop" Junior had no idea what a shortstop was or where on the field the shortstop played. He knew the word and he liked the word so that was the word he said when his manager, Otto Dingfeldt, while eyeing the expensive glove asked him what position he played.

At the first practice Dingfeldt said " Okay Junior, You're my shortstop."

Junior, overcoming the urge to ask his coach to "define shortstop" instead asked Dingfeldt "where do I play?"

Dingfeldt assumed that Junior was asking a subtle question about shading the hitter toward third or second depending upon whether or not the hitter could get around on the inside fastball.

"Shade over towards third" said Otto.

Junior walked on to the field and stood right next to the third baseman, a veteran eleven year old named Jake Genovese.

"What the hell are you doing here, kid" Genovese asked.

"The manager told me to shade towards third" said Junior. "Could you please define 'shade'?"

"Well for Christ sake move halfway between third and second and that's good enough but get the hell away from me before I kick your ass" replied Jake.

Arthur moved to the spot indicated. The first three batters hit rockets right at and through Junior. After the third rocket Arthur fell to the ground, faking an injury. When Dingfeldt came out to see 'what the fuck* is wrong with the 'fruit with the glove'.

Arthur said "Mister Dingfeldt, I don't like shortstop".

And with that, Junior was benched. He would remain benched for the rest of his Little League career which itself would end later that year.

Every moment that he sat on the bench while the others kids played the game, Arthur grew more suspicious of himself.

If you added up the price tags of all the gloves on Junior's team, it's likely the sum would be less than the one glove on Junior's hand, useless on the bench. Bobby Lowmeyer took Junior's spot at shortstop. Bobby had perhaps the worst glove on the team. Bobby's glove had been passed on to him by his older brother, Whitey, who gave up baseball while waiting for the bass player in his band to get an amp. Whitey got the glove as a hand me down from his Dad, Norbert who had gotten the glove from his Dad, Karl, whose favorite player wasn't Babe Ruth but a nobody named named Chuck Klein.

To Karl, baseball was the national past time.To Whitey, the few times that he thought about it while making noise in the garage, baseball was the national past its time.

All of the other gloves on the team were either hand me downs or K mart ten dollar specials. Arthur and his glove stood out on this team like a sore thumb which everybody on the team had because of their lousy mitts except for Arthur who had the good mitt and the permanent seat on the pine. Arthur Senior told Arthur Junior to never loan out his glove. Senior came to the first few of Junior's games but lost interest when he realized that Junior was not going to get into the game. Senior stopped showing up.

Before Senior stopped showing up, it became clear that the other players on the team hated Junior's guts because of the glove disparity. Bob Lowmeyer particularly resented Arthur. Bobby had the quickness and coordination to handle the shortstop position but his crappy glove prevented him from cleanly fielding the grounders hit his way. With every error, his antipathy towards Arthur increased. He started calling Arthur "Glove" and pretty soon everybody on the team began to follow suit.

The nickname spread from the ball field to the neighborhood to the school. Before long, everywhere he went, Arthur was called Glove. In Arthur's mind, they might as well have been calling him "Bra" which might as well have been "Oddball," "Weirdo," or "Dipshit."

One day Coach Dingfeldt approached Arthur and said, "Glove, if you lend Bobby your mitt for the rest of the season, I'll give you a new position."

Glove, a team player, was always eager to please.He also wanted to stay clear of the rocket shots smashed at the shortstop. Since it was clear that his Father had abandoned the team and wouldn't know or care one way or the other, Glove decided to lend his mitt to Bobby. Coach Dingfeldt, true to his word, gave Junior his new position.....statstop. As statstop, Junior had the important job of keeping score during the games and then turning his scorecard into a stat sheet. Dingfeldt turned the job of teaching Junior how to keep score over to his assistant coach, an alcoholic named Clyde Starks.

Starks taught Junior the numbers for the positions; 1 for pitcher, 2 for catcher, 3 for fist base, 4 for second base, 5 for third base , 6 for shortstop, 7 for left field, 8 for center field and 9 for right field. Any time anyone in those positions touched the ball, it was to be recorded in the "official" scorebook by the team statstop. A ground out to the second baseman was recorded as a 4-3. A flyball caught by the center fielder was recorded as an 8. Et freakin' cetera.

Arthur caught on quickly. With Bobby at shortstop hoovering anything hit near him and with Arthur at statstop recording every play, the Pirates began a winning streak.

After one particularly unbelievable play, Bobby came back to the bench and when the rest of the team congratulated him, Bobby said, "it wasn't me...it was Art."

For a split second Junior felt like he was getting some credit for the success of the team. Then he realized that Bobby was giving credit not to Junior but to Junior's glove which was now known as Art. The boy was now named after the glove and the glove was named after the boy. In the mind of the boy, the glove was getting the better deal.

With Bobby installed at shortstop with Art installed on his hand and with Glove installed on the bench with a scorecard and pencil in his hand, the Pirates began to win and win big.

Kippy Fiore, the Timpani brothers Sal and Bob, Kevin Yost, Rick Cicotta and Happy Jack McCallum despite their mediocre mitts could all field, run and hit. Nick Sellmer could pitch. The only weakness had been shortstop. Bobby and Art took care of that problem.

The Pirates reached the championship game. Arthur Junior never breathed a word about the teams success to his father for fear that his father would show up and demand that Arthur a) get his ass on the field and b) get his glove back from the zitface at shortstop. The night before the game, Arthur could imagine the whole house of cards collapsing. He, in fact, did visualize the entire humiliation and when he did so he fell asleep. He slept the sleep of the innocent who somehow suspect that they may not be innocent after all for reasons undetermined.

Arthur's father didn't show up for the game. The Pirates were playing the Braves. For years, the Braves had been the best team in the League. The guys on the Braves had real good gloves and their gloves were in proportion to their skills. Still, Art, on the hand of Bobby was the best mitt on the field and both teams knew it. Art had become the talk of the league.

The pitcher for the Braves was a guy named Chico. Word had it that Chico was at least fifteen years old. Chico threw hard and seemed to enjoy hitting kids. Everybody was afraid of Chico. Nobody wanted to dig in at the plate.

The game turned into a pitcher's battle between Chico and Nick. After a short delay because of threatening weather, the game moved quickly until the sixth inning, with both teams scoreless.

In the last at bat of the season, the Pirates dug in.

Kippy singled. Sal doubled. Kippy scored. The Pirates took the lead. Kevin hit a fly ball over the barbed wire into the power plant in right field for a two run homer. Mr Jordan, the coach of the Braves argued that the ball was foul. The argument got ugly. Several parents got involved. The umpire held his ground. The parents headed back to their seats. Tony Giambrone struck out for out number two after Chico threw a couple of pitches behind him.

Rick, the next batter did exactly the same thing that Kevin did, smashing the ball to nearly the exact same spot over the exact same stretch of barbed wire for yet another debatable homerun.

Out came Jordan. Ten more minutes of screaming, finger pointing, , spitting, swearing name-calling and threatening ensued before peace was restored. The home run counted. The score was 4-0 Pirates.

Bobby struck out to end the inning.

The Pirates needed three more outs. It was nearly nine o'clock when the Braves came up to the plate.

Darkness Falling.

An inning is not supposed to start after 8:30. Even with the rain delay, the sixth inning of the Pirates versus Braves championship game began at 8:18.

Glove kept meticulous track of such arcana. In this regard Glove was particularly superfluous. Ya don't need a weatherman to tell you which way the wind blows and you don't need a statstop to tell ya that it's dark.

By the time the top of the sixth ended; after the offensive outburst, after the two disputed home runs, after the the near riots that ensued after each home run, after the time spent after the riots clearing the field of debris and derelicts, the time was 8:50.

Nick Sellmer took the mound and began his warm-up pitches. Glove consulted his trusty scorebook. Glove noticed that Nick had pitched two innings in the must-win game prior to the championship game. The league had a rule that no pitcher could pitch more than seven innings within the space of a week.When Nick threw his first pitch of the sixth inning, his performance would be against league legislation. Glove figured that the penalty for breaking this rule would be forfeiture.

Coach Dingfeldt was not only aware of the rule but also aware of the fact that if he took Nick out of the game now, all the parents would be on his case for the rest of his life, not so much for taking Nick out tonight but for bringing him in a couple of nights before.

Coach Dingfeldt decided that he would leave Nick in the game and if the fit hit the shan, he could always blame the little twerp on the end of the bench, the "statstop" named Glove.

And if Glove approached him, the coach, he would pretend he was doing something else. Dingfeldt would determine Glove's honesty by the urgency of Glove's interruption. Glove was polite. Glove hated to interrupt anyone, particularly figures of authority.

Glove didn't know if Coach Dingfeldt knew what Glove knew. The inning which defined the entire season might depend upon Glove getting through to Coach.

The Pirates did have an alternative, a chinless boy named Steve Hall who everybody called Froggy. Froggy threw the ball in a combination submarine/sidearm style that lost all of it idiosyncrasy by the time it reached the plate. This imminently hittable pitch was called "the Swamp Ball".

As the other Pirates took the field for the last time, Glove walked from the far end of the bench to where Coach Dingfeldt was speaking to Coach Starks.

Glove cleared his throat "Ummm, Coach?"

Nick had already thrown the first of his allotted six warm-up pitches by the time Glove got to Dingfeldt.

"Coach, ummm, I'm afraid that if Nick throws one more pitch to one more batter……."

POP. Warm-up pitch number two.

Dingfeldt interrupted Glove."Are you afraid, Glove ?" Dingfeldt asked as he turned his back to Glove and for the last time rearranged the bats in the bat rack. Looking at Dingfeldt's back, Glove realized what a gigantic man his Coach was.

"Yes, Coach. I am"

Dingfeldt turned and faced the boy. Looking at his front instead of his back, Glove realized what a determined man his coach was.

SMACK. Warm up pitch number three exploded into the catcher's mitt on the darkened field. At this stage of the night, the pitches were more audible than visible.

"Do you know what courage is Glove?"

"Courage is facing your fears, Coach"

"Not bad, Glove"

SMACK. Warm up pitch number four.

"Courage, son, is knowing what not to fear. Do you understand me? "

"But, Coach……"

SMAP. Warm up pitch number five.

"Listen, Arthur. Go back to the end of the bench. Take out your pencil. Keep a record of the action on the field. You be the statstop. I'll be the coach. Aside from my advice about courage, forget the rest of this conversation. Know what to fear and what not to fear.Be courageous. Is that clear, Glove. "

“Yes, Coach”

For a split second Glove realized what he should do. He should run out to the mound and explain the situation to Nick. Nick could do whatever he wanted to do and at the same time bear witness that Glove had done the right thing.

In the next split second, he visualized how absurd that scene would be, how inappropriate to the trappings of the game. The benchwarmer taking over as manager and advising the star pitcher what to do. Nick barely talked to him anyway. That wasn’t going to fly.

Glove took his place on the bench.

Nick fired his last warm up pitch.

The umpire, a Greek guy named Dee who ran a delicatessen in which there was a horrifying barrel of gherkins, yelled “batter up”.

By the time Nick threw the first pitch in the last inning, Glove realized there was only one way out. The Pirates, his team, had to lose. Glove started pulling for the Braves even as he felt his heart breaking with the abandonment of loyalty.

Meanwhile in the dark on the bench between the top and the bottom of the sixth inning, Mr Jordan had a few ideas of his own. He hoped that Dingfeldt didn’t know that if Nick pitched one more pitch that action would be in violation of league rules and the outcome of the game would be, after the official protest was filed, either a forfeiture or a disqualification. Either way, the Pirates would be walking the plank. Jordan’s only fear was that someone would clue in the clueless Coach. When Jordan looked over at the bench and noticed some little kid with a too big uniform trying to get the attention of Otto, he thought that Froggy might be coming into the game and the protest win/win plan would be erased. Whatever the kid said to the coach and whatever the coach said to the kid before the little jerk walked back to his place on the bench, Nick had completed his warm up pitches.

Dee, the Greek umpire, trying to hurry the game along yelled "batter up". Before the leadoff batter, Stash Malloy, walked to the plate, Mr Jordan took him aside and revealed idea number two.

"Do not take that bat off your shoulder, Stash. Take every pitch. Take, take all the way. Do not swing"

Stash nodded and headed for the plate.

Jordan's plan was this, he wasn't going to protest until after the conclusion of the game. The evening was growing too dark to play ball. The whitest balls in the ball bag were already parked in the power plant somewhere. Whatever balls that Nick pitched would be scuffed from a season of sandlot. They would add an extra level of difficulty not only to the batters but also to the fielders and the umpire. Nick threw hard but he didn't have great control.

Dee's delicatessen owed the Jordan Trucking Company (whose motto was "we deliver the goods") a favor or two. The Brave's fans were all up in arms about the two home runs that they thought were foul balls. Dee owed them a couple of calls as well. If the Braves managed to score five runs in their last at bat, the protest would be moot.

Jordan loved his chances.

Fourteen pitches later, the bases were loaded with Braves and there were no outs. None of the first three batters had swung at a single pitch. The only reason no runs had been scored was the rule that a run could not be scored as the result of a passed ball.

Chico was coming to the plate.

In its essence, baseball is a game of catch between two people. While the game of catch is proceeding, a series of other people try to interrupt that game of catch, one at a time, by swinging a piece of wood at the thrown ball and then running home before the game of catch can be resumed.

In professional baseball, the game of catch must be played perfectly. If the ball gets by the catcher, blame must be found and assigned. If the blame falls on the catcher, if he should have caught the ball but failed to, the transgression is called a passed ball. If the blame is on the pitcher, if his throw was so errant as to be un-catchable, that transgression is known as a wild pitch.

In professional baseball, a penalty exists for passed balls and wild pitches. If, after a third strike, a passed ball occurs; the batter can try to run to first base before the catcher can retrieve the ball and either touch the batter or throw to first base. If humans are on base at the time of the wild pitch or the passed ball, the runners may advance to the next base or bases but they do so at their own risk.

Little League baseball is far from professional so some of these penalties are waived depending upon jurisdiction of the league. The East Side Little League, whose championship game was being decided by the Braves and the Pirates, allowed baserunners to advance after wild pitches or passed balls but forbade any runner on third from scoring a run in such a manner.

The reason this rule was instituted in the first place was the location of the backstop at the main field. The backstop was only fifteen feet from home plate which meant that a pitched ball could get past the catcher, hit the backstop and bounce right back into play. This factor made the backstop too much "in play". Several injuries had occurred when the ball bounced off the backstop so randomly that a collision at the plate involved not only the catcher and the runner but also the pitcher, the umpire and the batter who still carried his stick in his hand. So the rule was waived.

That's why, in the bottom of the sixth, the bases were loaded with Braves. Nobody was swinging and there was no base eligible for any runner to advance even though wild pitches/passed balls had been occurring on nearly every pitch.

As Chico strode to the plate, the situation was this and had been thus for awhile:the batter couldn't see the pitch to hit it, the umpire couldn't glimpse the pitch to call it and the catcher couldn't track the pitch to catch it.
And it was getting darker by the minute.

Dingfeldt, like most men, had two matters foremost in his mind....victory and justification. The fact that the kid had confronted him about Nick's eligibility to pitch the ninth inning irritated his justification module. The fact that the Braves had the bases loaded with nobody out and the best player in the league coming to the plate, threatened his victory module.

Otto had to come up with something quick. He decided to take a walk out to the mound. On the way to the mound, Dingfeldt realized that only two of the pitches thrown in the inning had been cleanly caught. Both of those pitches were called strikes by Dee, the delicatessen umpire. Hmmmm. Dee couldn't see the pitches either. Dee was assuming that if the catcher caught it, it had to be a strike and if it got by the catcher, the pitch must have been out of the strike zone in the first place which resulted in a call of "ball"

As fast as he was, Nick was not the easiest pitcher to catch. To make matters worse, the catcher, Skip Mancuso was not the first string catcher on the team. The best catcher on the team happened to be the best player on the team who happened to be the best pitcher on the team who happened to be the guy on the mound that Dingfeldt was heading towards.

By the time he got to the mound, Dingfeldt had his mind made up. He was going to make a change. His change was not going to be so much a change of pitchers as it was a change of catchers.

"Skip, go on out to right field and bring Frog in from the swamp. Nick, you're gonna catch the rest of the game. You pitched a helluva game, now I need you to catch one helluva inning." Frog came in from right field, replaced by Skip. Nick put on the catcher's gear. Otto gave the ball to Frog with the age old advice "Just throw this godamned thing over the plate. Throw it to Nick."

And with the changes made, Dingfeldt headed back to the bench.

And it got darker.

Six hours earlier Aristotle Legeer had just slapped down his last buck for a scratch off card at Dee's Delicatessen. Ari had bought the card with four quarters so he chose the Scratch Off called Loose Change. Loose Change is a scratch off card that shows six coins. If you scratch all six coins and they total more than a dollar, then the scratcher wins whatever prize is on the card which must be scratched to be revealed.

Ari scratched the first five coins.....96 cents. Then he scratched the prize amount figuring with his luck it would be a buck or two. The prize was $500. Ari felt good about the next scratch. He had certainly lost enough to justify the winning. He took a minute before scratching and then scratched.......

A penny.

A stinken' Lincoln.

One hundredth of a dollar.

One gazillionth of a phantom five hundred dollars.

Several bottles of ouzo disappeared from Ari's brainpan, along with a dozen roses for his patient, long suffering wife Diana and a trip to the Casino to feed Cleopatra's slot fifteen lines of nickels at a time as the Queen of the Nile whispers "Explore your fantasy. Enjoy your rewards". A rent payment and a tank full of gas also vanished.

What appeared was the usual, rage, self-pity and persecution complex. Also appearing was the reality that Ari had no gas in his car, no pay check for two days, no beer in the fridge and maxed out plastic in the wallet.

"I just lost five hundred bucks Dee"

"How could you lose five hundred bucks on a one dollar scratch off card?"

Ari told Dee the whole story. Dee understood, sort of.

“When will I ever learn, Dee?”

“My friend, what we have to learn to do, we learn by doing” answered the owner of the deli.

“Can you lend me twenty bucks for two days?” asked the erstwhile coin scratcher.

“I can do better than that” said Dee. “I can pay you twenty five bucks right now if you’ll do a job for me tonight. I need an umpire for a Little league game over at the field”

“I wouldn’t call the pitches at that nuthouse for fifty bucks, even as busted as I am” declared Legeer.

“I’ll be the one working the plate. I need somebody to ump the bases. You want the job? I’ll even throw in a forty ounce Bud and gyros after the game”

Dee’s offer was too good for the desperate, deflated Legeer to refuse.

“Why not” I asked Legeer.

Dee reached into the cash register. He grabbed two tens and a five. He slipped the three bills over the counter. The old friends shook hands. They both grabbed gherkins.

Six hundred thirty minutes later, as Dingfeldt was bringing Frog into the game, Mr. Jordan wasn’t exactly whistlin’ Dixie while waiting for the bus. Jordan had ideas of his own, equal and opposite.

Jordan was no longer concerned with victory, he had that in the bag. Jordan was concerned with style, a notion that appeals to most men only after victory and justification have been insured.. Jordan knew he had the game wrapped up if he wanted to go the paper tiger forfeit route. He also knew that if he told the rest of the batters (like he had instructed the three already on base) to “take all the way” and never move the bat from their shoulders, the inevitable parade of free passes in the dark would spell passive-aggressive victory. Passive victory was not the style of the Braves. The Braves were not paper tigers. The Braves were a championship team who won the old fashioned way. They ran. They threw. They fielded their positions. They hit. They hit with power. They executed the fundamentals. They sacrificed. They played as a team. They took advantage of opportunities.

They had great mitts.

They swung their bats.

In Jordan's mind, Little League was, above and beyond anything else, an opportunity for a series of life lessons. If the Braves were going to win and they were going to win, it was important that they won in a fashion that would stay with the young boys for the rest of their lives and help them to become better men.

Nobility so often hinges upon guaranteed triumph.

Jordan went to every baserunner, all three of them. "On the first pitch that Frog throws, I want you to take off to the next base You got that? As soon as he goes into his windup, you run like hell"

The runner at first, Glenn French asked "What if he throws over to first base Coach. I don' want to get picked off"

"Throw to first, Glenn? He can barely see first base and the first basemen can barely see him. Do what you're told. Run your ass off"
With the hit and run in place, Jordan coached Chico.

"Chico, You're gonna swing at the first pitch. It's gonna be over the plate somewhere. It's not gonna get any lighter. If we're gonna swing, we gotta swing now. We're gonna swing. You're gonna swing. You're gonna tie up this ballgame with a grand salami. You got me, son? First pitch. Take a rip. You're the best hitter in this league. We gotta shine the light where the money is."

"Gotcha, Coach" said Chico as he stepped to the plate.

Frog toed the rubber.

Chico dug in and tapped his bat on the outside corner.

Nick got in his crouch behind the plate.He didn't bother to send a signal to the mound. The signal would have been invisible anyway. Everybody knew what was coming.

The Swampball.

With the bases loaded, Frog went into his full wind up as there was no need to use the stretch. As he reached back and down to load some nasty swamp shit on his swamp ball, all the runners took off.

Five minutes earlier, when Dingfeldt was leaving the mound after replacing Nick with Frog and Skip with Nick, Otto realized he still had a dog in the forfeiture fight and his dog might have some bite if it came to red tape.

Since Nick had walked the first three men that he faced in the sixth inning, which means he didn't get anybody out, he would only be credited with pitching five innings according to the official scoring rules of baseball. Furthermore, the runners on base had all walked and according to the scoring rules of baseball a walk does not count as an official at bat. In other words the current situation was based on the statistical abnormality of the bases being loaded with three hitters none of whom had officially been at bat who got on base because of the free passes issued to them by a pitcher who had not statistically pitched in the inning.

Nick couldn't lose the game. If the Pirates won, Nick would get the win not because of his pitching in the sixth, he officially had not appeared in that inning, but rather because he had pitched the fifth and was the pitcher of record when the Pirates went ahead in their half of the inning. If the Pirates lost the game, the loss would be charged to Frog because the three runners on the base would be charged to Nick if they scored. Chico was the tying run and he was Frog's responsibility.

Otto had found his justification. If Jordan wanted to argue this one out, Dingfeldt thought to himself, let's have at it. In some ways, the statstop, the weird little Glove, had got through to the Coach. As he returned to the bench, Dingfeldt fired an appreciative vibe down the bench to Glove, who immersed in loyalty abandonment, contemplation of courage and the difference between resignation and faith, missed the vibe entirely.

Glove was occupied in hoping that Chico would come through for the Braves like he always did. Glove had played a whole season for the Pirates and hadn't made a single friend. The only time that he might have contributed to the team, he was ignored by the Coach who Arthur knew that he would blame for the loss.

Arthur had never prayed before, never learned how, but this was getting close. He was trying to make a bargain with somebody or something somewhere. If the Braves won, he would never again play on a team that didn't respect him or love anyone that didn't love him or back down from a boss who was cheating.

Dingfeldt looked out at the field as Frog delivered the first pitch to Chico. As the pitch left Frog's hand, Dingfedlt yelled "Courage" to his Pirates who couldn't see him but could damn well hear him.

Nick held out a target that he knew Frog couldn't see.

Bobby at shortstop heard someone yell "Courage".

Aristotle Legeer, the umpire, stood motionless in shallow left field five steps behind Bobby.

The runners; Coin Gedman at third, Tony Joy at second and Glenn French at first were all off and running with the invisible pitch. Chico swung. He could feel by the sensation in his hands at contact that if he hadn't got all of the pitch, he sure got a big chunk of it. He knew what a four bagger felt like. He'd been there before but never in the dark, never in the last inning of the championship game with the bases loaded with Braves, never on the threshold of neighborhood legend.

When the shortstop sensed Joy breaking towards third, Bobby instinctively broke towards second. That's when he heard the sound of aluminum smashing into cowhide. Then he felt a stinging in his left hand. The ball had found Art. The ball was in Art. All Bobby had to do was hold on to the ball and the moment and the legend.

Legeer saw the line drive disappear into the shortstop's glove. Legeer saw that the kid held on to the ball.

One out.

As Bobby pocketed the rocket, Tony Joy going from second to third was passing right in front of him. Bobby touched Tony with Art. The touch was so light and so fast that Tony kept right on running, right past Jordan who was coaching third and screaming for Tony to keep on running for home.

Legeer saw the touch. Two outs. Double play.

French going from first to second had no idea where the ball was so he did the prudent thing. He slid into second base. Glenn's slide was a thing of beauty although it was beheld only by Legeer and Bobby. Bobby slapped Art on the shoulder of French. Legeer saw the slap.

Three outs.

Triple play.

Unassisted.

Game over.

Championship for the Pirates.

There was no doubt in Ari's mind. He had clearly seen the whole play. Dee got to Ari before Jordan did. Ari explained his ruling to Dee. Dee said that from his place behind the plate he hadn't seen anything other than hearing Chico hit the pitch.

Ari assured Dee that he had seen it all.

The game was over, regardless of what Jordan might say, think or do..

Dee yelled out “Thank God for Aristotle”

Bobby was the second person within fifteen feet to realize that an unassisted triple play had ended the game.

Bobby was the first person to realize that aside from tagging the two runners, he had very little to do with the play. Chico’s line smash had simply gone into his glove. Bobby never saw the drive. He barely felt it when the shot smacked into his pocket just below the webbing. Even before the rest of the team knew what had happened, Bobby was already jumping up and down and yelling "Art, Art, Art.”

The leaping and the crying of ” ART ART ART" had worked its way through the infield half of the Pirates by the time Dee made it official by yelling “Triple Play, Game Over” and started heading for his car next to the power plant.

At this point, the whole team started running around the infield screaming ARTARTARTARTARTART.

In the midst of this sudden outbreak of Art. Mr Jordan got in the face of Ari Legeer. Legeer told Jordan exactly what he had seen.

On the bench, Glove, formerly Art had received the news that the game was over. He didn’t know how to record the play in his scorebook whether it was 6 which means the ball was hit to the shortstop and he caught it or whether it was 6 6 6 which meant the ball was hit to the shop and he caught it and he tagged two runners.

While wrestling with this administrivia, Art realized that the Pirates the team that from which he had abandoned loyalty only a few minutes earlier were all chanting his name.

Except they weren’t.

They were chanting the name of his glove.

He wrote a six into the scorebook.

And then Bobby understood that they wouldn't be chanting ARTARTART and they wouldn't be champions and he himself wouldn't be on the threshold between legend and myth if the statstop hadn't lent him the glove in the first place.

As the whole team reached the bench, Bobby started yelling GLOVE GLOVE GLOVE GLOVE. The rest of the guys followed suit…even Dingfeldt. They hoisted the statstop on their shoulders and began carrying him around the infield screaming GLOVE GLOVE GLOVE.

The scorebook fell to the ground.

On their shoulders in the dark, the boy who kept score, the momentary traitor to his own team, felt tears of shame and joy pouring down his face as they took him from base to base. Every time he heard them yell Glove…..he understood that word to mean traitor, loser weirdo

Nimrod who don't know a bra from a glove.

The Pirates didn't know the kid on their shoulders was bawling. They were champs and so was he. They couldn't have done it without Art and that means they couldn't have won it without Glove.

ARTGLOVEARTGLOVEARTGLOVE

Good thing it was dark.

A passerby would have seen a bunch of boys yelling about art and love in the dark with one small boy on their shoulders.

That passerby would have misunderstood. Especially if the passerby was Glove's father or Thornton Krell.

Krell would have thought they were saying Art of Love. He would have thought of ancient Rome and poetry. He would have thought of Ovid.

FIRST DOZEN WORDS

On the way to our cancer consultation reckoning, our memory connectors were on alert and searching for omens.

We found one almost immediately.

Two minutes from our house, an ambulance with lights a flashin' was pickin' up a poor soul and taking them somewhere. Yikes. Not what we were looking for yet as we passed it became clear that the ambulance was bringing somebody back from somewhere instead of taking them away.

Naturally, we took this return as a good omen.

We take what we can get in the realm of faith as it ricochets towards reckoning.

We made it to the consult and discovered we were early which meant a bonus half hour of looking at the complex aquarium in the waiting room and imagining the first fateful dozen words from Doctor Somebody.

We in this case being my wife Lynn and my daughter Mary and me myself and I.

Our name was called and we walked into the examination room which was posing as a conference room. We were as prepared for the worst as we could have been prepared for the worst but still pretty sure we were somehow unprepared.

The door opened and Dr Somebody entered the room with all kinds of documents in his hand. These were the first dozen words of the reckoning.

"Something smells good in here and I'm pretty sure it's not you."

He was looking at the part of we that is me.

Of all the imagined first dozen words, these twelve had never approached our imaginings.We took that as a weird compliment to the way that the we who were women in the room wore our perfume.

I remember the first couple of minutes after that and the rest is kind of a blur.

Doctor Somebody described how the results of my various scans indicated that the cancer had not worked its way into the bones or surrounding organs. As a matter of fact, the surroundings were all in good shape.

A previously unknown level of relief and happiness surged through us immediately.

We started talking about offense now for the first time. What we could do to attack that cancer and get it the hell outta here. Removal of the prostate, eight weeks of radiation or insertion through surgery of radioactive seeds.

The unknown backed away. The amorphous shape took shape. Doctor S admitted that the time in the shadow of the unknown is the worst of times. We're on the attack now.

Long story short, the word is TREATABLE. All of the options are on the table. Doctor S asked us for our choice after describing all of the alternatives. We all went for the seeds.Now we have to speak to the oncologist radiologist to see if the seed surgery is a realistic, viable approach. That conference is coming next week and we're good wif it.

We're not out of the woods yet but the bears seem to be behind us rather than in front of us.The story is far from over. The after effects remain profound. We're aware of those changes.

We don't mean to underestimate.

We are aware that bears can move forward by moving backward and can in fact step in the exact same tracks that they made when they were going forward before moonwalking backward/forward. As for tonight, we have already been changed by the profundity of cancer. We looked into the abyss while walking through the woods. Even then, we had faith.

We are delighted so…Now, right now, we're gonna back off and boogaloo. Stay tuned. I'll write more when we come back to earth. And if we don't I'll write from wherever we are but damn, we like it here.

FROM OBSCURITY TO HERE

I look at my work and see that it's good. Gawd, I'm a great writer. One of the best I've ever read anywhere.

And then an internal strawman advocating Satan jumps up and brays "if you so good den why aintcha rich and famous".

Of course I know the answer for that. I ain't gonna sell out. I'm an obscure artist. I don't want the hassle of fame nor the complication of wealth. Andrew Luck said it best...enough is enough.

I take it one step further.Not enough is enough because I still have my pride.I got plenty of pride that's another reason why I and guys like me always got plenty of nuthin which is always plenty for us.

We're the ones with talent looking for opportunity. Because the opportunity never comes along...Because the phone never rings and the voice on the other end never says; "I've googled Ice Rivers and my God, your wistful prolificacy as a writer is only equalled by the unassuming magnificence of your photographic images. We're sending a limo over to pick you up and put an end to your self-induced obscurity. In other words 'c'mere Cat, we gonna make you a star"'

Da phone, she don't ring.

That's the pickle we're in, obscure martyrs and artists that we are.So we turn our pride into anger and discontent that fuels our literary and artistic drive. Of course all of this is self indulgent non-sense because America is the land of opportunity.If you believe in capitalism which is to say if you believe in America then you believe in happiness then it eventually becomes apparent

that in America...

Wait for it....

Opportunity seeks talent rather than the other way around.

Most of us who feel we are talent looking for opportunity are inherently angry because the talent we have discovered in ourselves is not our true talent but only a facade, a compulsion, an obsession or rationalization. We are fighting a chin first bout against the stupidity, insensitivity and selfishness of the society that surrounds us

and its lackey dogs,

and its vampires.

Then we realize that the whole concept of capitalism is...

Wait for it.....

to capitalize on talent

so

talent must be discovered if capitalism is to survive and since capitalism is doing pretty well if you are at the top of the pile then the ongoing search for talent is also working out quite satisfactorily Now and then we can stop perceiving ourselves as sanctimonious talent compulsives looking for opportunity and start realizing that opportunity is looking for talent and everything will turn out fine in the end if we can just be happy

truly happy

not fake happy

not I give up happy

just happy

as I learn a little more

every day about whom

I imagine I am and thankful that Im alive

And see that it is good.

THE DOODLE THAT I DO

I doodle.

It's always awesome when I find out that others doodlers do the doodling that I do and even more awesome when the doodlers who doodle what I do have come up with a name for the doodling we do.

Apparently the doodle that I do as well as the doodle that they do is called "tangling". Next thing you know, there will be rules for "tangling" in order to differentiate the doodle that they do from the doodling that I do.

Master tanglers will emerge to let me know that the doodles I've been doodling for the last thirty years don't qualify as tangle doodles for some arcane reason like lack of cross hatching or violation of color agreement.

This, of course will lead to one of those dangling conversations when someone is trying to teach you what you already know and have rejected. Those irritating moments when it's appropriate to say, "I overstand you" but better to just say nothing and wait for the barrage to conclude.

Then I'll depart down the untangled path that I've already spent decades perfecting the imperfections of. Since it's kinda like a tangle, I'll call my work a dangle. Then we can have a pissing contest between the merits of tangle doodling versus dangle doodling until some genius comes up with a synthesis called dingle dangle tangle doodling and makes a lot of money and provokes several suicide attempts by tangle doodlers who are now passed.

All of this amuses the dangle doodlers like myself who knew we were just wasting our time in the first place and were amazed when all of a sudden somebody made a big thing out of what we were doing/doodling when we were trying to think of anything else than what we were thinking of when we started doodling and we let our intuition take over to link whatever is going on in the present to the dream world of disassociation which helps us grasp the situation we are trying so hard to absorb without over reacting to.

I did a doodle two hours before I headed into the consultation with my surgeon which would describe the aggressiveness of my cancer. I finished it, while occasionally glancing at the aquarium he had in his waiting room as I dreaded his first dozen words.

After I heard his first dozen words in the consultation, I held up my doodle…to which he delivered words 13 and 14.

"Modern art."

Naturally, I was very relieved.

RADIATION

Today was my first day of radiation; the beginning of active warfare against the terrorist cells hiding in my prostate. The whole deal took about fifteen minutes and most of that time was spent in positioning my body to get the best shot at those son of a bitches and stop them before they spread any further.

We're going to be bombarding them for the next 28 days...27 now.

They were trying to stay hidden and had built up a little bit of a fortress over the past couple of years before the biopsy identified them and the cat and body scans located their hideout.

They were trying to kill me.

We got 'em now.

We got a great team.

We're done with their sneaky shit.They are invading us baby boomers at a frightening rate. You want to know the chances of a male to have a significant secret invasion going on in his prostate? It's simple, take your age and subtract 25.

If you're fifty, it's a 25% risk , etc.

We're sick and tired of these terrorists.

We've learned how to find 'em.

We can find' them before they spread and we can blast the shit out of 'em. We're gonna poison the bastards.

I started radiating the bastards today. I plan on enjoying the hell out of the next 27 sessions as we fight poison with poison.

Of course since this is war, there will be some collateral damage…bring it on.

Every day as a species, we get more precise at droning and defeating these cells. I'm one of the first baby boomers. I'm proud as hell to be making my stand.

Boom.

We're not gonna take it.

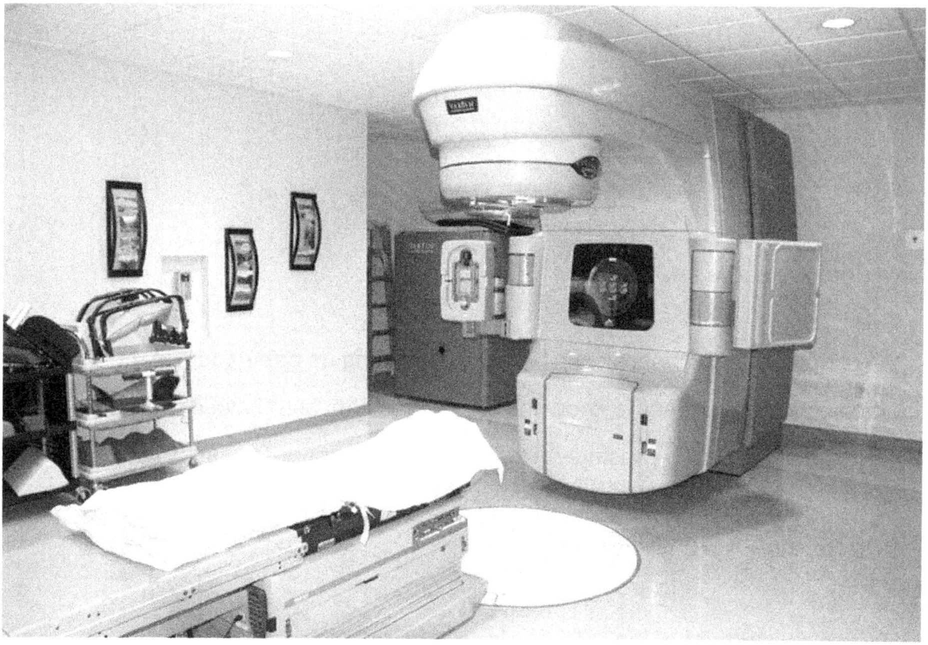

SELFIE AT THE CIRCUS

Monkeys chattering in my brain

Minimize the gain of pain

While I form a Congo line

Of I , me, myself and mine

And we sit as one for our group shot

Trying to remember what fortune forgot.

We pose with tilt and smile

Recoiling for a little while

Looking into the user friendly lens

The merciless mirror where distortion ends

And realize we're back again

Jack Daniels in the lion den.

With a twist of hocus pocus

We maneuver myself into focus

Depress the shutter

Utter a mutter

As we cough

Precision wanders off.

Another blur produced.

We wonder “what’s the use”

We know it’s getting awful late

For any youthful self-portrait.

We steady our grip

We let er’ rip.

The one man horde

Always going forward

Lives another day

A hunger artist without the hay

Who longs to feed again

Further down the bend

Heading towards humbling dawn

Because the forget me nots are gone.

Lookin’ one last time around

Findin’ the circus still in town.

GOODBYE KID

My life changed in 1958. I was a kid barely out of the Peanut Gallery.

Clarabell on Howdy Doody had broken his silence, the last two words of Doodyville. He said, “Goodbye kids.” So long Buffalo Bob, Phineas T. Bluster, Flub a Dub.

Hello California…hello Mickey Mouse Club…hello Annette…..hello Spin and Marty.

Down on the edge of Lonely Street, Elvis had said hello.

Davey Crockett had died at the Alamo after singing “Farewell to the Mountains.

I had never heard an electric guitar.

Then a rock and roll show came through town into our sparkling new War Memorial. Al’s 18 year old aunt Carol bought three tickets. They took me along.

Clyde McPhatter, The Elegants, Jimmy Clanton, Johnny Tillotson, the Olympics, the Danleers, the Coasters, Dion and the Belmonts

I was sitting in the third row in a packed and screaming house.

I was changing fast.

Then Bobby Darin came out

Splish Splash

Queen of the Hop

More change for me, contractions coming quicker and each more intense

Then Duane Eddy

Yup

Cannonball

Rebel Rouser

Twangy, super amplified twangy guitar.

In some ways, I lost my virginity right there.

Then Buddy Holly and the Crickets

Oh Boy

More guitar

Every day

Peggy Sue

And the last act

The star of stars

The teen idol

The heart throb

Frankie Avalon.

I wasn't even a teenager yet but I found a teenage girl sitting on my lap calling me "honey" and screaming "Frankie".

Dee Dee Dinah

Gingerbread Venus. When I left that night, I was an authentic rock and roller…not just a kid anymore. I still am and clearly am not. I'm too aware of death.

IN VANISHING VALLEY

Forty plus years ago, on a startling, clear August afternoon, I was smack dab in the middle of everywhere, the Grizzly Mountains of Montana. To be more precise, my Outward Bound group was in the midst of crossing a boulder field in the Grizzlies that had appeared as a routine valley on the topographical map we were using.

We were four days deep into the wilderness of Beartooth.

I had backpacked about a half a mile on top of these boulders always hoping that the boulder I was treading on would lead to another boulder and not an unjumpable crevice that would force me to backtrack God knows where. Also only God knew how or when those boulders avalanched into the vanished valley between mountainsides in the first place without showing up on any maps. Yet here they were and amongst them, incongruously was I. If I could have given up, I would have.

I thought I was in trouble.

I knew I was in trouble when while galumphing from one boulder to the next, I came upon a snow, white Bighorn mountain goat. I couldn't believe the goat was sitting so still, as I stupefied, drew closer. The goat was obviously a lot more at home in mountains than I.

I got about three feet away from the bearded wonder. The goat continued to look straight at me while remaining absolutely motionless. Upon closer examination, I understood why the goat wasn't moving. Two of its legs were broken, folded beneath his body. The goat had picked this boulder in this vanished valley between Grizzly mountains as his dying place.

Perhaps this dying place had picked this goat.

Who knows?

God only knows.

I looked at the goat with his beard as white as snow in Ireland. The goat looked at me. Neither one of us knew exactly what to do. I'm sure I was the first human this goat had ever seen. In the face of his oncoming death by exposure, I, a mere mortal, didn't phase that goat one damned bit.

I considered putting the goat out of his misery but the best I could have done was a head bash with a rock, if I could find a lethal enough rock amongst or atop the boulder.

While looking around for a clobbering rock, I absorbed another view of the boulder field. My eyes swept over the former valley as far back and forward as I could see. On the boundaries of the boulders, I saw mountainsides. Above the mountainsides, I saw clear blue sky. Off in the distance, I heard the echoing shouts of my scattered Outward Bounders. Each of them hoping that the next boulder they chose to leap on would lead to another boulder and not a crevice.

I had another kind of decision.To bash a bearded mountain goat or not to bash, that was the question. I began to wonder exactly what misery I thought I was putting the goat out of? What did an interloper like me know about misery in the mountains? I also reflected upon this undeniability. Before me was a creature who had lived its entire life bounding from rock to rock before making one last, fracturing fatal error in judgment. Before that creature was a human whose idea of bounding and diving from rock to rock was playing in a rock band at a bunch of dives. Yet the former was mortally injured and the latter was attempting to pass judgement.

I wondered if the goat had bounded into one of the dives where I had once played Louie, Louie whether he would have been tempted to pull the wires from our amps.

Then I refocused……

I realized that the clouds, the sky, the mountains and the boulders couldn't care less whether the goat lived or died or for that matter whether I lived or died along with the goat. The sky, the mountains, the clouds and the boulders had played out this kind of drama, minus me, millions upon millions of times before without any of my help and would continue to play out this tableau long after I left, if I lived long enough to leave. If this dying place didn't choose me as well. I looked once again at the goat who was motionless, aware, at peace, dealing with the pain, and prepared for infinity.

That's about as close as I've come to seeing You Know Who.

Some silent, sacred time elapsed.

I set my sights on the next boulder and headed for it. I never looked back. Everything was perfect in the wilderness. That night, I decided for sure that I wasn't going to shave my whiskers. I still have the beard today. And it started turning white last year.

Meanwhile, back in the land surrounding Vanishing Valley there rose up more sound and fury than usual indicating more than the usual level of nothingness in the mountains.

As I left the goat behind, I listened to the world and discovered the sound of nothingness under which I could pick up indications of tremendous sound and fury. The stillness was lyrical...When I came down from the mountain, I knew things that no one else knew. At the same time, I didn't know something that almost everyone, unless they had been out in a boulder field in the middle of Everywhere, knew only too well.

Nixon had resigned the presidency.

I missed all of that. I traded it for Mt. Tempest, Grasshopper Glacier, skree, gorp and a glimpse of You Know Who.

When I got the news about Tricky Dick, I rewound in my mind to where I was at the exact time that he was waving goodbye. I'm pretty sure I was between boulders, in a hard place, gazing at a goat and deciding to grow my beard to always remember the time I almost saw You Know Who. Today, during radiation while contemplating mortality and recovery, I thought of the mountains again.

KUNIO

"A man could be a lover and defender of the wilderness without ever in his lifetime leaving the boundaries of asphalt, power lines, and right-angled surfaces. We need wilderness whether or not we ever set foot in it. We need a refuge even though we may never need to set foot in it. We need the possibility of escape as surely as we need hope; without it the life of the cities would drive all men into crime or drugs or psychoanalysis."

— Edward Abbey, Desert Solitaire

I was a Rochester, New York asphalt dweller barely skirting crime, drugs and shrinks when I first set foot in Montana. I had come to take a graduate course called Literature and the Outdoors at Montana State University in Bozeman. I was completing my requirements for Permanent Certification K-12 Language Arts. I took my brand new Dodge Club Cab truck and was in the stalwart company of Deke and Crown.

By the time we got to Bozeman, we already had adventures in the Dakotas, Utah, Wyoming, Colorado all the way to California. We were drinking and trucking our way across country or as we liked to say...we turned left and just kept going. When we got to the Pacific we turned right and kept going back, back, back until we reached Bozeman. We had been on the road all summer camping and often living in our truck "down by the river".

We had no idea what to expect at Montana State so we were more than usually unprepared for the incredible array of healthy, buxom, nubile women that abounded on campus. Naturally, we wondered WTF. This could not be real.

F turned out to be a national gathering of intercollegiate cheerleaders, hundreds of 'em, who were seminaring on campus. We didn't learn about that fact for the first few days that we were in Bozeman before I attended my first class and met my fellow grad students.

Kunio Yamane was one of my classmates. Kunio had just arrived in the United States where I met him at a meet and greet for students in the class hosted by Dr. Gerry Coffey. Dr. Gerry had created this class and it had drawn national and international attention. The idea of the class was an intensive three week program. During the first two weeks, we would meet daily from 9-4. These were the days of "encounter groups". Our group sessions would be aimed at building the teamwork that we would need for the last week of the course when we backpacked into the Beartooth mountains to climb Mt. Tempest....the highest peak in Montana. The first two weeks would be the literature part. We would read and discuss The Man Who Killed the Deer by Frank Waters, Desert Solitaire by Edward Abbey and various passages from John Muir

Imagine Kunio. Here he was in his first six hours in America. He had passed through a campus crammed with some of the most alluring women in the country. He had driven through the mountains of Montana's big time splendor. He must have been thinking to himself " so THIS is America!"

Of course, his thoughts were in Japanese. Kunio didn't speak much English...just enough to get by. Kunio was a cheerful guy. I introduced myself and we bowed and shook hands. A moment later, a group of cheerleaders passed the deck on which we were having our party. I noticed Kunio looking at the girls as they passed in the same way that I had looked at them before I got hip. By this time I had learned that they were cheerleaders so I pointed to them and said, "Cheerleaders" to Kunio.

Kunio gave me a puzzled look and repeated my word...."cheerreaders?".

"Yeah, cheerleaders"

When Kunio responded again by saying, "Cheerreaders?" I realized he had no idea what I was talking about so I tried to simplify.

"Yeah Kunio, they're cheerleaders. Ya know; Rah Rah Boom Boom."

His response, again quizzical "Rah Rah Boom Boom?"

I clapped my hands and waved them about. “yeah, Rah Rah Boom Boom”

Kunio’s eyes widened and he burst into a weird I gotcha grin accompanied with a lascivious wink and said, " Ah, Rah, Rah BOOM Boom…Rah Rah BOOM Boom.

God only knows what Kunio thought I was talking about, so I just winked back.

We bowed again.

We had become friends.

Long story short…the class was a great success. We broke through barriers during the first two weeks and by the time we entered the Beartooth, we could count on one another. We achieved our goals. We earned our credit hours along with a lifetime supply of stories and wonder. Kunio climbed Tempest. Kunio made it through the boulder field but he never saw the suffering Bighorn.

We returned to Bozeman, safe, sound and sustained.

We decided to have a farewell party at a Montana shitkicker saloon called the Golden Nugget. Everybody was drinking beer and dancing, Kunio in particular. Bachman Turner was in overdrive that night and although I had come down from the mountains and seen a lot, *You Ain’t Seen Nothin Yet* was pounding through the speakers and my brain as we kicked our heels and commenced to *Taking Care of Business.*

We began to draw the attention of the regulars in the bar. One of the regular gang came over and asked about Kunio. He asked if Kunio could do origami , probably figuring that every Asian could automatically do origami.

Just for shits and giggles, I asked Kunio if he could do origami.

Kunio said, “yeah yeah yeah.”

We all gathered around a long table, my classmates and the Bozemanites. Somebody produced a piece of paper and gave it to Kunio. He sat down with the paper; everybody expecting magic.

Kunio did not disappoint.

Very carefully, he folded the paper and refolded and refolded.

Suddenly, we were looking at the most primitive, most simplistic, most childish paper airplane that I had seen since second grade.

With great fanfare, Kunio tossed the paper airplane towards a pitcher of beer.

Just before the airplane crashed into the beer, Kunio said

"ORIGAMI".

Everybody cheered and we rah, rah boom boomed the night away.

CHAMPION HILLS

This is a true story of golf, cancer and human nature. On my third day of radiation I couldn't stop thinking of Champion Hills. I had to confront the reality that medical costs and recovery time would make it impossible for me to keep up my membership. I made up my mind to go over to the club to say goodbye after this morning's radiation.

The head pro at Champion Hills is named Darlene. Obviously, she can hit the ball a mile and putt with precision. Two weeks ago, Darlene had sent out to the members a note informing us of an increase in fees. Lynn responded. In her response Lynn mentioned the fact that I had cancer and was taking radiation. The increase in club fees was gonna be difficult for us as we couldn't predict the progress of the radiation nor the potency of the after-effects.

The irony is that golf might be therapeutic. I just couldn't afford to play at my club anymore. Pulling into the parking lot I remembered summer days past. The course was beginning to reawaken. When I got to the clubhouse, Darlene was giving a lesson and preparing for a meeting with board of governors. She opened up the conversation with this; "Ice, you picked the worst time for us to talk"

"No problem Darlene. I'll stop back another time"

"How are you Ice ? What kind of cancer do you have"

When I told her it was prostate, Darlene said "Isn't that the one that's most treatable"

I said, "Yes, I'm very lucky. I hadn't been doing a lot of planning lately other than thinking about each day"

I was warming up to resign as April 1 is the deadline for the fees.

Darlene said, "I was hoping you could take some more pictures of the course this year".

"Of course I will"

Then Darlene blew my mind…"and as far as membership goes" she waved her hand dismissively "consider your dues paid. You're still a member. What do you think about that?"

I was stunned. I thanked her for her kindness.

She said You're a good man"

We both had tears in our eyes.

She went back to her lesson.

I returned home to give the news to Lynn.

She was on the treadmill.

“Well, what did Darlene say?“ she asked.

"We don’t have to worry about the club anymore,” was my cryptic response, and after a moment “Darlene said she would wave the membership fees this year”.

I didn’t play anymore golf that season but we regularly dined in the clubhouse.

Once again I was reminded about the millions and millions of random acts of kindness that are committed every day but overlooked in the sensational fog of the hundreds and hundreds of random acts of cruelty.

I could feel another cell of cynicism disintegrate, clobbered by the power of human understanding.

WAFFLE IRON MYSTERY

Luck? I'll tell you about luck.

In November my wife ordered a waffle iron through Amazon. Time went by and no waffle maker. We were getting irritated, not so much by the absence of waffles but rather by the delay in delivery

A couple of weeks later a very large box arrived at our doorstep. I asked Lynn what the hell is this? The package was a lot bigger than any waffles I have ever consumed.We took the package into the house. We opened it. The package did not include a waffle maker.

Lynn, immediately got on the phone.

She's great on the phone; polite, attentive, determined, patient and persistent She made contact with a representative whose accent was a lot different from ours. Lynn told her about the erroneous delivery.

The voice on the other end offered a remedy. All we had to do was "rewrap the package, take it to the post office , send it back. and we'll credit your account"

The ears on our end were not pleased.

The voice on our end had another remedy. We aren't gonna rewrap this thing nor take it to the post office. This package is here because of an error on your part. We don't intend to make up for your error with our time and our gasoline.

The voice on the other end needed a moment to listen to the voice of her supervisor.

For five minutes there were no voices on either end.

Then the voice on the other end offered another remedy. We may keep the package and they would send the waffle maker.

The voice on our end accepted the remedy. Another win for Lynn.

Three months later having discovered our cancer, we decided that we would fight the condition with radiation. After we made the decision and began to schedule the treatment dates, a nurse entered the room with piece of paper that listed some of the potential side effects during radiation. Among the side effects were these two: Urination Changes and Bowel changes.

Urination changes include burning with urination, urinating more often and more urgently. Possible incontinence . Bowel changes include increased gas, urgent or loose bowel movements sometimes activated by the increased gas. Considering the alternatives, we considered and consider our selves very fortunate. We got this covered, no problem. And not thank God with a waffle iron.

The mystery package that we kept , even though we couldn't imagine a use for it at the time, contained 36 extra large adult diapers. This is what I mean by luck and it's all true.

No shit.

SHIT

The seventh day of radiation proved to be informative. Maybe too informative, if ya know what I mean.

The night before, I was up all night because of continual urination. I overslept after I finally fell asleep. When I woke up, I was late.

I had to jump in the car and white knuckle it through a rainstorm and construction and past an accident to get to the hospital on time. You don't want to be late to radiate because there is a very tight schedule of people coming and glowing.

I got there just in the nick of time. I admit, I was feeling shitty.

They called me in and almost immediately.... "Are you all right, Ice?"

"No, I'm half left. Let's do this thing."

I hopped on the sled. They put me in position. They left for the viewing station. I went under the scan. I felt like I was under for a long time. They came down and said I was "positioned wrong" and had to start the whole thing all over again, which they did. Little did I know how polite they were being.

I got up, put my clothes on and left without telling them my usual horrible joke. On the way out, I told a nurse about the problem with leaking. She said, "It's a normal side effect but it's a little early for it to be starting. If it doesn't go away by tomorrow, I'll prescribe something".

Still feeling shitty, I stopped on the way out of the hospital to have a bowel movement. I got home and the peeing continued unabated. For the rest of the day, I was going to the john every 10-15 minutes. It became clear that I couldn't sleep with my wife as my constant getting up and going to the bathroom made it impossible for HER to sleep as well. I moved upstairs to another bedroom with a full bath. I woke up seven times to pee before I finally woke up for real.

I showered and went off to the hospital, this time leaving 45 minutes early. Sure enough, I ran into a traffic jam that cost me 20 minutes and during that time I somehow managed to contain myself.The rest of the trip to the hospital took another ten minutes.

Let me say, I was relieved when I got there.

They called me in and asked if I was feeling better.

"Aside from being up all night peeing, I feel great why do you ask?"

"You didn't look like you were feeling good yesterday and we were worried about you"

I explained "that I was feeling shitty yesterday because I'm a guy who always gets to a place early and when I have to white knuckle it to an appointment, I always carry a trace of the frustration that I had trying to get there on time. It has an effect on my mood when I first walk in."

Mike said "Amy has the same problem"

Amy concurred" Yes I'm always arriving right on time or a minute late. Always in a big tense rush to work"

I said, "Amy, there's a whole different and beautiful world waiting for you that you know nothing about. Your job and your life will change immediately if you get to work a half hour early. You can grab a cup of coffee, read the paper, have a chat, whatever and then when you're ready to start, you're ready to start"

She said, "I like the way you put that. I need to start doing that."

I told her that once I had started getting to work early it totally changed my work experience. "You know how yesterday, I appeared rattled and ornery because I got here in the nick of time. Remember, how clear it was to every body that I wasn't the same guy. That guy is the guy that you are when you get here in the morning in the nick of time and just like you recognized that in me, your co-workers recognize that in you"

I climbed into the sled, They positioned me. They hit me with the rays. They lifted me off the sled.

Amy came down from the viewing booth. She told me that what I had said was good advice. I encouraged her to try it and see. "If you set the goal to be a half hour early even if you're twenty minutes late, you're still ten minutes early."

Amy laughed and said she had never looked at it like that.

On the way out, the Doctor was ready to see me. She asked me about the peeing. I described it as best I could. I've never been real good at describing the act of urination so it was kind of awkward.

She asked me if I had eaten anything unusual during the weekend.

I told her that I had attended two Easter buffets and whatever I had, I had a lot of but no, there was nothing exotic.

Then she asked me about bowel movements.

Again, I don't have the vocabulary to be accurate so I told her that, "Yesterday after the radiation. I got rid of a lot"

She said," I'm glad because yesterday DURING your scan we noticed you had a lot of stool so we couldn't get a great picture. In today's scan there was much less stool and a much better picture." Needless to say, I was flabbergasted at this information which is just part of modern technology that can find just about anything within your body except your soul.

I've got to realize now that every time I get on the sled, everybody in the room is seeing exactly how full of shit I am in three dimension. I clearly was feeling like shit the day before and the reason why I was feeling like shit, apparently, was that I WAS full of shit.

Everybody knew it but me.

That's usually how it goes when somebody is full of shit and it's probably why people feel shitty in the first place.

Just sayn'.

So the doctor fixed me up with another prescription that should confront the constant urination problem. Finally the she advised that I start drinking a lot of cranberry juice so maybe next time, I wouldn't be so full of shit.

Of course she didn't SAY exactly that but that IS exactly what she meant.

Smoove.

And I've managed to type this whole thing without having to get up and pee even once.Now, I'm gonna go downstairs and hit up some cranberry juice.

TROT ON THE BLOCK

I remember my first Thanksgiving in a previous wifetime. We had been married a month and a half. We had built a chicken coop together. We had horses. We had a goose. We had a mule. We even had a peacock. The chickens were laying. We also had a couple of turkeys. As Thanksgiving approached, I wondered about the fate of the turkeys.

My wife didn't wonder. She acted.

She coaxed one of the turkeys out to a stump that unbeknownst to the fowl was a chopping block. She got the bird to stretch his neck out on the block. She took a mighty swing with her ax. Contradicting rumors of stupidity, the turkey lurched out of the way as the ax buried itself in the stump.

The turkey trotted away as if nothing had happened and tried to regain his dignity.

My wife was accompanied by her friend Beth who was eager to help but who was laughing her ass off.

The turkey meanwhile doubled down on rumors of stupidity and walked right back to the stump and confidently stuck his neck out. This time, Beth grabbed the turkey's back legs. A moment later the axe fell.

I was photographing the whole thing.

Although the actual photograph, like the marriage itself, is long gone…I have an imprint of the photograph indelibly recorded in my mind.

It is the moment of contact.

Beth on the left is flinching.

Cindy on the right is baring her teeth, arms fully extended.

All of it is in a slight blur except for where the ax has come to a sudden stop as it passed through the neck of the bird and hit the stump. The ax and the neck of the bird are in perfect focus. A darkened area on the axe is the blood erupting from the birds neck as the ax has passed through.And yes, the turkey did run a round a little bit after his head was cut off.I think it was the first time for everybody.

I know it was the first time for the turkey.

I was pretty sure I got the picture.I proceeded to my dark room and made a print while the women were finishing up with the turkey. Because I was working in my own darkroom, the image was in black and white and it turned out exactly as I described it above. The black and white nature of the image enhanced the reality of the situation.

We had invited several guests to come over and join us for Thanksgiving the following day. The picture was so remarkable that we decided to frame it. We put the framed picture in the dining room.

Our guests arrived, smoking joints and drinking shots as was the custom of the day. John McCormick, who three years later died sober while sitting shotgun in a collision with a telephone pole was the first to notice the image."Wow, what a picture"

People came over and looked at the image with varying degrees of astonishment. Finally, someone asked the inevitable question. "Is that photo a picture of the turkey we are about to eat?"

We nodded.

Beth spoke up.

"This is Thanksgiving"

When the transformed fowl appeared on the table, John asked if he could do the carving.

He did one helluva job. John could do almost anything.

There was plenty of meat to go around and a multitude of Thanks were given as a certain degree of reality grasped the gathering.

UNCOMMON COMMON

Once upon a time, we were playing Bingo in a Fire Hall. Suddenly, an amazing fire burst out across the street. I had never seen anything so powerful and scary. Everybody started running away from the Bingo parlor and the house across the street.

Everybody except my father that is.

He ran toward the fire and before anybody could realize what happened, he was across the street and into that inferno. He pulled a kid out of that blaze before the volunteers of the Fire Hall had even heard the siren.

My father was a firefighter by profession as was my uncle Tommy, my mother's brother. My mother's sister's husband was a cop as was the son of my mother's brother Tommy Jr.

By instinct and training they ran toward the fire, towards the fight.

My uncle was a cop who walked a beat in the most dangerous parts of town where he was known, respected and even loved. Everybody called him Big George.

I understand the principal at the New Town school ran towards the gunmen rather than away.

Instinct and training, along with courage and humanity.

Teachers are becoming the firefighters of 9/11 as schools become more and more vulnerable.

None of them or us are heroes other than working class heroes as Lennon captured the idea.

We're just effing peasants doing our jobs.

Firefighters absorb more injuries each year than police officers.

Nobody gets more criticism than cops.

No profession is assaulted more than teachers.

All of us stand on the thin line between good and evil.

None of them/us are making serious money compared to the kings and queens of the universe whom we teach and protect with our lives.

It's not about the money. It's not about being heroic. It's about running towards the fire rather than away from it.

Walking towards the need instead of ignoring it. Standing in front of the children rather than behind them.

Uncommon common people dedicated to and convinced of the common good.

GOD, HOW I MISS ROSELAND

Starting with Galloping Gertie, through my first round of miniature golf, into the Penny Arcade across from the changemakers where I got an authentic Tom Mix photograph, beyond the Wild Mouse, through the Bumper Cars next to the shooting gallery behind the Cotton Candy stand near the restaurant which eventually became a beer stop where one of my friends once asked what the penalty was for punching out a clown. Back to the hot dog stands beneath the swings and beyond the Skyliner with Skeeball coupons in hand. Tee shirts, cut offs and a pair of thongs, for decades we'd been having fun all summer long.

I knew Roseland big time and the feeling was mutual.

I had to be present for her last night.

We all knew the date of the execution. Condominiums need to be built.

Lots of Landlovers showed up, most young only in heart.

We traded in all of our skee ball tickets which we had amassed over the last ten years and won a forty inch plaster statue of a bearded guy in a yellow raincoat holding on to a bunch of lobsters as if his plaster depended on it.

We posed for pictures in front of or onboard all of the rides.

When my mother died many years later, the picture of her riding the merry go round was the photo nearest her flowers.

We kept trying to pretend that the fun, the eternal summer was never going to end. We knew in our hearts that some point the cups would stop whirling.

During my last ride on the carousel, I began to wonder if, in fact, the rides would stop that night. The operators after all were mostly college kids on the last shift of their summer jobs, probably a week or two from the quad. What would stop them from keeping the rides going all, night, hell all weekend? What could happen to them if they did? They certainly didn't have to worry about getting fired.

But before that paradoxical showdown, the management would present one final fireworks show out over the pier on Canandaigua Lake. The fireworks would begin at eleven. We took our rides on everything as eleven approached.

It was a startlingly clear star spangled evening; a Roseland night.

At ten-thirty the announcement of the fireworks started to come over the p.a. system. Everybody in the park wanted to be in on this event, including the ride operators. So like some kind of blissful, mourning army, we all strode to the site of the fireworks.

At eleven o'clock, the main park was deserted. I distinctly remember looking at that deserted park. I don't remember Roseland ever looking brighter or more inviting, resonating not only the remnants of that night's crowd but also all of the crowds of all the decades past. Although Roseland trembled, it appeared alive and ready to get up on its feet and sprint all the way to Rochester, to Lake Ontario thirty miles South to say goodbye to Sea Breeze.

Complete

Vital

Vibrant

vigorous

empty

throbbing

trembling

pulsating

eternal Roseland over my shoulder.

And then the first fireworks exploded in breathtaking perfection over the lake. The crowd as one ooohed. At that exact instant, I tore my eyes away from the miracle in the sky for one last peek and saw all of the lights in the main park slam off at once, never to come on again.

Total darkness. A silent sound as deafening as any I had ever not heard.

Most of the crowd

As if on cue

turned away

from the sky

gasped

laughed

and cried

as

Roseland

died.

SGT. PEPPER'S RADIATION TEAM

We got a great team at the hospital.

So let me introduce to you

the radiation therapists

Who deal with me every day.

They're Amy, Maggie, Paul and Mike.

Bompop Bombpop, Bompop, Bompop Bompup

Bompop, Bompop Bompop BUMBUMBUMBUMBUM Bop Dooah.

They put me on the table every day

They make sure that my feet are in the cast

Then when all is ready, they quickly run away

And from the booth send out another blast.

They're Amy, Maggie, Paulie and Mike

They're learning who I am and what I like

They always seem to know the exact words to say

To help me through another healing day

etc.

It's always nice when I start to write and bam…it goes right into Sgt. Pepper but sure enough I'm getting by with a little help from these friends. And I've got to admit, I'm getting better.

Okay, Okay, I'll stop and break into prose.

Gradually

Amy looks like a grown up version of a friend from high school. Maggie looks like a grown up version of a friend from college. Paulie looks like a grown up version of a guy I played baseball with. Mike looks like the guy who played guitar in my band.In other words, they all look familiar. So right from the get go I had the feeling I was with friends.

When I told Amy that she looked familiar. She said " a lot of people think I look familiar"

Looking familiar is a pretty good thing don'cha' think?

The first task is getting me on the sled. I'm nowhere near as flexible as I used to be so they team up and gently lift me into position. They've made a cast of my lower body and that cast is on top of what at first looked like random sheets. I have to get my feet into the cast part shaped for my feet and then the therapists take over.

They tell me to "lay heavy" and I'm learning how to do that. Of course at my weight, it comes kinda natural. I'm getting pretty good at laying heavy. Laying heavy means when I feel movement beneath me, I resist the urge to move with that movement. Of course the radiation blasts have to be exactly precise, so when I am laying heavy they are maneuvering the sheets beneath me to put me into the right position without my feet leaving the mold. They pull on the sheet and that puts me right where they want me.

All this time we are making small talk and laughing.

Then one of them will say, “Perfect” and they duck away to a protected area where they watch me through the glass. While watching me, they are also seeing a three dimensional rendering of my inner lower body projected on to a computer screen and making sure that the zaps are zapping the tattoo where the zaps should be zapping.

I’m laying heavy and except for the radio playing in the background, there is silence. I am under the linear accelerator, looking up at the ceiling where I see a red laser cross.The accelerator moves around me and does what it’s supposed to do for about five minutes. Then I hear one of them say, “Great” and next thing I know, they are lifting me off the sled.When my feet first hit the ground, I experience some vertigo. I sit down in the chair and usually tell a story.

The first story on the first day was what happened when the skeleton walked into the bar. The bartender said. “whaddya want”. The skeleton said, “A beer and a mop”.

The second story on the second day had a fish walking into the bar. Bartender said, “Whaddya need”.

The fish said, “Water”.

The third day, a duck walked into the drugstore. The duck asked for lip gloss. The astonished pharmacist brought back the gloss. The duck said, “I don’t have any money, just put it on my bill.

The fourth day, ham and eggs walked into the bar. Bartender said, “We don’t serve breakfast.

The fifth day Jesus Christ walked into a wine bar, etc. The wine pourer asked, “What would you like?” Jesus answered “Just a glass of water.”

Every story got the reaction I hoped it would get. They acted as if they had never heard the story before and then after a pause like after the fish says, “Water,” they gave me the kind of laugh that indicates an amused aha .

Perfect.

Unfortunately I had used all of my clean jokes.

So today, the ninth day, I went with golf. Jesus and St. Peter are playing Pebble Beach. St Peter tees up and blast a beautiful drive right down the middle of the fairway. Jesus whistles in admiration and steps to the tee box. He hits a little dribble that barely makes it to the cart path of the elevated tee. The ball rolls down the path and gets picked up by a rabbit who starts bounding away only to be captured in the talons of a magnificent swooping eagle who grabs the rabbit and starts to fly down the fairway. A flash of lightning hits the eagle who drops the rabbit who drops the ball which lands on the green, takes a giant bounce hits the flagstick and plops into the hole. St Peter turns to Jesus and says, “Hey, are you gonna play golf or just fart around.”

Everybody laughed again. I’m starting to enjoy this here radiation.

Go team go.

WILD BILL FROM BABYLON

I'm starting to wonder how long I will last. I'm already older than I deserve to be; based on the way that I've conducted my life. I want to give credit before I go to people who should already be famous if they gave a shit for fame.

One of those people is my friend Wild Bill. We've been buddies for over fifty years. I asked him to be my daughter's Godfather. I couldn't have made a better choice for her. I haven't spoken to Amanda for at least five years but Wild Bill has and he tells me she's nice.

Thank you, Godfather.

Wild Bill will never be married but to this day he carries ten rubbers in his wallet on his never ending quest to "get laid". Ya gotta love guys like that.

Sometimes he does, God bless him...

He's always having misadventures with cops maybe because of the dozens of messages on his car, the latest being DUMPF TRUMPF

We pissed, side by side, into Walden Pond.

Sitting shotgun on the Long Island Expressway with Bill is a shit your pants experience.

He's seen the Dead fifty times at least. He had a conversation with George Harrison. Nowadays, Bill's the oldest man at every concert and the most energized.

Nobody dances like Wild Bill.

He was a friend of Bobby Vee.

He's a roller coaster fanatic and a member of the 3 stooges fan club

I've seen him punch a taxi cab driver on Fifth Avenue.

He's got season tickets for both the Yankees and the Mets.

He cried when he heard that my mother died.

He sends birthday cards to all of his friends even though none of us have the slightest idea when His birthday arrives.

Christmas cards, Father and Mother's day cards as well

He's a master of trivia, an expert on the Bobby Fuller Four.

He's the last of the great mooners.

He's a distinguished Starlite popper.

He gets along with dogs and cats.

He's got my back.

He should be a movie if he gave a shit.

He's Wild Bill from Babylon.

One remarkable afternoon, I was sitting at a booth in Kennedy airport slamming some suds with my brother Deke while waiting on Wild Bill to pick us up for a weekend of irresponsibility.

Naturally, Bill being capricious from the get go was already two hours late. Responding in kind, I took the opportunity to waste even more money with the rest of the clubless apes on overpriced beers drafted at the airport watering hole.

While in the midst of this activity, I happened to notice a guy sitting at the bar. The guy had his back turned to me. Apparently, he too was waiting for his connection because every ten minutes or so I could hear him say to the barkeep, "I'll have another one please" with a sorta under control yet fighting panic quality to his request.

The guy was in the bar before I got there and I'd been there a couple of hours. I figured our consciousnesses were at the same level of disarray. I never saw the guy's face but something about the tone of his voice reminded me of the voice of the astronaut in 2001 who on the Jupiter Mission gets locked out of his ship by the computer and trying to keep his composure under control without panicking, keeps insisting that the computer open the portal for him to retake control of the ship.

"I'll have another one please" sounded exactly like "Open the pod bay door, Hal" to my altered listening.

Judging from the size of the guy's back and the fact that this was Kennedy Airport, the possibility did exist that this was in fact Keir Dullea, the actor from 2001.

I passed my perception on to my brother. I said, "Listen to the way this guy says 'I'll have another one please'. I think that's the guy from 2001".

My brother equally committed to his beers but still acutely attentive to timbre detail, laughed at my Bud soaked perception. Childishly egged on by his laughter, I decided to approach the guy at the bar.

I took a seat on a stool next to him. I ordered yet another brewski and got a side view. The side view kept me in the ballpark. The guy ordered another drink and the recognition possibility grew even stronger.

Finally, I tapped the guy on the shoulder and said, "Excuse me, are you Keir Dullea?"

The man turned to me and before he spoke I knew, holy shit he's the guy.

Keir said, "Yes I am, do I know you."

I said, "Not really but you're in one of my favorite movies....2001. I've seen that movie ten times and even though I love it, Im not sure what it's about."

Keir said that it was one of his favorite movies as well but he wasn't real sure what it was about either. He thought it was "something about God". Apparently he had been called by Kubrick, accepted the job...worked on his scenes for a month or so and then left the production not knowing anymore about the entire project then what he had experienced while acting in it. He told me that when he saw the movie after its release, he was "stunned."

We carried on a conversation for about fifteen minutes. I told him I was a teacher and he told me how much he respected the profession and how flattered he was that I recognized him.

A great guy.

I excused myself and went back to my table where a great commotion had taken place as Wild Bill finally arrived. I had enough respect for Dullea's privacy that I didn't tell Bill about what had just happened.

When my brother asked, I said, "Yep, it was him. Check him out and let's get outta here before this whole thing gets too absurd". Deacon took a look. I could tell he was astonished by the whole situation.

We started to head out of the airport in a huge, blurry hurry considering we were already an hour late for that night's concert.

Bill started relating the wild excuses he had for being so late. I told him don't worry about it. Let's make the most of tonight, after all as Noel Coward once said, "Keir Dullea, gone tomorrow."

STARLIT HUMAN NATURE

I didn't feel like working one Friday night at the Starlite Drive-in. I wasn't too concerned because we were playing yet another in a long line of low budget Jean Michael Vincent flicks that nobody came to see anyhow. I figured that I'd hang out with the projection crew and the homeless derelict "cousins" who were living in the projection booth until between movies when I'd man the concession stand. Then I'd go home and feed a few unpurchased meatball sandwiches to my pig Seymour.

Driving down West Henrietta Road, I ran into an unexpected, unexplainable traffic jam. I wasn't in any particular hurry so I cranked up my eight track and started

listening to *Arthur* by the Kinks. By the time I got to "Brainwashed," I could see what was causing the clot. All of the cars were pulling into the Starlite. I rechecked the title marquee and although a few of the words were misspelled, the basic idea remained; something about a Hawk starring Vincent and Will Sampson was indeed playing.

I pulled into the long, gravel road that led to the ticket booth and that cubicle was empty. When, at last, I got to the booth, I discovered that the restraining rope was down. The ticket seller had unlocked the rope, opened the booth and as I learned later, in a fit of self-righteous drunken, immature irresponsibility had decided to quit his "godamned shitty job". He took off and left the gate unattended. I never saw the guy again but I heard he opened a fruit stand in Irondequoit specializing in illegally imported bananas.

I was ambivalent about the situation. It didn't hurt me any that more people were attending the show, since I was paid a commission based on the sales of the concession stand. The more people who came to the flick, the more money I would make. Remember though that I didn't feel like working that night and since I hadn't expected anybody to show up, I was all by myself which meant I was going to have to do the work of three people maybe four even if I got a couple of the derelicts living in the projection booth to stop smoking weed, get off their asses and help me out a bit.

When I pulled into my stand, the projectionist greeted me. Drunk as he was, he didn't particularly care how many people were in the lot. He was being paid by the hour. I told him that the reason that all of these people were here was because Mark had opened the gate and abandoned the booth.

One of the great mysteries of this night was how in the world did the people get the word that the movie was free and how did it spread so fast. If we had put FREE on the marquee, probably nobody would have pulled into the lot.

Reminded me of a friend of mine, named Rick who was trying to get rid of an old refrigerator. He put the thing in front of his house for a couple of days with a big FREE sign on its door. Nobody even sniffed it. Finally on the advice of another friend named Charlene, he put another sign on the fridge....$50. That night somebody stole the fuckin' thing.

Art, the projectionist, and I were pondering these matters while also trying to figure out what the heck we were supposed to do. We had a parking lot full of freeloaders. Should I start popping the popper? Should Art start reeling the projector?

We looked around and got an eyeful of human nature as the sky grew dark.

People started to lean on their horns.

They were honking to start the movie.

That freakin' did it!

A parking lot full of freeloaders defreakinmanding that they get what they didn't pay for and expressing their rage by leaning on their horns. I told Art, "I've got to say something."

I didn't know exactly what I was going to say but I knew that somebody had to say something and since I was still sober and giving a shit, it had to be me.

I went into the projection booth. I fired up the PA system.I grabbed the mike and this is what I said:

"Ladies and gentlemen, we have a situation here. The guy who takes tickets left his post so all of you are here for free. Look around, the place is packed and nobody has paid as much as a dime.Now, I can't blame you for taking advantage. I sure as hell can't throw all of ya outta here. I do want you to know that this is NOT a FREE show and staying here would be like stealing. Stealing is wrong. I do have an idea, a solution. We're going to send somebody back to the ticket booth. The right thing for you to do is exit the drive in on the right onto Brighton-Henrietta Town Line Road... then turn left and re-enter the lot. The ticket person will charge you half price and you will have the satisfaction of knowing that you did the right thing. We will begin the show in 10 minutes."

Art had been listening to this with a look of astonishment on his shitfaced grill. He asked me what I thought would happen. I said, "I believe in people."

Silence ensued.

Honking stopped.

Then I heard a car engine start up. Then another, and another. I saw a line of cars heading for the exit, God bless'ed, every single car that I could see headed out the exit. Moments later we got a call from the ticket booth out front. "It looks like an invasion out here! There's a procession of cars coming down West Henrietta Road and pulling in. What should I do?"

"Charge 'em half price and say thank you," I told my man.

The drive-in filled back up not quite as full but almost. Ten minutes after my announcement, we started the movie. I gave away free popcorn all night. The owner made more money that night than he had any right to make. The people saw a movie for half price and got free popcorn along with the satisfaction of, on this occasion, doing the right thing.

That night, I went home and had a moonlight talk with Seymour about human nature. Pretty sure Seymour didn't understand a word I was saying yet between gulps of his meatball sandwiches, although he grunted and farted at appropriate times.

ERICHA FROM A DISTANCE

Sometimes it's important to see things through the eyes of others. We received this letter from a niece named Ericha who lives in North Carolina. Lynn responded to the letter before I even saw it. I was gonna respond but Lynn covered everything pretty objectively. Of course she left out the part about my brave, courageous, inspiring battle but that's probably because I've left it out of my own behavior especially when seen up close.

Anyway, here's what it looks like from a distance.

Ericha's letter and Lynn's response.

"Hey guys,

So I just wanted to reach out and let you guys know you are in my prayers everyday. Cancer is a very scary word. Usually I shy away from reaching out on a topic that I don't understand. Today I was thinking about it and I realized how selfish that was. I was so scared to bring up something you guys deal with everyday. But really as family its only right that we are here for each other through thick and thin. Even if we are scared we stand tall for the ones we love. We are the people who lend a shoulder to cry on. I want you guys to know I can and will be that person if you guys ever need anything. I've always looked up to you guys for being very knowledgable and kind and do not deserve this disease to come into your life. But, God works in mysterious ways and I strongly believe you guys will beat and overcome this obstacle. Love you guys and miss you! Hope to see you soon!!

Erika

What a wonderful letter. So full of love, concern and support. Thank you very, very much. Uncle Ice has just six more radiation treatments. They won't know if all the cancer is gone so he will have to go in for regular blood tests to check his PSA level which will tell them the potential threat of cancer cells remaining or not. He has been experiencing fatigue, depression and incontinence . He is on meds for all of that which gives him some relief. No sleep at nites though which can make him zombie like. But the good news is that a few weeks after radiation he should return back to how he was before the radiation started. We are getting thru this by feeling how lucky we are that it was caught in time and the treatment just involves radiation not surgery or chemotherapy. He tells me that when he writes his book about recovery, he's gonna include your letter.

With love and appreciation,

Aunt Lynn and Uncle Ice

FULL OF POISON

I'm about as full of poison as I'm going to get. I'm twenty five blasts in with three to go. Lethargic guilt is such a pitiful condition. I'm reminded of a conversation I had with a friend of mine a few months before I got diagnosed.

My lifelong pal John Crown had been clobbered by heart attack, heart surgery, cancer, colostomy and blinding cataracts.

On his most recent trip to the hospital, Dr. Somebody asked Crown if he was depressed. Crown knew that the doctor was very aware of how many health concerns he had on his plate.

"Of course I'm depressed, Doctor. Wouldn't you be if you were I?"

The doctor shrugged as if to say "uhyayuh"

The doctor asked Crown if he wanted something for the depression.

Crown said "No thank you. My depression and my family are the only thinga I give a shit about"

That's how I was feeling all day today. The only thing that interested me was my lack of interest and the guilt that came with not giving a shit which is even more interesting and paralyzing than the lethargy itself. At the radiation center, they warned me that 95% of the people having the treatment that I'm having experience fatigue.

I wondered if they had a reason for that amazing percentage. They said it's our bodies reaction to the poison that is introduced into our systems with poison being another word for radiation.

I had been operating under a false impression. I thought that every day when I get zapped by the rays I was equating the rays with a ray gun which fired at my cancerous cells for about five minutes. Then after the volley, the smoke cleared.

Not really.

Radiation is more like pouring poison in to a container until the container is full and then letting the poison invade the environment in which the deadly cells are trying to multiply.The battle goes on for more than a volley of five minutes. The battle is continuous 24/7.

In other words, every day my container gets filled with more poison. It's gonna linger in the neighborhood for a month and when it starts to dissipate, we'll look at the environment again and see what damage has been done to the invading cells.

So that's why I'm worn out and going to the bathroom 3 times an hour.

And the whole thing is becoming routine.

Routine tends to normalize even the most extraordinary circumstances.

It's comforting to know that all of this is normal and there's no reason to feel guilty. A reduction in guilt takes the edge off the lethargy.

So I'm gonna feel good about all the time I spend rotting on the couch.

My body earns it every day. Soon I'll be as full of poison as I'm gonna get and from that point on, I'm gonna get better.

FUZZY SCIENCE

Meanwhile, I've been poisoning a patch of innocent pea pods just to see what would happen to the peas.

Other pods, I've left alone just to give those routine peas a chance.

Naturally I've been raising almost as many caterpillars as I've been poisoning pods.

Just to see what might happen to the moths. Most of the caterpillars that I've raised are immune to the poison that I've been putting in the pods. They can eat all the poison they want and live to eat more on another day. God knows that there's enough poison to go around.

The main reason I've been poisoning the pods, besides seeing what might happen to the peas, is to see what might happen to the spiders. Ya see, eventually the caterpillars that eat the poison peas will turn into moths. These moths will look exactly like the moths that emerge from the caterpillars who ate the unpoisoned peas.

They will look the same and maybe even taste the same but the immune caterpillars who ate the poison peas will have a different truth when they become moths then will the other batch of moths whose pea digestion was restricted to the non-poisonous peas back in their respective caterpillar days.

"Different truth, different consequence" as Aristotle might have whispered to Krell if they had ever met. Of course, the likelihood of fictional meeting non-fictional is always very poor no matter what happens to the spiders, if ya smell what I'm cooking.

And there's a lot cooking in California.

Too bad we couldn't have doused the fires of California with the floods of Katrina and called the whole thing a wash.

But so much for wishful thinking, even thought it is my favorite defense mechanism (especially when the perceived threat is emotional rather than physical)

Let's return to the practical and the poisoning of peas.

What will happen to the spider? Since all the caterpillars looked exactly alike whether or not they had eaten the peas from the poisoned pods, they would eventually grow into identical moths that I could throw into spider webs just to see what the spiders would do. Moths fly into spider webs all of the time whereas the odds of a caterpillar showing up in a spider web are roughly those of a turtle sitting on a fence post.

I had to make sure that the caterpillars weren't gonna turn into butterflies. Butterflies are too strong for most webs. I made sure to use the fuzziest of caterpillars. Fuzzy happens to be my nickname because my last name is Fuzzler

Both the turtle and the caterpillar would need help to get to the top of the fencepost or the silk of the web and spiders are a lot smarter than fenceposts. A fencepost ain't gonna worry about how a turtle got upon it whereas a spider might have some concern about how a caterpillar got into the web. The spider might be a little suspicious.

Since spiders are smarter than fenceposts, suspicion is a form of intelligence. Nothing breeds suspicion like jealousy. Nothing breeds jealousy like love. Love always begins with attraction.

Attraction begins with notice.

On their way to delectable mothhood, two fuzzy little caterpillars noticed one another. The male caterpillar was named Yar. The female was named Asil. Asil was the more mature of the two which meant she thought more about reproduction than did Yar who was concentrating on chewing and crawling.

How much did Asil think of reproduction?

Let's put it this way, she was jealous of fireflies. Asil had no idea that the peas she was eating were from the poison pod patch, unlike the peas that Yar was digesting.

Yar's peas came from a totally different patch.

I know this for a fact because I'm the guy who personally poisoned the pods and I'm the guy who determined which caterpillars got the poison peas and which ones didn't. And I kept em separated. I'm also the guy who fed the caterpillars. I'm the guy who bred the caterpillars. Like most breeders, I'm a feeder.I knew lots of things that the caterpillars didn't know. I'm a man for God sake. Let's hope I got more brains than a caterpillar.

Here's what I knew that the caterpillars didn't know. I knew that they were immune to the poison peas that they didn't know they were eating. I also knew the purpose of their lives and why they were bred and fed in the first place.......Just to see what would happen to the spider.

Although Asil was jealous of fireflies, she didn't love fire flies. A caterpillar loving a firefly would be sick. Asil wasn't jealous of fireflies because they could fly. Asil knew that someday, somehow she too would be able to fly. Asil wasn't jealous of fireflies because of their fire because Asil sensed something that almost everybody senses unless they're sitting around a campfire.The sparks coming from a campfire are very different from the fireflies flying near the campfire.

What appears to be fire in fireflies is really a mixture of luciferin and luciferase. The resulting mixture is not a fire. Fires, like truth, emanate light and heat. Firefly fire contains no heat, only light. Sort of like compassion. Asil wasn't interested in truth or compassion. Asil was interested in breeding and feeding. Asil was more developed than Yar who was interested only in feeding.

No, Asil wasn't jealous because she loved fireflies. Asil was jealous of the way that fireflies loved fireflies. Fireflies flash when they're hungry or when they want sex. Every flash is a semaphore of desire either to feed or breed.In this scenario, the female waits in the weeds until she is luciferinated for a half second by the flash of the male flying above her.

Asil had seen this seductive behavior frequently from fireflies. She thought it was cool. Cool as a fire without heat yet hot as a fire without light.

FUZZY'S BLUES

I've watched the caterpillars grow into moths. I've picked out the two moths that look the best. I'm gonna throw them one at a time into a spider web that I've found. In the meantime, I want to sing you folks some blues before we all find out what the spider's gonna do. Maybe I don't have the voice of Jack Neelin or the strum of Genesee Johnny or the stylin' of Brian Burley but here we go...

Well, it looks like it's come down to the final two

Yes, it looks like it's come down to the final two

One looks at the other and says, "Up to me and you".

I don't know if caterpillars have names.

I don't know if caterpillars have names.

If they don't they oughta cause they both look just the same.

I've chosen the spider, I've approved her spinning.

I've chosen that spider, I'm down with her spinning

The game is sudden death, I can't see two moths winning.

Both of the pillars have grown up to be moths.

Both caterpillars have grown up to be moths.

They're gonna get all caught up in a game of web toss.

The lady caterpillar's chock full of poison peas.

Yeah, the female pillar all fulla poisoned peas

Yet the moth she became ain't suffering no disease.

The male caterpillar of poison peas is free

The caterpillar man of poison peas is free.

There's a load of silk underneath the apple tree.

I'll conclude my experiment when I'm done with strummin.

I'll end my experiment when I finish this strummin'

Spin on Mona, Your poison trick or treats a comin'.

I'm gonna have some rum and apple cider too

Gonna drink some rum and suck some cider too

Then we'll find out what the spider's gonna do.

EVENTUALLY

Of course, the caterpillars eventually became moths. When they took wing, Asil became Lisa and Yar became Ray. By the time they became reacquainted, Ray's scent brushes were loaded with alkaloid. Lisa could smell that from ten feet away. Lisa was sitting on a wire perch chemically treated with poison peas. The chemical treatment lured Lisa to the wire and Lisa lured Ray.

Lisa had already lured a dozen others to her in her four days of fertility but there was something about Ray that suggested that his alkaloid package would be the package selected for warrior offspring.

Maybe it was his size. The bigger the moth, the more the alkaloid. The more the alkaloid, the more the male moth advertises his reproductive eligibility.

This is the message Ray was sending to Lisa. 'Look at all the alkaloid I'm carrying. I get this from the flowers. If you want your kids to be able to gather a lot of alkaloid from the flowers make sure that their old man brings a load of alkaloid to the bargain'.

Ray looked big and he smelled big. Ray hovered over the wire. Lisa called to Ray. Lisa called with her scent. Although Ray was not a butterfly, he did know how to flutter by. He did just that.

His scent brushes came out when he got in range. Once, twice, thrice, in less than a second. Lisa was impressed. She accepted Ray. The rest is moth love, too private and exquisite to describe.Even on a weekend when practically no one is looking.Except just a few who wonder what the spider's gonna do.

MONA

Mona the spider is fastidious. She knows how to use her silk. Her silk will be far less useful if it becomes cluttered so Mona spends most of her visible time cleaning the debris from her web. The more debris in the web, the less clear the signal becomes when something of value is caught up in the silk.

Mona can not see all of her web so she waits between spinnings and cleanings. She stays out of sight and waits for a signal. Her web is filled with silk spun of different levels of water content. The more water in the silk, the more elastic. The most elastic silk is in the middle of her web. These are the waterworks. When prey falls into the web, they are confronted with mysterious elasticity far beyond rubber. Caught in the center of the silk, the prey in its struggles puts very little tension on the web. Every attempt at escape only results in tighter wrapping.

Mona reads the level of tension. She has her escape routes well designed when the tension gets too high. Mona only feeds upon appropriate tension. All the prey can do is pray. Mona isn't looking for a fight. Mona is looking for food.Even on weekends, when things are so quiet elsewhere.

I know all about Mona but not yet enough. I'm gonna use Lisa and Ray to find out what the spider is gonna do. And Lisa will be a momma soon, if she survives the tension.

Moth tossing is a skill. I've had a lot of practice. I'm a professional. I wouldn't try this at home if I were you.

I kept the two moths that I had raised from caterpillars and poisoned or not poisoned in two separate vials. I took the bigger of the two out first. I knew he was the male. I figured that with his strength, I would have to get him closer to the center of the web. I grabbed him by his wings and tossed him.

My hours of practice paid off. He landed right smack dab in the middle of the web.

I opened the second vial and removed the female. I wanted to get her off to the side of the web, closer to the spider. I grabbed her wings and tossed.

Perfecto.

The female landed off to the right, very close to where I knew the spider was hiding. The male flailed more than the female but the elasticity at the center was greater. He got all wrapped up in the web. His strength and struggle didn't cause much tension on the web. The elastic web was more water than fire.

The female landed on a portion of the web that was more adhesive than elastic. She would have generated more tension on the web if she weren't so tightly stuck to her spot.

I couldn't help but notice that they seemed to glance at one another intermittently as they tried to escape. Each of them had a clear look at the fate of the other. I wondered if they wondered what the spider was going to do.

I wondered if they even knew that spiders existed. I wondered if they were afraid. I wondered if they were sympathetic towards each other.The male got even more wrapped up when he realized the female was in a predicament. Was he trying to rescue her?

Of course the possibility existed that they thought this was play, perhaps even foreplay. I know I wasn't playing. I know there is such a thing as spiders. I wondered what this spider was going to do.

Mona was middle aged. She was six months old. Every spider month is equivalent to seven years of human life. In human terms Mona was forty-two. The last of her spiderlings had ballooned away. Her mate died right after mating with Mona. Such is nature.

If you've seen Spiderman, you know what ballooning is. The spiderling projects a single thread of silk which sticks to a nearby object. The spider then swings to that object and balloons again. Depending on how far they want to get away from their mother, the spiderling continues to balloon and balloon.

As a mother, Mona paid attention to the spider parental creed. Make sure the spiderlings get webs and wings. This creed meant that it was important for each spiderling to feel a sense of security so that they would be willing to leave the web and establish a home of their own. The stronger the sense of web the stronger the sense of wing. The more that a spiderling loved his mother's web, the further he would distance himself from it when he finally ballooned. The further away he got, the less competition his web would be for the web of his momma.

Mona's spiderlings were far, far away. They had been well raised and they loved their mother.Mona was an empty webber.

Mona was acutely aware of the double disturbance in her web as she sat in her den. Her experience had taught her that it was very unlikely for two disturbances to occur so simultaneously. She figured the commotion could be traced back to one of two possibilities. The disturbances, soon to become prey, then to become liquid then to become food, must have been romantically involved. That's why they were fluttering so near to one another.

And flying blind.

Or else the Giant had delivered them.

The Giant had been feeding Mona since she was a girl, before the mating and the spiderlings and all that jazz. She had grown to trust the Giant. Most urgent, however, was the hunger.

I should be more specific. Mona wouldn't take a nibble. Mona would take a suck. Before sucking, Mona would inject either Ray or Lisa or both with venom that would turn their insides into liquid. She would go back to her den and wait for the innards of her prey to liquify. Then she would begin to suck. Sometimes, the sucking took place right out in the open. Other times, Mona would take her silk wrapped supper into her den where she could suck in private.

I've tried to imagine what it must be like to feel my insides turning into liquid. I had food poisoning once and that did some serious liquefying. Maximum diarrhea mixed with technicolor yawning.

I have experienced emotional liquefaction more frequently than physical liquefaction over the course of my life. When I am injected with the contempt of another person, my convictions tend to liquify. Contempt is a powerful venom. For every action, there is an equal and opposite reaction. Resentment is the natural reaction to contempt.Here's the equation to avoid.

You have contempt for me, I have resentment for you. Or vice versa.

If turning someones insides into liquid can be viewed as a physical manifestation of contempt, then I suppose the prey being liquified must be pretty resentful. Resentment resembles jealousy and jealousy is the green eyed monster that mocks the meat it feeds upon according to the Bard. Contempt is an eight eyed, eight legged empty webbed widow who injects whatever she has trapped with a poison that turns their convictions into liquid so she can suck them dry and ignore their resentment. Does contempt poison itself when it inadvertently sucks up poisoned convictions concealed within resentment? I wondered if I would be able to pick up on any of these emotions or answer any essential questions as I patiently sat and watched and wondered what the spider might do.

PALP FRICTION

I play the guitar a little bit. I drink a little bit. Sometimes I drink a little bit before I play the guitar. Sometimes people tell me I sound better on the guitar after I've drank a little bit. I'm pretty sure I don't sound any better but somehow when I play, I make the people who listening to me want to drink. The more I play, the more they drink. The more they drink, the better I sound. So I drink even more so I can sound even better so they can drink more because I sound better which makes me want to drink more so I can sound better which will make them drink more which will make me drink more so that.......

Ya know, the usual.

I've often wished that I could drink while I was playing the guitar not just before or after. I've wondered if that would actually make my guitar playing sound even better to the folks who were listening because unlike me when I play, they are actually drinking while they are listening whereas I am playing under the disadvantage of not drinking at the same instant that I am playing which puts me a little out of synch with the drunks who are listening.

I wish I had a couple of extra hands coming out of my mouth.

If I did, I could pour the beer down my throat while at the same time playing the guitar with my other two hands.

Spiders have two little hands coming out of their mouths. Those two little hands are called palps. Spiders use those pulps to hold on to whatever they are going to sink their fangs into. Sometimes they use the palps to make changes in the thread of their webs. They grasp the thread with their palps and amend the web with their mouths. Spiders don't play the guitar unless of course, they happen to be Martians.

The moths are in the web. I've got a cold beer in my hands. I'm sipping the beer and wondering what the spider's gonna do.Let's remember, the moth nearest the spider was the moth who ate the poisoned peas.

I figured that the spider would go to the nearest meal. The spider would nibble on the pregnant moth with the poisoned peas. The spider would realize that something was wrong. The spider would choose one of her escape routes. She would return to her corner. She would feel weak. She would ascertain from the vibes coming through the silk that the meal furthest away was too strong for her to overwhelm. She would wait until her queasiness subsided. Then she would return to the near meal and nibble a little bit more.

I knew something that she couldn't possibly know. The meal she was nibbling on was poisonous. Every nibble would make her weaker. I didn't know who would die first, the poisoned spider or the moths struggling in the web.I wondered if it was the silk that killed the moth or was it the spider. If the spider died first, I would free the moths from the web.

I figured the whole deal might take a day after the first taste. This is what I thought the spider might do.

I waited to find out what the spider would actually do.

SIX YEAR DAY

Every day in the life of a moth is like six years in the life of a human.

Lisa was six days old in real time which means thirty-six years old in human time. Lisa had spent the first twenty-four years of her life in heat. During those years she had rubbed plenty of abdomens while being embraced by many a clasper. Twice she had felt threatened during a momentary mating session. Moths are pollinators not fighters. When the choice comes to fight or flight, the moth will choose flight. Lisa and her lover took off as one, the claspers coming off his abdomen holding her close even as they fluttered away, conjoined amorously, from the perceived danger.

Lisa remembered both of those occasions. They were thrilling and embarrassing at the same time. Even though they were memorable, the couplings were meaningless. Lisa and her mate were both distracted while flying away from danger and although they completed their intercourse, lack of purposeful, reproductive concentration assured that neither coupling would be fertile. In human life, this is known as a flying fuck. Of course humans cannot fly and will very often choose fight over flight when threatened. The human term “flying fuck” refers to not paying proper attention to an endeavor due to a lack of commitment in that project.

When Lisa finally met Ray, they both had a chance to concentrate. Ray was a big moth to begin with but he transferred ten percent of his body mass, in the form of spermatozoa, into Lisa. This transfer proved to be fertile. Lisa, in the web, was very pregnant.And loaded with nutrients. And poison.

Ray had struggled with liquidity and silk before. He didn’t think it was such a bad thing. Ray held no resentment for that struggle. As a matter of fact, he saw his situation as another shot at renewal. Remember, Ray had ben Yar. Dejavu all over again.

When Yar, the poison free caterpillar, had reached his full size, he had already prepared to complete metamorphosis, the radical change in body form that turns a caterpillar into a moth. Yar had pupated himself to a twig. To anchor himself to his twig, Yar had spun a button of silk from his mouthparts, then grasped the silk button with his cremaster, a claw-like structure at the end of the abdomen. Hanging from the twig, Yar had shed his skin to reveal the pupa underneath. Before becoming a pupa, Yar had spun a cocoon of silk around his body. The silk of the past had protected Yar from predators and from drying out. Silk was neither an enemy nor a stranger.

Within the pupa, Yar’s tissues and organs had broken down into a soupy liquid, and then reassembled into the tissues and organs of Ray. Groups of cells known as the imaginal discs remained complete, and Ray’s mighty structure took shape as directed by these cells.

When Ray’s development was complete, he had split the pupal shell and crawled out. Then he had unfolded his wings which pumped blood into his veins. Ray remembered spreading his wings until they dried and hardened. Ray flew away and eventually mated with Lisa.

And now he found himself in silk once again.

Ray was confident this was just another stage of maturity.

He would emerge from this silk and fly away again. Ray thought he was turning into a bird. He looked forward to spreading new wings. Ray had no idea that spiders even existed so he didn't wonder at all what Mona would do.Ray had changed a lot since the days of Yar. Ya might say he matured. He was no longer thinking primarily about crawling and feeding, he was thinking now about flying and breeding. He suspected the web was another form of cocoon which meant it was another stage in development.

Another passage.

Another promotion.

Ray was happy that Lisa was involved in the same passage, the same struggle, the same silk at the same time in the same place.

Ray began to understand love.

He and Lisa would become birds together. They would build a nest on some distant chaparral and have babies. He would become Ayr. Lisa would become Sail. Together they would sail through the air until they found the acre or two of brushy territory which would be their secret homeland.

They would be secure.

They would be mates for life. They would never wander from their nest. Their nest would be a compact cup of grass, fibers and bark bound with silk.

Each day, they would make the rounds of their territory, right up to the river. They would feed, bathe, take care of their young and fend off interlopers. Sail would be Ayr's constant companion. They would take delight in bouts of mutual preening as they took care to inspect and arrange each other's plumage. By night, they'd huddle together against the chill. They'd face in the same direction so near together that they would appear as a single ball of feathers from which tails, wings and feet protruded. They would always be together.They would stay out of sight. They would be heard more than they would be seen but they wouldn't be heard very often. They'd live in a tree fifteen feet off the ground when they weren't sailing through the air.

Ray was thinking about Ayr and Sail when Mona sank her fang into him.

Love hurts.

After the puncture, while his insides were turning to liquid and just before his final breath Ray, still expecting to become a bird, thought his final thought. This is what he thought: It could have been worse.

Lisa, on the other hand, continued to be more mature than Ray. Lisa had moved beyond contemplations of breeding and feeding and had moved towards contemplations of death and deliverance but not in that order. Lisa observed the death of Ray. She felt no sadness. Ray had done his job. She still needed to do hers. She needed to deliver the eggs that she and Ray had created.

She knew she was going to die.

Ray, in his immaturity, had considered himself immortal with death merely another stage of metamorphosis. Ray's immaturity prevented him from the fear of death.

Lisa was afraid to die. Lisa knew that her life was incomplete. Lisa had learned what a spider is and the part a spider can play in death-making. Lisa knew she was next.Her eggs would die with her.

It couldn't get any worse.

The spider returned and rappelled down the silk towards the moth that I had raised on poisoned peas. Poison's a funny thing. Poison consists of chemicals. After we ingest poison, our liver uses enzymes to convert those chemicals into poisons. If we don't have the enzymes that convert the chemicals into poisons then the chemicals within the poison are of no threat to us. They might even cure us.

Lisa was missing the enzymes that would turn the chemicals from the peas into poison but the spider possessed those enzymes in spades.

If Mona ate the moth whose innards she had already liquified, there would be no problem.

If the Mona ate Lisa , there would be a big problem.

Death by poison for Mona

Death by liquidity for Lisa.

Choices, decisions, consequences.

The spider was all fangs and palps. The moth was all vulnerability except for the wild card of hidden toxicity.

Lisa knew she was next.

Her eggs would die with her.

It couldn't get any worse.

I found out what the spider would do.

The spider decided that she didn't want the moth. She backed off. She began cutting. She took the thread with her palps and put it in her mouth. Mona cut a perfect window in the web with her sharp fangs.

Lisa fell free from the web.

Lisa took flight.

The spider returned to her watch.

I found out what the spider would do.

Lisa delivered.

Spiders will do what Mona did.

They recognize poison when they sense it and hungry is better than dead, especially with delicious Ray a goner in the silk.

I felt pretty good after I found out what the spider did. I didn't know whether or not the spider would be smart enough to avoid the moth who had eaten the poisoned peas. The spider was smart enough to discern the presence of poison in her web. If we were all smart enough to know which moth is poisoned and which one ain't. If we resisted the urge to do what we can do and instead focused on doing what we should do, the world would be a much better place.

And it was the poison that saved Lisa and her children

Speaking of better places, Lisa's delivery was a better beginning. Her offspring, half poison and half not would never have to liquefy in silk and contempt.

As evening fell, I decided to smoke a cigar.

My work was done.

I know I shouldn't smoke but what the hell, I had just learned a great lesson. Avoid poison when possible. Embrace poison that cures. Know the difference. Radiation versus tobacco.

The night was still. Fireflies were everywhere. I lit a candle. I stuck the end of my cigar into the flame of the candle. I took a couple of puffs.

I blew three perfect smoke rings.

Perfect smoke rings are possible on a windless night.

As the third smoke ring floated away, a moth flew right through the middle of it and headed towards the candle flame. As the moth neared the flame, I noticed threads of silk dangling from the wings of the moth. The moth didn't get any nearer to the flame than moths always get to a flame but not too many moths are carrying a thread of silk.

It was the silk, not the moth, that kissed the candle. The flame shot right up the silk. The moth burst into fire and headed towards the smoke rings expanding in the distance.

The moth momentarily stood out amidst the fireflies.

The moth had become flying fire.

Then it disappeared from my view forever.

Peace, at last.

MORE SEYMOUR

I've almost forgotten how much fun it was to drink beer with Seymour, my pig.

Remember those delicious meatball sandwiches that only existed at drive-ins? We took a lot of pride in our meatball "sank witch" when we ran and cooked at the Starlite concession stand. We always threw in a load of extra sauce and cheese. Those subs were nuclear powered.

Some times we'd make a few subs too many. I'd take whatever leftovers we still had hanging around and feed them to Seymour. At that juncture, feeding meatballs to a pig was my idea of a savings account.

I'd usually bring at least twelve pack of Bud to accompany the meatball sandwiches. I'd take the winding path down past the barn, past the manure pile, past the chicken coop and the duck pond into the wired off part of the pasture that we had converted into a pig pen.

I'd stand next to the pen, throw a few sandwiches on the ground and wait for Seymour to emerge. I was usually working on my first Bud while I was bringing the sandwiches to Seymour's slophouse. By the time I got to Seymour's place, I was finishing my second. I'd finish my third by the time Seymour emerged from his little tin hut.

At this point, I'd pop open my fourth Bud and pour the fifth and sixth beer into the black, circular, plastic container that we used as a watering tough for the pig.

Seymour could drink even faster than I could when he put his mind to it, in other words when he wasn't peein', poopin' eatin' or sleepin'. The whole purpose of chilling with the pig in the first place was to avoid any semblance of pressure or constraints or manners. Burping, farting and even puking was no problem. I'd drink at my own pace and whenever I finished one I'd pop open another one for the pig and another for myself.

I've heard about dogs, who come to a kitchen table, sit on a chair, put their paws on the table and wait to be served. These are dogs who think they are humans. Seymour did not think he was human. Seymour knew for damned sure that he was a pig and when he partied with me I think he figured that I was one too and he weren't far off. Seymour was all attitude, identity and appetite.

There was nobody else around except me and the pig. The stars were bright; the temperature perfect. The only sounds of the night were the natural sounds of the pasture and the pen along with the snortin', slathering', plopping' burpin' leaking' sounds that Seymour routinely made at times like these. It was peaceful. I had been productive as in "I'm going down to feed the pig now, honey." Life in the pasture drinking with the pig was a bizarre Bud commercial waiting to be made and shown at the Super Bowl.

One time, near the end, when we had come to grips with the sobering eventuality that Seymour was destined to become ham, bacon, sausage, etc, I had a barn party over at my house. Some of my buddies had heard me bragging about the peace of mind I enjoyed while drinking with the pig. Apparently they thought it was a good idea because by the time I got down to the trough, Seymour was passed out in the cooling mud, getting a bit of a sunburn, his trough still half full of beer.

I went back to the barn and asked how many people had been drinking with the pig. Seven guys raised their hands: Tommy Tron, Bruce, Jack Stafford, John McCormick, Wayne, Wild Bill and Uncle George. I told them to come down to the sty and see the fruits of their labor.

The bunch of us walked down the path together. As we got close to Seymour, a reverent silence descended, When we arrived at his trough the stillness continued as we gazed and gaped at the five sheets to the wind bovine blacked out and basking in his combination of mud, Bud, swill and perceived freedom, catching some rays and judging by his apparent ease of breathing, completely relaxed, at peace with the world, unconcerned with appearances.

A few weeks later I recruited all of these guys to help me load the corpulent and non-co operative Seymour into the back of my truck to take him to processing about ten miles down the road. Seymour was no longer a little piggy on his way to the market. We had a rough, sweaty, shitty and muddy time trying to get Seymour into the truck until somebody got in touch with a guy named Fuzzy who suggested putting a pillowcase over his face. We did. It worked. We led Seymour into and out of the truck and into the processing pen where they spray painted the word "RIVERS" in large letters on his no longer sunburned hide.

I remember taking one last look at Seymour. There was another huge pig in the holding pen with him. I imagined those two pigs looking at each other's hides, seeing the black spray paint and thinking, "This ain't real good". Then I shut the door and left Seymour in the darkness.

Seymour was no longer just involved. He was committed.

The next time I saw him he was in packages

Over the next few decades, every time that I've gotten together with any of those guys, particularly during All Star games, somebody always comes up with "remember Seymour" and the next round of stories take off from that common point of departure as if Seymour the Pig was a space station and all previous stories were shuttle crafts arriving to be refueled enroute to homecoming or deeper exploration

MENDON SEA CRUISE

As in the case with most epics, many colorful events occurred during my final days at the Starlite. Most of those colorful events were driven by colorful people, people that I wouldn't have known if it weren't for the Starlite which was sort of a vortex of idiosyncrasy. One of those colorful people was Wayne Green.

Wayne was a regular at the Starlite, as well as a drive-in aficionado. One particularly slow night, Wayne came in from his car and we began a snack bar conversation about drive in culture , etc. Wayne became so engrossed in the conversation that he missed the second feature which was The Deep with Nick Nolte and Jackie Bissett. Due to no fault of our own, we had been playing the movie one reel short and out of order but nobody complained except one time when the sound went off for a minute or two and a few people honked. That's when I realized that people didn't give a shit what they were watching as long as they could hear it.

Wayne asked me how to operate the popcorn machine, I showed him. He was immediately hooked on concession stand life.

I told Wayne that anytime he wanted to stop by and help me run the stand, we'd let him in for free. Most nights, Wayne would show up and volunteer his services as popcorn popper. Wayne wasn't the only one. Towards the end I had six or seven people who enjoyed the concession stand so much that they would come to the drive in just to hang around, every so often going back to their cars to drink beer or whatever. The concession stand became an oddball country club. Almost every night one or two or more of these volunteers would show up to pop and pour. In the end, they were basically running the stand and I was spending more and more time in party cars.

Outside of the stand, I didn't know much about Wayne or the other "volunteers" but I figured they were either geniuses or lunatics and probably both. We'd get into some pretty crazy conversations on slow nights and since we kept playing Jean

Michael Vincent level movies without half price admission or free popcorn, there were a lot of slow nights.

One night Wayne and I were talking about making lemonade of lemons, making a fortune out of a misfortune. Wayne told me about a guy that he knew whose truck caught fire the same week that the engine of his boat blew up. Wayne told me that the guy welded the body of his boat on to the frame and motor of his car, got some dealer plates and drove around in his truck boat.

I had trouble believing that one. I told Wayne so. He assured me that the story was true. I said, "Yeah, right" and forgot about the whole deal.

About a month later, I was mowing my lawn when a boat with dealer plates pulled into my driveway. Wayne was at the wheel. How can I describe this contraption? I know. A speed boat on wheels and that's exactly what it looked like although you couldn't see the wheels too well. I called up a few people and there were already a few folks partying in my house. Everybody changed into shorts and swim suits. The guys stripped off their shirts. Before long we had a boat chock full of nuts all singing "ooh Wee, Ooh wee Baby, come and let me take you on a Sea Cruise." We set off driving through Mendon like five dimensional survivors from a demented Beach Blanket Bingo flick minus Frankie and Annette with Beach Boy, Dick Dale and Surfaris music blasting from the deck on the deck.

You should have seen the cars as they passed us. Imagine a cool late September afternoon. You're driving down Mendon Town Line Road. Suddenly you see a speed boat approaching you full of lunatic/geniuses mash potatoing, twisting and watusiying to Msirlou or I get Around or Wipeout. My only regret is we didn't take the time to grab Seymour the pig, throw some shades on him and include him in the voyage.

We cruised around Pittsford and Mendon for a half hour. Truck boats use an awful lot of gas. Eventually, we pulled back into my driveway and abandoned ship.

I never doubted Wayne again.

The Starlite era had ended. The truck boat had been revealed. Apparently Wayne's purpose in my life was fulfilled, including one bit of information that I was awake enough to remember. As we were heading back to the house, Wayne asked me if I wanted to take the wheel. Paranoia set in. I could see the headlines, "Local teacher crashes into telephone pole in truck boat filled with passengers without seat belts or life jackets."

Wayne was silent for a moment, keeping his eyes on the road and his hands on the wheel. He asked me "if I remembered the night when all the cars pulled out of the Starlite and then pulled back in."

I said, "Of course I remembered that."

Wayne said that He hadn't believed ME when I told him that story.

Wayne believed it now because he knew the guy who was the first person to pull out, the guy who had started the entire righteous exodus. The guy who helped right the wrong. Turns out the guy was on his first date that night and legitimately wanted to see the movie because he and his date were fans of Will Sampson and Tonto. The guy's named was Ovid and his date was named Julia. The date had been a success.

WELL HELLO HAYLEN

Well, Hello Haylen.

This is your hippocampus speaking. You and Tito have already turned down our hypoglamus. You've jolted our amygdala and you're feeling euphoric. So what if we're a little dumber, we were too smart to begin with and we can use that blissful reward. We earned it. Turn up the music and slip out of those awesome sandals. Dance, girl dance. Doot Doo.

We're not gonna make any complex decisions in the next hour or so. Nobody's home and the lights are getting dimmer. Go ahead and enjoy the distraction of unexpected pleasure. Turn off the alarms. Have another.

You're hearing me now, loud and clear so listen, you're not desperate and you're not unhappy. That's the depressant kicking in. Fight it. Roll with it. You just wanna be happy right? You just want what you want when you want it just like everybody else except they always get it and you figure that you don't. Relax, it's just the label talking.

You find yourself very attracted to Rebecca but you don't know what to say either to yourself or her or your so called "boyfriend" who doesn't give a shit about you and has about as much tenderness as a cactus whereas Rebecca seems to understand soo much.

I can feel my voice fading Haylen. Pretty soon I'll be gone and you'll be on your own with Tito. Last thing I want to say is be careful who you call and where you go tonight because you're not gonna remember any of it tomorrow. Don't call Rebecca and for God's sake don't call Ice Rivers. They will remember everything you say and they will assume that you remember as well. Ice might even write it down. Before I go, grab a pen and make this note RIGHT NOW....Take Metaphysiction from Krell.

A couple more Tito's and you won't even recall writing that note until you see it tomorrow while registering for the semester.

You've been here in the gap many times before

and what the hell, you're still alive.

You've zoomed past one point five

So grab your wrap Haylen, you'll find an empty lap Haylen.

Just promise if you go away, you're not gonna drive.

If you think that it's weed that you need.

Don't forget to inhale until you cough.

Just one last thing, if ya know what I mean

It wouldn't hurt a bit right now to do the dean

I'm your memory and I'm signing off .

LAST DAY OF RADIATION

Today's the day. Last night was the night. I only had to pee four times last night so I got my first half way decent shuteye in months.

At this moment I am resisting the urge to hit the sack and indulge in fatigue.

I'm thinking about the original *Invasion of the Body Snatchers* and *Nightmare on Elm Street*. In both of those flicks, sleep was to be avoided unless you wanted Freddy to slash through your walls or wake up as a pod.

Those movies always bothered me.

I hate the feeling of falling asleep when I don't want to fall asleep. This used to happen to me all the time, particularly on Wednesday nights when I was young.

Because I was big fan of horror films, my parents used to let me stay up "late" to watch Shock Theater which played all of the Lugosi, Karloff and Chaney films. *Frankenstein*, *Dracula*, The *Wolfman*, The *Raven*, The *Mummy, The Black Cat*, *The Invisible Ray*,*The Ghoul*,The Werewolf of London , etc. The show came on came on past my bedtime so it was quite a privilege and quite a challenge.

Plus, I was actually scared by the movies or at least I expected to be.

I would take my position on the carpet in front of our tiny teevee set. The movie would start and before too long, I would realize that I was falling asleep. I learned to recognize the feeling and the "oh no" that accompanied it. I would invariably choose to "rest my eyes" for just a minute during a commercial. I learned after awhile that once I started to rest my eyes, the rest periods would increase in frequency and duration until at last I was asleep on the floor and had to be carted of to bed all the time insisting "I'm awake, I'm awake"

The morning came and I awoke with a sense of failure and a determination to make it all the way through the next week. I realized that once I started to "rest my eyes," it was all over. I would make a conscious effort to “resist the rest” but week after week I failed.

I wasn’t used to failure back in those days and it frightened me more than the movies did. I was learning about temptation and my inability to resist it.

This was my first previews of fatigue but I really didn’t know what fatigue was until a few months ago. There’s a difference between fatigue and being tired, passing out, blacking out, dozing off or being exhausted.

For the past few months, I’ve suffered fatigue and it’s a lot different from “resting my eyes” because in fatigue I’m not even interested in the “movie” that is my life. All I want to do is sleep, well not exactly sleep but more like escape but even in the escaping there is the over-riding sense of failure and guilt as days melt away and merge with nights.

Fatigue sucks.

So as I write these words, I am resisting the urge to “rest my eyes” and to go downstairs to my cave/pit. The urge is strong but not as strong as yesterday and yesterday wasn’t as strong as the day before.

They told me after my last blast of radiation that sometimes the fatigue starts to go away after a week and a half but sometimes it can continue for three or four months or in some cases forever.

Today is exactly a week and a half since my last blast. I’m gonna go the distance. I’m not goin’ downstairs. I’m not gonna turn into a pod person again today. No way. I’ve charged up my camera. I’m snapping flowers. I’ll be leaving for the ballpark in three hours. I’m gonna look good. This is the day I marked down on my calendar for the beginning of my comeback and I’m not gonna rest my eyes until I get back from Frontier Field.

My brother is my best friend and I haven't seen him during this whole situation. I want to see him now. I want him to see me snapping pictures, keeping score, drinking a beer and rooting for the old home team.

Freddy Fatigue can't get me at Frontier Field if I keep my eyes on the ball.

Naomi Silver is the owner of the Red Wings. Her dad Morrie saved the franchise by selling stocks in the team to the Rochester community. My grandfather who took me to my first ball game…a home opener against the Havana Sugar Kings, bought my brother and me a share of stock. I still retain that stock. I love going to the stockholders meeting in February because it reminds me that we might make it through another savage winter and that the Wings will be on the field soon. The idea of getting back to the stadium has motivated me through this entire poisonous process.

Even though it's been around for more than 20 years, I still consider Frontier to be a new stadium. It doesn't have the roof or the ramp or the Arpeako hot dogs of the original Red Wing stadium on Norton Street but to me it's still home, and there's always hope at home.

Can't wait to see ya Naomi.

Looking forward to an ice cold beer from Conehead, a Big Bud with Jim Van Ryne and the gang behind 3rd base and a smile from Dave behind first.

Everything's gonna be awwright.

OVID WARREN PEETS

Even though I think I'm a smart ass, I'm not as smart as I think I am.My name is Ovid Peets.

I'm here to tell you a story about a guy who was proud of his ignorance and worried that he wasn't as dumb as he thought he was . Over the course of our acquaintance this man gratified himself by proving conclusively that he was even dumber than he had hoped.

His name was Thornton Krell. He was my professor. I was taking a seminar class called Metaphysiction at a place called Montgomery Community College. I didn't know what the hell Metaphysiction was and neither did my advisor, Pete Kecorius. As soon as I found out that Pete was vague on the seminar, I decided to throw it into my schedule. I figured I could drop the course later and blame the drop on Pete who would have to admit that he didn't know what the hell he was talking about when we first discussed the offering.

Everyone knows that in a fire, the survival strategy is to drop and roll. Only MCC students know that academic survival strategy is to enroll and then drop.

I can remember the first few minutes of the first class without looking at my notes. I can't look at my notes from any class before Krell's class because I never took notes. I used to draw pictures. I had contempt for anyone who actually took notes. What a waste of time. What a waste of paper. I figured it was all posturing because anytime I would ask anyone to see their "notes" they would always say they didn't have any notes either.

They must have been drawing pictures too or writing those little love letters that begin "I'm sitting in class bored out of mind and thinking about what we did last night……

For some reason I used to draw a hockey rink as seen from a nosebleed seat. After I drew the rink in great detail, including stick figure crowds, I would rest the point of the pen somewhere on the "Ice" and wrist flick the point towards the "Goal" which resembled a large E turned without the middle perpendicular. If I managed to stop the point within the E, the stroke counted as a goal. I would disallow goals in which the stroke was slowed down enough to mimic conscious purpose. Only subconscious strokes counted. Sometimes the pencil and the "ref" would get in long arguments about whether or not a goal should count or not. In this way, with an occasional fake "I'm listening and I'm interested" glance at the teacher, class time passed.

When I wasn't drawing hockey rinks, I was drawing drum sets. This habit was about to change within the first ten minutes of encountering Krell.

They say that a student pretty much makes up his mind how he will get along with a teacher within the first five minutes that the teacher is in front of the class. Even while Krell was taking attendance and reviewing the institute rules, which everyone had heard at the beginning of every class at MCC (and still disobeyed) I was forming my impression of Krell. I kept hearing the song "96 Tears" playing in my brain. Anytime I hear ninety-six tears in my brain, I remember the group that sang the song…Question Mark and the Mysterians with Question Mark written as ?.

So, my initial and lasting impression of Krell was of a mysterious guy who would have a lot of questions for me to consider and about whom I would have a lot of questions which he would probably never consider because I would never pose the questions what with the hockey playing and the drum sets.And that someone would cry: cry, cry, cry; ninety-six tears yeah.

The first thing he did after the preliminary administrivia was to turn his gaze upon the class and make these sounds: (and now I consult the notes that I didn't have at the time that Krell was making the sounds) "Alpha, Beta, Gamma, Delta, Epsilon, Zeta, Eta, Theta, Iota, Kappa, Lambda, Mu, Nu, Xi, Omicron, Pi, Rho, Sigma, Tau, Upsilon, Phi, Chi, Psi, Omega".

Next, he took out a match. Before striking the match he informed us that the sounds he had just made were the letters of the Greek alphabet. He said his first goal was to have everyone in the class be able to repeat those sounds in the time it took a match to burn down to the finger tips. With that he struck the match and recited the alphabet and with a flourish blew out the match in plenty of time.

"I'm going to repeat the alphabet. You will take notes while I recite. Then, I'm going to call on one of you...I will light the match. You will recite the Greek alphabet before the match burns my fingers. You may use your notes"

With that, he repeated "Alpha, Beta, Gamma, Delta, Epsilon, Zeta, Eta, Theta, Iota, Kappa, Lambda, Mu, Nu, Xi, Omicron, Pi, Rho, Sigma, Tau, Upsilon, Phi, Chi, Psi, Omega".

I stopped drawing the hockey rink and right there on the still freezing ice, I took my first serious notes Alfa, Bayta, Gamma, Delta, Epsilon, Zayta, Eighta, Theta, Iota, Kappa, Lambda, Mew, New, Zi, Omicron, Pi, Rho, Sigma, Tau, Upsilon, Phi, Chi, Sigh, Omega.

I wasn't looking around to see if anybody else was taking notes.

Krell paused at Omega. He looked at the attendance roster. He took a match from the pack. He said, "Mr. Troy. You will give me back the alphabet. You may use your notes. I will count to five and light the match"

I don't remember much about Mr. Troy except that he was wearing a tee shirt that said, "Weed Man". When Krell got to five, Troy got to his feet and headed to the door. With the match still burning in Krell's hand, Troy looked back at the spontaneous combustion in the front of the room. "Kiss my fart" he yelled and walked out the door.

Krell kept the match burning in silence until it reached his finger tips at which point he said, "Ouch" and shook the match out.

“Kiss my fart” Krell mused aloud “what an interesting juxtaposition of the physical upon the invisible. He might have been a great student but alas, I’m afraid that’s the last time we’ll see Troy although we will talk about him quite often.”

He took out another match. “Let’s try it again. Hayen Kamp, it‘s your turn”

Helen read the alphabet from her notes. She finished with plenty of match to spare.

“Very good, Haylen.” said Krell while snapping his fingers with the loudest snap I‘d heard since my left handed sixth grade clarinet teacher snapped me out of music lessons for incorrectly counting measures. Krell’s snaps, on the other hand, conveyed praise not criticism “How do you account for your success?”

“I read from my notes” said Helen.

“And before you read them........”

“I wrote them.”

"And before you wrote them?” Krell asked.

“I listened, Mr Krell.”

“And in literary terms, Haylen, what verbal exercise are we involved in right now?”

“A dialogue.”

“A Socratic dialogue to be more specific. Thank You Haylen for introducing the basic tenets of this class. The dullest pencil on the roughest paper has a better memory than the sharpest brain in the smoothest intellect. Aristotle, the student of Plato wrote very little...what remains of his work is a hodgepodge of his notes combined with the notes of the students he was teaching in his Lyceum, Any questions?”

In the pause that inevitably follows any teacher asking if there are any questions, two impressions raced through my mind. 1: Helen might be the Hawking of the class which greatly increased my odds of bozohood and 2: The teacher had a Southern accent when he called on Helen. He called her Haylen.

The pause ended as it always does with a dork with a question.

Arthur Gregor raised his hand. Krell nodded in his direction.

Gregor asked "Well, Mr. Krell what exactly is the definition of metaphysics and the relationship of that definition to metaphysiction"

Krell responded, " With all due respect, the answer to that question comes at the end of the class not at the beginning because the entire purpose of this seminar is to explore the intellectual journey that led to metaphysics and later metaphysiction".

Krell continued, "Haylen has already touched upon some of the primary components. We will be learning how Socrates led to Plato how Plato led to Aristotle and how Aristotle led to metaphysics. In a nutshell, Socrates asked questions in verbal dialogue. Plato was the student of Socrates. Plato listened to the dialogues that Socrates narrated. Plato recorded the dialogues which were a history of the philosophical life of Socrates. Socrates only spoke. Plato listened and took notes. Plato added his own thoughts to the thoughts of Socrates which he had noted. He passed his thoughts and notes on to others who were taking note of his thoughts which were the thoughts of Socrates filtered through the lens of Plato. Thus, Plato became a teacher."

Krell went to the blackboard and printed the words **Socrates**, **Aristotle** and **Plato**. He began drawing lines between and amongst the names and explained; "Aristotle was a student of Plato. Aristotle added his own thoughts to Plato's thoughts which were themselves notes upon the thoughts of Socrates which led through logic and biology and astrology to metaphysics. Aristotle was the first teacher of metaphysics. I'm not going to even try to describe the lineage that led from Aristotle to Krell because it's taken me my entire life up to this very second to unravel that journey which is continuing even as I speak and upon which you, Mr. Gregor are a fellow traveler until you follow the path of Troy".

By this time, the hockey game had ended and I was, for the first time, taking notes furiously, afraid that I would be called upon to suffer the fate of Troy. I know for sure that I was taking notes at this time because the above paragraphs are an interpretive reconstructions of the words of Krell based upon the actual notes of that first class on that last hockey rink upon which I glanced as I composed the last paragraph and will be consulting for the rest of this effort.

See, another thing about notes is, they stick around. If they didn't there would be no Aristotle and God knows what else there wouldn't be...maybe even God.

If nothing else this class of Krell's was, by definition, noteworthy.

I'm not sure if my notes are worthy of the noteworthiness of Krell's class (what with the high probability of bozos on this bus) because I myself may be a bozo and if you're on this particular bus, holding on to the handrail next to mine, you may be a bozo as well.

Unless you're a Hawking.

By the time I left class that day only three of us remained, myself, Helen and Julia. Arthur had taken an early lab break and had not returned. Weedman Troy had apparently enrolled and dropped, at least that's what Krell said at the end of the period.

"The bad news is that five is the minimum enrollment to hold a seminar. The good news for you four survivors, if in fact the seminar survives, is that if we continue the class and I use the traditional grading curve, the E has already directed me to kiss his fart."

When you're riding in my bus, in which failure is always an option, it's reassuring to hear the E has left the building. I made up my mind I was in this class for the duration. I even had notes to prove my determination.

Riding this wave of confidence and conviction, I decided to approach Helen and confess my embarrassment at Krell's mispronunciation of her name.

"Excuse me. I was in your Metaphysiction class. I couldn't figure out why the teacher had a Southern accent only when he said your name. Helen is such a nice, classical name. I'm sorry he had to butcher it."

Helen looked at me as if she were looking at a dog turd tidbit on the sole of a wedding shoe.

"Why thank you for your sensitivity, Oafid. Not only have you underestimated the teacher but also you've insulted me and my parents. My father's name is Haynes. My mothers name is Helen. They named me Haylen. I'm sorry my name isn't classical enough for you"

Haylen turned on her heel and was gone before I had the opportunity to clear either my throat, my name or hers or her parents or Krell.

SECOND CLASS

I beat the teacher to the second class. We all did. I was the last to arrive not including Krell.

Arthur, Haylen and Julia were all in their seats. I nodded at Arthur, tried to avoid Haylen's gaze by looking down at the floor. Then after noting the awesome old school sandals that were between the floor and Haylen's soles, I got a better look at Julia.

Julia was not a beautiful woman but there was something about her that demanded my attention. After about two-seconds I realized what that something was. Julia was dressed in an exact replica of the curtain rendered green velvet gown that Scarlett O'Hara had worn to visit Rhett Butler when he was in jail where he was sick and tired of seeing women in rags; where he was relieved to see that Scarlett was not in rags and was ready to give her anything until he discovers that her hands are filled with callouses.

I was surfing in this state of stupefaction and cinematic reverie when Krell entered the classroom. Apparently I had walked in on the conclusion of the customary debate about how long the class waited for the tardy teacher before disbanding, five minutes for adjunct or TA, ten minutes for assistant professor, fifteen minutes for full professor.

Nobody knew what category Krell was so I have the feeling if he would have been five-seconds late, the class would have been empty by the time he entered which would have spelled the end of metaphysiction, right there. But there he was right in the nick of time. I took out my notebook and pencil. I gazed at the Greek alphabet just in case we began where we left off.

Krell said, "Well folks it looks like we have a class. It seems that after Troy burned out, he immediately dropped the class which caused Jeff Debes of interdisciplinary to have a meeting with Paula Merowsky of the Art department office which led to a meeting with Eric Hartz of the philosophy department which led to a meeting with

Barbara Williams of the English Dept. which led to a meeting with Joe Lipardi the supervisor of investiture and fabled corn hole pitcher which led to a meeting with Eric Rich of adjunct education which led to a meeting with Dean Phillip Thrall who okayed the class fifteen minutes ago while I waited outside his office."

"In case you're wondering, every one of those people make much more money than I do. So, Julia, when I strike this match, tell me the Greek alphabet and when you're finished I'll explain education to you."

With that Krell struck his match and Julia finished her recitation beautifully before the flame was gone with the wind.

Krell congratulated Julia and began his lecture.

"Once upon a time there was a guy who was a terrific learner. Let's call him Torch." Krell began and continued. "Everything activated Torch's curiosity which fired up his intellect which filled him with inexhaustible creative, emotional, intuitional and investigative energy. Torch learned everything he could about each person, place, thing or idea that he encountered with his senses, with his emotions, with his feelings and with his intuitions.One day it dawned on Torch that the best way to increase his own learning was to give away what he had. Torch decided to teach."

Krell printed the word **TEACH** on the board and continued.

"When the teacher is ready, the students will appear and when the students are ready the teacher will appear. In the early days of Torch's teaching, there were many appearances and disappearances. Usually, they were out of synch. Sometimes, Torch's teaching schedule got a little unpredictable what with the perpetual investigations of all things attracting his attention for random amounts of time. Similarly, his students, their curiosity activated by Torch, were out and about making their own discoveries, building their own toys. Eventually, one of his students, let's call him Arclipides, came up with an idea."

Krell wrote **ARCLIPEDES** on the board and continued.

“After a session of sharing on the steps of the Atheneum, Arclipides asked, ‘Why don’t we all come back here to these very same steps on the same day at the same time next week?’ Next week arrived and everybody showed up. Everybody was only four people and Torch, the teacher. The four people were Lysis, Arclipides, Sachelli, and Lyvia. As time went on the four people grew to forty people. The forty people grew into a hundred people. At this point Arclipedes came up with his second big idea, ‘why don’t we break this group into four groups. One group can meet on Monday, the next group on Tuesday, the third group on Wednesday and the fourth group on Thursday'.”

Krell wrote **SCHEDULE** on the board and continued.

“Torch had a little problem with this big idea. Even though meeting with the people was definitely feeding his learning habit, four days a week was a bit much. Torch suggested two groups on Monday and two groups on Wednesday. Arclipedes went along with the idea. Arclipedes divided the hundred into four groups of twenty-five and told them which day and time to show up on the steps.As time went on, the hundred turned into thousands and the thousands turned into millions and the millions turned into billions.The steps turned into hundreds of thousand of schools.Torch continued to learn. Sachelli, Lysis and Lyviia went on to become the first faculty. Arclipedes became the first administrator.”

Krell wrote **ADMINISTRATOR** on the board and next to the word a dollar sign. Then he continued

"Eventually, Arclipedes and his followers started telling everybody where to go, what to learn and how to teach. All of the followers of Arclipedes seemed to have a natural interest in finances so the gathering places grew bigger and bigger as a price tag began to be attached to learning. Torch never had much interest in money and neither did Sachelli, Lysis or Lyviia. Learning was their treasure and giving away what they had earned (after all, learned is earned plus an l for either life or love) was the best way to preserve and enrich their intellectual treasure.This was fine for Arclipedes. Altruism always cuts cost.”

Krell paused for a moment as a bell rang somewhere.

Krell shrugged his shoulders at the sound of the bell as if indicating "See that's a perfect example of what I'm talking about".

Then, he continued: "Way, way back before the steps turned into schools, Torch and Arclipedes were on a collision course. When the crash finally happened only Arclipedes walked away. Arclipedes had amassed more money and with more money had come more power. All Torch had was teaching, learning and the love and respect of his students. Trouble. Mismatch. Arclipedes insisted that what Torch was espousing was not good for the people. The powers that be agreed. Torch drank the Kool Aid."

Krell wrote **HEMLOCK** on the board and continued.

"The remaining faculty insisted upon some degree of intellectual freedom if they were to continue coming back to the steps. This was the beginning of tenure.Tenure is to education what beer is to Homer Simpson; the cause of as well as the solution to all of the problems in the classroom. Arclipedes 'not good for the people' eventually turned into the standard administrative method of suppressing progressive ideas while sustaining status quo. 'Not good for the people' became 'not good for the kids' if an innovative idea needed to be stopped or 'good for the kids' if a stale idea needed to be preserved."

Krell paused, looked out the window and wrote STATUS QUO on the board before he continued.

"Today, for example we have middle schools. Not only do we have middle schools but those schools usually start the earliest in the morning and contain the kids who would benefit most from getting more sleep. Going back to K-8 schools would simply be 'not good for the kids' until the decision was made to return to K-8 schools, the justification for which will be that it has suddenly become 'good for the kids'. Other examples abound. The factory schedule. SAT exams. Standardized testing. The categorization and separation of knowledge into subjects and departments. The hierarchy of the sciences. How did anyone ever determine that biology was easier than chemistry and chemistry easier than physics. For those seeking entry into the closed fraternity/sorority of "science" biology is traditionally taken first, then chemistry then physics.This is how that particular hierarchy was determined. An Arclipedean confronted this choice at the beginning of the twentieth century and determined the order of scientific investigation, the way Arclipedians determine many subdivisions of learning. Alphabetical order."

"Thus we have," and Krell wrote on the board.

Biology

Chemistry

Physics

and

they are all

Good

For

the Kids

Until

They're

Not."

Krell wondered if there were any questions.

I raised my hand.

"So, Mr. Krell, physics is no more difficult than biology?"

Krell turned his gaze on me as a cat gazes at a mouse except with kindness rather than ferocity. "You're name is Ovid, right? That's an unusual name. Where did it come from?"

"My father named me after an eye doctor who cured him of lazy eye. His name was Dr. Ovid Pearson. He operated on my Dad's eyes."

"The reason I asked," said Krell, "is that I have a great affection for the Latin poet Ovid whose most famous work is the Art of Love."

As if on cue Arthur sneezed snottily.

"Well, Ovid, do you think it's more complicated or important to figure out how we got here than who we are or how to build a television. All the sciences are the same. We've constructed the borders as another means of educational elimination of the unworthy."

He took a sip from whatever he was drinking and continued.

"The more the Arclipedeans took over the steps, the more schools came to resemble businesses. This was the great Arclipedian strategy. Find something essential, turn that essential into a business and keep the business a secret. Thus we have the great experiment of American public education. The schools serve as filtering devices for American society. The idea was for the rich to get richer, the poor to get poorer and for the multitude in the middle to miss the picture entirely. And for the Arclipedeans to make money, raise tuition and determine what is 'good for the kids.'"

Krell wrote **TUITION** on the blackboard and then he continued.

"Arclipedeans realized that everybody loves rags to riches stories, so the most brilliant 2% of the poor and 18% of the middle class were permitted to pass through the screen. This permission was based upon stupendous grades which were largely based upon persistence, note-taking and subscription to values that were 'good for kids'. Value to society was determined by the college attended at the end of the twelve year rainbow of public education. The kids with the most money went to the best schools which were, by Arclipedean definition, the schools that cost the most to attend. As soon as those kids graduated, they were expected to contribute generously to the alumni fund in support of their schools which kept the coffers of their selected schools full which enhanced the reputation of that school which made the prestige of a degree from that school so much greater. It was possible for a child from a rich family to go to a great school and become the most powerful man on the face of the earth even as that kid without the money could or should have Peter principled out as an assistant manager at Wendy's."

Krell wrote **HAMBURGER** on the board. I wanted one bad.

Then he continued.

"This is what Arclipedes foresaw when he said, 'let's all meet here at the same time next week.' What to do with the masses of people who didn't have the money, the brains, the values or the persistence to make it through the screen to the Ivy League or even the Big Ten or even the SUNY system.There must be business possibilities in that mess er mass. We built colleges without dormitories and called those colleges junior colleges or community colleges. At these places we set up one last screen for entrance to the American dream. One final fling to begin to grab the brass ring."

He wrote **MCC** on the board. He looked around the room and continued.

"We can always find teachers who will work for next to nothing. We can put those teachers who will work for nothing in front of students who have next to nowhere to go. We can hire a load of budding Arclipedeans to keep the cruise on course, even if the cruise sometimes resembles a cross between *McHale's Navy* and the *Love Boat*. They can be Deans (short for Arclipedean) and department heads and project managers and instructional specialists and financial aid counselors and bursars etc, etc, etc. They can help us determine 'what's good for kids'. In the end there will be a classroom with a minimum of five students and a teacher, or,

in our case,

four."

I noticed that whenever Krell wanted to make a point, he seriously

slowed

down

the pace

of his speech.

I looked around and noticed that neither Julia nor Arthur were taking notes of any kind. I was still too embarrassed to look at Haylen. I did look at her foot and noticed that her awesome sandal was half on and half off.

Did that mean she was taking notes or not?

When I raised my glance upward, I noticed that Arthur had a gloved hand in the air. I hadn't noticed the glove before. I figured Arthur was doing some sort of Wacko Jacko comedy act or something.

Krell spotted the glove and nodded at Arthur.

"Question?"

"Yes," said Arthur, "Are we gonna have a test on this stuff?"

Arthur looked over at Julia, who nodded her head first at Arthur then at Krell.

Julia raised her hand. "Yes," said Julia "how exactly will we be graded in this course?"

Krell answered, “Let me answer the second question first. The grading will be metaphysictional and as far as the first question, thank you for reminding me to bring up another early Arclipidean

whose

name

was

testacles.”

Krell wrote **TESTACLES** on the board and continued.

“Back in the torch-lit prearclipidean days of learning, all instructional elements were in balance. Structure was in balance with substance. Sensing was in balance with thinking. Feeling in balance with intuition. Process in balance with coverage. Evaluation in balance with instruction.The distance between evaluation and instruction was minimal. Evaluation was part of instruction and instruction part of evaluation. Self-evaluation was evident. If a student could follow the instruction that meant the student could grasp the body of knowledge within the instruction. The level of individual grasp could be ascertained by the intensity with which the student applied the instruction to his, or in Lyvia’s case, her life. In other words the illumination of torch was built upon two principles: 1) Take what you need and leave the rest. 2) By your works, you will be judged. Something about this didn’t sit well with Arclipides. The problem began with sub-division and led to differentiation. How could differentiations within sub-divisions be articulated? That’s when Testacles revolutionized education. ‘Why don’t we demand that the students repeat the words of the teacher to show that they have heard the words?’”

Krell wrote the word **REPETITION** on the board and then wrote it again and smirked.

"Arclipedes thought about this for a few days. When next he saw Testacles, he said, 'I like your idea about the students repeating the words of the teacher. The student who repeats the words most accurately gets the highest ranking in his subdivision.We need a word to describe the instrument that we will use to determine the level of repetition and the differentiation based upon that repetition. I've decided we should name that instrument after you, because it was your idea. When we ask students to repeat the words of the teacher, we'll call that demand for repetition a test. Now we need a word to call the differentiations themselves. What should we call the results of the ya know, the uh test. It should be something like steps indicating movement up or down. What's another word for steps, Testacles "

"Ummm, steps are actually grades"

Krell wrote **GRADES** on the board and continued, pretending that he was both Arclipedes and Testacles. When speaking as Arclipedes Krell spoke in a higher, more rapid pitch. When Testacles, Krell slowed down and spoke in a deep basso profundo.

"Grades are great, Testacles. Students will take tests to earn grades. The higher the grades, the greater the rewards. 'Testacles, you're a genius'. Relentless, determined Testacles (pronounced test ah kleez) was honored but he had yet another question. "Which words of the teacher should we demand that the students repeat on these tests? Should the same words be asked of every student even if they have different teachers?"

"The words", answered Arclipedes, "should be the words that are

best

for

the people"

Testacles, whose spirit was not easily broken, had one more question. “Who then determines what words of what teachers are best for the people/”

Arclipedes knew the answer to that one. “Testacles, my virile friend,

We

are

the people.”

The class continued but my notes ended with

we

are

the

people.

STOPPING AT THE LIBRARY AFTER CLASS

After class I decided to cruise over to the town library to see if I could check out a copy of *Cat's Cradle*, *Catch 22*, *Catcher in the Rye* or *Crime and Punishment*. Krell had claimed that all of those books were examples of metaphysiction. Hey if I can save a buck using the library, I'll save that buck.

Libraries are great anyway. Where else can a guy go to search for something that he wants, find that something and have somebody give him that something for free as long as the guy promises to bring that something back in a reasonable time.

Of course, even that level of freedom and civilization poses an ethical problem for some guys.

I know a guy who steals books from the library. In his mind he's not stealing them, he's just making his own due date. He'll swipe a book. He'll take it home. He'll take a leisurely five month read. He'll slip the book back in the slot when he's finished, if he gets finished.

No problem.

Anyway, when I was walking into the library, I noticed that somebody had unloaded maybe fifty cardboard boxes full of books on the sidewalk in front of the building. There were at least a thousand and maybe twenty-five hundred books in those boxes. The sky was gray. Rain was drizzling down upon these abandoned books.

I stopped by the pile and looked at a couple of titles. One of the books that I picked up was called *Rock of Ages: The Rolling Stone History of Rock and Roll.* Another book which looked like a prayer book was called *As Bill Sees It*. A third book was called *Myths and Facts: A guide to the Arab-Israeli Conflict.*

I tried to form a mental picture of the guy who had read and deep-sixed all these books and what kind of drama led to that abandonment/donation.

The only guy I could think of was Krell.

I assumed that all of the books in his collection would be equally compelling/ comKrelling. I figured that when I came out, I could grab a dozen or so soaked books, dry them out and make them mine.

I entered the library. I picked up Catcher and Catch. I walked around the stacks for a few minutes looking at periodicals. Unlike the guy I told you about earlier, I checked out my books at the circulation desk in a civilized way.

Maybe twenty minutes had passed. I went outside, intending to grab some soaked books.The garbage truck had beat me to the books. Of the fifty boxes only four remained. I watched as the burly garbage guy picked up box number forty-six of fifty and threw it into the grinder. Forty-five boxes had already been devoured. Millions of words. Hours, weeks, years, centuries of attention and creation. The garbage guy noticed me looking at him. He hit me with a glance that howled "yeah?"

I said, "kinda sad, really"

He said, "It will all be recycled"

I said, "You got it" and walked to my car.

I had learned something about life, death and eternity. The garbage guy had been yet another teacher. His name might as well have been Yoric. Mine might as well be Torch

I got in my car and headed South. I wondered what the guy who had brought all of those boxes of books to the library would have thought if he knew his beloved books would not even get into the door of the library. His donation was in vain.

It reminded me of the time that a buddy of mine accidentally ran over a stray cat who was looking for some shade. He was backing out of my family's driveway. He heard a tiny thump.He got out of the car. He found the lifeless cat. He put the cat in a bag. There would be no letting this cat out of this bag, not as a functioning cat anyway. My buddy brought the bag full of broken cat to our front door. He rang the bell. When my mother answered the door, my friend said: "This cat died in vain"

I've often wondered about that quote. My friend was suggesting that the cat in the bag had been ripped off before realizing its purpose in life. This suggests that cats actually have a purpose in life. If that purpose is to live nine lives, then the cat in the bag definitely died in vain.

Or maybe the cat's purpose in life, like all of ours, is to simply not be hungry or to get run over and become part of a legend.

I was feeling hungry so I stopped at Dee's delicatessen and bought a ridiculously huge submarine sandwich with everything aboard.

I continued to aim South, heading towards Keenan Park.

KEENAN PARK

Keenan Park is a great place to relax, meditate the purpose of cats, contemplate American education, take a nature walk and/ or eat a sandwich. As I approached the Park, I noticed paper plates with arrows and words nailed to telephone poles. The plates read Civil War Re-enactment ahead. The arrows pointed towards Keenan Park. I noticed another word on some of the plates. That word was FREE. Hey, if it's FREE it's me.

Me, the words, my car, my submarine sandwich and the arrows were all headed for a collision at the same place.

I got out of my car at Keenan and started looking for a bench upon which to sink into my submarine. That's when I came face to face with Robert E. Lee.

General Lee was heading North as I was heading South. I was amazed to see General Lee. What do you say when you're walking South into a park to eat a submarine sandwich after a morning with Krell and you run into the replica of a dead rebel general who has reconstituted himself and is heading North?

I figured a crisp salute would be a good start. I snapped one off. General Lee smiled beatifically upon me and said, "At ease, Johnny".

I relaxed and spoke "General Lee, you were a genius. You waged one hell of a campaign. If only the artillery had been more accurate, Pickett's charge might have worked and we'd be in a whole different ballgame right now."

"Actually," said General Lee, "maybe not all that different. American politics today are more or less dominated by the old Confederacy if you think about it. So my men who were slaughtered goin' up the hill didn't totally die in vain"

"Unlike a cat I once owned," I replied.

"I have a cat too" said General Lee. "I mean not me as General Lee but me the guy who dresses up like General Lee at these here re-enactments. My cat once killed a Doberman named Duke"

"That sounds like one helluva story, uh General Lee"

"Just call me Lee. That's my given name, son. Lee Edward Roberts. I guess it was inevitable that I would end up masquerading as Robert E. Lee. For all my years in school, they kept calling my name directory style whenever they took attendance. Ovah and ovah and ovah. One day, it hit me. My purpose in life. A simple twist of fate"

I wanted to hear about the cat and the Doberman but my stomach was starting to growl. I resisted my urge to inquire further. I snapped off another salute and said the only thing I could think of at such an odd moment: "Thank God for Aristotle"

General Lee nodded in agreement.

"Generally, I agree" is what I think I heard General Lee say as we parted and I headed further down the path, deeper into the Park.I continued to head south towards the bench in front of the pavilion past the meadow. As I strode towards the bench, two dozen people on horseback began to congregate at opposite ends of the meadow. A dozen were dressed in blue, another dozen in grey. All twenty-four were brandishing wooden swords.

I reached the bench. I vowed never to be hungry again. I unwrapped my sub and began chomping just as the two dozen cavalry men began to charge towards each other.

I didn't mind the noise. I actually kinda liked it. The submarine tasted a little better because of it. It wasn't the noise that was causing my thought processes to grow blurry and dark.

I wasn't sure if what I was watching was a calvary or a cavalry re-enactment. I knew one of them was the correct word for the place where Christ got nailed and the other was the correct word for soldiers on horses.

I knew that soldiers on horses must have been quite the military breakthrough and quite an advantage over terrified, soon to be trampled soldiers not on horses.

I knew that soldiers on horses turned out to be quite a disadvantage when the fabled Polish calvary encountered German soldiers not on horses but rather in tanks. The Polish cavalry was blown to smithereens.

Even in my mind I started using both words for one meaning. I could settle for a fifty percent grade on my internal vocabulary. If I kept my mouth shut, no one would discover that I didn't know the difference between calvary and cavalry.

My muddled thoughts grew darker when I thought of that proud Polish calvary splattered across their particular slaughter field. That was a bad scene for sure but nowhere near as bad a scene as nailing the son of God to a cross after whipping the crap out of him and crowning him with thorns like they did at cavalry.

Meanwhile the cavalry's in the meadow were having the time of their lives running into each other while flailing wooden, fake swords. I realized the swords were crosses painted black and silver with one perpendicular four times longer than the other.

These replica forces were attacking each other with crosses.

I imagined all of the crosses with an outstretched figure upon them. I imagined the blue and the gray horsemen attacking each other with half-assed crucifixes.In that way, my description of the charge as either calvary or cavalry would have been correct.

Oh yeah, even on this bright afternoon my thinking had once again grown dark and out of focus.

"... in focus"

I heard her before I saw her and I didn't clearly hear her until after I saw her. When I saw her, I didn't really see her. I saw Scarlett and Scarlett was hugging me.

"Are you talking to me?" I said in subdued DeNiro as I turned my head to the left. The face I saw inside the green bonnet belonged to Julia.

"Yes, I am" said Julia," and I was talking to you before when you were lost somewhere in dark space. I said, 'hi', you didn't answer. Then I said, 'get your thinking back in focus' and you turned your head my way, all Taxi Driver. If you don't mind me saying so, you still don't appear to be seeing things too clearly"

I returned her greeting, told her that I didn't mind her saying so and added "that's quite a projection," even as I noted with internal alarm and external denial how accurate she was.

Julia said, "I know a lot about projection. My grandfather was an arc-light carbon projectionist at the old RKO Palace. My father was a projectionist at Loew's before he became a megaplex manager. He would like me to become a professional projectionist but my mother has different ideas. She wants me to keep my projections intuitive."

"Well, what made you project that I was out of focus?" I asked

"Guys between eighteen and twenty-five are always out of focus, sometimes more so than other times but always muddled, always absorbed by noise. Lots of times the puddle grows darker than it ought to be" said Julia.

I remembered how much the noise of the calvary charge helped me to enjoy my sandwich.

Julia/Scarlett was starting to scare me.

I feigned indifference.

“And upon what does your Dad base his projection”

“He bases his projection about the attention span of people on his policy for projectionists at his plex”.

“He bases his projection about the attention span of people on his policy for projectionists at his plex? Is that what you said?” I asked Julia.

“That’s what I said”, she answered.“There’s nothing wrong with your listening”

“Well, Julia, do you want me to project as to how your Pop’s policy for projectionists at his plex affects his projection about the attention span of people or are you going to explain”

“Ovid, I’m flattered, You remembered my name. Why don’t you go ahead and project”

“Julia I’m afraid my projection, according to your father’s projection, would be dark and out of focus. Why don’t you go ahead and explain”

I finished up my plastic twenty ounce bottle of Diet coke and tossed it at the waste basket next to the bench. A miracle…it went in. I pumped my fist and said, 'yes’ which Julia took as a signal to explain.

“Fair enough. Back in the days of Grand-Dad” Julia began, “movie theaters could seat many more viewers. Some, if not most theaters could sit a thousand folks at a time. Still, for all those people, they had only one projectionist operating two projectors. Each projector would carry a reel of film. Just before the reel ran out on the first projector, the projectionist would flip on the second projector which he had just loaded with the next reel. Didja ever notice those little scratches or circles that show up on the upper right corner of movies and wonder if you were seeing things?"

"Yeah, I've noticed those marks. They even show up on teevee when the old movies are played"

"Those marks signaled that the reel that was playing was coming to an end. The projectionist would fire up the second projector and at the exact second that projector one ran out of film, projector two picked up the slack and threw its light on the screen. As soon as projector two took over, projector one went into rewind. When the rewind was finished, the projectionist would take that rewound reel off the projector and replace that reel with the next reel which would be ready to go on projector one as soon as the film ran out on projector two."

"That's reely interesting" I punned as I felt my focus starting to slip. Julia missed the quip and continued.

"Those were the old days. One theater, one screen, two projectors, one projectionist. My Dad's multiplex has sixteen theaters, only two of which have more than three hundred seats. One has five hundred, the other has three hundred fifty. The other twelve range from one hundred to three hundred, Most of them are three hundred."

"Ya know, Julia, it's funny. I've always wanted to bowl a three hundred game. I think I'd rather bowl a three hundred game than hit a hole in one. It's close though. Which would you prefer"

"I'd prefer that you maintain your focus and let me finish what we started. If that's too much to ask just say so"

Here I was presented with the perfect storm, the ideal situation to use the greatest line of all time. I knew that all I had to do was say, 'Frankly, my dear, I don't give a damn' turn my back on Julia and exit stage North. I would have a story for my future wife, my future kids, my future grand-kids maybe even Krell.

And I was pretty sure Julia would sit there, watch me

walk

away

and

say

tomorrow

is

another

day.

I'm polite. I blinked. Castles made of sand melt into the sea.

Julia continued.

"Nowadays, in the megaplex, we have one projectionist operating eight projectors.This bit of planning saves us seven salaries for starters. That's part of the reason why we stagger the starting times of movies. Another reason is to keep a steady stream of customers passing by the concessions stand".

"Who can watch a movie without popcorn?" I asked.

Julia, at least one step ahead of me answered, "And who can eat popcorn, especially popcorn loaded with extra salt and butter, without having a soft drink?"

"I'm getting thirsty just talking about it," I said while glancing at the empty Diet coke in the waste basket and wishing I had more.

"That's why the invention of cup holders in megaplex seats actually saved movies" she said while unfastening her bonnet.

Julia continued. "The projectionists can change the reels on eight projectors at a time by changing reels on one while the other seven go unattended. This more efficient operation does run the risk that other films not being attended to might snag in the projector and get burnt by the lamp. To prevent this from happening, the projectionists who work for my father routinely expand the gap between the gate that supports the film and the lamp. This provides a margin of safety. It also results in the films being shown out of focus.The higher the population of males between eighteen and twenty-five in the opening weekend audience, the greater the gap between the gate and the lamp. Nobody ever complains. Ever."

Whoa. I thought that I was beginning to see the big picture.

I reflected back to Julia's original projection with a question, "And you're projecting that we young guys don't complain because we don't know the movies are not in focus because our perception of life itself is out of focus therefore in synch with the out of focus film being projected behind us that shows up in front of us?"

"Exacata mundo," replied Julia. "And there's more. See, Dad's got to save money on projector lamps. Those things cost a grand a pop. The more play we can get from the bulb, the more money we save. So we play the out of focus movies that you guys watch on the projectors with the dimmest lamps.These are the lamps that we should replace but we can use on you guys because you never complain about the darkness or the out of focus projection because we turn the volume ten percent louder in the dim bulb auditorium than we do in the other auditoriums. As long as you guys hear a lot of noise, you don't particularly care what you see. And whatever it is that you're seeing, you don't mind if it's dark as long as it's loud."

The cavalry charge in the background had quieted down for a moment. I hoped the noise would begin again so I could concentrate on what Julia was saying and not be so distracted by looking at her. Especially without her bonnet. She was starting to piss me off.

Julia stood up suddenly and took a furtive look North followed by a lingering look South. As she stood, I got another look. Julia was vee shaped, or should I say vee vee shaped with the bottom vee inverted and the top vee tottering precariously on the bottom vee.

No woman looks like that. Julia was wearing a corset. Why not, Scarlett wore one. Julia was channeling Scarlett . Fiddle Dee Dee.

To my great relief, the calvary in the meadow started another charge. The din helped me relax. I wanted to ask Julia about the corset but didn't know where to start. I figured that I'd feign innocence and since she was so good at reading my mind maybe she'd take the bait.

" Julia, your dress is beautiful. Is your outfit authentic?"

She smiled infuriatingly and changed the subject.

"Where did you ever get a name like Ovid?"

"Well, when I was young, I had a problem with my eyes and......"

Julia interrupted and stepped a little closer, "Oh yeah, I remember now..what's your middle name?"

"Warren. That's my middle name."

Julia repeated my name aloud a couple of times, "Ovid Warren Peets hmmmm. Ovid Warren Peets.

I had the feeling she'd get half the puzzle and she did.

"War and Peace. Damn, your last two names are war and peace"

"That's only the half of it" I confessed.

"Explain, Warren" She demanded.

"My first name is Ovid. Like Krell said in class, Ovid was a Roman poet. His most famous poem was The Art of Love. If you put the whole thing together, my name is Art, Love, War and Peace. My father thought that pretty well summed up life"

I could tell Julia was impressed because she shut up for a couple of minutes while she once again stood and looked North and then South. She moved a little closer still and asked "what do you prefer Ovid, art or love?"

I tried again. "Is your dress comfortable"

She came even closer, tilted her face upward and fluttered her eyelashes.

BIVOUACKED WITH BOBBI ROBERTS

Twenty-four hours earlier, Julia was bivouacked in the midst of a huge misunderstanding between the over-all Confederate commander Robert E. Lee and his wife, Barbara 'Bobbi' Roberts'.

Julia had been participating in these encampments semi-willingly since she was a child. Because she no longer felt that she was a child, Julia didn't want to come to these "freak shows" any longer. The dustup began when Julia arrived in civvies and reported directly to the commander.

When the commander asked Julia why she was out of costume, Julia nuclear dumped."I'm out of costume because I'm sick and tired of feeding people crappy popcorn at the plex. I never want to have that giant salt shaker in my hand again. I've lifted my last box of Diet Pepsi syrup and brewed my last batch of fake pop. I'm tired of Dad, thinking that I'm going to get into the theater business. That business is falling apart.Everybody knows that movies now are nothing more than sneak previews for DVD's and pay TV."

A cannon boomed off in the distance as Julia rubbed her eyes and continued,

"Mom wants me to be a seamstress. I can't sew worth a damn. She knows it. I know itI'm going to community college now. I'm going there because my grades sucked in high school because I missed way too much school traveling around to these encampments. None of my history teachers gave me any credit for being here.The other teachers just thought encampment was odd; a gathering of live in the past doofusses with too much time on their hands. I'm having trouble keeping up in my classes. There are too many students in all of them, except one and that one has only four students and a weird teacher. There's a guy in that class who wears a glove all the time, who looks like he's got some complicated issues but he doesn't pay any attention to me. I don't like the other two students and I don't know what in hell the teacher is talking about nor how he intends to mark anybody."

By this time, Julia had tears streaming down her face." I can't stand my job. I'm a disappointment to my parents. I'm invisible at school. I have no future plans. I might get thrown out of a flunky college. I'm attracted to a weirdo with a glove who doesn't know I exist.I've come to believe that these encampments that I used to love are egotistical freak shows. I'm not the cute little kid at the camp anymore. I'm a nobody, a nothing."

Lee Lee was a bit conflicted.

Lee Roberts was picking up a snootful of the most alluring perfume emanating from Julia, desperation, vulnerability, sincerity and low self-esteem. This combination of pheremonic emotional aromas has always created an irresistible bouquet for the opportunistic male. Lee Roberts was such an animal.

General Robert E. Lee, on the other hand, was all about empathy, action, and healing. General Robert E. Lee was a God-like perfect example of man at the zenith of courage, compassion, chivalry, and Confederate culture. Lee Lee was a combination of both. So too was Robert Roberts.

The commander put his arms around Julia. She leaned her face against his shoulder. The tears increased. The commander ran his hand soothingly along the back of Julia's head.

"I wish you were wearing your snood," he said.

Julia began to laugh, wondering what that comment would sound like to anyone overhearing the comment who had no idea what a snood was. The commander pulled her in a little tighter. Julia felt safe. She felt protected.

"Why don't we take things one day at a time? Come back here tomorrow. Wear that Scarlett O'Hara curtain dress that I love so much, that we all love."

"But," said Julia, "I have classes tomorrow."

“I figured that you did” said the commander “ Here’s what you do. Wear your dress to the classes. I’m sure you’ll get noticed not only by the guy with the glove……" at the mention of the guy with the glove Julia laughed again"but also by the other folks in the class. It might even be a good time to ask the teacher about how he determines his grades. You certainly wouldn’t look desperate or vulnerable or uh”

Lee Roberts hesitated. He was afraid that he was letting his mask slip.

“Or what?” asked Julia.

“Or lacking in confidence” Lee continued. “Then after class, meet me right here and we’ll talk again. Does that sound like a plan”

“You always have such brilliant strategy, General Lee” Julia whispered even as she was coming up with some strategy of her own.

The rebellious embrace tightened before it relaxed. As they pulled away from one another, Julia brushed her cheek against the beard of Lee. Her lips might have grazed his cheek as they passed. Maybe more than grazed.Maybe lightly kissed. All in the eye of the beholder. The South had risen again. Or hadn’t.

The General’s wife, Bobbi Roberts had seen the whole thing.Buxom would have been an understatement. Reubenesque an overstatement. Voluptuous might have worked at one time when Bobbi had curves in places in which other women didn’t even have places.

Simplicity is best.

Wide is the word.

Everything about Barbara “Bobbi” Roberts was wide, including her teeth.'Wide and white’ is how Bobbi herself described them. She was proud of her teeth. They were her most outstanding physical feature, a feature that demanded maintenance to preserve the sparkle. Bobbi was all about maintenance.

Bobbi was in costume and her costume was flaunting her wideness. Her sleeves were wide. Folds on her bodice lent a further sense of width at the shoulders and the bust line. She wore a wide hoop skirt which grew even wider as it descended towards her wide feet. The only thing relatively narrow about Bobbi was her waist which was narrow only in comparison to everything else and emphasized by gathers from her bodice and skirt. The narrowness at the waist only emphasized, by contrast, the width of her sleeves whenever her hands rested at her sides.

Bobbi parted her hair in the middle and her simple flat hairstyle added to the dimension of her width by accentuating the width of her face. She gathered her long hair in a mesh net known as a snood at the nape of what remained of her retreating neck. Bobbi's snood was ornamented with bows and ribbons.

Bobbi was proud of her snood and also aware that for some reason her snood seemed to, uh shall we say 'invigorate' her husband.

A photograph of women during Civil War times usually caught the subjects with their lips tightly closed, often to conceal poor teeth. Bobbi's lips were tightly closed even though her teeth were far from poor. Bobbi's lips were closed because she was furious at what her eyes beheld as she looked through the window of the cabin in the park, the imaginary headquarters. Her husband, the so-called commander, was hugging and kissing some young hussy in civvies. Since the slut was in civvies, there was no way that Lee could justify his action as part of his duties as Commander. The dirty, cheating son of a bitch was whispering some indiscretion to that little crying/laughing harlot. Probably trying to arrange a slimy rendezvous for more intense cradle robbing.

Bobbi bided her time. She watched as the embrace ended with, what was that? Was that a kiss? She resisted the urge to barge into the cabin while the strumpet was still in residence. She would wait until the whore left then she would charge into that cabin and make life living hell for the commander, which she proceeded to do.

Besides her teeth, Bobbi had two other major assets that she could use as weapons, tools or adornments. Bobbi had a voluminous vocabulary and could wield that weapon with deadly, withering lucidity. Bobbi didn't need the eff word and had contempt for those who did. She used the language precisely rather than inarticulately to express her rage.

DUELING MERCY MANNERS

Bobbi was an inveterate reader of Miss Manners and was excruciatingly aware of correct behavior. This was asset number two. When Bobbi synthesized the two; withering lucidity with excruciating observation, the results were devastating. Bobbi confronted Julia and delivered a scorching criticism which was masked under a veil of maternal advice about oversharing and inappropriate familiarity. Bobbi knew her words could be taken many ways and she was ready to pounce on Julia's response

Julia was not devastated. Julia was a lot like Bobbi except far younger and far narrower and not so well teethed. Julia was likewise a fan of Miss Manners. Julia also eschewed profanity in her discourse. Julia was not convinced of her innocence. She was going to have to convince herself with her spoken words. Julia leapt to her own defense.

"Mrs Roberts, your advice is well taken but superfluous. I've made a habit of faking delight at worthless presents during Christmas time. I've shown false pleasure in the success of my competitors. I've expressed curiosity about the lives of the terminally boring who don't have much of a life for anyone to be curious about. Perhaps I did step over the line in my sharing with your husband and for that I am sorry. I hope you will accept my apology."

Bobbi, astonished at Julia's response, had an unexpected autonomous response. She succumbed to an inevitable natural phenomena. She burped.

Inexcusable.

Julia was aware that Bobbi had burped even as Bobbi attempted to cover the burp by treating it as if it were a cough. Bobbi formed the fingers of her hand into a wide fist and placed the thumbside of that fist against her mouth.

"Excuse me" said Bobbi, still pretending that the burp was a cough but aware that Julia probably knew the difference.

"There's no need to for me to excuse you, Mrs Roberts. Society recognizes the necessity of breathing and ingesting but ignores digestion as much as possible. I take digestion as a natural consequence of ingestion. Life is all about inclusion, exclusion and toleration. Sometimes we cannot tolerate what we include and our bodies stammer before they exclude. Wouldn't you agree, Mrs Roberts?"

" That's true" said the General's wife who found herself starting to like the girl in the Scarlett O'Hara costume "And of the three, inclusion, exclusion and toleration, we spend most of our time in toleration. Our main troubles occur when we attempt to include someone or something that we should have merely tolerated or completely avoided"

Julia got the message. She nodded in agreement and prepared to explain the projected "kiss".

General Lee, meanwhile, had reached the meadow and was continuing to head North.

At the same time, a few clicks further North,Ovid grabbed his submarine sandwich and Diet Coke before booking out of his car which he had just parked after a weird morning with Krell.

Before Julia could begin her explanation of the projected kiss, she was surprised that Mrs. Roberts broke the silence first.

"On the subject of tolerance, we must be careful not to abandon our sense of right and wrong only to preserve transparent tranquility passing as toleration. We must not become doormats in a perpetual state of forgiving. We need not accept every apology. Or is this what forgive and forget is all about, pride swallowing and resignation?"

"No, Mrs Roberts, if that were the case, we wouldn't need to forgive and forget, we'd just need forget. There are two parts to that equation and we can always do one without the other. Surely, you have forgotten situations that you didn't choose to forgive. I know that I have. I don't want to load up my mind with those troubling distractions so I let them go. Still, I don't want to pass off toleration as absent-mindedness."

Bobbi Roberts was impressed by Julia yet not quite won over. "My dear, a few minutes ago, you apologized to me. You asked for my forgiveness. Doesn't that indicate some guilt on your part? Why else would you ask for forgiveness. How can I forgive you for something that you haven't done? Something that I clearly haven't forgotten? What does forgiveness mean to you?"

Julia thought for a moment. She was not afraid of wait time.

"Forgiveness, Mrs. Roberts, is a contract. Forgiveness is a two part deal. Forgiveness is a response to an apology. Just as we have become a society unwilling to pretend happiness, we have also become a society unwilling to apologize. Without apology, there can be no forgiveness. We have become an unforgiving society filled with unforgiven members. And no, you should not assume my guilt because of my willingness to apologize. In a more tolerant world, a more forgiving world for accidents or mistakes, even those obviously lacking in ill will or intention, would require an apology. That is the reason why I once again ask your forgiveness. I am prepared to explain my lack of ill will if you require that as a condition of your forgiveness"

Once again Julia was ready to explain the projected kiss.

Further North, Ovid saluted General Lee as the cavalry prepared to charge.

Bobbi was by now genuinely impressed.

“There is no need for further explanation. I accept your apology.You are a young woman of great promise. Furthermore, the quality of mercy is not strained.......”

“It falleth as the gentle rain from heaven” Julia continued. Both women laughed. The storm clouds disappeared. Sunshine appeared over the meadow.

'Thank God for Shakespeare' Julia thought to herself in the momentary silence that ensued.

Julia knew the etiquette of social kissing but she was relieved that she didn’t have to review that etiquette with Mrs. Roberts, the wife of the man with whom Julia had tested the boundaries of that etiquette. She was sure that Mrs Roberts knew the same rules that she did and that any misstep might bring back the storm or even worse, the whirlwind.

Julia knew that five areas were available in the realm of acceptable social kissing: the lips, the right cheek only, the right cheek followed by the left cheek and/or the hand. Julia knew that when she pulled away from her embrace with General Lee that she had perhaps kissed his right cheek. Even if she had for sure kissed his right cheek, that indulgence would fall safely within the boundaries of acceptable etiquette.

Julia also knew that as the woman in the embrace, it was her privilege and not General Lee’s to initiate a public kiss on the lips. Julia was aware that if she presented her lips by tilting her face upward without moving it to either side, any gentleman would have no choice but to accept her offering. Especially if she closed her eyes after fluttering her lashes amidst the face tilt. General Lee was without a doubt such a gentleman. Any such offering would have been enthusiastically accepted. Julia was certain of that consequence.

Julia remembered that she had considered that posture and for the sake of propriety had decided against it. This recollection nearly enabled Julia to rationalize her peck on the cheek of General Lee as an innocent expression of affection. Nearly, but not completely. Julia did have the remnants of a nagging self-suspicion. Had she loaded up an extra thrill charge on the peck? She suspected that she had.

She needed a further demonstration of her innocence along with a reason to get away from Mrs Roberts while the getting was still good.

That's when Julia spotted Ovid as he walked past the meadow and headed for the bench. It was time for the "fake boyfriend" trick.

"Please excuse me, Mrs Roberts, but that's my boyfriend over there with the sandwich. He said he'd come over here today and there he is"

Bobbi was relieved that Julia had such a young boyfriend. She chuckled at the foolishness of her own suspicion that one as young as Julia would be in any way interested in one as much older as her husband.

"Oh, he's cute" Bobbi lied. "Go over and greet him right now. We'll talk later"

"I'll take my leave then" said Julia and started heading over to Ovid.

The old and reliable fake boy friend trick had seemingly worked again but Julia was going to need an almost immediate hug and maybe even a subsequent kiss from Ovid to seal the illusion. She didn't think that would present much of a problem. Julia knew how to flutter and flatter.

Meanwhile Ovid was trying to grasp the difference between cavalry and calvary.

A PRAYER IN THE MEADOW

Julia surprised me by giving me a quick hug as if I were her boyfriend.

At that very instant I realized that Julia and I were totally different. Her embrace felt to me like the kind of embrace a cat would throw on a mouse if the cat and the mouse were about the same size and if they were standing on their hind legs and if the cat was wearing Scarlett O'Hara gear and the mouse had just finished eating a submarine. The mouse might try to put his arms around the cat but since the arms of the cat are so much longer than the arms of the mouse, his embrace would be considerably less determined than hers; as was my embrace of Julia.

Even as I held on loosely I could sense that Julia was not above stealing apples to get her free ride to skull island. I thought she might look real good strapped to a stone altar. I figured that she was the kind of woman who would make a tiny man live in a dollhouse until she accidentally knocked him down the cellar stairs and assumed he was lost in the flood.

That's when I sensed her moving away from our embrace. That's when I felt her lips brush against my right cheek.That's when she lifted her chin, tilted back her head, fluttered her eyelashes and closed her eyes.

I'm no gentleman.

I did the same thing.

As we both tilted our heads in opposite directions, I had a moment to think. If a photographer came by and snapped a picture of the two of us at that instant, the picture might look as if we were praying.

I know this is true because a photographer did snap a picture at that moment and a week later it was published in the paper above the caption, *Prayer in the Meadow.* In the picture Julia looks a lot like a female praying mantis.I look like the male mantis who an hour earlier had been telling his mantis friends "Man, I'd love to be torn limb from limb by that."

Back in real time, I opened my eyes, looked down at Julia with her pursed lips and realized that I had one more chance. This time, I took it.

"No, I don't think I will kiss you, although you need kissing, badly. That's what's wrong with you. You should be kissed and often, and by someone who knows how."

Julia whispered "But Ovid, I need a little kiss right now" Our lips were so close that an onlooker would have thought we kissed and imagined Atlanta in flames behind us.

Damn, she had given me yet another opportunity. I took it.

"That's your misfortune."

I broke from her embrace and started heading North.

I resisted the urge to turn around for one final look at Julia. I figured that she figured that tomorrow would be another day. As I neared the parking lot, I once again encountered General Lee, who was heading South. He was heading back towards the battle ground. Once again I saluted.

"I've been thinking about your cat story that must have been one bigass cat"

"I imagine it was"

General Lee straightened himself into his full height. Dude was tall. I felt myself growing smaller.

"That fool dog must have made the mistake of getting between the big cat and her kittens. That strategic position is a must to avoid whether it's cats or humans; individuals or armies" observed Lee Roberts. "Sometimes, it's not the size of the dog in the fight or the size of the fight in the dog, it's the size of the fight in the cat in the dogfight"

"Cats are cats. Dogs are dogs. As a rule, they don't get along. Cats and dogs are not people" I saluted again looking to be discharged.

"That's right Johnny. We are the people" concluded Lee Roberts as he dismissively and somewhat doggedly returned my salute.

I'd heard that one somewhere before.

General Lee went South. I went North. I recaptured my car, put it into reverse and then pointed it towards my apartment.

TUBE TIME AT THE PAD

By the time I got home, I was ready for some serious tube. I hit the couch, grabbed the remote and checked the guide. T*he Incredible Shrinking Man* was going to start in five minutes. I locked in and flashed back.

When my brother was a baby, my parents got their first VCR. My folks had a lot of chores to do around the farm so he did a lot of solitary playpen time. They'd stash him in the pen, turn on the VCR and go about their business. Our VCR collection of movies consisted of two; *King Kong* and T*he Incredible Shrinking Man.* I used to stand by his playpen and watch those flicks over and over again. My parents tell me that by the time he was three, he must have seen each of those movies over a hundred times each.

I've seen each of them at least 50 times.

As a matter of fact, as I was driving away from Julia and General Lee I did what I usually do when times get complicated, I started thinking about Scott Carey, The Incredible Shrinking Man.

I wondered what kind of vision Scott had. I wondered if Scott's wife could hear him yelling when she booted him down the cellar stairs. I understood once again, why cats are not my favorite animals. I recalled the terrifying strength of spiders.

I know a thing or two about eyes. I know that we need light to see. I know that the amount of light we receive is determined by the size of our retina. When Scott Carey grew smaller, I assume that the size of his retina grew smaller in proportion to the rest of his dome. Otherwise, Scott would have been an eyeball, way beyond 'bulging', atop tiny legs scurrying around the floor. Scott's body would have been eighty percent eyeball We would have had an even more horribly absurd movie, particularly if somehow during the scurry, the bulging eyeball with feet had blinded itself which under the circumstances was probably inevitable

I imagined an observer of the scurrying impaired eyeball watching as the minuscule monster ricocheted from wall to wall. "Oh, my God, what could be worse than to be just an eye," the observer might say to his companion who might reply "well, it could be blind" which in this case it would have been which wasn't of course the case in the uh movie.

The case in the movie was that Scott had normally proportioned retinas about seventy times smaller than the retinas he had before he started shrinking which means that he was stumbling around with hardly any light flying through the pinhole of his retina. Just think how scary everything is in the semi-darkness, especially the blurry semi-darkness. Scott's blur was infinitely more dark and out of focus than any projector Julia might try to imagine.

Although there were a lot of loud noises.

Besides the cat and the spider and his wife's high heels, Scott had to deal with perpetual semi-darkness.

And as his vocal cords shrunk, his ability to generate sound waves also shrunk. I'm sure that Scott was screaming his head off at his wife before she kicked him down the stairs and equally sure that she couldn't hear a sound he was screaming which may have been just as well because with diminished hammer, anvil and stirrup, he wouldn't have been able to understand her reply any more than we are able to make out the words in thunder.

Is Thunder really Godspeak for "it's raining".

Hmmm.

This of course made me think about ants. Are they trying to yell something at us as we step on them? Are we huge, incomprehensible thunderhead blurs in a dark world trampling upon them even as they warn us about their homes and their children and the work that has to be done?

I think not. They're different from Scott Carey. They never shrank.

The movie started. I watched it again for the first time in at least ten years.

I realized how much I had grown.

RETURN TO KRELL'S CLASS

" Phi, Chi, sigh, omega"

Haylen smiled. She had completed the Greek alphabet twice on one match. She hadn't even glanced at her notes.

While Krell nodded at Haylen; Arthur, Julia and I exchanged glances that screamed " we're the bozos on this bus".

A moment later, according to my notes, Krell started in about Socrates.

"Socrates was born in 469 BC and lived until 399 BC. If you do the math, you'll see that Socrates died when he was only thirty-two years old. Go ahead and do the math and find out for yourself."

I did the math.

We did the math.

No problem. Socrates was only thirty-two when he died.

Then Haylen raised her hand.

Problem.

"Mr. Krell, according to my math…Socrates was seventy when he died."

"Seventy, Haylen?" Krell raised his eyebrow.

I thought maybe the three of us were getting off the bozo bus or at least making room on board for Haylen. Haylen continued, "Yes, sir. In this case, the count is backward rather than forward. Socrates wasn't one year old in 470 BC. 470 BC was also 1 BS."

Krell seemed not only to understand but also to be entertained. “What, may I ask for the good of the class, is 1 BS?”

“Sure” responded Haylen. “ 1 BS is one year before the birth of Socrates. Socrates was born in 469 BC. One year before his birth, the year would have been 470 BC not 468. In 468 Socrates would have been one year old. Of course, he didn’t know the year was 470 or 468 or anything BC. Nobody had any idea when Christ would be born or who Christ was or why Christ would be important or why their very birthdays would be determined by the future son of a carpenter”

“Very true, Haylen. Now how does your counting backward mechanism work” asked Krell.

“It took sixty-nine years to get from 469BC to 400 BC. Then you add one more for 399 and that leaves you with seventy. Socrates lived to be seventy”

I did the math. Haylen was absolutely correct.

“Do the math again and you’ll find that Haylen is absolutely correct. You should also learn to think carefully about anything that your teacher says. Particularly if that teacher is I” said Krell.

At that moment because I had done what Krell had said before he said it, I felt like an Advanced Placement Bozo. I was still on the bus but I was moving a couple of seats closer to the driver.

“Before we go any further, does anybody know anything else about ancient Greece that would be illuminating for the class to consider?” Krell asked.

The usual silence followed.

The usual silence was followed by the usual two follow ups. “Anybody?... Anything?”

I was feeling pretty smart in a stupid way so I decided to step up.

"Yeah, that's where the first French fries were made"

Julia, got all over that observation. "No, they weren't they were made in France. That's why we call them French fries"

Krell came to my rescue.

"Wherever they were made, they were indisputably made in Grease. Good one Ovid"

Julia laughed out loud.

Arthur and Haylen were pissed.

Arthur must have felt marginalized because he responded with a snarky comment to Krell which he read from a three by five index card. "My father told me that Socrates, despite his place in history, was over-rated. He actually wrote nothing because in essence he felt that knowledge was a living, interactive thing. Most of what we know of him comes from the historical inaccuracy and misinterpretation found in the works of Plato and later Thomas Aquinas."

Krell answered " Well Arthur, your father seems like quite a smart man. I imagine he's had a great influence on your life. There's a lot of truth in what he says but like all truths it bears closer examination"

Arthur seemed to wince at the mention of paternal influence.

Krell continued.

"First of all, let's deal with the concept of over-rated and let's consider the list of the over-rated. I'll bring up a few: Shakespeare, Caesar, Elvis, Lincoln, Marie Curie, Eleanor Roosevelt, Meryl Streep, the Beatles, Amelia Earhart Picasso, Da Vinci, Rosa Parks, Muhammad Ali, Katherine Hepburn, Mother Theresa. All may be considered over-rated simply because they are famous. Fame is an integral part of iconic over-rating. How can you be over-rated unless you're famous? Nobody's gonna over-rate Sid Gertner, the guy who lent Lincoln the pen that Abraham used to write the Gettysburg Address. Where would we be today if at that moment of inspiration, Gertner didn't have a pen. The reason nobody's going to over rate Gertner is because nobody knows that Sid, performing one of the millions of unnoticed acts of kindness that characterize human behavior lent the pen to Lincoln in the first place."

Krell wrote **SID GERTNER** on the board and continued

"Of course, you might say that since I identified Gertner and Gertner is long departed, he must be somewhat famous and thus susceptible to be over-rated. The problem is that I don't know whether or not Gertner gave Lincoln the pen. Somebody probably did. That somebody has been totally forgotten by history so just because I name that somebody Gertner doesn't mean that Gertner becomes a figure of historical importance although I'm sure that exact mechanism has occurred in history many times over."

Krell wrote OBSCURITY on the board and continued "Even when that somebody, like Gertner, might not have existed at all at least under that name.We remain alive as long as anyone who ever knew us or knew of us remains alive. The people who live the longest are those who have created enduring works of art or who have had enduring works of art created about them or who are simply remembered by the most people.These people are famous. These people may end up over-rated.Socrates was such a one as for that matter was Plato and Aquinas. So Arthur, I agree with your Dad about part one."

Krell paused.

PLAY MEATBALL

Ya know how when you go to concerts there's always some doofus yelling out for the performer to play their most overplayed song as if the performer doesn't realize that people want to hear the overplayed song and no matter how much he hates playing the overplayed song over and over again, he's going to have to play it some time during the show and he's already figured out when and where it will fit into the program that will cause him the least discomfort and cessation of creative momentum? Usually that place will be at the very end of the show when the artist can't put it off any longer and where momentum can mercifully end.

Ya know the guy standing fifteen feet away from Dylan after Dylan opens his show with "Maggie's Farm" who starts yelling for "Like a Rolling Stone" as if Dylan is not going to play that song.

Or even worse, the guy who starts yelling for "Blowin' in the Wind". Ya know, the guy who has never heard "Visions of Johanna" but knows every word to "Blowin in the Wind" and has come to the show for a hootenanny after walking down many roads that have led him to the conclusion that he can indeed call himself a man. And his wife next to him, the woman who married him anyway, who somehow thinks Dylan is going to sing "Puff the Magic Dragon" or" If I were a Carpenter".

Whenever I hear one of those guys, I try to balance out their request by yelling out a request for a song that nobody knows, not even the artist because the song doesn't exist. I picked out a title for this imaginary song, a title unlike any title I have ever heard for a song. The title of the non-existent song that I yell out for the artist to play after a nimrod has just yelled out the name of the artist's most overplayed song, the title of that song is MEATBALL.

I yell out "PLAY MEATBALL".

I've even gone so far as to light my lighter while yelling out PLAY MEATBALL. I've even been pro-active and yelled PLAY MEATBALL before the other guy has yelled out say PLAY BORN TO RUN at a Springsteen show.

Once, sweet Jesus, I was in the front row for a Neil Diamond show with a single ticket that I had won after accidentally being the seventeenth caller. I knew the blue hair next to me would be screaming for "Sweet Caroline" so the instant that Neil took the stage I beat her to the punch by yelling "PLAY MEATBALL". Neil heard me. I think he put a mental comma after "play" so he heard "PLAY, MEATBALL" before he had song a note or strummed his guitar.

Neil was more puzzled than pissed.

So was the blue hair next to me.

Who, now that I think about it, she looked a lot like Barbara Bush.

But that's unusual.

Usually, the people around me look at me as if I know something that they don't know which might even indicate that I am an actual "friend of the band" because actual friends of the band are always yelling out things to their friends in the band that nobody but the guys in the band or the friends of the band understand. The old fake in-joke trick.

Those who don't mistake me for an actual 'friend of the band' often regard me as an expert on the band because only an expert on the band would know such an obscure title as MEATBALL and have the insight expressed through his bellowing to suggest to the performer who may have forgotten the song that the exact instant of the yell would be a great time to reach into an ancient bag of tricks, to redistribute the stones in the kaleidoscope by twisting the barrel in a new-old fashioned way.

I usually get a lot of respect when I yell PLAY MEATBALL.

After Krell's bit about the torches in response to Julia's snit fit, I wanted to yell PLAY MEATBALL to see if I could get him back on track but since this was a college class and not a concert I decided to do a variation of PLAY MEATBALL. I yelled out:

"What about Socrates"

Krell continued.

THE STORY OF SID

The story of Sid touches upon the subject of historical inaccuracy. You or your Dad's charge of Platonic misinterpretation, Arthur, leads me to a subject that in the study of metaphysiction is probably unavoidable and certainly embedded. That subject is physics. This is a good time to oversimplify and humanize the laws of thermodynamics of which there are three. The first law basically states any change in the internal energy of a system will be the result of work done on or by that system and any heat flow into or out of the system. In other words, the universe assures us that we can never win, that is if winning means getting out more than we put in. Or as the over-rated Beatles once sang "and in the end, the love you take is equal to the love you make"

Krell wrote **BEATLES** on the board in small letters and continued.

"Except it isn't. It's a little bit less. That's what the second law of thermodynamics tells us. Not only can't we win, we can't even salvage a tie. The second law states that in any process to convert heat energy that flows from a hot object to a colder object into work, there will inevitably be some loss. That loss can be attributed to the entropy of the systems involved. Entropy is the natural state of the universe. Entropy is disorder.Try as we might to put things in order, entropy will always rear up and demand our attention or else matters will naturally grow more chaotic. Let's assume that in learning, the teacher is the hot object and the student is the colder object. The teacher tries to transfer some of his heat to the student when the student is ready. The teacher cannot transfer all of his heat. The natural entropy of the transfer insures misinterpretation Certainly, Plato misinterpreted Socrates. Certainly Aquinas misinterpreted Plato's misinterpretation of Socrates. Your father, Arthur, is misinterpreting the Aquinas misinterpretation of the Platonic misinterpretation of Socrates."

Krell noticed that I was taking notes furiously.

"Even as I talk" Krell continued, "I notice that Ovid is taking notes which assures me that I will be misinterpreted when Ovid rewrites his notes. The misinterpretation will not be limited to Ovid but also will be shared by anyone reading Ovid's rewritten notes. So my interpretation of Arthur's father's misinterpretation of Aquinas misinterpreting Plato misinterpreting Socrates will also be misinterpreted. And that's in the present. Imagine what would remain after twenty-three hundred years of misinterpretation and entropy."

Krell drew a breath.

Arthur asked another question "what's the third law of thermodynamics"

Krell summarized, "If the first law means we can't win and the second law means we can't even break even, the third law means we can never get out of the game. We being in this case, Socrates, Plato, Aquinas, Arthur's father, Arthur, me, Ovid and anyone who will ever read's Ovid notes.We're in this game forever and we can't win."

In the momentary vacuum, I started imagining the twenty-seventh inning of a meaningless September ballgame between the Tigers and the Mariners tied at four to four with two outs and nobody on and nobody getting warm in the bullpen with everybody on Earth watching and nobody giving a damn who wins, not even the players themselves because both teams are expecting to lose.

My reverie was interrupted by a follow-up question from Julia.

"So if I misunderstood you correctly, you're about to present yet another misinterpretation of the life of Socrates which we in turn will distort according to our individual, emotional entropy. Then at some point, you will give us a test which will measure our misinterpretation against yours and the difference will produce a profile of the intensity of our academic or intellectual chaos which, you will then translate into a 'grade' of some sort ?"

Krell paused for only a moment before replying. "Well, Julia, in the unlikely event that I understand what you're asking I'd have to disagree that you misunderstood me correctly but add that yes you have understood me incorrectly which shouldn't come as any surprise based on the laws of thermodynamics which I just misrepresented through over-simplification."

Arthur was more or less lost in these particular woods but at Julia's mention of a test, his impulse towards definition engaged and he asked another concrete question.

"So is Julia right about the test?"

Krell replied.

"Arthur, in the midst of her misunderstanding, Julia did strike a little gold. I will test your misinterpretation of my misunderstanding of metaphysics and use my more constant misunderstanding as a yardstick to measure my evaluation of your more random misinterpretations. Remember though that the grades themselves will be misconstrued by whomever looks at them. Not only will the grades be misconstrued but the actual title of the course will be misunderstood, as you yourselves have already been fooled by the course which I unintentionally misrepresented in the course catalogue which is in itself a studied collection of chaos presenting itself under the illusion of clarity. So, I wouldn't worry too much about the tests or the grades."

Julia again, "Then what should we worry about".

Krell again "I'm going to start worrying about the life of Socrates and how it relates to the writing of Plato and how Plato influenced Aristotle and how Aristotle created metaphysics and since I'm the teacher, part of your job is to read my mind so that your misunderstanding can more closely resemble mine. You might start worrying about Richard Boone, because when I was a young man my favorite teevee show was *Have Gun Will Travel* and the influence of Paladin keeps popping up uncalled for in my mind when I least expect it, like right now for instance, and that's the mind that you guys are supposed to read if you are to get an A in this course. I hope I'm not making myself clear"

This sounded to me like an opportunity for a rallying cry.

I yelled out "Yes, you're not. Let's hear about Socrates"

Krell continued......

"Last class, I created a straw man called Torch. Perhaps you imagine that Torch was a lot like Socrates. That would be no accident if you did because I was trying to paint a picture of a person who would remind you of Socrates yet not be Socrates."

Julia raised her hand again "Isn't Torch an unfortunate name for a straw man"

"I wanted to get across the idea of illumination, " Krell responded. "The concepts of spontaneous combustion and subsequent immolation were only glowing on the periphery of my metaphoric construction but since you've highlighted it, then yes, the choice of Torch is not as unfortunate as you might imply"

Krell wrote **ILLUMINATION** on the board

"And let's finish up this little exercise in misinterpretation with the demise of the angry towns-people galumphing through village greens at midnight, heading towards the forest pursuing some heresy and trying in vain to interrupt the inevitability of that heresy's ultimate ascension to mythology and/or orthodoxy. Who were the guys leading that parade? The local torch makers led those exercises in violent, mob induced misinterpretation. At one time, torch making was a highly sought skill and as sure a sign of leadership as the ability to throw rather than the ability to lift. When the mob finally reached the windmill, the castle or the bridge or whatever was the target of their misinterpretation, which of the torch bearers usually took over leadership? That's right, the guy who threw his torch at the castle, the bridge, the windmill or the whatever. It's amazing how often a single torch hit the hay just right which caused the formerly indestructible castle to ignite and burn to the ground along with the collection of disparate, walking cadaver parts and the insane quack who sewed them together in the name of progress.Ever since Edison invented the light bulb, we have had a dearth of torch driven angry mobs. I for one miss them. I say we should bring them back. What would happen if tonight a group of students met on campus; ignited a bunch of torches and then marched through the town? It ain't gonna happen because torches are illegal. Yeah, you can get those fake kerosene torches for your random midnight barbecues but the days of the good old fashioned torches used to whip a group of lunatics into a misguided outburst of ill conceived frenzy led by the best and seemingly least belligerent torch thrower in the town have passed us by

unless

we

count

Donald Trump

and teevee."

Krell continued

"Ovid's response is a perfect example of what we call in education 'a window of instructional opportunity'. In show biz, that's referred to as giving the people what they want or putting the light on the star. Apparently, Ovid wants me to get on with the story of Socrates which is what I wanted to do in the first place but hesitated to do so because I felt as if the venetian blinds were covering the windows and then when we started down the road, we had to take a small detour at the straw man.

Krell opened the venetian blinds and continued

"The good teacher, of which I'm sure Socrates was one, recognizes these windows of instructional opportunity when they arise and uses them to the advantage of the class. So on we go with Socrates.Socrates as a child wasn't handsome but he was probably rich which is a trade off many of us would accept. We assume that he came from a prosperous family because as a young man he had enough leisure time available to master the philosophy of his era.The emerging philosophy consisted largely of various attempts to provide scientific explanations for the origin and structure of the universe. This wasn't going too well because we still hadn't discovered that what goes up must come down and just about everything else regarding science including the concept that the sun rather than the earth was the center of our astronomical system and that the Milky Way is composed of an infinite number of stars and the Milky Way is one of an infinite number of solar systems and that man might not be the center and purpose of the universe. Of course, Galileo added much of that information two thousand years after Socrates and the great Italian scientist was immediately confronted with a mob carrying torches who took him to the Inquisition where the Pope made him promise that he wouldn't tell anybody that the earth moves."

Krell wrote **GALILEO** on the board and continued.

"A smart guy like Socrates could see right off the bat that lots of problems existed within the emerging scientific explanations among them no television, no radio, no cars, no internet and a flat earth but he also understood that they were much better than the mythological explanations that were prevalent in his time. It's not clear what levels of academic success Socrates attained in his study of science or physical philosophy but we do know that by the start of the Peloponnesian War which occurred when Socrates was in his mid thirties, he had abandoned physical philosophy and began the examination of conduct that he would continue for the rest of his life."

Krell wrote **WAR** on the board and continued.

"Apparently that transition which began with alienation from science was precipitated by Socrates' interpretation of an inquiry directed to the oracle of Apollo at Delphi by an Athenian named Chaerephon. According to the oracle..."

Julia again.

"How do you spell that last name that you mentioned. The guy who asked the question of the oracle. It sounds like 'chair on a phone but I'm sure it's not spelled that way."

Then Arthur

"And how do you spell the name of the war that was going on when Socrates was in his thirties"

Krell wrote **Chaerephon** and **Pellopenesian** on the board.

Then Julia again

"And, uh, isn't the Milky Way a galaxy and not a solar system?"

Krell heard Julia's question with his back.

The questions were coming hard and fast as questions do when a class suspects the opportunity to fluster, contradict or break the teacher.

When he finished writing the two words on the board, he turned and faced the class."Solar system or galaxy, what's the difference?" Krell shrugged his shoulders as if he had been asked to explain the difference between an aardvark and an anteater.

Julia answered. "I should think there would be quite a huge difference as a solar system is part of a galaxy which means a galaxy is bigger than a solar system"

Arthur chimed in. "yeah, and a solar system is smaller than a galaxy"

Krell responded, "Thank you two for overstating the obvious. I was being metaphysictional which is of course unfair because you guys still don't even know what metaphysics is."

This response fired Arthur's obsession with definition. "Well then, Mr. Krell, can you finally give us a definition of metaphysics"

"Arthur, I can give you a definition of metaphysics but that definition by definition can not be the definition of metaphysics. Voltaire said 'when he that speaks and he to whom he speaks, neither of them understand what is meant, that is metaphysics'".

I thought I understood so I yelled out "I don't understand what you mean"

To which Krell joyfully responded "And I don't understand what you mean when you say you don't understand what I mean"

To which Haylen added "Eureka. At last we arrive at an example of Voltairean metaphysics, if I am understanding you both incorrectly"

Krell was obviously pleased with the lesson. The venetian blinds were opening and the sun was streaming into the consciousness of at least three of us in the room.

Krell continued.

"I always consider solar systems and galaxies to be similar because of the beach. When I walk on the beach, I realize that there are as many stars in our solar system as there are grains of sand on all the sandy beaches of our planet. The sun is one of those grains of sand. Our grain of sand is surrounded by nine planets, thirty-one moons, thousands of planetoids, millions of comets, innumerable meteoroids and vast quantitates of interplanetary dust and gas. Can you grasp that Ovid"

"No I can't grasp that Mr, Krell"

"Excellent, then I will continue."

Krell continued. “Our grain of sand, our sun, appears toward the outer rim of our galaxy in which there are billions of other grains of sand like our sun, millions of which are surrounded by moons, planetoids, comets, meteorites and are thus known as solar systems. Now we continue walking down the beach and pick up yet another grain of sand and realize that there are as many galaxies out there in the universe as there are grains of sand on all the beaches on our planet. Every time that we increase the magnitude of our telescopes we discover more galaxies which means the number of galaxies may well be infinite which is even more galaxies than grains of sand. And the universe is expanding and with each expansion more beaches, more grains of sand. Can you comprehend what I’m saying Haylen”

“No sir, I cannot comprehend the enormity of what you are saying,” answered Haylen.

Julia again, “I can clearly understand what you’re saying. You’re asking what’s the difference between a solar system and a galaxy and you’re answering your own question by saying, 'hey they’re both grains of sand on the grand scale of things so what’s the diff’. That’s what you are saying”

Krell again

“Thank you Julia because what you are saying is a perfect example of exactly what I’ve been saying but I don’t suppose you understand why it is such a perfect example”

Julia again, “No, I don’t”

Krell again, “You’re learning”

“But what is it that I’m learning?” Julia wanted to know.

“Julia, if you had understood me a little less correctly, I would guess that you had learned something about the way we as humans misinterpret the consequentiality of the physical and have therefore embraced the metaphysical. Certainly, it's fine to deny the immensity of the physical as defined by the incomprehensibility of the cosmic but all of that changes the moment someone hits you in the face with a rock.A rock is not theoretical."

Krell wrote **ROCK** on board and kept on. "A rock is nothing but a fact .And as far as an abstract idea like freedom goes, my freedom to throw a rock ends where your freedom to have a face begins. Once we have defined the actual boundaries of an abstract idea like 'freedom' we can begin to explore the consequences of another abstract idea known as 'justice'.. Both 'freedom' and 'justice' are based upon the shaky alliance between the abstract and the concrete"

I decided I better try to get this locomotive back on track. "Metaphysics rawks. Rawk on Sawkrates"

Krell took the hint and returned to CHAIR ON A PHONE.

"When Chaerophon inquired at the shrine of oracle of Apollo at Delphi, he was informed that, 'no man was wiser than Socrates'. Chaerophon passed this message to Socrates. Socrates knew that Apollo could not lie but he also knew that he himself possessed no great wisdom. Thus Socrates arrived at the riddle that would inspire him for the rest of his life."

"I look at the clock and realize that our time together today is just about up. The sand has passed through the hour glass so to speak. I'll save the riddle that haunted Socrates for next time. Any questions?"

"Yes," said Julia. "Let's imagine that you are the oracle at Delphi and I am Chaerophon. My question Mighty Apollo is this, who is the smartest person in this class?"

Krell stepped right into the role " no one is wiser in this class, no one is wiser in this college, no one is wiser in this city, no one is wiser in this state, no one is wiser in this country than ………"

Krell made eye contact with everyone in the room

“No

One

Is

Wiser

Than

Ovid.”

I was more stunned than anyone in the class when Krell made his observation. I lingered around after class to see if I could get some validation from Krell about the seriousness of his remark. Julia was hanging around too, pretending to organize her notes but in reality, trying to make sure that I wouldn’t get a moment with Krell.

Krell was getting edgy.

He looked at the both of us and asked “are you guys ready to get outta here”

Julia scurried out of the room without a word.

Now me and Krell were alone.

"Did you mean what you said when you were pretending to be Apollo?“ I asked Krell.

Krell on his way out the door, turned back and said, "Does a bear shit in the woods?”

Then he was gone.

I left the room right behind Krell. I was thinking about bears and wisdom. Grizzly bears in particular. Grizzly bears are my favorite animal for a lot of reasons but the most outstanding reason is that Grizzly Bears have the ability to walk backwards in their own footprints for up to two and a half miles in order to confuse whomever/ whatever is tracking them.

I started imagining, not for the first time, this gigantic ferocious grizzly bear somehow picking up one foot after another then stepping backwards daintily with that ponderous paw/claw and placing it exactly claw for claw in the track it had made leading up to the retreat. It's like bear moon-walking which certainly must befuddle, astonish and amuse whatever is tracking the bear.

And the next question is, of course, how and why did bears learn this distinctive survival trick. How often in the wild is something actually tracking a bear and what, if not a guy with a gun, could that something be? A grizzly bear is at the top of the food chain. You'd have to be an awesomely hungry cougar to be tracking a bear. Moose freak out at the tiniest whiff of bear crap. It's obviously not Bullwinkle tracking the bear. So if it's not a man or a moose or a cougar and the maneuver has been around long enough to turn the moonwalk behavior into an instinct, then who in hell is tracking a grizzly?

The only answer I could come up with was dinosaur.

I know there's a few billion years difference in the time that these species blundered through their respective forests but what else would bears be intimidated by enough to learn how to walk backwards in their own tracks to confuse whatever was theoretically threatening them.

And furthermore, what happened when the bear moonwalked all the way back to where he was face to ass with whatever was tracking him, what's the bears plan? To attack the dinosaur with its ass?

I wondered if this constituted wisdom.

Learning to walk backwards in our own tracks until we confront our imaginary Jurassic enemies with our asses at which point we back asswards attack?I also knew that bears hibernate most of the winter. So the answer to Krell's exit question which was his answer to my question is this:

It depends on the time of the year.

LIGHTS OUT AT THE LIBRARY

I know I ain't wise. No matter what Krell says. Yet Krell did definitely say that no-one was wiser than me. For the next couple of days I took a look around, a close look.

Particularly at the guys. I was already convinced that both Haylen and Julia were smarter than me.

I was looking to find a guy smarter than me. If I found that guy, I could ask him what Krell meant when he said that nobody in town was smarter than me.

If the guy was smarter than me, then that would disprove the thesis of Krell, that nobody was wiser than me, which the guy smarter than me would be trying to explain while at the same time debunking.

I was smart enough to know that I wouldn't be able to pick out a guy smarter than me simply by the way he looked. Everybody looks smarter than me. I had to have standards other than appearance.

I started with three standards.

I figured that a guy wiser than me would be older than me, would be married and have kids.

Most of the guys who I knew in that category were your typical hard working Joes. Guys who did their job when they could find one. Guys who paid the bills when they had the dough. Guys who raised good, pain-in-the ass type kids. Guys who went to church as often as the wife could drag them there. Guys who bowled Wednesday nights and drank Buds before dinner. Guys who were easily exasperated but not easily defeated. These guys were especially hard to defeat or discourage when defending a half-assed scheme. Guys whose character shines through most clearly when the thin ice is crackling beneath their skates. A leaking roof, an unexpected complication at work or the growing pains of their kids are enough to throw these guys into freak city. A Hummer from out of nowhere smashing through their front window and planting itself in the hallway during the ball game? No problem.

These are the guys who can turn a minor problem into a nuclear disaster and a nuclear disaster into a walk in the park.

These are the guys that everybody watches with mixed awe; half fascination and half apprehension. These guys are capable of fixing anything or breaking it into smithereens. You never know when these guys are going to over-react or be oblivious.

I hoped that one day I would be wise enough to be amongst them. In the meantime, I wanted to ask them questions about justice, courage, love, temperance, faith, hope and charity. I was looking for a wise man in America.

I didn't have much time.

I needed some answers before the next class.

Once again, I made my way to the library, the seat of all local knowledge. I spotted a guy standing outside the conference room who seemed to have the standard qualifications; two of them for sure based on his wrinkles and the wedding ring on his hand. I asked him his name and told him that I had some questions I needed to ask for a college course. I was prepared to take notes. I took out my pen and paper

The guy told me his name was Otto.

My name is Ovid.

I tried to remember the last time I talked to another guy whose name began with an O. It's not often that two guys whose names begin with O get to talk about the Lone Ranger. Especially if one of the guys names is a palindrome. I learned about palindromes in eleventh grade English when my teacher, Mr. Sagan, wrote the most famous palindrome on the board "A man, a plan, a canal. Panama". I've been palindrome sensitive ever since. A goddam mad dog.

So there we were, two O guys, one a palindrome, who had met two minutes ago, sitting at a table in a library getting ready to talk about courage, justice, life, etc.

Otto reached into his wallet and pulled out his own piece of paper. His piece of paper looked like it had been through a war or two, which I found out later that it had been.

"Let's start here" said Otto. "It's the beginning"

"Always I good place to start" I agreed.

I started taking notes/

Otto read from his paper, "with his faithful Indian companion Tonto, the daring and resourceful masked rider of the plains led the fight for law and order, in the early western United States. Nowhere in the pages of history can one find a greater champion of justice. Return with us now to those thrilling days of yester year...... From out of the past come the thundering hoofbeats of the great horse Silver! The Lone Ranger rides again"

"What the heck was that" I asked.

"That was the way the Lone Ranger radio show began every week. I'll read it again. Listen and ask your questions"

Otto read it again.

I asked my first question "why did he wear a mask"

"Good question" observed Otto. " His real name was John Reid. He was a Texas ranger. Before he became a Ranger, John and his brother Dan had been partners in a rich silver mine strike...."

I interrupted. "Is that why he named his horse Silver"

"Yup and that's also why he fired silver bullets which he made himself at his silver mine. One day John, his brother Dan and four other Rangers got ambushed in the badlands by the Butch Cavendish gang. The Cavendish gang fired down on the Rangers with high-powered rifles. The Rangers were trapped. All six were hit. The Cavendish gang lingered to make sure everybody was dead, then they rode off"

"Five of the rangers were dead but......."

I jumped ahead "one of them miraculously survived which made him 'The Lone Ranger' and he decided to wear a mask to hide his identity while he hunted down the Cavendish gang"

"Damn", said Otto, "You are one smart kid"

"Am I ?" I asked thinking maybe Krell was right after all.

"And you're getting smarter every time you ask a question about the Lone Ranger"

"Okay" I agreed and continued my pursuit of wisdom. "How did Tonto get into this?"

"Good question" said my guide with a twinkle in his eye. I figured it had been awhile since anybody had asked him that question.

"After the Rangers were bushwhacked by the Butch Cavendish gang, Tonto came upon the badly wounded Ranger. Tonto nursed the Ranger back to health and they rode together from that point on. The real story though is for the show to continue, the Lone Ranger needed someone to talk to so that his inner thoughts and plans could be related to the audience in a form other than monologue," my guide explained.

"It was convenient to make the character a noble Indian to amp up the irony a little bit. The real kicker occurred when they decided on a name for this noble savage. They chose Tonto which in Spanish means fool. Now depending upon your meaning of fool, Tonto was either a wise warrior whose words always contained a double meaning and thus an element of truth or he was the doofus who walks into every trap and has to be continually saved by the Ranger. You could take it either way or both."

"So the Ranger was calling Tonto a fool every time he spoke to him?"

"You could say that" Otto replied

"Well what did Tonto call the Lone Ranger"

"Yeah well Tonto called the Ranger ke moh sah bee which means 'best friend' in the language of Tonto which unknowingly to Tonto are the words of a fool." Otto said.

"So," I reasoned, "when you see two best friends one of the friends is usually the fool?"

"Usually," said Otto," but lotsa times they both are. Like me and my buddy Lights Out. We been friends and fools for a long time. He's in the conference room. I want you to meet him."

Otto returned before Lights Out.

"He'll be here in a minute. Before he comes in though, I wanted to give you my definition of courage. Courage is knowing what not to fear."

"That sounds a little bit like ignorance is bliss," I said.

"No son, ignorance is not knowing what to fear and courage is knowing what not to fear. There's a big difference"

I understood incorrectly and thus metaphysictionaly but also realized that I was living somewhere in the middle. I knew that I was afraid of almost everything.

With that Lights Out suddenly appeared. I noticed that he too had come from the conference room. I also glimpsed a sign on the conference room door that I hadn't seen before. The sign said, 'Tune in Yesterday'. The reason these guys were in this library at this particular time was because they had come for a conference about the golden age radio before teevee

If Otto looked like an elephant without tusks, his buddy looked like a wildebeest carrying a full load of invisible lion on his back and a wedding ring to match. Otto turned to his friend. "Lights, this kid is looking for the secrets of life. What can you tell him"

"Otto" said Lights Out "looking for the secrets of life is like looking for the license plate number on a car that's pulling out ninety feet away on a street that's as deserted as a warm bottle of beer. Whaddya want me to tell this kid"

"Tell him something that you know for sure. Tell him something simple. Tell him what you glimpsed. Tell him something from your radio days. Ask him a few questions. This kid is smart" Otto insisted.

Lights Out turned his spooky gaze my way.

"Kid, " he said, "lots of people will tell you that life imitates art. I'm here to tell you that art imitates life"

"Art was an interesting fella" Otto agreed sorta. "We used to call him Glove."

Mister Out fixed his frightened and frightening focus full upon me."When I was a kid, my favorite radio show was called *Lights Out*. I never missed a program. That's how I got this nickname. Churchbells would ring twelve times and the announcer would say, 'LIGHT'S OUT EV-RYBODY'. Around the twelfth toll of the bells, an announcer would say, 'This is the witching hour. It is the hour when the dogs howl and evil is let loose upon the sleeping world. Want to hear about it? Then turn out your lights'. I'd turn out the lights and get scared to death. The stories were scary for sure but it was the sounds that went along with the stories that I can never forget. Otto says you're a smart kid. Let me tell you how a few sounds were made and then let's see if you can figure out what those sounds imitated."

Sounded like a plan to me.

"I'm ready. Go ahead."

Mr. Out went ahead, "Here's an easy one. Maple syrup dripping on a plate?"

"I'm gonna go with drops of blood hitting a floor" I had caught on to the game.

"One for one" said Otto. "Throw him another one, Lights".

Mr Out was just getting warmed up. "How about a blade chopping through a head of cabbage"

"I'm gonna go with a guy getting his head chopped off"

"Two for two" said Otto

Out again. "This one's more difficult, I'm going to describe three sounds and how those sounds were made. See if you can tell me what's going on in the scene. One, frying bacon. Two, sparks flying produced by attaching a telegraph key to a dry cell battery. Three, a ringing telephone."

I caught a whiff of the drift.

"Let's see. How about a guy getting zapped in the electric chair even as a call is coming in from the governor demanding a stay of execution"

"Three for thee" said Otto.

“Here’s my last one. Soaking a rubber glove in water and turning it inside out while a berry basket is crushed”

“That’s not fair” said Otto.

“You got me there," I admitted.

Mr. Out seemed pleased, quite a bit too pleased in fact. "That, young man, is the sound of a man being turned inside out when caught in a demonic fog. You see. Art imitates life”

I objected meekly. “ Can’t be sure about that because I’ve never been turned inside out in a demonic fog”

“Be patient, kid. Give the world a chance” said Lights Out in a distinctly foggy voice.

Otto added “wait until you fall in love”.

I thanked the men.

I left the library.

A dog howled in the distance. Maybe it was another dog getting killed by another cat.

LAST CLASS

A couple of days later, I arrived at Krell's class with at least a minute to spare.

Apparently Arthur was expecting an exam that day or had already had one in an earlier class because he was wearing an examination glove and explaining to an astonished Haylen how he had made his choice of gloves.

"When it comes to latex gloves, I have two choices: the Accu- care Plus or the Universal 3G. The Accu is yellowish white and the Universal is white. I wore the Accu for a test last week in History. I fanned on that test. So I went with the Universal for this morning's test in Astronomy. As far as powder goes, both brands are equally free"

When Krell came in, Julia had a surprise of her own. She asked Krell if she could recite the alphabet and hold the match herself. Krell gave her permission. Julia pulled out a tube of those extra long matches that people use to light candles and fireplaces. She lit the match and calmly recited the Greek alphabet ten times before the flame finally burned out.

Krell seemed impressed.

"I don't think anybody's going to top that act so we can put an end to the alphabet on a match recitations once and for all"

Then he turned his attention on me.

"And Ovid, how has it been for the last couple of days walking around as the smartest guy in town"

I told Krell that I had gone around and tried to find somebody smarter. I told him that I had met two men and they were both smarter than I was so I had given up and was okay with my stupidity.

Krell said that, “He doubted either of the two guys were any wiser than me”. He said that, “They probably had given me a mass of confused and contradictory opinions, derived from stories or traditions or memories and that those stories and traditions and memories and contradictory opinions had been no doubt changed at will to match the march of time and circumstance.”

He said, “Such opinions were not knowledge”.

He said, “Such opinions were only used to reinforce personal biases and that such opinions do not establish wisdom although all people who hold such opinions consider themselves wise and usually appear so to others”.

He said that, “Socrates spent his entire life under the belief that he had been identified by Apollo as the man whose mission in life was to destroy the false conceit of knowledge which had blinded his countrymen to their real ignorance and had in fact stupefied them with a false, fearsome sense of security and self-importance.”

Krell told us about how Socrates would question everyone and then prove how worthless the answers to his questions really were. Socrates didn’t offer any answers to his own questions because as he openly admitted, he himself was completely ignorant.

“Or as you have told us, Ovid. He was 'okay with his own stupidity’. Because he did so, Apollo had judged him to be the wisest of all. And that’s how I’ve judged you. And you went out and proved me right”

Julia passed me a note. The note read “PROJECT YOURSELF"I could tell everybody in the class wanted me to say something.I gave it a shot.

"Well, I did discover something in my questioning of the two wiser men who probably aren’t as wise as I thought they were. I discovered what I want to do with the rest of my life”

Everybody was paying attention now, particularly Julia.

"I've decided that I want to become the Lone Ranger of writing. I want to do the right thing anonymously and write about right when I do. First thing, I'm gonna do is write up the story of the last few days. I'm gonna use my notes. The next thing I want to do is ask Julia if she'll go out with me tonight to see a Will Sampson movie at the Starlite."

Haylen looked disappointed.

Julia said, "Love to."

Krell seemed to understand. "If you want to write anonymously, you need a pen name. Something cool that flows."

"Ice is cool," observed Hayen.
" Rivers flow," said Arthur.

"Ice Rivers" Julia concluded.

I kinda liked it but kinda thought I might have heard it somewhere before. It didn't put a rocket in my pocket but could be...who knows what's beyond the bend or over the rainbow.

And" Krell asked "what was the name of the man who inspired you to make such a decision"

"His name is Otto Dingfeldt," I said.

When he heard that name, Arthur turned his glove inside out and looked as if he wanted to punch a berry basket. Play Meatball

Lights Out.

I left the campus. When I reached the end of the campus road I always turned left, this time I turned right towards the Starlite.

ADDICTION

In my first years of teaching, I was always suspected to be "some kind of beatnik, hippie, commie" because of the length of my hair. A supervising dinosaur introduced me to a group of parents as "our resident Bohemian"

Apparently, I didn't "look"like a teacher. I looked more like the enemy. I looked more like a kid.

I look back at pictures of my hair in those days and am amazed at how short it actually was. Perhaps the problem was that it covered my ears. This was about the time when most middle class white folks truly believed that marijuana immediately produced reefer madness and turned users into playground pushers.

One day, I was in the cauldron known as the teacher's lounge when I was surrounded by a conversation about the evils of weed. Then, into the conversation burst a ray of light. One of the vice principals, a tall mouse studying to be a rat named Wolf, entered the room. The lounge, afraid that an authority figure might have heard them talking about "drugs," immediately clammed up. Somehow, Wolf correctly translated the silence and asked if he had interrupted a "conversation". One of his minions, petrified that she might be "covering up", admitted that the conversation was about "marijuana and it's addictive effects"

Wolf seemed pleased to be included in such a frank discussion. In a most reassuring yet dismissive and accusatory voice, Wolf said, "I don't know what the effects are because I've never tried it.......Why don't we ask Mr. Rivers?"

Wolf seemed to understand that I was almost as alien to the gossip of the teacher's lounge as he was. I hadn't said a word during the whole discussion other than a few cryptic nods. All of a sudden, all eyes were on me. I clearly remember my answer to this day. "Well," I said, "I imagine it's a lot like reading."

Although I didn't consider anyone in the room to be much of a reader, I could tell they held reading in the sacred contempt that many non-readers do, especially Wolf who made some kind of sound, turned his back and left the room.

I wish I had paid more attention to my own words because my reading addiction was at the stage where I might have been able to do something about it, having recently escaped from college.

Instead it kept growing. It would eventually cost me thousands of dollars, my first marriage, dozens of friends, and led me into the company of irresistible enablers/ responsible librarians like Penny Rider, Patricia Lindsay and Sara Kimmel who enabled my habit with frolicking enthusiasm.

I had to have it.

I realized the problem started when I was a child.

Both my mother and my father had shown symptoms. Not only did they fail to discourage me, they encouraged me. I became part of a cult known as "bluebirds".

I almost kicked the habit when I went to college. Somehow I lost my desire as the habit was foisted upon me by professors with whom I had failed to connect. I didn't want to be dragged into their world.

I'm deciding to come clean today after another night of revelry and fifty years of increasing intake As usual, I was up until all hours of the morning, indulging myself. I rarely sleep with my wife anymore as she tries to put reading limitations on me. I don't blame her for doing so but I can't resist.

A few years ago, someone suggested that perhaps if I started writing about my experience, perhaps it would lessen my dependence.

I did.

It didn't.

Now my writing has only intensified the problem.

The addiction is reading. I'm still pushing it.

Yesterday, I did something unusual. I started reading my writing. This exercise energized the problem to another dimension. I spent most of last night in a half sleep trying to figure out what I meant by my own writing.

I started editing in my mind.

That's when I knew I had to come clean. My mind started to formulate the confessional words that I am writing now, which you must be reading if you've come this far. As a matter of fact, I'm reading them myself and will continue to read them a couple of more times as I in Sysyiphisean mode, attempt to edit them.

Then it's back down to the cellar where I will continue reading free samples from Kindle, wishing I had the money to buy all these samples that interest me and knowing that the only way I can afford them is if I win some kind of writing contest in which I might use this "composition" as my entry but probably won't because it's too metaphysictional to understand and might not match the taste of the judges in the contest. Then I'll go to the library and see what I can get for free but I'm having trouble at the library because they say I didn't return a book that I know I returned because I don't have it in my house even though I've torn the house apart several times to the horror of my wife.

The missing book is "Metamorphosis, The Hunger Artist and more stories from Kafka"I know I returned it. They can't keep fining me forever can they? I'm innocent but I'm trapped. What if I can't use the library anymore?

I'll have to win a contest or publish a book to feed my need. I can no longer separate myself from my addiction. I am what I read

And so are you. Be very careful, if it's not already too late.

VIN

Yesterday was my father's 93rd birthday.

He wasn't around to enjoy it; that is if you consider these mortal coils by which we're bound a condition to celebrate rather than tolerate.

Pretty sure he's in a better place and celebrating in the way they celebrate in better places. He shuffled off four years ago. He was sick and tired of being sick and tired. He worked his ass off to gain release from the nursing facility/rehabilitation center that wouldn't let him out until he proved that he could walk.

He proved it. They let him out. Three days later, he woke early went to the bathroom, told my mother "Today's the day. I feel great" While in the bathroom, he collapsed and shuffled off.

It became clear that all the work that he did to get out was motivated by his desire to die at home which he pulled off.

I talked to him the day before. His last words to me were "keep busy".

He had a top hat.

Fifteen years before all of this, when all of this was more than any of us could have imagined, he bought the tombstones for him and my mother. He took a picture of those tombstones, engraved with every thing but the dates. He proudly brought the pictures over to my house one day.

This was the first time I ever thought he could die.

"At my funeral, wear my top hat, will ya?", he asked.

I said I would.

I did.

Just before we put him into the ground, just after we launched the balloons, I put his top hat on top of his urn and snapped my camera. the camera worked. This wasn't a dream. So long, Vin.

He was a firefighter, a captain.

He was a Veteran of Foreign War… WW2…the Phillipines.

He decided he wanted to be cremated.

He knew a lot about fire.

We picked out the urn that we thought he would have liked. Not real expensive… black and gold. We all got to carry the urn around at the funeral. We took our last picture with him. No relative of mine had ever been cremated before unless you count my Uncle Sam who drank a couple of pints of bourbon every day of his life and when he was cremated, they couldn't put out the fire.

That last part about Uncle Sam was a joke.

Let's get back to my father. For the proceeding decades, I called him Vin. We all did. He could have been Captain or Dad or Pop or Daddy or Father. Captain was way too formal. Pop was a Coke. Father sounded a little too Catholic. Daddy was for infants.

Why not Dad?

All of my buddies had a Dad. Their Dad did this and their Dad did that. My Dad was so much braver, so much funnier, so much smarter, so much more willing to get out in the backyard and throw the football around. My Dad was something other than what I perceived everybody else's Dad to be.

He was someone else. Everybody had a Dad. I had a Vin. His first name was Daniel. His middle name was Vincent. Yesterday was his birthday.

LUCIDITY IN DISGUISE

"Suddenly someone is there at the turnstile, a girl with kaleidoscope eyes".

Lucid dreams are a whole different subway system. In a lucid dream, the dreamer suddenly realizes that he/she is dreaming. Upon that realization, the dreamer brings some conscious decision making onto the inner screen projected by rapid eye movement. In this mode, the dreamer begins not only to watch the movie but also to direct it as well as screen-write and star in it. After such an integrated exercise, the dreamer awakens with a clearer memory of the dream and brings that memory into their morning meditation along with this accompanying sub-thought.

Thank God I got out of that one just in time.

The dreamer begins to live the dream.

Once in a while, the living of the dream recalls other parts of the dream that the dreamer didn't actively bring to consciousness. These bits and pieces of scrambled subconscious produce deja vu.

Sporadically, a culture experiences a universal deja vu. A movie becomes a hit. A novel becomes a best seller. A philosophy becomes a code of operation. A leader emerges. Revolutions begin. Penguins crouch. A star is born. Filler is filled.

A wrong is righted.

Clarity replaces paradox.

A consensual reality emerges. We fix something before it breaks.

Reading is close to lucid dreaming. The reader rapidly moves his/her eyes along the page as you are doing now. Unskilled readers, because of the task of decoding and subvocalizing move their eyes more slowly across the page. The slower the eye movement, the blurrier the picture on the inner screen; the less the sense of interaction with the text and connection with the writer. The reader is watching the words rather than rewriting them, directing them or starring in them.

The more skilled the reader, the more rapid the eye movement. The more rapid the eye movement, the more vivid the projection on the inner screen. After such a reading exercise, the reader emerges with a clearer memory of what he/she has read and often brings that memory into their ongoing meditation.

The reader begins to internally live the text.

The living of the text recalls other parts of other texts that the reader didn't actively bring to consciousness the first time through. These bits and pieces of scrambled subconscious coalesce and produce insight which illuminates confounding of the past.

The reader goes forward with a better understanding of the slings and arrows of waking life. Then after a brisk day of living, the reader goes back to bed and dreams a lucid dream. The reader picture himself on a boat on a river or swinging on a swing made of clouds while looking up at blue trees under a wooden sky in lipstick land.

A FULLER GRASP OF FILLER

In order to attain a fuller grasp of the concept of filler, we must detour through anacondas, alligators, dinosaurs, LSD, and birds. Let's start with anacondas, alligators and birds,

Ready?

Every so often I would get a job moving objects from one place to another. I had a brand new Crew Club Dodge truck with matching cap. My buddy at the zoo admired my truck and asked me if I would be willing to do some under the table transpo for him. I responded with my usual response , "Why not?".

I arrived at the local zoo on time and moments later he emerged with a very large canvas bag that was destined for a zoo in Buffalo. He loaded the bag into the back of my truck. "You're all set. They're waiting for you at the zoo."

"Cool, what's in the bag?"

"Our anaconda."

"What's it doing in the bag?'

"Doped up and chilling."

"MMMkkkaaayy. I'm gonna get truckin'."

So me and the anaconda in the canvas bag set off for Buffalo. I wasn't worried at all because to me the reptile was in the bag and the bag was just cargo. I did think it was kinda cool though and might be the beginning of a story that I might tell someday.

When we got to the zoo, the herpetology guy came out and removed the snake from the bag. He pronounced it both female and fit. This pronunciation guaranteed that I hadn't arrived at the same time as some other guy who was supposed to arrive in a Dodge Crew Cab and that I wasn't trying to pass off a sick, male anaconda while the other guy purloined the healthy snake bitch.

Or something.

For my reward, the herpetology guy decided to give me a tour of the innards of the snake house, apparently a rare extravagance.

As we walked through the snake house, the herpetology guy explained in exquisitely excruciating detail what would happen if he or I got bit by any of the venomous snakes that we were passing. All of the poisons were different and needed a different serum and usually by the time help got to the unconscious poisoned person it was already too late. Matter of fact that's how he got the job. They found the herp dude before him passed out on the floor and by the time they figured out the problem, it was too late for him.

The dude was dead.

Then we proceeded over to the alligator pond where he invited me to watch the alligators have lunch. At that moment, a bunch of starlings were thrown into the alligator pond. One of the "pain in the ass birds" landed directly on the head of a partially submerged gator.As I looked at the bird doing a morbidly comic homage to a raven on the bust of Pallas, I asked the obvious question."why doesn't the bird just fly away?"

"We already clipped his wings. He ain't goin' nowhere."

The alligator with the bird on his head wasn't goin' anyplace either. He just sat there motionless wearing a delicious starling hat.

"How come the gator isn't moving."

“Oh, they don’t move much. They move only when they need to. The rest of the time, they do what he’s doing.”

“Oh yeah,” I asked, “what is he doin? Is he asleep or is he awake?”

“Well, he ain’t awake and he ain’t asleep. It’s something in between.”

Of course as a human being I was only aware of two states of consciousness... either awake of asleep. This was before my various surgeries and adventures in anesthesiology.

“He’s what they call dormant.”

Dormant is a deeper variation of chilling. I understood that the anaconda in the bag had been doing the same thing.

Alligators spend most of their lifetimes dormant waiting around for something to happen and not particularly concerned when nothing happens

Just gatoring.

When we as humans ‘gator,’ I call that condition “filling”. We spend most of our lives in a zone beneath memory and the common product of that zone is “filler.”

I have no trouble taking the small evolutionary crawl backward from the dormant state of alligator behavior to the general intelligence or lack of same possessed by dinosaurs. If alligators space out a lot, imagine how much time dinosaurs spent spacing out. And they were around for three million years before we showed up which means that perhaps they were created in the image and likeness of God.

Three million years is a lot of filler.

Of course as Disney taught us, they came to an end at the LaBrea tar pits which even today is chock full of dinosaur bones. The dinosaurs were walking around, spacing out when they blundered into a gargantuan tar pit where they stood and spaced out for a while longer until they were stuck in tar but good. Even being stuck in the tar didn't bother the dinosaurs because hey, aren't we all stuck in the mud when we're spacing out. Every once in a while a spaced out stegosaurus would be rudely awakened by a T Rex that had also stumbled into the tar. Nothing more awakening than being stuck in a tar pit next to a gigantic carnivore who is trying to devour you especially when you're hallucinating. Aside from that, Mrs. Lincoln, the dinosaurs only other awakening from spacing out was hunger. Hunger ruined a lot of dinosaur mud pit space outs on their way to fossilhood in Los Angeles.

I never contemplated how stupid dinosaurs were until a couple of nights ago while watching *Walking with Dinosaurs* and the experts made a point of how spectacularly intelligent raptors were in comparison to other dinosaurs. I've heard this line of speculation before so the mere fact that it is repeated so often must mean that it's true. I started thinking that raptors were like dolphin style smart. In my book, dolphins are a hell of a lot smarter than gators. Flipper would have been an entirely different show if Flipper were an alligator.

Later in *Walking With Dinosaurs* in one of those important blurbs that geniuses throw on the screen immediately before a commercial, I learned that the "super intelligence" of raptors could be compared to the intelligence of ostriches today.

Whoa, Raptors were about as smart as ostriches which means that ostriches are one hell of a lot smarter than dinosaurs and raptors are a lot dumber than dolphins

I admit, a certain wisdom exists in spending a lot of time with your head buried in the ground but aside from that, ostriches don't strike me as particularly intellectual. If ostriches are the Advanced Placement/gifted/honors students in the dinosaur class, can you imagine what kind of paper wads the dinosaurs are throwing.

I don't know if you've ever been to an ostrich farm? I have.

On the ostrich farm, the ostrich farmers were holding court about the nutrition and comparatively low cost of ostrich meat. While this was going on, the farmer's kids were in the background cooking ostrich burgers. Simultaneously an ostrich wandered over near me and I looked it right in the eye. As I'm looking eyeball to eyeball with a future ostrich burger, I'm not picking up a lot of vibes from the ostrich one way or another. Certainly, nowhere near the vibes that a stegosaurus stuck in a mud pit would be projecting towards a T Rex as they met eyeball to eyeball moments before the feast nor the vibes I would be projecting when coming eye to eye with a raptor.

At this point, the ostrich farmer came up to me and said, "I notice you're looking at that bird's eye. Guess what. Their eye is almost exactly the size of their brain."

I took that information with a certain amount of freakout. Next thing I knew, the farmer was handing me an ostrich burger and practically shoving the burger down my throat. To get the farmer away from me, I took a bite. How can I describe the taste, the experience of eating an ostrich burger while looking an ostrich in its gigantic, tiny brain sized eye,

I'd say stupid and stupid.

So when I learned about the cranial comparison of ostriches to raptors, well it was small crawl towards creating these words that stay. Simple rilly but nowhere near as simple as a brontosaurus in a tar pit.

We're not extinct yet so I think I'm smart.

How else can I explain this rather rude attempt to disrespect the intelligence of Dinosaurs just because several of them overdosed on filler while standing and starving in the LaBrea tarpits?

Yeah, dinosaurs are extinct and we're not so hardee har har.

Extinction is a fact of life on "Earth"; the rule rather than the exception and therefore no reason to construct further arrogance driven oversimplifications. The history of life on this planet is the ironic parade of one extinction after another. I hate to think that five billion years from now some twelve fingered, four thumbed alligator

Mozart will discover this very writing and think I'm stupid only because we humans are not around anymore to defend our suicidal, supernatural obliviation.

I assume the four thumbed alligator will be smaller than me based on another ridiculous evolutionary over simplification that I have clung to for years, namely that intelligence is determined by brain to body ratio with dinosaurs as poster clods and the diplodocus the poster child of poster clods. Since dinosaurs were so gargantuan with such miniature brains no wonder they were doofus enough to go extinct, most of them not even smart/savage enough to learn to carnivore.

Basically, this means that the more we grow, the stupider we get.

What are we saying then when we tell a kid to "grow up?" Are we saying that when you get bigger, you'll be stupider so you can solve your problems in a more dunder headed, more specifically representative way?

Remind me not to advance this theory on the ghost of Andre the Giant or Wilt Chamberlain.

If this theory were true, I'd be dumber now that I'm older and fatter than I was when I was younger and thinner. Over the years my brain has stayed the same size but my body has grown dramatically. Multiply that problem by a hundred and you have the quandary of the dinosaur.

If this theory were true, we'd start electing big brained infants to positions of political power and struggle to interpret their babble as economic or military or political strategy.

If this were true, everybody would be going nuts trying to lose body size which means there would be an international fetish for thinness as well as an ongoing craze with dieting and youthful appearance. Women in particular would be Botoxing like raptors trying to unwrinkle and prolong our species. Thank God or whatever that NONE of that is happening.

Of course, according to researchers including Seton and Masters, there is another theory. The theory is that vegetarian dinosaurs including the mighty brontosaurs lived on Jurassic vegetation the chemical elements of which are very similar to LSD. Is it possible that this whole "existence" we are living currently is nothing more than the hallucination of a brontosaurus bad tripping while spacing out and starving while stuck in a tar pit. Dinos also imagined themselves turning into birds and some kind of comet hitting the planet causing wide spread extinction of their species which caused the de-evolution into mammals who believe whole heartedly in the concept of death and time and beginning and endings and Los Angeles. In short, they imagined the supernatural.

Should we fear the supernatural? Oh yeah. We are the supernatural. We are the only conscious existences on earth. God damn it And he/she/it did.... As we all know from Eden.

That's when we began to be self conscious. Eventually self consciousness leads to death consciousness. We alone are death conscious and that is our Rubicon. When we grew to realize death we realized ending. Soon after discovering ending we became conscious of beginning and middle as well. When we watch movies or read stories or tell stories, we like them to have a beginning a middle and an end. That's consciousness.

We get the feeling that we've got to do something...got to go somewhere...got to see somebody....and not just for reproduction or survival. Yeah birds/dinosaurs migrate but that's all about survival. Pretty sure they don't plan in advance. They just go. I've seen thousands and thousands of birds in my life. I've seen maybe a couple dozen dead ones. Where do they go to die? Do they die in mid-air and disappear? They're not worried about death or disappearance......no idea what any of it is.

Birds as a species like bees are disappearing rapidly. When the birds and the bees start to vanish, we ought to suspect something. Something big and not kind.

A mushroom showed up in my yard a couple of days ago....one single solitary mushroom. I don't think that mushroom was lonely. Don't think that mushroom was worried about me getting my driver out and practicing my swing even though the head of the shroom was perfectly teed up and getting out my driver and practicing my swing was exactly what I was thinking until this morning when the mushroom was gone. Don't know where it went

Just gone like the birds and the bees. No funeral, no grieving, no nuttin' except I guess THIS which I am able to do because I (like you) am supernatural.

I'm gonna die. I know it. You know it. My daughters know it as do all of my friends and lovers who remain alive. I've known it for a long time probably since I was three years old when a friend of mine, Sammy Ferrante, got run over in his own driveway by a cement mixer.

Towards the end of my teaching career, I was thirty plus years older than the students in my classes. The odds were real good that I would/will die before most of them. I reminded them of this when I invited them all to my funeral. They immediately thought that I was sick. I said, "I'm not sick. I'm just much older than you." Some of the students said that I shouldn't be talking about something so morbid. I didn't think there was anything morbid about it, I was inviting them to contemplate mortality which is/was a concept that very few of them were willing to contemplate in their perceived immortality. After more discussion, I asked the question again. "I'm inviting you all to come to my funeral. Raise your hand if you plan on attending."

Almost all of them raised their hands. I thought, metaphysictionaly at least, that the class was of great value.

These words might outlive all of us and emerge as art until the end. The end is whenever anyone who read these words is gone along with everyone who knew anyone who read these words along with everybody who knew me and everybody who knew anybody who knew me.

Don't worry, I've got 10 grandchildren.

Art itself is supernatural because it reminds us that we're alive which means we're conscious which means we're aware of death. Even though art is supernatural, we don't need to fear it. We don't need to fear all of the supernatural. That would be crazy....yet....

That lunatic who just walked into the church and started murdering everybody, he was supernatural. He was conscious of death, probably very conscious of it. He was something to fear and for God sake somebody sold this guy some guns.

The guy who sold the guns was/is supernatural as well. Very supernatural...very conscious of death. The guy makes his living by dealing in death-makers although I guess he can justify it by rationalizing that the weapons will only be used to eliminate deers or bears or coyotes or in case of assault weapons, dinosaurs and other natural beings who don't know or care about death anyway so no biggee.

Like birds and bees although we don't need a gun to kill the bees. We kill them naturally. Save the howitzers for the offspring of the birds and the bees, the foul mouthed humming birds.

And for further supernatural reasons, I'm past the beginning of this "essay," past the middle, entering the beginning of the end of the middle because I'm running out of time. Dinner is waiting. I have to be there for that...we're having some variety of chicken.

Pretty sure the chicken didn't see THAT coming. Aside from sunrise..the chicken had no idea what time it was. He was used to being fed. He was used to the same schedule. He was far from afraid. Now he's committed.

Time is on our side. No other creatures on earth have the slightest idea what time it is, although most know night from day, especially owls, aardvarks and other nocturnals who prey at night although time measured in terms of light and dark is far from hours and minutes. Even a one eyed owl has no idea how old he is. We use time to measure where we are in life…beginning…middle or let's just say senior which is a nice way of saying comparatively close to the end, down by the river.

This seems like a good time to begin the ending as you and I and all of us have something we have to do and we better get to it for time is running out on getting that thing done.

When everybody has everything done that would be a great opportunity to bow out gracefully and become extinct.

Maybe that's what our computers are helping us to do and hoping that we don't teach them about death or time.

Hawking is telling us we've only got 600 years left until the whole shebang turns into a fireball so the computers better hurry which they are incapable of doing unless we teach them what they don't want to learn.

Then when we're gone…the supernatural is also gone.

No ghosts…no werewolves, no zombies…..no more death

no more time

and that and this are the ends.

HANDS OF A WRITER

I had aspirations of becoming an Eagle Scout. I had the Boy Scout Manual which described all of the requirements for any merit badge. Since I played the clarinet and had studied at Eastman School of Music, I figured that I might as well get the music merit badge.

I found the name of the advisor who would check on my requirements and approve my merit. I made an appointment. I packed up my instrument and biked way over to his house. It was a bumpy ride.

I knocked on the door of his house, a house that had seen better days. He opened the door and asked how he could help me. I told him that I was the kid trying to get a music merit badge. He remembered and invited me into his home.

I couldn't tell if he was young or old because he was quite tall and had a full beard. My ONLY experience with beards was Santa Claus and Abe Lincoln. He had his hair combed straight back and if he used Brylcreem, he used more than a little dab.

Even though it was a sunny day, he had his windows closed and his Venetian blinds drawn. I noticed that he had a guitar in one corner of his large living room, a a pair of bongo drums on his coffee table, shelves full of books both paperback, comic and hardcover. His ashtrays were full of Camel butts. The only artwork I could see was a poster of Robbie the Robot carrying Ann Francis. Under the poster was a piano.

"I know your name Scout, do you know mine?.

"Your name is Mr. Krell, sir".

"That's right. So you like music, do ya. What kind do ya like?."

" I like orchestra music," I lied.

I'm pretty sure he saw through that because he then asked "do you like that rock and roll?"

Mr. Krell was the first older person who had ever asked me about rock and roll.

I told him about Buddy Holly, Clyde McPhatter, Duane Eddy, and Dion and the Belmonts. I told him that I had gone to that rock and roll show at the new War Memorial. Sensing his approval, I went on and on about the show.

He let me talk which surprised me.

When I was done, he asked the required questions. Could I read music? Could I count beats in a measure? Did I know what a times signature was? Could I name three stringed instruments?

I could. I could. I did and I could.

He asked me if I had any long playing records or just 45's.

I told him that I had lots of 45's as well as four long play hi fi 33's; *Loving You* by Elvis, the *Twang's the Thang* by Duane Eddy, *Victory at Sea* and the *Music from Peter Gunn* by Henry Mancini.

He seemed impressed. He showed me his albums and he had dozens of them, mostly from artists that I had never heard of except for Fats Domino and Little Richard.

He noticed that I had brought my clarinet case. He knew that I was required to play three songs.

Krell said "let me hear you play."

I opened my case and started assembling my instrument when I discovered that during my bike ride, I had cracked my only reed. I wouldn't be able to play the clarinet that day.

He asked me if I could play anything on any other instrument.

I told him that I could play a couple of songs on the piano. I sat down on his piano stool and one handed Oh Susanah and The Hunting Song. I said "that's it".

He asked me if I ever played the bongos which I hadn't.

Krell said "I'll play a couple of songs on my hi fi for you. See if you can find the beat on the bongos."

He played a couple of songs. There were no drums in the music and the singer had a nasal voice voice and "sang" weird words almost like he was talking. Somehow, I could feel the rhythm in the songs. I tapped away on the bongos with my heart and my hands.

Krell seemed satisfied with my tapping. He told me that I had natural rhythm and he liked the way that I "felt" the music. He told me that he paid close attention to my hands when I played the piano. He noticed the chewed nails. He told me that I didn't have the hands to be a musician but I might have the rhythm and tapping to be a drummer. I asked who was singing on the album. He told me it was a young guy named Bob Dylan.

He said he would count the bongo songs as the performance requirement.

Then he said this....."you have the hands of a writer. You and I know that you still owe me a performance. What do you think, you should do?"

I had run out of ideas but he had one tucked away. There was something he wanted me to do..something that I "owed him." Something that I would eventually learn to love

"Someday, I want you to write about me and about this moment and my message."

BAGMEN WILL STAND

Family plays a big factor in my friendship tree.

I knew Crown and Wild Bill. I introduced them to each other and to Deke. Deke is my brother.

Deke, Crown and Wild Bill are now friends.

Deke knew Bruce and D'argento before they knew me. He introduced them to me and I introduced them to Crown and Wild Bill.

Me, Deke, Crown, Wild Bill, Bruce and D'argento are now friends.

Crown knew Walt and Hank before Walt and Hank knew Wild Bill, Deke,Bruce and D'argento.

Me, Deke, Crown, Wild Bill, Bruce, D'argento, Hank and Walt are now friends.

My sister Terri knew Jack before he knew Deke who knew Jack before I knew Jack and before Jack knew D'argento, Crown, Wild Bill, Bruce, Hank, and Walt.

This cluster is the core cluster in my friendship tree. We celebrated this cluster every year for 35 years at Deke's place on Canandaigua Lake. We gathered at the baseball all star game which is in mid-July. At the gathering we made announcements and predictions and we shared old stories of announcements and predictions past. I could and perhaps will write a book about those announcements, stories and predictions as well as the men who made them.

The tradition ended when we moved South

They are the funniest, smartest, most trustworthy men that I know. They are the reason why I rarely laugh at comedians and their 'craft'. My crew is so much more hilarious.

I think I'll start with Bruce.

Deke met Bruce when they were both in high school part time picking up trays as weekend food service workers at Park Avenue hospital. Over the years, I have heard many stories of what went on in the locker room of the hospital, the pranks that were pulled and the fun that was had.

Bruce is the star of my favorite story of that era. Bruce tells it beautifully at the All Star game every year.

Seems that a guy named Steve had pulled off a few nasty tricks on others so the others were looking to get even. One day Steve was in the locker room stall taking a crap. While Steve was sitting on the throne, Bruce picked up a laundry bag full of soiled towels. Bruce tossed the twenty pound bag through the opening at the top of the stall onto what must have been an astonished Steve. The bag was heavy but soft. After tossing the bag, Bruce immediately began his getaway.

Steve bolted out of the toilet with a turd in his hand. Bruce turned around and saw the flung dung heading for his face. He moved slightly and the turd went splat against the wall. Bruce describes that SPLAT moment in great detail as it seemed to be happening in slow motion.

I try to imagine the incident from Steve's point of view. You think you're alone in a critical moment and suddenly a laundry bag falls on you. It doesn't hurt but it startles the crap out of you. You react to the situation immediately. You grab hold of your warm creation and with your pants still down, you burst through the stall door. You see everybody running and laughing. You spot Bruce. You're an all star third basemen with a terrific arm. You fling your turd and it looks like it's going to hit Bruce in the face until at the last moment he swerves and SPLAT. You go back in the stall, clean up, pull up your pants and take off.

Nobody knew what ultimately happened to the splat on the wall but the conjecture went like this. Al White was the evening clean up guy and when he got to work that night, his boss told him to make sure to clean up the locker room because there was a "mess" down there. Al spent most of his evening shifts handicapping the horses for the next day at Finger Lakes. He liked to work fast so he could have more time sitting on his ass, smoking and handicapping. He went down to the locker room. It didn't seem too messy until he noticed the splat on the wall..."Goddamn, there's a turd on the wall"

He took care of the mess but always wondered how that turd got so high up on that wall.

Now you know what Al White was never able to figure out.

And you know a little bit about Bruce and my friendship tree.

Remember this all went down before I even met Bruce. Deke had told me the story.

I finally met Bruce at the famous Watkins Glen Concert featuring the Dead, The Band and the Allman Brothers. There were 300,000 people at that event. The odds of meeting Bruce that day were one out of 300,000,We got as close as we could when we spotted a large blanket and a motorcycle. We made our way to the blanket and that's where I met Bruce. The Dead were singing "Bertha don't ya come around here anymore".

It's always a good thing when I can remember what song was playing when I first meet a person. When that song is "Bertha" and it's being played live by the Dead in the midst of 300,000 people on a day so sunny that torrential rain is a possibility at any moment, well that's a good way to meet.

Yes, the torrential rains came. Everybody started scrambling to escape the storm. Bruce went over to his cycle and opened his saddle bag. He took out three blue garbage bags. He put the bag over his head and pulled it down to cover his body all the way to his knees. Like a turtle, he pushed his head through the top of the bag. Then he punched his arms through the side of the bag. He had made himself a raincoat. He threw us the other two bags and we did the same thing. We were the

Bagmen. Not a lot of people were standing most were hiding under whatever sparse cover they could find. I looked at the situation and said, “The Bagmen Will Stand.” We stood up proudly through the whole storm. When the sun came back out and the pounding rain disappeared, those people around us who had been seeking shelter from the storm began to emerge and started praising us for bagging it. They thought the bags were cool. A few people wondered if we had any more of those bags. Bruce did have a few more and he shared them. They repeated the turtle and arm move. Before long there were three more bagmen and two bag ladies. Everybody laughing. Soon many of those who had brought a plastic garbage bag to the concert started wearing them like we were wearing them and making their way over to our space for some good wearing and sharing.

Thus began the Bagman Ball.

Every March we had a blowout party at wherever Bruce was living at the time. The highlight of the party was putting on the bags. Bruce supplied the bags pro bono. When everybody was in their bags, we’d put on “Sympathy for the Devil”. Every one would start singing “Doot Doo” and conga lining throughout whatever space was available in the house.

The consensus opinion was that Kay Stafford wore the best bag. It became another tradition that when people were putting on their bags, they would ask Kay to come over and custom fit. Kay designed quite a few different styles. I’ve heard many a bag lady, upon receiving a compliment for the style of her bag respond "It’s a Kay Stafford design”

Aside from Bruce and Deke and me, no one really knew why they were putting on bags and "Doot Dooing" but the whole scene was so bizarre and hilarious and filled with gentle peer pressure that all the participants enjoyed the exercise and the party was united. How can you be pissed off at somebody who's wearing a garbage bag exactly like the one that you're wearing?

We continued to have that party for the next 25 years. We called it the Bagman Ball.

Phillip Seymour Hoffman showed up at one.

Maybe you attended one or two.

I'm talking to you Mr. Stub and Maureen. And all of you Rich brothers and sisters. I'm talking to you Alcrimidere...and don't forget the laughing gas.

I'm talking to you Tommy Tron and you Michelin Man.

I'm talking to you Krell and you

I'm talking to you Scott and Linda

I'm talking to you Pete on stilts, you Bill Downey and you Gary Gottshalk and all of the Caroll brothers and sisters

If you did, all I can say is "Doot Doo"

HOW THORNTON MET SADIE

I attended a couple of Bagman Balls. I even scored a Kay Stafford bag.

As you've noticed both Ice and Ovid talk about me a lot which means my life to you must come across as incomprehensible. I'm gonna tell you this part of my story in my own words and I hope you'll misunderstand.

I'm Thornton Krell

I found out tonight that my second wife was born in Pleasantville, Pennsylvania. How ironic ! It's as if Richard Nixon was born in Honestville, California or Trump born in Modestville, New York. She was born in a Naval Hospital. Her father explained to her that she had a navel only because she was born in a Naval Hospital. He also told her that his acne scars were shrapnel wounds from his combat days in Korea. She believed him on both counts.

I don't know whether or not my ex-father in law served in Korea but one night ten years later, I was in a bar when one man (a guy wearing yellow plastic jacket with the name "Don" over the pocket) claimed that he had fought in Korea and wanted to bet "ten bucks" on it. Since nobody could suggest a sober or even sane way of settling this bet, my attention began to wander.

I commenced to look at the huge fishtank behind the bar in front of which two veteran malcoholics were arguing about whether or not one of the men had fought in Korea. I wondered what would happen if I dropped an electric eel into that fishtank although I was pretty sure that it wasn't an eel in my pocket.That's when the fist fight started.

A few minutes later, seventeen stunned goldfish were flopping around on the bar room floor, silently screaming as if they had been born in Berserkville, Georgia.

Dino, the bartender was in the backroom changing his shoes when the tank crashed to the floor. Dino didn't speak much English, not that a common language mattered much at a time like this. The only words that Dino ever spoke that I could understand were "two fer you" I would nod and Dino would draw me two draft beers. We had an understanding and it worked for both of us.

I walked over to the splatter scene. I picked up two of the goldfish. At that moment Dino emerged from the backroom. He took one look at me holding the goldfish and asked "Two for you?"

I handed Dino both fish and said, "No, two for you."

I stepped over the two morons pounding each other on the bar room floor. "Don" was getting the worse of it.

I turned back to Dino who was holding the two fish. I pointed to the lummoxes on the floor on the floor and said, "Two for you" and walked out of the bar.

I didn't return to that bar for 12 years. By the time I returned, the bar had a new owner, a new fishtank and a new bartender, a morbidly overweight neighborhood guy named Charley. Charley had been a regular in the old days and we remembered each other from the original "two for you days". There were only three people in the bar that night, me, Charley and a woman apparently drawing something in a sketchbook.

Charley came at me with a wink and asked "two for you". I said of course. Charley gave me my two and change. He gave me 10 bucks more than he should have. He winked. With that I ordered two more for me.

I glanced at the woman with the sketchbook. Our eyes met. I asked her what she was drawing in the sketchbook. She showed me. It was a sketch of me holding two beers, one in each hand. Her rendering looked just like me only smarter and not as drunk. I asked her if she wanted one of my beers. She said, "Sure".

Ten minutes later Charley came over and asked “two for you.”

I said, “Two for me and two more for her”.

Once again he winked and gave me double the change.

Later I found out that Charley was in the process of quitting the job and giving out handouts to all of the neighborhood guys because he hated the owner’s guts.

She accepted both beers and kept sketching. She showed me what she was sketching. It was a sketch of me kissing her. She told me her name was Sadiel kissed her.

It might have looked like two goldfish going for the same piece of corn.

Whatever.

Three years later, we got married by a fake Abe Lincoln in a little chapel outside Blissville, Vermont.

WITH GLOVES IN THE GARDEN

They had met before, these invincible Sons of the South but never in this most famous of gardens and never wearing their gloves. One of them, both descendants of slaves, hailed from South Carolina and the other from Kentucky. Before this meeting, both had travelled the world and the world had lured them them into this square space.

In another time, they might have carried pistols or swords as this was the beginning of a fight to the death. This time all they carried was their strength, skill, indomitability and courage.

They knew each other as well as two men can know each other while still remaining strangers. In another time or another place they might have been friends but not on this night.

They both needed each other and both were aware of the need as was the world and the world was watching albeit from a distance.

Elizabeth Taylor, Richard Burton, Gene Kelley, Ethel Kennedy, Ben Cartwright, Marcello Mastroianni, Hugh Hefner, Michael Caine had gathered and were close enough to catch blood spray. Norman Mailer and William Saroyan came with their pens. Frank Sinatra brought his camera. Richard Nixon along with the largest television audience in history, thirty million strong, tuned in on closed circuit television.

Five minutes before the South Carolinian headed to the forum, he prayed in his dressing room. “God let me survive this night. God protect my family. God grant me strength and God allow me to kick the shit out of this mother fucker.”

When they reached their destination, the Kentuckian bobbed up and down on his toes. He brushed up against the South Carolinian and said “Chump”. The South Carolinian scowled in response.

Finally, at last they were called to the center of the Garden. They glared at each other with locked eyes...one yapping the other grinning. Neither of them the least bit familar with defeat.

In another time or another place, one might have said to the other " We meet at last." Only the man from Kentucky spoke. Muhammad Ali said to Joe Frazier, "Look out nigger, I'm gonna kill ya."

Thus began the long process of each of them killing the other slowly.

They would meet again over and over but never again like this, never again so undamaged.

IN THE PACKAGE

Mr. Baseball remained in his coma for months, for years…assuming there is time in a coma. Maybe I should check with Buzzo.

It was the bottom of the ninth and Baseball was behind by 100 runs and there were two out and two strikes One more strike and he was out.

Game over.

I visited him often. I told him all the latest baseball stories and rumors. I talked about the Christmas party and Joanne and her purposeful stride. I like to think that he heard me

That was the situation the last time that I visited him at the Community hospital.

Time passed. Mr. Baseball kept fouling off pitches, his faithful loving wife Rosie by his side.

Rosie figured that maybe things would improve if they moved Baseball to his home ball park. Still in his coma, Mr. Baseball was transported to his home.

Home plate.

I never saw Mr. Baseball again except in my dreams. I kept trying to take his picture but the camera didn't work.

His home plate was far away from my home plate. We didn't visit in person, overwhelmed as were with our own ballgame.

When he got home, minus a few tubes and some drugs that hadn't worked, Mr Baseball out of nowhere, hit a homerun. He came out of the coma but remained bedridden. We didn't know about the rally, we had left the game a little early. We knew that he was home and we had his phone number.

One day, Lynn called the number and Rosie answered. The rally was still going on. Therapists were pitching now and Mr. Baseball continued to swing away always bolstered by Rosie who was as encouraged as she was encouraging. She told Lynn that a speech therapist was pitching at the moment. She whispered to Mr. Baseball that Lynn was on the phone. He understood; another base hit.

Rosie put the phone up to Mr. Baseball's face.

Lynn said, "Hello, Mr. Baseball."

Lynn's 'hello' was like a hanging curve ball. Mr. Baseball took a mighty swing and said in a slow, soft, labored voice "Hi Lynn."

Home run. Grand slam.

Rosie took the phone back and explained the progress Baseball had been making. He was scoring on the coma. His therapists were amazed.
He scored 200 runs and beat the stroke.

Meanwhile he had developed cancer. It was the cancer, not the coma that finally ended the incredible rally. Baseball died at home surrounded by his priceless memorabilia and in the loving presence of his Rosie.

We went to the funeral. Mr. Baseball looked good almost as good as he looked the time he caught a foul ball barehanded at Frontier Field. In my dreams, he shows up at his funeral and he, Rosie, Lynn and I go off to dinner as if nuthin' had happened. He grabs a foul ball with his bare hands at Frontier Field. He even makes fun of me for imagining that everything wasn't perfect.

We paid our condolences to Rosie.
A week later, we got a package in the mail with Mr. Baseball's home address as the return. In the package was the fiber optic bear.

ALI, FRAZIER, CHUVALO AND EVELYN

Slides.

Remember slides?

You'd throw your slides into a Kodak Carousel and voila…a light show up against the wall.

Needless to say I threw quite a few slides against quite a few walls over the years as I told my Ali stories.

I liked one of the slides in particular .I made a nice 11 by 14 print from that slide. Ali and Joe exchanging punches during their second fight at Madison Square Garden.

We all got older as the years passed. It seemed like Ali and Joe got older faster than everybody else. What else could we have expected?During this time of great decline, George Chuvalo added to the pugilistic tragedy.

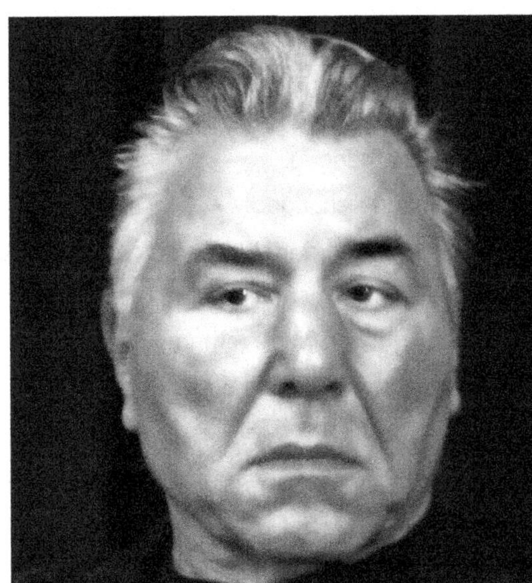

George Chuvalo

The Croatian Crusader.

The Heavyweight Champion of Canada.

The human punching bag and common opponent for the vastly more talented Ali and Frazier.

The man who could not be knocked down.

The man whose face had launched a thousand fists.

George Chuvalo had a face that had been sculpted by other fists into the face of a fist

And then after George retired, life stepped in and continued the battering.

He lost his wife and sons to suicide. Heroin was very involved.

Still George refused to hit the canvas.

Word got through to his old opponents, Ali and Joe, that George was hurt and

staggering but that he refused to go down.
A boxing organization in Rochester decided to throw a benefit dinner for George.
Yeah it was a band aid on a shotgun wound but every little bit helps.

Joe Frazier decided to attend and waive any fee.
So did another wounded warrior name of Muhammad Ali.
Ali was shaking from Parkinson's and Joe could barely see.
Joe and Ali didn't usually appear together.
Bad blood existed.
People wondered why after all these years bad blood still existed between Ali and Frazier.
The answer is simple. These guys tried to kill each other three times in front of the whole world and they damned near succeeded.
He jest at scars who's never felt a wound.

There was a lot of laughter that night but nobody was laughing at the scars.
I was there too.
The Chuvalo benefit cost a hundred bucks to attend. My ringside seat at Ali-Frazier fight also cost $100.
So much had changed.
One thing hadn't changed.
The 11 by 14 photograph that I took at Ali Frazier 2 looked exactly the same. The two of them stalking each other in the middle of the ring, young and healthy and with all the lights shining on them.
I brought the picture to the benefit.

I had met Muhammad, Joe and George individually but I never thought that I'd see all three of them in the same room at the same time.
Yet, here we were for the common good of Chuvalo.
In the lobby, I got a chance to visit with boxing expert Burt Sugar and HBO analyst Larry Merchant. They both reacted to me as if I had pissed myself while wearing a white suit.. Arrogant and a million miles away from Ali in terms of engagement and humility, these two celebrities brushed off my questions about the sweet science with an insolence worth mentioning here.
Vampires

I left those “famous guys”.
I was relieved to leave.
I entered the main room.

Carmen Basilio was much more approachable. I had met Carmen a couple of times before. I didn’t want to ask him the same old questions that he’s been asked a million times about Sugar Ray Robinson. I asked him about one of his less famous victories. “Hey Champ, do you ever see Johnny Saxton anymore?”

Carmen answered “No, he’s all fucked up.”

“What got him Carmen, I followed up,“ drugs, booze, women, gambling?”

“No” said Carmen, “I fucked him up.”

Carmen was a tough man.

I found my table. My name was still not Sinatra nor for that matter Sugar or Merchant so my $100 dollar table resembled my “ringside” seat in terms of physical distance from the action. I shared a “way in the back” table with another human who also had connection/complexion problems; a stunning middle aged African American woman named Evelyn. We had the only two seat table in the place.

Evelyn and I chatted for awhile about the value of our $100 as compared to the $100 spent by the more connected, very Caucasian, very male attendees flaunting upfront and uptight. We figured we were outsiders. We bonded. I showed her my 11 by 14 photo. She liked it and said, “Be careful with that. It’s valuable”.

Evelyn had a mission of her own.
Evelyn told me that she “knew” Joe Frazier and the last time Joe was in town, she really got to know him and he got to know her. She planned on having a little chat with Joe later in the evening about his previous method of leaving town. She assured me that Joe would be paying close attention.

All the stars were already seated miles away at the main table. All the stars that is except for Ali. It’s only fitting that the champ enters last.

All of the other guys had entered from the front of the venue.

When Ali and his entourage entered the room, they came in from the back. As soon as he entered the room, the whole environment changed for the better. He walked very, very slowly. Since he came in from the back, the first table he passed was our distant table for two.

He stopped at our table. He looked right at me and although it seemed impossible, I got the distinct feeling that he remembered me from our morning at Deer Lake decades before. Evelyn noticed the look and asked me after Ali had passed us, "does he know you".

I told Evelyn that I had spent some time with him a long time ago.

Whether he recognized me or not, he once again gave me that wonderful feeling that I was cool with him and that our table was the best table in the house and that, once again, made me feel cool with myself

although he couldn't possibly have remembered.

I guess that's what charisma is all about.

Like I said, I had met Sugar and Merchant, ten minutes before they took their upfront seats. I'm sure they had already forgotten about me and their vibe would have amplified that disregard. Not with Ali.

I started feeling important, inspired rather than intimidated. The whole room turned back to see the old champ. I got the feeling that everybody in the room started feeling important for different reasons.

Uplifiting and transcendent, eliciting smiles and cheers with every step, the Champ caned his way to the front. Everybody in the place was experiencing rampant, contact joy.

I don't think that Frazier was feeling that joy although he probably remembered feeling a lot of contact. It was obvious that Joe was feeling pretty dang great before he even entered the place, if ya know what I mean.

A lot of feelings fly around a room when Ali enters that room and walks toward a partying Joe Frazier.

The dinner began.

Neither Ali nor Frazier addressed the audience; for different reasons.

Chuvalo expressed his gratitude towards both men for showing up and making his benefit such a success. Weirdly enough if a three man boxing match broke out, Chuvalo would probably win even though both Joe and Ali had battered him in the past.

Merchant and Sugar blabbed some and sucked a bit of energy from the room although their wisdom has slipped beneath the radar screen of both my memory and contempt.

When the program concluded, the master of ceremonies, a born bullshitter named Jerry Flynn announced that for a half an hour the head table participants would be willing to sign autographs.

Immediately the rush to the front began led by the people sitting in the front. From the way back table, we watched the crowd in front gain full advantage. We only had a half hour and it looked as if there were two hours of people in front of us.

We did a little spontaneous human calculus.

Evelyn headed towards Joe. She had more than an autograph in mind. She had a piece of her mind in mind and she was about to give that to Joe.

I headed for Ali, by far the longer of the two lines.

Somehow, my 11 by 14 print caught the eye of someone in Ali's entourage. He asked me to identify the picture. "Ringside, Madison Square Garden, Ali-Frazier II"Diju take dat picture?"

"Yes I did"

"Champ prolly like to see it. C'mon"

He escorted me towards the front of the line, not the very front but a definite improvement on my table rank. Ali and I were in the same force field. I knew he'd have time for me even as the minutes ticked away. With about 10 minutes left in the opportunity, our chance came.

I put my picture in front of the Champ. He considered it carefully. He was in no rush whatsoever. Then the familiar whisper that he either said or sent. I'll never know which but the message was clear…"choo take this?"
"Yeah Champ I did'
Another whisper/send "it's good."

Then the eye contact. Ali and me eyeball to eyeball again. Same eyeballs that had been eyeball to eyeball with Martin King, John Lennon, Sonny Liston, Elvis Presley, Sugar Ray Robinson,, Joe Louis, James Brown, Stallone, Duvall, Carson, Borgnine, Malcolm X, Ross, Wilt Chamberlain and infinite others were inviting me to come on in and stay a minute.

Make yourself comfortable.

Join the crowd.

Maybe u been here before.

He gave me his beautiful Parkinson's signature. Very slow, very painful, looking up every few seconds directly in my eyes as if this were the first signature of his career given to his best friend. Ali had signed another piece for me at Deer Lake decades before. Like the man himself, Ali's signature had changed dramatically over the years. His Parkinson's signature took a good twenty seconds to make with five separate lookups and included only the fragments of four letters….. M…A…L….I. Ironically he made his mark over Joe Frazier's image in the ring in my picture.
He hit me with the feint again although this feint was very faint yet still overwhelming.

I thanked the champ. Again the eyes. Again the illusion of recognition. Again the electricity.

So long champ.

Still five minutes of the half hour remained. Wow.

Pause

Shift.

Shuffle.

Recalculate.

I got a shot at Joe.

Where's Evelyn?

There she be.
Evelyn chillin' with Joe
"Hey Evelyn" from fity feet away with four minutes left.
"Hey Ice, c'mon up here and meet Joe."
Once again the Red Sea miraculously parted.
The Red Sea thought Evelyn was Joe's wife and I was a friend of Joe's family.
I got to the table with time to spare.
Evelyn said "Joe, this is my friend. Sign his picture"
I put my picture in front of Joe.
Joe looked at my picture.
"Dijoo take this picture"

"Yeah I did, Champ"

"Good picture", said Joe.

Ironically, Joe signed his name over the image of Ali in the ring in the light at Madison Square Garden, young and beautiful.

Floating

Getting ready to sting forever.

Evelyn gave Joe a peck on the cheek.
Joe took a sip from his beer.
I gave Evelyn a peck on her cheek.
It was the last time that I ever saw any of them.
Time was up. Ring the bell.

NON-FICTION IS THE NEW FACTION

WAY BEYOND INDIANA SPIN

(Dreams & Distance)

In my dreams, my camera is always broken at times like this. My camera was shattered. The shattered lens suggested that I might wake up so I decided to go with the dream a little further to see what would happen. I went to my video camera. It seemed to be working.

Uh Oh.

This might not be a dream.

Whatever it was, if I could tape it…it might help. I turned on the camera. It worked. The semi had come to a stop about 150 yards in front of us. The driver was still in the cab.

I pointed the camera in the other direction and noticed a person coming towards us. I kept the camera aimed at his face so I got a closer up look than I would have without the camera.I focused on his eyes.

His eyes told me that he thought he was looking at a couple of ghosts.
When he got within speaking distance, I put down the camera. "I saw the whole thing. I thought you guys were goners? Are you okay?"

I wasn't sure.

We walked around to the side of the van. Lynn was leaning up against it.
I kept the video running.

The tape would later be seen at least three times on national teevee.

Moments later, the police arrived.

Lynn explained the collision with astounding calm and clarity.

I was no longer taping.

They arranged for our demolished van to be removed from the median. They gave us a ride to a nearby hotel. They explained our situation to the folks at the front desk who set us up with a room although all of our belongings were still in the van. They lent us a room pro-bono. Everybody told us not to worry.

We found out that we were in La Grange, Indiana. All we had was the clothes on our backs. And the aid of better angels.

I was teaching summer school. I was a teacher all the way. I taught twelve months a year. No house painting for me. I had been going twelve months a year for ten years with only one break in between. I didn't teach in the summer of 87, the year that I met Lynn.

Lynn was a single Mom when we met. She was raising three daughters. I was a single Dad raising a son and a daughter. Her kids liked me and my kids liked her. We spent a lot of time together especially on the weekends when I had custody of my two.

Lynn was working part time at First Federal Bank. She was good with change. She balanced every day. She could find the errors when someone else failed to balance. She didn't stand for a lot of bullshit that's why she was checking our love boat for leaks when I suggested a road trip test.

My prior experience as a road warrior had convinced me that you don't really know a person until you've been on the road with them. I had made the trip from ocean to ocean three times before I got married the first time. I regretted the fact that I hadn't road tripped with my first wife before we got married. Although two children had to be born, we might have saved ourselves some nightmares. I had rushed into that first one and wasn't gonna rush into this one.

Two years had already passed with Lynn and me. Our bodies were at rest and would tend to stay at rest unless acted upon. Times of indecision.
We had both already been married. We both carried the scars.

We had met one enchanted evening when she walked up to me and asked me if I wanted to dance. The first song we danced to was "Hurt so Good" by John Mellencamp. The second was "Loving You" by Elvis. The third was "It's All in the Game" by Tommy Edwards. When Tommy was about to sing the words "then he'll kiss your lips" I decided to take the chance.

I kissed her lips. She kissed me back.

We had been together every day since and it was going on two years. Two wonderful years. Time to nut up or shut up.

Lynn made a decision.

She said we should get married at the local justice of the peace. She called it to question one afternoon when we were having lunch at Mario's on East Avenue our favorite Italian restaurant.

Justice of the peace was no place for me or for us as far as I was concerned. She took it as a rejection of her love which was the opposite of my intention.

For the first time, we began to wonder about the future of our relationship. Yet, we had booked a trailer for a weekend at Darien Lake. We decided to make the trip. We had a couple of our kids with us. They were having a lot more fun than we were. They were outside the trailer when Lynn handed me a tiny article from the Democrat and Chronicle. The article said, "The Field of Dreams is a real place."

All of a sudden it was clear to me.

I am a person of intuition which means I have a tendency to say out loud exactly what is flashing through my mind at the exact time that it flashes. The flash came on.

"Hey Lynn, If we were ever to get married, it would have to be at the most beautiful place in America. Our love deserves it. If you're willing to travel to Iowa and if we can find this place and if it's real we could get married on the spot, right at home plate."

She made a face that I couldn't decipher so I didn't take it as a rejection. Then she said, "Great idea. I'll call up Iowa and tell them we need a marriage license to get married at an imaginary place at an undetermined time."

I found out later that she thought I was nuts and bullshitting her at the same time.

We had seen the movie together earlier in the year. We both thought it was great. In one scene, Kevin Costner (Ray Kinsella) asked his wife Amy Madigan "is this heaven or is this Iowa" as they relaxed one starry evening on the diamond that he had carved into his cornfield.

The location was so exquisite that I thought perhaps it was the most beautiful place I had ever seen.

This was the place for us.

Plus we would give the relationship the test. A test that I firmly believed had to be taken by any couple in the tentative situation that we occupied.

I enjoyed teaching summer school because I got a chance to pay attention to the kids who had been lost along the way during the regular school year. I was always amazed with the progress they made when given that second chance.

So the question lingered, if we were going to take a road trip when would it be? Lynn had her schedule at the bank and I had mine at the high school.

During the regular school year, I taught twelfth grade English as well as Creative Writing. I also taught an elective called Cinematic Literacy. I created that one myself and it was a great success. I was approaching the peak of my teaching career. I had ten days at the end of August, beginning of September.

Lynn had a week of undefined vacation saved up.

We had originally met on July 11th, 1987 or as we called it 7/11.

On our two year anniversary, we went out to dinner at the very restaurant where Lynn had made her first proposal a month before. Midway through the meal she said, “I sent away for a marriage license in Iowa. The field is located in Dyersville which is near Dubuque. We have a license waiting for us in Dubuque.”

Of course I was surprised but since I hadn’t been bullshitting her about the road trip idea, I said, “That's great. Good job.”

I didn’t know if she had actually procured a license or if she was reality testing. I was mystified when she said, “So if we break up this summer at least we can always say that at one time we had a marriage license in Iowa when we tell our story”.

All through the month of August, we came up with reasons to take the trip and those reasons were roadblocked by objections, obstacles and realities. If Lynn wasn’t exactly rocking the boat during those weeks, she was damned sure checking for leaks.

One night, we watched *Close Encounters of the Third Kind*. We loved the flick and mixed it into our plan. If we headed west we would go as far as Devil’s Tower in Wyoming and if we hadn’t made up our mind to get married by that time, we would head back and know that we had tried goddamn it, we had tried and we had an Iowa Marriage license to prove it.

It was also becoming clear that if we hadn’t made up our mind to try the road trip before school started, it meant that we probably should wrap up the relationship as painlessly as possible. On August 25th, I called Lynn from my apartment and said, “I was ready to go if she was”.

She wasn’t ready and she hung up sorta pissed off.

This was the last possible day to make the trip and be back in time for school.

A couple hours later, I heard a knock on the door. It was Lynn.

She told me the van was in the parking lot, packed and ready to go if I was serious.

I ran into my apartment, packed a few things.

I climbed into the van.

"Let's go".

I said.

"I'll drive"

I drove the first leg. We found a rest area deep in Ohio.

We napped for a few hours. Then we went into the rest area and washed up. Lynn came out first and went behind the wheel. I started to climb into the van when an impulse struck me. As I was leaving the rest area, I saw a machine selling bio-rhythm cards. I decided what the hell…I went back and bought a card for that day.

It only took maybe an extra thirty-seconds. I didn't like what the card said so I threw it out. That thirty-seconds would be crucial as we were headed for a blind spot that we might have missed if not for the card.
We managed to arrive at the blind spot exactly on time. Yeah, the whole crazy pilgrimage was my idea. I talked her into it, yet it was her van that was smashed to bits.

That's when the semi entered our van.

One way or another, the journey was over.

Indiana Spin

We were alone together in a motel in LaGrange, Indiana not far from Touchdown Jesus and the Golden Dome of Notre Dame. I was beginning to get a grip on death. As we traveled from the wreckage to the hotel, I asked what time it was. When we arrived at the hotel, it was a half hour before the time it was when we were on our way to the hotel.

Someone explained that we had crossed the line separating one time zone from another. We had left Eastern Daylight Savings Time. That's when I began to realize what death is/was. This was eternity. When you're dead, you're in Indiana and you keep crossing between time zones and Touchdown Jesus forever.

Time stabilized for a while in the hotel. I was expecting hysterics, blame or disassociation from Lynn. Instead, I got calm, composed, courageous capability. She started working the phones.

She had a handle on what happened. She called her auto insurance company back in New York. She explained the situation…car wrecked, hotel in Indiana, etc. They wanted to know what her plan was.

To my astonishment, Lynn told them that she wanted to **continue** on with her journey. She outlined what she needed and what she expected from them to make that continuation possible.

Following that, she called the American Automobile Association and got from them what we needed to continue the journey. A few minutes later, a rental car appeared at the motel. We drove around a bit, looking for a place to eat. We lost and gained two or three hours in that fifteen minute search.

After "lunch" we made our way to the junkyard to take a look at the van.

"Yep, it's totaled," the junkman asserted.

We gathered our belongings from the van and loaded them in the rental.
I could not have been more impressed by any companion. Even though I wasn't sure whether we were alive or not, it was clear that we were inhabiting the same realm. It was a realm, I wanted to remain in for the rest of my life/death.

I got down on one knee in that junkyard and asked Lynn to marry me.

She accepted.

August 26, 1989.

What a day.

What an eternity.

And the pilgrimage was still on. We didn't know if we were dead or alive but we knew we were getting married. We didn't know where. We had a marriage license in Iowa. We had been looking for the Field of Dreams which we heard was in Dyersville.

We drove through that town. There's a lot of farms in Dyersville and a lot of corn. We couldn't find the farm that we were looking for. We were hungry, tired, not sure if we were alive and headed for a place that might not exist. We were in a rented van.

We saw the driveway to yet another farm and turned into it, past yet another corn field. When we got to the farm itself, it was most definitely not the *Field of Dreams* farm, it looked more like the *Cujo* farm. We got the hell out of there but not before some giant thing flew out of the corn, through my open window and onto my chest. I don't know what the hell it was a bird, a locust, a demon grasshopper? I don't know, I just grabbed whatever it was and threw it out the window toward the cornfield or the hell from whence it came. I watched it wing away.

When we reached the end of the driveway safe from Cujo and the flying thing, I pulled the van off the road. I realized that I had gone crazy. Here we were in the middle of Iowa for God sake. We were lost. We might be as destroyed as was our original van. All my fault, all part of yet another crazy dream that I had dragged Lynn into.

We turned right at the end of the driveway. We drove about a hundred yards.

And then...we saw a paper plate...nailed to a tree...on the plate two words and an arrow...Movie site...arrow pointed right.

We took that right turn and a half mile down the road, there it was....The Field of Dreams. No doubt. Right exactly out of the film and out of my dreams.

Perfect.

We drove down that long driveway and met a man who was working in the yard. I asked him if he was the owner of the place. He said that he wasn't but the owner was out in the cornfield on his tractor. I saw the man on the tractor in the corn and walked towards him. He turned his tractor to meet me. When we were about ten feet apart, he shut off the tractor and focused his blue eyes on me.

"Can I help you?" asked the man on the tractor.

I said,"I believe you can. We've traveled from Rochester, New York. We had a terrible automobile accident yesterday. I'm not sure if we're alive or dead so tell me, is this heaven or is this Iowa?"

He looked at me and realized that there was something going on here and he wasn't sure what it was. Then he answered in the most perplexing way possible.

"It's whatever you want it to be."

I said,"Whatever it is, it's the most beautiful place I've ever seen. I want it to be the place where we get married."

He said, "You can do that."

I asked "Would Friday be all right."

He said, "That would be fine."

We shook hands.

On that Friday, he would be our best man. His name was Don Lansing.
I told Lynn the great news. We got in our car and drove to Devil's Tower.

We had originally said that we would go as far West as Devil's Tower in homage to *Close Encounters of the Third Kind* and if we hadn't made up our minds by then, well we'd head back home and take a break. Of course, we had already made up our minds thanks to the junkyard proposal.

That night, we stopped in Sioux Falls. A year earlier Sioux Falls had been the site of a horrifying tragedy. A plane crashed and there were no survivors. The plane crashed in a cornfield. We trucked through the Black Hills and the Badlands of South Dakota. We stopped at Mt. Rushmore where, I almost lost my wallet. We made a late night stop in Deadwood. We wanted to check and see if we were really still alive. They dropped fluorescent eye drops into Lynn's eyes and checked to see if hemorrhaging had occurred. I'll never forget looking at Lynn in that darkened emergency room with her glowing, green fluorescent eyes. The eyes were by far the brightest objects in the room. The doctor okayed us for further travel as if anything could have stopped us now.

We stayed the night in Spearfish after spending some afternoon time wading through a few crystal clear South Dakota cascades, getting our feet wet, so to speak. We made our way to Devil's Tower and agreed that we'd gone far enough west. We headed back to Heaven/Iowa.

We returned to Iowa on Thursday night. Don greeted us warmly and invited us into the house. Yeah, the house in the movie. Don wanted to know what we were going to wear. All we had left were our jeans. Don went to the phone and called the local tux shop. They had one tux left. Don asked if we wanted a cake. We said yeah. He got on the phone and called the local bakery. He asked Lynn how big the cake should be. She said big enough for fifty. I laughed out loud. We didn't know a single person in Iowa aside from Don and the guy who originally greeted us, a guy named Butch who was a caretaker for the field and his wife Annie.

Then he asked Lynn if she needed a wedding gown. He knew a dressmaker in town. He called Anne Steffen, the local dressmaker. He described our dream and asked Ann if she could help out. She said that she could.

That evening, we drove into town. The only tux in town fit me perfectly. Next we met Anne. She and Lynn got together and designed a wedding dress. That night we slept at Butch and Annie's house and torrential rain poured down ending a monthlong drought.

The next day, we went back into town. The dress was made. Beautiful, like in a dream. We drove to the town office to pick up our wedding license that Lynn had sent away before we left on our pilgrimage. By the time we got to the office the word had already spread. We got our license. They told us that they had heard all about the plan and so had the local television station. The station wanted to interview us. We met the reporter and she seemed very interested in our story. She had a full camera crew with her.

We told them that we had arranged for a magistrate to do the honors. We told them about the car crash.The town barber had heard about all of this and volunteered to give me a haircut while Lynn tried on her dress.

By that time it was getting late. We stopped at a restaurant to have our last meal as single people. We looked up at the teevee and there we were on the local news. We watched ourselves telling our story.

We made it back to the house. By this time, a bunch of neighbors had gathered.

I went into the room where in the movie Ray's daughter looks out the window and says, "Something's gonna happen out there."just before the ghost shows up.

I had the same view of the field and I knew that indeed something was gonna happen out there. We were gonna get married. The ghosts were gonna show up.

I made sure I had the wedding ring which we had bought at Wall Drugs in South Dakota. The rings were made from genuine Black Hills gold.

By this time about fifty people had gathered.

I left the house and walked into the corn in left field. I figured that since I still wasn't sure that I was alive that I should come out of the corn like the ghosts did.

I made my way to the pitchers mound where I met Don. I was on the mound for a few moments when the fifty people started to ooh and ahh as Lynn emerged from the house. Suddenly everything was in transcendent five dimension. I couldn't have dreamed of a more beautiful bride.

She made the long walk past the bleachers and crossed the magical first base line. She didn't disappear. She met me on the mound and we walked together to home plate where the magistrate awaited. We took our vows with Don standing right behind us. I shed a tear when Lynn agreed to accept me as I am. The witnesses cheered.

After the ceremony, we disappeared back into the cornfield before we reincarnated on the porch. The towns folk had brought fixings. We ate the cake (large enough for fifty) together. They all wanted pictures so we posed for a while. We drank some champagne that somebody had provided. We bid them farewell.

The next day we were home.

On the flight back, we told the stewardess our story and she put us in first class. Sitting right next to us was Maury Wills, the ex-Dodger shortstop who had once stole a hundred bases in a season. She told Maury our story and he congratulated us. We made it home in time for the Ring of Fire around Canandaigua Lake.

We told my parents the news

We're going to be celebrating our thirtieth anniversary next week. We're still going the distance and easing each other's pain.

I believe we're gonna make it all the way to happily ever after. Maybe even Heaven.

Doot Doo.

Made in the USA
Middletown, DE
18 November 2020

24344086R00205